The Big Book of Bootleg Horror
Vol. I

The Horror Anthology

HellBound Books Publishing LLC

Edited by Mitch Workman

**A HellBound Books LLC
Publication**

www.hellboundbookspublishing.com

Printed in the United States of America

The Big Book of Bootleg Horror
Vol. I

Compiled and Edited by Mitch Workman

A HellBound Books Publishing LLC Book
Houston TX

Dedication

To the wonderfully named Annabel de Vetten of *Conjurers Kitchen* for the conjoined fetal skull pictures – they are actually made out of chocolate, for people who like to imagine they are consuming the heads of such unfortunates – an ultimate taboo if ever there was one!

True artistry; check 'em out for yourselves…

www.conjurerskitchen.com

Foreword

First of all, thank you, Dear Reader for buying this mighty tome – we hope that it brings you entertainment, dark thoughts and those long, pitch black, sleepless nights where every creak is the anguished moan of some ethereal creature slithering beneath your bed and each brush of branches against the window pane is the spindly, skeletal claws of unimaginable horrors begging to be let in.

For this anthology – our first of many – we at HellBound Books Publishing have brought together the brightest stars to inhabit the indie horror scene right now, names who – be in no doubt at all about this – will be as commonplace upon the tongue as King, Barker, Laymon, *et al* by the time The Big Book of Bootleg Horror is skulking amongst the musty shelves of bargain bookstores across the US and beyond.

You will note, as you dare yourself to venture ever more forward into the darkness and terror within these pages, that some of our tales are written in 'British English'. For this, we make no apologies; we have deliberately left in the Brit' syntax and spelling because to have Americanized those stories would have been to spoil their wonderful uniqueness – and the Brits did *invent* the language, after all!

And so, it is on we march fearlessly to the main event, the twenty yarns that you have parted with your hard-earned to enjoy; stories of the taboo, the forbidden, and the downright disturbed.

Time to brace yourself, Dear Reader, and enjoy…

HellBound Books Publishing LLC

The Big Book of Bootleg Horror
Vol. I

Contents

Burning Bridges and Broken Fingers

S E Rise

There is a darkness inside me that should never be unleashed. They say everyone has an animal inside them. A beast that is at the core of our center. If you push a man far enough and take away everything that keeps him civilized, you risk releasing that beast. The beast is there for a reason. It is part of our base survival instinct. Some people never have to worry about their inner beast because it is such a small, timid, little animal. Some of us have a lot more to be concerned about.

"What do you mean you're letting me go?" I asked incredulously at the twenty-something-year-old punk.

"I'm sorry, but you have not made the corrective actions I have asked of you. I see no other choice but to terminate your employment with this company," he countered without looking up from his shuffling of papers.

"I don't have the money..." I said and this jab was a sharp stick into the wound. The guy had been riding my ass for the past two months. If it wasn't this, then it was that. We can't be afraid of change. Change is good for growth within a company.

Fuck your change. You change and fix things that are broken. If it's not broken, then don't fix it.

Twice, I had nearly knocked the smug little motherfucker on his ass. This got me a lecture from him about remaining positive, open to criticism, through the diversity of a group.

I had told the prick to just stay away from me, let me do my job and leave me alone. Did he listen? Of course he didn't. Now he thinks he can fucking fire me?

"Then I see no other..."

"Wait! Goddamn it. Just wait a goddamn minute," I responded and it was ten times too loud. I had been working for this company for almost twenty years. I was this close to retirement. My wife left me and took the kids, I paid a quarter of my check to alimony and another half of it went to child support. My piece of shit car blew a gasket and my rent was a month overdue. I was working my fucking ass off. There was a time... fuck it. Take a deep breath and try to calm down.

"Are you seriously going to fire me because I can't buy new clothes?" The beast inside me stirred and began to pace.

"Policy requires you to come to work clean and serviceable. Those clothes are not clean and serviceable. I asked you to get new ones and you did not. You did not do what I asked. I am your direct line supervisor and I'm tired of having to answer to my boss as to why you look like shit..." He said and the corner of his mouth went up because internally he thought it was funny that he said shit.

The beast inside me lunged forward against the door of the cage.

Jesus, I fucking hate this guy.

"Are you married? Do you have kids?"

"I don't see why that is any of your business, but yes, I have a wife and two children," he said and if I had been paying attention, I would have seen the family photo of his Porky the Pig looking wife and their two little Piglets.

"What would you do if you found yourself in this situation?" I asked and seriously wanted to know. Does this idiot have any idea what the consequences of his actions are going to be?

"That is a false hypothetical. I could never be in your situation. I still have my wife and children, I have clean new clothes, I drive that red beamer that you more than likely have seen, and I went to college."

I felt the snap and the chain around the beast let loose at the words "I went to college."

I went to college as well, you fucking idiot, but it sure didn't help me a whole hell of a lot because I am working for a stupid motherfucker like you. Then it dawned on me. It wasn't about the clothes I wore or the ones I didn't—or couldn't—buy. It was about me. He was going to fire me no matter what I did. He was toying with me and enjoying it. This was a no-win situation.

I didn't believe in no-win situations.

"True, you are absolutely right. You more than likely will never be or even find yourself in my situation," I said, and that's when the animal inside me began to howl. The door to the cage swung open and it took its first step of freedom. I glanced at the little clock beside the Porky Pig family photo.

You want to play games, idiot? You want to sit there, smug in your own self-righteousness? You want to quote shit from your little books?

That's when the beast stepped forward and growled his idea to me. I listened and I liked it.

"You're going to give me all the money in your wallet or I am going to break one of your fingers." I enjoyed the look of shock that replaced the look of contempt. Shock I could deal with.

"Excuse me? You're going to collect your things and leave the building. You're fired," he said and I saw the fear and shock slip into the background as the smug contempt returned. He really enjoyed that. Good.

His hands were flat against the desk in front of him. He thought I was bluffing, but the beast leapt forward with unnatural speed and grace. I grabbed his right arm at the wrist, latched onto his middle finger and bent it backwards until it snapped, cracked, and finally lay flat against the back side of his hand. The action was so smooth and quick he wasn't able to react. The horror of what I had just done rocketed through me and I liked it. I liked it a lot. His mouth opened to scream out in pain and I punched him in the throat. This stopped the noise of his scream dead in its tracks. He gagged and choked as he grabbed at his throat with his free hand. I could hear the air exchange so I wasn't worried about if I had crushed his windpipe or not. I grabbed onto his ring finger and his eyes went wide.

"Give me your wallet or I am going to break another one of your fingers. And if you scream, I am going to hit you again."

Apparently, he didn't understand and reached for the phone.

I snapped his ring finger back, felt the satisfying crack and pressed it against the back side of his hand. I hammered a fist against his chin and felt the satisfying crunch of his front teeth shattering. Now that felt amazing. The animal inside me howled again and my anger soared to unexpected heights.

"You are the reason my family left me!"

I hit him again in the face. His head rocked back and on the rebound I hit him again. His cheek split open and the red of exposed meat made me hungry.

This time, on the rebound, I let loose of his wrist, grabbed hold of his not so pretty shirt and pulled him up onto the desk. He flopped down like a fish and a spray of blood shot out across the desk with the exhalation.

If he wasn't going to give me his wallet the easy way, then I would have to get it the hard way. I held his head against the desk with my left hand and reached into his back pocket to fish out his wallet.

Unfucking believable. The motherfucker had five crisp one hundred dollar bills hiding in there.

I hadn't seen five crisp one hundred dollar bills together at one time in over a year. Before my wife left me. And, do you know why my wife left me? Because this idiot cut my hours and docked my pay for three months and the goddamn accident wasn't even my fault.

"It wasn't my fault, was it? And, you fucking knew it wasn't my fault," I said into his ear.

His eyes fluttered at the sound of my voice and I smelled the unmistakable stench of piss.

"Guess what, piss pants, I don't believe your clothes are very clean and serviceable now. Do you? I'm going to have to dock your pay and cut your hours." The beast inside me loved this; loved seeing me destroy my enemy. Rage began to replace anger and I wanted to hurt him more. I wanted to hurt and maim this mother-fucker. My jaw clenched and I felt the saliva gush. Before I could stop myself, I leaned over and sunk my teeth into the cartilage and flesh of his ear. The blood tasted salty but delicious.

With a twist and thrust of my head, I felt a large portion of the man's ear tear away. Why hasn't someone heard us by now? I would like to think that I spit the chunk of ear out onto the floor, but with all honesty, I can't remember.

The rage turned into something different then— something controlled. Something sadistic and evil. I felt incredible. Clarity and enlightenment coursed through me.

He was merely middle management and therefore was not assigned a secretary. The sun had set and our smart, hardworking employees had punched their time cards out, then sailed away to their Islands of Paradise called home.

Good for them. Speaking of that... I fished the dumbass' cell phone from his pocket and slid my thumb across the screen. Damn, this is a nice phone. Apparently, he wasn't too worried about it getting stolen. No passcode.

The screen flashed up and I regretted saying anything about the passcode. Fingerprint identification required. Easy enough. The sight of his deformed broken fingers thrilled me.

We couldn't stay in the office all night, so I thought of a wonderful place we could go.

I scrolled through his top five contacts and found his wife.

I glanced over to the Porky Pig photo. Okay, maybe she didn't actually look like Porky the Pig. She was kind of hot. This gave me an idea.

I pulled up the message screen and set my plans into play.

"Going to be a little late tonight. Put the kids to bed, lock their doors and prepare yourself for me. I am serious."

SEND

"K" Her response was quicker than I could have imagined. My wife would never have responded that quickly. You got yourself a big dick there, buddy? I gave him a quick glance. Unable to respond, she was nice enough to answer the question for him.

"Do you want me to wear the big black strap on again?" The message asked and I nearly laughed myself into tears. The idiot's cheek was swelling his eye shut, the blood drooled from his broken mouth and his two broken fingers would make anybody a bit nauseous. I was past the point of no return. I either followed this through or I was fucked.

"Not tonight. I am feeling cock strong and lusty. I want to play a game tonight. I want you blindfolded, face down with your ass and cunt in the air waiting for me. I am hard just thinking about it," I sent in reply.

The beast in me liked the idea and I felt myself growing hard.

Fuck it. Why not?

I pulled out my hard cock and snapped off a dick picture for her and pressed Send.

"OMG!!! You're serious? OMFG!! Your dick looks so fucking big." She sent back and I couldn't help but smile.

"Be ready, I am coming for you. I am going to take you." I sent back.

"I'm wet just thinking about it...oh do you want the lights on or off?"

"Off... I have to finish up here. Be ready." I sent back and didn't wait for a response. I sat him back into the chair and took a good look at my handiwork. All you had to do was just leave me the fuck alone.

***

I brought him back around to consciousness by stapling his good ear to his head.

Twice.

"Still with me, buddy boy?" He squirmed in the chair and tried to get up. I slammed the stapler into his ear again, pinning it for the third time. He tried to bring his hand up to cover his ear and forgot about his fingers being broken. He started to scream, but I was ready for him and jammed one of his expensive wool socks into his mouth.

His broken teeth were sharp and I felt it tear a layer of skin off of the back of my hand. He saw it too and tried to bite me. I brought the stapler down onto the crown of his head and put a staple there too. This must have hurt pretty damn bad, because he recoiled from it like I had a loaded pistol.

"How much money do you have in the bank?"

He stared at me stubbornly and I raised the stapler. He issued a noise through the sock gag and I realized the problem.

With the sock gag removed, I only had to staple him once more to get him to give me a truthful answer. "How the fuck do you have that much in the bank?"

"I budget and invest. My wife and I are very frugal," he said and the words were mangled by his broken teeth.

"Bullshit, that's three times your annual salary. There's no possible way you saved that much," I said and saw something in his eyes then.

That's what I thought. Someone's been stealing cookies from the Cookie Jar. Good, that's going to be mine as well. "Get up. It's time to go home."

"Fuck you. I'm not taking you to my house."

"Really? It's okay. I've already talked to your wife. She's expecting us."

His mouthed opened to protest again.

"If you don't, I am going to staple your eyelid open... or maybe just put a staple through your eyeball." That got his attention. I brought his cell phone (my new cell phone) up to my mouth.

"Siri, show me home. Map it."

***

Getting to the car was a challenge, but he was middle management and had a parking spot in the front row.

I sent the text. "I'm on my way home."

"K, I'm ready." He saw her response and tried to protest. I slammed my fist into his jaw and drove the rest of the way to his house in peace. I woke him up by pressing down on his broken fingers. His eyes snapped open and I brought the stapler up in front of his face. "We're going inside. If you say a word or make a noise I am going to kill your children while you watch. I will cut their heads off and make you and your wife eat soup from their skulls. Then I will kill your wife and make you eat her. Do you understand? Have I made myself perfectly clear?"

There was terror mixed with resignation in his eyes and I fed off of it.

All you had to do was leave me alone. Let me retire and collect my pension. Now I will probably have to kill you and your entire family.

I saw him realize the outcome as well. It's never good to leave a man without an option. So, I gave him one.

"Give me what I want and I will go away. It doesn't have to end that way."

I saw the anger return in his eyes and I grabbed onto his broken fingers. His knee buckled and he opened his mouth to scream.

"If you do... they are fucking dead." He shut his mouth and ate the pain. "And speaking of fucking... your wife is waiting for me. You're going to love this part."

***

I pushed the door to the bedroom open and the light spilled across the bed. Good to her word, she was in position, the blindfold was in place. Her nice full tits spread out against the comforter, and her ass was pushed up into the air awaiting me. I felt my dick getting hard and I looked over to confirm his silence. His eyes were smoldering with hatred, but he remained quiet. In the dark, we crossed the room and I sat him in the chair positioned against the wall and in front of the bed. That way he had the perfect view of what I was doing to his wife.

"Oh my, is that a burglar?" she said in mock concern. Obviously she and he had done the role playing thing before.

I pulled open a drawer and tied his hands behind his back. His broken fingers tried to get in the way and I tied them in place as well. I quietly pushed him against the chair. I was curious though and feeling mighty powerful at the moment. I reached down and stripped the man's pants and underwear to his knees.

His pink little boner sprung up and I smiled. I also stuck another sock in his mouth.

Boy, was she going to be surprised.

I pointed my cock in the right direction and brought it to the edge of her sex. I could feel the wet heat coming from her and it turned me on.

"You're not going to hurt me are you, Mr. Burglar?"

I smacked her ass hard, told her to shut the fuck up and plunged the entire length of my manhood into her.

"OH MY FUCKING GOD...WHAT THE FUCK?" she gasped and moaned in surprise. Her ass shot forward, then back as she slammed it back against me. "Oh fuck, yeah." Over and over she slammed that ass against me, each time burying me to the hilt. She came, oh my god, did she orgasm. Over and over, thrust after thrust. I could not believe how well this woman could fuck. I felt my own orgasm beginning to rise and decided to change tactics. I wasn't even near being done yet. I pulled it out to the edge and made sure it was slippery wet. I slid the head up to her spider hole and heard a noise escape her mouth.

"Ooohhh..." The sound was low and deep.

I pressed the head into her and let the length of me slide in. The low deep ooooh became a deep, primitive womanly moan. The kind of moan a man is never supposed to hear or see.

I nailed that ass like it was mine and she took every inch like a goddamn champ. I looked back and his pink boner was rock hard and he was watching us and getting off on it.

Good, then you're going to love this...

I pulled it out of her and smacked her ass. Leaning over, I grabbed a handful of the woman's hair and pulled her onto the floor, then backwards and close to her husband. I pulled her head back by her hair and she opened her mouth in invitation. I plunged my cock down her throat and began bobbing her, up and down upon it. I watched as her hand found his pants, then his naked leg. If it had surprised her she didn't miss a beat. If anything, she started sucking even more vigorously. Her hand slid down the seated man's thighs and she found his hard, pink cock. I felt her mouth change as she smiled. Her hand came away and went to her wet pussy and then back to his cock. Her hand slid up and down him with ease as she sucked me off and hand-jacked her husband.

Her mouth worked wonders and she felt me begin to engorge. She pumped me faster with her mouth and her free hand fist-pumped the first stream of spunk down her throat. I buried it deep for the second stream, pulled it out and let her fist pump the rest onto her blindfolded face. Dutifully, she took the last stream on the tongue and then turned to begin sucking off her husband. With his hands tied behind his back, he could do little but buck his hips into her wanton mouth.

***

She collapsed backward onto the floor, stomach and chest heaving with the effort and exhaustion. She kept the blindfold in place and slowly started to giggle like a girl.

"Oh my fucking god. That was fucking incredible!!" she said and her hands slid down to her throbbing freshly fucked sex. "Oh my god, you are the best husband ever." Her hand found my foot and she turned and began to crawl up my leg where I sat on the bed. Revenge is sweet and the beast was still turned on. She found what she was looking for and after a few slides of her mouth, I was hard again. She kept the blindfold on and enjoyed herself by pleasuring me.

He just watched from the chair with his swollen, cut face and broken teeth.

***

All good things must come to an end. She took all of me to the last drop and I turned her to face her husband. She had a bright sheen of sweat across her tits and stomach and her tongue licked at some of my spouge that had escaped her.

She was ready for more, but I held her by her shoulders and slid one hand around to her throat. She arched and squirmed like a whore and I smiled.

"Tell her what I told you to tell her," I said and the volume of my voice startled her. She froze in my grasp and her hands dropped to her sides.

I watched him as he tried to sit forward. His eyes met mine and I could still see the hatred in there.

Good.

"Did you enjoy yourself?" he asked. And I tightened my grip on her throat. This was not what he was supposed to say.

"Oh god baby, yes. This was fucking incredible. Thank you so much," she said and I watched as his eyes came up to meet mine.

"Good baby, I liked it too. Tomorrow morning, I need you to do me a favor..."

"What, baby?" I felt her throat move up and down as she formed the words. She was reacting to the tension in the air and might be getting the feeling that this wasn't a game. Her hand started to come up to take off the blindfold.

"Leave it on," he said and that surprised me.

"Okay baby," she said and let her hand fall back down to her side. "Tomorrow, I need you to go to the bank and withdraw all of the money in our account. Can you do that for me?"

She remained silent and I felt her relax in my grip. This told me she knew there was too much money in there too. She hesitated and chose her words carefully. I could feel her neck tense with anger. "Do you want that in large bills or small bills?" She asked as she titled her head back towards me.

"Big and small will work just fine," I said and she did something strange then. She left the blindfold on and gave her husband an unspoken message. To me it felt like "This is your fault. I fucking told you." She leaned back with her elbows resting on my knees and her hair cascaded across my cock and balls.

I guess someone else is in the mood to get a little payback.

She rode and fucked me for the rest of the night. Her unbridled passion destroyed him more than any wound I could have inflicted.

***

As the sun rose, we slept where we collapsed. He was still in the chair asleep and she laid butt ass naked and sprawled; her face resting against my manhood. She felt me stir and started my day with a nice bit of lip service. When she was done, she got up, showered and got dressed in a nice business suit. I lay in the bed and watched the ritual.

Once complete, she stood and turned to me. She was actually a very attractive woman.

"You're not going to hurt me or my children are you?" She asked and stood patiently, awaiting my reply.

"No, I am not."

"Good, then I will be back soon with your money." She started forward and grabbed a t-shirt up in her hand and tossed it onto her husband's pink manhood.

She returned with a suitcase full of embezzled cash and handed me the keys to his car.

Stood on her tiptoes and pulled me down to slide her tongue into my mouth.

There were no words exchanged, she simply turned then and opened the front door. I heard her mom voice kick in and she said something about going to grandma's house. The door slammed shut and I turned towards my new car.

He stood in the window and watched as I got into his car. His hands were still tied behind his back.

It sucks losing everything, doesn't it? I told you to leave me alone. Maybe someone will care. But it won't be me. Call the cops; maybe they can help.

The animal rested behind the iron cage. It was satisfied for now, but the promise of its return was guaranteed.

Eroticide Triptych

Kevin Wetmore

The jealousy of a goddess had shattered her joy and driven her to darkness. She had not yet known a man, but that did not matter as her virgin knot had been broken by a god – by the god. The father of the gods had seen her from above, and in seeing lusted, and in lusting taken, and she knew pleasure none of the girls in her village had known when they laid down with the village boys, with their clumsy hands, nervous embraces, and over-too-soon passions. She had been penetrated by lightning, cauterizing her hymen even as it was broken. Waves of pleasure and pain poured through her as she felt the god thrust home and make her a woman, and more than woman – the paramour of the Thunderer. Heights of pleasure were hers as she climaxed over and over as only those taken by the divine can.

But the joy of coupling with him soon turned to despair. The rage and jealousy of a woman scorned is nothing compared to the rage and jealousy of a goddess scorned. His sisterwife – mother of gods, homekeeper, hearthmistress – knew of his infidelities; one cannot hide marital inconstancy from a celestial spouse. The fury of the mothergod could not fall upon her husband for the transgression, though, and so it fell upon the young nymph.

Her beauty, her grace, and the exquisiteness of her young, innocent sexuality was what had caught the eye, lust, and eventual attentions of the immortal. Thus, the mothergod decided to remove such temptations, not only from her consort, but from all males who might feel desire for the nymph. Her revenge upon her rival who had stolen her husband's desire was to rob the unchaste plaything of her ability to entice.

The nymph's hair, which his hands had stroked in the heat of carnal desire, became serpents. Her eyes, that once held his while his seed burst forth in her, turned the color of blood. Her skin, once so soft and hot to his kisses, became that of a dragon. The price of a god's passion was to become a terror, a destroyer. Her sensuality, only newly discovered in the arms of her lover, lost forever to the ravages of the curse put upon her.

She fled across the waters. She who had been the fantasy of every boy in her village, who had been the lover of the greatest of gods, became a story with which to frighten children; a beast whose visage could turn human flesh to the burnt umber color of basalt. Her loneliness and pain made all the worse by having copulated with a god and knowing she would never know his, or any being's, touch again. If mortal rutting produced such heights of ecstasy, few are those who know or can stand the climax brought on by coitus with the eternal. The loss of such joy is among the greatest of all losses. To know she would never feel it again broke her heart again and turned it to stone.

The first man to come to her after the transformation was simply a hunter lost in the woods. She watched him longingly, from a distance. Her rage was deep, her sense of loss overpowering, as was her solitude. She wanted and hated at the same time. As he spotted her, his eyes looked deep into hers and his body stiffened. He trembled as the transformation took him, solidifying his flesh and removing all sense and sensation from him. He gasped his final breath as he hardened, frozen forever in the moment.

Unexpectedly, his death moved something inside her. As his body shook with the metamorphosis, and his eyes never left hers, she felt a warmth growing within her. Pleasure washed over her. With each tremor of his limbs she gasped, spasms building within her. She bit into her own tongue, the taste of her blood heightening the pleasure of his stiffening death throes. Floodgates she had not felt since He was inside her opened and overwhelmed. She unleashed a fierce cry and collapsed, exhausted, to the ground. Her flesh tingled. She breathed deeply. A cruel smile formed on her lips. She licked them slowly, the copper taste of blood mixing with the smell of the earth she lay upon. Though she would never know a man's touch, his death would give her more pleasure than such a quick and joyless trifle ever could. The mothergod's revenge would be her rapture.

II

She awoke with a headache and a haze. Stiff. Pain. Bandages between her legs. Memory. Anger. Shame. Loss. The mattress felt raw and rejecting, pushing her from the bed, even as she only desired to fall back asleep and forget. Wake up, perhaps, in a different place, to a different day.

Slow. Sore. Flame, dying to a dull throb under the bandages. Grasping the headboard, she pulled herself up and walked to the mirror, not wanting to look, afraid of what was there. She did not look different, but nothing was the same. She reached out and seized hold of the dresser, dizzy and afraid of falling. She went back to the bed when it felt safe enough to move and wept.

***

He had been charming and handsome when they met. Good to her. He did not go out and look for other women. He did not hit her or say mean things. Her friends were slightly jealous, even as they were happy for her. Her parents were also delighted. "He's a good Ijaw man, from a good Ijaw family," they said. They liked that he valued his traditions and his culture. He had been to university in Dakar and was now a successful businessman back in Warri. He was educated, but it did not turn him from the ways of his people. He worked hard and had a good house and he wanted to marry their daughter. She was young, just out of school herself. Not university, but the local school. She was pretty, and known in the town as a hardworking girl who would make someone a good wife someday. She did not think they day would come so soon or with a man who had known ten summers before she had seen the world.

On the day of their wedding her father sacrificed the biggest bull they had and her mother took her aside and told her all the things that she would need to know to be a good wife and mother. She was told he was a good man and that she was lucky and should obey her husband because he was a good man.

The night of the wedding he brought her to his good house. She laid with him. She was not entirely inexperienced, but had never taken a man inside her before. He did not wait. He simply climbed on top of her and took her. She bled. She felt a fire burning between her legs. Tears of pain rolled down her face as she held her new husband while he deflowered her. Then it was over. He kissed her tears and smiled. He held her and told her he loved her.

Soon they were making love regularly, but her newfound pleasure in the act after her initial pain did not seem to please her husband. In their second month together, he told her that he believed in the traditional ways and that, though he loved her parents as his own, they had let him down as she had not been circumcised, as tradition and the ancestors demanded. She could not believe her ears. He told her that he was taking her to the doctor and having the ritual performed so that they could live a good life together. She told him her parents did not believe in the practice and that she herself had no desire for it. He grew angry. He told her that she was his wife and she would do as he pleased. She would honor his ways and she would obey.

The next day, a smiling nurse, nearly ninety years old, reassured her and brought her into the doctor's room in the "clinic." The doctor her husband had brought her to was waiting with a table and a tray of instruments and a blank facial expression. She cried once again as she was taken.

Lovemaking with her husband held no pleasure for her after that. She felt violated every time he touched her. No doctor's knife could hurt her as much as his insistence of her obedience. He sensed her resentment and in turn resented her. Their marriage grew cold and loveless, but he still demanded his rights as her husband. She would lie under him and allow him his pleasure, but also let him know the complete absence of hers. He began insisting that she work more actively to pleasure him. He insisted that he would be the one to lie down and that she must ride him until he was satisfied. She would stare at his closed eyes, her own burning with rage until his seed flooded her. She would withdraw him from inside her and lie next to him, wishing that she could make him feel the way that he had made her feel.

The passion of her anger burned within her. Her rage became her lover until she decided to give in to this new paramour. One night, he came home and insisted on her submission. He laid down on their bed as she mounted him. His eyes closed as they always did, and she felt his tension building. Reaching behind her with the knife she had hidden under the pillow that afternoon, she felt his sac with one hand and then cut with the other.

His eyes bolted open and he screamed and tried to push her off, but she held him down with her weight and held him inside her, even as he began to lose his tumescence. Blood began soaking into the mattress. He lost consciousness from the pain. She knew if she did not get him help he would most likely bleed to death. She cradled him inside her and felt herself climax for the first time since her "surgery" as he slipped out. As her orgasm drifted away, she slowly inhaled and exhaled and bent over and kissed the man who had pleasured her in his pain. Climbing off, she left him in the bed to go wash the blood from between her legs.

III

Three candles guttered on the nightstand by the side of the bed, the only light in the room other than the streetlights and moon coming through the open window. She lay atop the covers wearing the black nightgown she had worn on the first night of the honeymoon. The man she had married was not coming to save her now, though. He was long gone.

He had come the previous two nights. Nothing like the man she married. Cold, violent - he came late, with the night, entering her bedroom and enjoying his power over her, knowing she was alone and helpless. She had always thought vampires were made-up things, something from the movies but not real. Then she came to the attention of one.

Two nights ago, as she slept, he found his way into her room. She awoke to find him standing at the foot of her bed, staring at her. His eyes were dark, cold and angry. For several minutes, nothing was said. They stared at one another. She remembered thinking their breathing was oddly in sync. Hers was terrified; his also quick and short, with anticipation she later assumed. Then he smiled and she saw his horrible teeth. The smile said he was going to hurt her.

"You are mine," he whispered.

"No. Please!" was all she got out and he was upon her, moving faster than she thought possible. She felt his breath on her neck and then he was biting her. With his mouth on her neck he reached down and tore off the boxer shorts she wore to bed. She realized in a panic that he meant to have her sexually as well. He bit her on the thigh as well, then slid back up to feed on her neck while entering her. Once she stopped screaming and settled down, he became less violent, almost gentle with her. It did not matter. She felt violated in every way. He took her in every sense of the word.

"The books and the movies lie," she thought after, sitting in the tub, warm water running the whole time. She washed the blood from her neck and body and examined her neck and face and thigh for bruises. He had been clever. Perhaps that is how he survived for centuries: he left no marks on her face or anywhere visible other than her neck for others to notice, and shame meant she would wear a scarf or a high-necked shirt tomorrow.

It was not like in the books and movies. The vampire was not romantic. He did not make her feel alive or sexy or like he wanted her to be his eternal queen. He just took her and drained her and left her after he got what he wanted.

He returned the following night. Again, she awoke to him standing over her. His black, soulless eyes looking down on her. "You are mine," he whispered, although to her it sounded louder than screaming. He took his time. Leaning over, he smelled her, sniffing slowly around her neck. He licked his lips and then gently bit her lip. She closed her eyes, wishing it over. He bit harder and drew blood. They both tasted it simultaneously, both inhaling sharply - her in pain and he in ecstasy. His claw-like hands grasped at her. Again, he took his time taking his pleasure from her. The tears running down her cheeks seemed to feed him as much as her blood did. As he took his leave just before dawn he said, "Don't forget. You're mine and I can have you any time I want you."

This third night she came ready. She put on the nightgown. She placed the candles on the nightstand and lit them. She knew he would arrive around two and would take her again. So she was ready. She did not sleep with anticipation.

She heard the apartment door open. She heard the tread of his boots on the living room floor. The bedroom door slowly opened and he stood there, framed by the light coming in through the living room windows. He stood there staring.

"Well, this is a change," he said. "Are you happy to see me?"

She did not speak.

He moved across the floor quickly and was on top of her in an instant. Unlike the previous nights, she immediately wrapped her legs around his and her left arm snaked up behind him.

"See," he told her, "I can have you any time I want."

She whispered in his ear.

"What?" he said, confused.

"I said, you can be penetrated, too," she repeated, and her right hand snaked up behind him, too, holding the sharp wooden stake that she had hidden under her right thigh. Before he could move, she held it in both hands and plunged it into his back. He screamed, his eyes and mouth opening wide and he began the push off her. She embraced him with her arms and legs, slowly driving the stake in further and not allowing him to lift off of her.

She understood in that moment what it was like to have someone in your power. What it was to penetrate. What it was to feel their life flowing in and over you. She wanted to look in his eyes as he was pierced. She wanted the moment to last. She felt his legs kicking against hers and smiled.

His blood flowed over her. It must have included the blood he had taken from her. She smiled again in ecstasy, her eyes closed. With each spasm she felt herself grow warm and happy. It wasn't like in the books or movies. He did not vanish, or explode or turn to ash or dust. He simply shuddered, as he did when he climaxed inside her.

She whispered in his ear, "You are mine now. But you will never have me again." His tremors began to lessen and she saw the light go out of his eyes. Every ripple caused her endless pleasure. She pushed the shell to the floor and for the first time in days she drifted into a content and dreamless sleep.

Two and a half hours later, Detective Gillespie arrived on the scene. "Talk to me, Marko," he said to the uniformed officer next to the door.

"Call came in from the neighbors. They've been hearing screams the last few nights, and finally decided tonight they had had enough."

"Better late than never," Gillespie remarked, surveying the apartment bedroom.

"Too late for him," Marko said, pointing to the sheet on the floor. "Wish they had called sooner, a lot of problems could have been taken care of."

"Who's the vic?"

"Her estranged husband. Guess she had a restraining order against him because he was abusive, but he's been showing up here the past few nights. Like I said, neighbors heard the screams but didn't do anything about it. Looks like she took the matter in her own hands. She stabbed him in the back with this." He handed the detective a plastic evidence bag with a blood-covered, sharpened stake. "Hit the aorta just right and he bled out in a matter of minutes."

"Jesus." The detective looked over and saw a young woman sitting in a rocking chair with a blanket wrapped around her. She was wearing what looked like a black nightgown, but her hair and body were drenched in blood. A female officer was standing next to her, quietly taking her statement. The bed on the other side of the room was a bloody mess.

She looked up at the detective and smiled at him. "He will never harm another woman again. His blood was so warm. You wouldn't think a vampire's blood would be warm. He lived to penetrate me. He died when I penetrated him."

And she closed her eyes and smiled as she relived the moment again, as she would every night for the rest of her life.

See?

Paul Stansfield

He stared at the wall, at the third cinderblock up, the eighth one over. The one with the crack in it. The crack was about three inches long, and split into two parts on one end. That was it. The sum total of his attempts to break out; kicking with his sock-clad feet, open palm blows, fingernail scratches. One lousy crack. It must be reinforced cinderblock, he figured. Or the equivalent. Who knew if it was real, actual cinderblock, as he had known it on Earth, when he was alive. Odd that they replicated it here in Hell. Or maybe not. It did add to his frustration somehow.

He frequently wondered why he was in a cell at all. What were they keeping him from? Outside meant he'd be in a different section of Hell. So what? There was no escaping, obviously. But the rulers of this infernal place must know what they are doing, he had to admit. They are the experts. Who was he to question their tortures? Where was he when Lucifer had created his domain?

He turned away from that particular section of wall and regarded the rest of his area. It didn't take long. Four reinforced cinderblock walls, one two-inch-thick mattress with two thin blankets and a skinny pillow, one specially-made commode. They'd given him a real porcelain and metal pipe one at first. They'd quickly realized the mistake of this. He'd demolished it the first night, and had dug a good way through the hole that the toilet had been connected to, using its own destroyed innards. One of the demon guards had received a nice gash in his head with a section of pipe, too, before they'd swarmed him, put him in a cloth straight jacket, and injected him with a chemical one. The next time he'd been really aware, lucid, he was in this room, with a new toilet. It was made of heavy Styrofoam; strong enough to support him, but too soft to use effectively as a weapon or a shovel. Plus it wasn't connected with anything. Emptying it was accomplished using heavily armed guards, while he was asleep (until they were in the room, that is), every few days or so. It had just been emptied in this way the night before, so it only had a couple of pissloads in it. So the smell was basically nonexistent. That was something.

He often wondered why they didn't use the chemical restraints all the time. He'd seen other damned souls in here obviously under their influence in his few times outside. But usually he was clean, and free within his cell. Why? Maybe it was more punishing this way, him being totally aware, and with a tiny taste of freedom. The zombied ones were—maybe—happier not knowing where they were or what was going on. Or maybe the other damned souls weren't really damned souls at all; maybe they were demons in disguise. He wasn't really sure. It could all be a ruse to fuck with his head.

And why was he damned at all? They'd stolen his memories, most of them, but in what remained he remembered being good, praying and all. He had been decent, and considerate of others, generous, and honest. Why? He ground his teeth. Unless, unless, a nagging voice cut in, maybe the memories he had were false, implanted by the evil spirits. He didn't know. He didn't know anything for sure.

The slot at the bottom of the door was opened, and the cardboard tray was quickly pushed through. He didn't bother running toward the door, knowing as he did that it would close very fast, as it did today. He stared at his dinner. Pre-cut chicken, green beans, buttered roll, applesauce, and cups of orange juice and water. Plus a napkin and a plastic spoon. No forks, or sporks even, anymore. In the past they'd been careless, and forgotten to collect every utensil. How that demon had howled when he managed to get that spork head into its brain! Or pseudo-brain, and pseudo-chicken, pseudo-napkin, everything. Who knew if anything was as it appeared to be?

He ate his meal, and even relished it. It was usually edible, sometimes tasty even. Another tease, this decent food in Hell? This could change, though, so he enjoyed every meal as if it was his last. Other shoes could be dropping at any time.

He gazed up at the camera, safely nestled high up on the wall, out of his range. They seemed to rely on it more lately. There were fewer visits by non-custodial demons of late, none at all for the past few days. Were demons scarce here in Hell? He chuckled to himself. Were even they tired of losing too many? So it seemed.

As he finished eating he ran though his memories of life. These were both vexing and entertaining. But he had little else to do. Plotting was another time waster. Unfortunately, he hadn't been able to think of a good escape or attack plan lately. His captors seemed to anticipate everything, and learn from their mistakes.

He moved over to his bed and lay down. He usually got tired after eating. Funny how he still needed food, and sleep. His body seemed unchanged here. Another mystery. Maybe it was yet another mockery, close enough to life to make him miss it more. Oh well. He wasn't complaining. Sleep was pleasurable, and dreams were a temporary (yet sometimes teasing and annoying) escape from here. His mind began a mental tunnel through the hated walls.

***

Tad adjusted the focus knob on the camera using the instrument panel, and Quinn Utz came into sharper view. Despite himself, knowing full well he was looking through a camera lens, Thad shuddered. Several of the patients in this ward were scary, but Quinn was by far the worst. And most prolific. He'd killed five medical personnel; two nurses, three doctors. Three back at Stonebridge, two here at Cinaminnson. He'd seen the tape of the ones here. He'd never seen anything so savage.

Tad jumped as someone sat down beside him at the console. Dr. Brison. He sat back down, and tried to simultaneously stop his heart from thumping crazily and prevent his cheeks from reddening. He failed at both.

"Evening, Tad. Sorry I startled you." Her smile revealed that she wasn't that sorry.

"Hey Doct-Donna. That's okay." Donna Brison was one of the few doctors here who didn't mind, and in fact preferred, to be called by her first name by other employees. She was pretty consistent in her overall lack of pomposity, a rare treat here. Some doctors didn't even bother learning the nurses' and techs' names, and instead referred to them as "you," or "nurse." "This guy makes me uneasy is all. I'm kind of Quinn-phobic."

Donna chuckled slightly. "It's not a phobia unless it's an irrational fear of something. Quinn has unfortunately demonstrated very rational reasons to fear him, in so far as he's killed many people."

"You shrinks and your jargon. Have to correct every little mistake."

"Of course. How else am I supposed to make myself feel validated and superior, but by making someone else feel dumb and inferior? Actual intelligence and competence? No sir."

Tad giggled. Most doctors had little or no sense of humor, and Donna's joke was funnier since it was so patently false.

"But seriously, anything new with him tonight?"

"Nope. Same ol' stuff."

"I see. Well, if I'm right, Quinn may be acting differently soon. Quite differently." Tad looked at her carefully as she finished speaking. Her smile had changed from jokey to triumphant. Her smile was kind of uneven somehow, which fit her overall bearing. Tad couldn't quite decide whether Donna was cute in a geeky sort of way, or geeky in a cute sort of way.

"Explain."

"You know that one of my areas of interest is how the brain and the senses are connected. And how damage to certain areas of the brain severely impact on the senses. Visual problems from brain damage are then called agnosias. Some examples are object agnosia, in which people can't properly visualize and describe a certain object, like a TV, for example. Or another would be a color agnosia, which is the same thing except for a certain color, and so on. I think that our boy has a particularly rare and unfortunate one. I think I've discovered which one. Some other doctors here go the other way, and say he's schizophrenic, or sociopathic, even. I think that's bunk. I've been looking over his case history, his blood tests, his stool samples—everything I can get my mitts on. Especially his CAT scans."

Tad jumped in as she paused. "Wow. I'm flattered that you chose me as the one to first hear your revelation."

Donna giggled again. "Shut up. You're the fourth one I've told—I was just hoping that you'd be more supportive and open-minded than my superiors, especially Dr. Johnson." Her smile faded. "Seriously, though, dude, I'm not 100% positive, but it fits. Hear me out. Everything suggests that Quinn has a weird agnosia called prosopagnosia, in which he doesn't recognize people's faces. He—I think—sees only separate features one at a time—a nose, an ear, a mouth, and can't put them together to recognize who the person is. Everyone looks like a stranger to him. Now, he was in extensive, multiple surgeries for the brain damage he got from that car wreck. So, to him, one moment he's driving in his car, then the next thing he's aware of is waking up in a hospital bed surrounded by people he's never met."

"Okay. Very traumatic, agreed. But that's just one sense. And why would he start killing people? That's kind of extreme."

"Because," her hand slapped on the desk top emphatically, "I saw something else. I think parts of his memory were affected too—not full on amnesia or anything, but some significant loss. And you said one sense out, but that's not really true. He's deaf, remember…"

"But he signs, and probably reads lips, so what?"

"Just that areas that may also have been affected. Look, I'll show you the charts. But picture this. He doesn't recognize anyone, and more importantly, he doesn't see his wife, or friends, or any doctors or nurses that he knows anywhere at all. They've abandoned him, and these imposters are around him instead. Weird, faceless ones. And, he can't hear them, and may have forgotten how to sign. He can't communicate with them at all. Who was the first one he killed? His wife, who was very physically demonstrative, hugging and kissing him. But she wasn't his wife to him. As to why kill, doesn't that sound nightmarish? Wouldn't you be terrified? And who's more dangerous than a person scared out of their minds?"

Tad digested this, taking his time. He went over the points that she'd made one by one in his head. He was fairly familiar with Quinn's history, and he had to admit that what she said did sound plausible. Could it be true? Donna watched him quietly, her legs tucked neatly underneath her on the chair, lotus style.

"You mentioned the brain surgeries that he had. Why didn't they correct the damage that causes this condition?"

"Quinn's brain was badly fucked up in his accident. The doctors had their hands full simply keeping him alive. In comparison, the damage still left which may be causing the condition is extremely subtle. Also, the prosopagnosia in his brain looks different from the documented cases that I've seen, and it seems to be much worse. Most people with it can recognize emotions on faces, and age, and sex, at least. I don't think he can. Not to mention his probable memory loss. It's like he won the bad brain damage lottery. Bear in mind, too, that I'm basing my theory as much on his behavior as from his CAT scans, and things."

"All right, you've come up with a reasonable theory for why he's like that. How are you gonna fix him?"

"I think he could learn signing again, learn how to talk with people again. Using that he can learn what happened to him, and become a normal, functioning person again. But how to teach him? How to make him know us, trust us enough to spend weeks and months learning? As we've discussed, he's very dangerous. Remember the five senses. Sight is out, since his agnosia makes him unable to recognize us. Hearing is totally out too. Touch is impractical since him touching us is risky to us, and touching him will scare him even more. Taste is impractical too, since it's so localized. So smell it is. He may have recognized people using this already, but I think his sense of smell is poor. Hell, his allergies are intense, some days not much must penetrate that phlegm. But a strong, unique smell—that could be the ticket. My hope is he'll associate a particular, chosen odor with me, and, using a lot of patience and effort, he'll relax enough to consent to be our pupil."

"Well that sounds cool to me. How come Dr. Johnson was less than enthused?"

"Fucking politics. He's arrogant, as you know. He has his own theories about Quinn, and he's not about to throw away his in favor of a young, new, female doctor's. He can't believe his brain surgery buddies would have missed anything, first of all. Plus, I think it's punishment—I believe on some level he thinks I may be on to something, but he doesn't want Quinn to get better. He's said as much, 'Two meals a day is plenty for the psycho murderer,' and such. A psychiatrist, can you imagine?" She paused for a moment, and took a deep breath. "Not that I'm for a minute condoning the killings of all those people—that was a horrible tragedy, and I feel for them and their families. But, this seems to be a horrible, yes, but fucked up, weird case. Is Quinn responsible for these killings, if I'm right about his condition?"

Tad stroked his chin. "I see what you mean. To refuse a possibly effective treatment for the guy is barbaric. And if he did learn to talk, and presuming he's repentant and all, maybe he'd do something to help make it up to the victims, in a way. Something. But anyway—when are you going to test out your plan?"

"Tomorrow night. That's partly why I'm here. Will you help me out?"

Tad shivered slightly, almost imperceptibly. "We're not trusting your theory too much, right? Full defensive protection and all, right?"

"Dude, I'm hurt. Of course. I'm not arrogant enough to risk other's lives for my own ego. And certainly selfish enough to protect my own ass at all times, too."

"Okay, I'm in. Just spell my name right—either in your triumphant report on this if all goes well, or on my tombstone if it doesn't."

"Great. Thanks, man." She was off in a shot, white coat billowing. Tad followed her with his eyes, ruminating still on the theoretical cud she'd given him. Hmm. That Johnson was so close minded, egocentric, and brutish surprised him not at all. He was by far Tad's least favorite doctor here. He still remembered his first day here, in the break room, when Johnson had made fun of him for being a nurse. And not in a playful way, either, but in a mean, bullying manner. "Back in my day almost all the male nurses were rump rangers. Is that still true?" Tad, for seemingly once in his life, had thought of a comeback right then, and not five hours later. "A good number of them are, Dr. Johnson. But I liked that. That meant more nursing school pussy for me." The other guys had given him a good laugh for that. Johnson, though, had gone silent, and bustled out in a huff.

Shit, though. Just thinking about confronting Quinn, even with all the defenses, chilled Tad. He felt like the stereotypical pansy that Johnson had inferred he was. He hoped Donna knew what she was talking about.

*****

The demons were up to something.

It had begun about a week ago. Three non-custodial demons had come in, as usual while he was dozing. They'd restrained him using the padded cuffs on his hands and feet before he'd been able to properly fight back. Relatively normal behavior for them. But what had come next was not. Instead of taking blood, or putting him into a torture device, they simply had sat him down in a chair they'd brought in. In front of him was a table. On the other side of the table a demon had been seated. The demons who had restrained and seated him had sat down themselves, a few feet away.

What had come next had been bizarre. Not painful, though, which was a refreshing change. In fact, they hadn't touched him at all for the duration of the event. The demon opposite him had begun holding up its hands. It then began to move them around chaotically, not hitting, not grabbing or holding anything, just moving them. After a while he could see that the hands started making the same motions repeatedly, and as it did it would indicate itself. Still later, it began to do the same with the table, the chair, the other demons, and various other objects it produced from a bag behind it.

He'd stared stonily at the flailing demon, and its fellows. He'd kept waiting for them to stop the strangeness and start the abuse. It hadn't come though. Instead, the demons had left, right after leaving his dinner for the night. It had been a better dinner, too. Larger portions, tastier. Two desserts.

They'd kept it up each day since. The total non-abuse had also remained intact. He'd taken to barely struggling at all during these times; it seemed okay for now. If, or more likely, when they stopped and went back to abusing him he could revert back to fighting as well. He might as well conserve his strength. The extra food was helping, too. He couldn't see his ribs anymore. He felt stronger than ever.

Yet another weird thing about the past week was the demons themselves. They'd always been interchangeable, faceless. Now there seemed to be certain individuals. The one behind the desk, the hand mover, for example smelled sweet and spicy, each time. The other non-custodial demons similarly had their own scents, all different and distinctive. Were they truly individual demons, or did they just adopt the odors for his benefit (confusion?)? This also didn't make sense. He couldn't figure it out. More of their torturous tricks, probably.

What were they up to? He would just have to wait and see.

***

Donna successfully traversed the gauntlet of drunken people (mostly med school students) and rejoined Tad at their table. He grabbed the bottle as she sat down, and read the label carefully.

"That doesn't look like The Dommer to me," he said, fake huffily.

"This ain't exactly a posh place," she returned. "Korbel's the best they got. Fuck you, it's champagne."

"True." He picked up the opener off the tray, and after removing the foil wrap, popped the top and extracted the cork without spilling any. He filled the glasses, and they picked them up in unison for the toast.

"To Patience, Labels, and Mental Health," she said. They clinked their glasses together and drank.

"Labels? Didn't some philosopher say, 'When you label me, you negate me?'"

"Again, fuck you. Assigning Quinn his label might stop him from negating others." Tad smirked and poured himself another glass. Donna shifted around in her seat. "Maybe we should have waited long enough to get showered and change. Our odors are overwhelming."

"That bad, huh?"

"Not negative smells, just too strong for my taste. Especially now. It's my time of the month, so I'm particularly sensitive now."

"Goddamn shrinks. Always revealing too much of their personal lives." She smiled in a rather perfunctory manner and stared off into space. Tad knew she was thinking about Quinn, and shut up and let her do it. When she was ready she'd talk. After about five minutes she was.

"That pissant Johnson still doesn't believe me. He still keeps saying that Quinn's a sociopath and is playing me, looking for a chance to kill more people. He must not look at any of my evidence! His mind couldn't be more closed."

"Oh well, screw him. At least he's not stopping you. Eventually he'll have to see the truth. 'Course then he'll try to take credit for it, I bet, but..."

"Yeah. Man, though, that's not gonna get me down. Today was great! When he signed his name, and pointed at himself, then did the same for me, I almost creamed myself. We're on the way. We've got identity, and trust, probably. The main obstacle is passed. It's still gonna take him forever to build up his vocab, with his condition, but he'll get it eventually. Then we can treat him properly, maybe even get him out of there and be productive again."

Tad stared at Donna. Her face was flushed with excitement, her eyes alive and vibrant. Cute in a geeky sort of way, he decided. Unless it was the champagne, he admitted. Never mind. Stay professional. "It was real cool. If Johnson or any other skeptics had been in with us today, they'd have caved. Quinn's changed. You can see it in his face."

"All right, English Leather-Vanilla. Enough shop talk. We have the night off. Quinn, who now knows himself as Quinn, heard from Donna that our next session is Wednesday. Wanna get your ass kicked in Foosball?"

"I'll take you on, Jasmine-Curry. But the results won't be what you think. You're obviously feeling extra cocky from your professional breakthrough. But the little soccer players' heads are already as shrunken as they'll ever get, and they're wooden besides. Your powers are useless."

Donna retrieved a handful of quarters from her purse. "We'll just see about that, Mister."

***

The session was progressing well. Donna held court behind the table, slowly and patiently signing various words to Quinn. He, for his part, stared attentively at her, (albeit it in his odd, disjointed way) his own hands repeating the words that she signed, occasionally forming one of the others he knew in an independent manner. Quinn's bonds had been modified to allow these motions; instead of his hands being locked tightly behind his back, or even in his lap, they were each attached by a good three feet of chain to a grommet embedded in the table. His feet, however, were still tightly locked together beneath him. Around them the nurses sat in their own chairs, watching the event closely; Matt and Jose behind Donna, Tad on Quinn's side of the table, about five feet away.

"Brain," said Donna, deliberately and exaggeratedly mouthing the word as she made the corresponding hand signs. She knew this was a long shot, as Quinn, by the nature of his condition, could only focus on one small body part at a time. However, she thought it was good practice for both him and her. Eventually he might become able to concentrate and even lip read. She believed in aiming high.

Quinn's eyes narrowed somewhat, and they seemed to be focusing on her hands. But it was so difficult to judge. Donna was used to repeating the codes many, many, times, and did so now.

"Brain," along with its nonverbal cue. Quinn's left eyebrow started to flicker upwards. This was often a signal that he was understanding the sign. He brought up his hands to mimic hers. He was close, but just a little off on one finger. Carefully, and slowly, Donna moved her hands toward his to correct the motion. For the past two weeks he had allowed this brief, gentle contact without becoming upset or violent. Even so, Donna couldn't quite get her hands to be entirely tremor-free as her hands got nearer over the table.

"Ummph, a wahwah," moaned Jose suddenly. All those with hearing in the room turned to face him as he began to flop about in his chair uncontrollably. His eyes rolled back in his head and saliva bubbled out between his lips.

Matt leapt up from his chair. He'd been sitting in it backward, his forearms resting on the chair backrest. As he stood his jacket pocket clinked against the chair. The bottle of Denim cologne nestled inside jumped out of his pocket and into the air. The cap disengaged as it catapulted, and a large dollop of its contents splashed across Donna's outstretched wrists. The bottle itself nipped the edge of the table and fell to the floor, the remainder of its scent gurgling out in a puddle.

Four things happened simultaneously. Matt, unaware of the odor missile he'd accidentally released reached Jose, who'd fallen to the floor. Tad leaped toward Quinn desperately, and by chance his right foot landed squarely on the cologne bottle that was stewing in its own juices. Donna murmured, "Oh shit!" and began to pull back her hands. Quinn, whose attention had been locked on Jose temporarily, inhaled. A split second after he did both eyebrows arched up dramatically.

The slippery bottle went out from under Tad, and so did his legs. He wasn't able to break his fall, and he fell face first onto the floor behind Quinn. Quinn, meanwhile, grabbed Donna's hands just before they passed out of his handcuff range. With a jerk, he yanked her small frame across the table towards him. Donna scrabbled for purchase on her side of the table, sending her purse flying, not achieving any kind of hold. Her head came flying toward Quinn's. Matt perceived the other emergency unfolding before him, and he also moved toward doctor and patient.

Keeping her hands pinned in an outstretched position, Quinn brought his mouth to Donna's neck. His teeth tore her jugular in one slashing bite. Tad landed on Quinn's back a second later, his eyesight blurred by the tears and blood that had resulted from his nose slamming the floor. Quinn dropped Donna's arms and lashed out viscously with an elbow, the three feet of chain on his cuffs giving him just enough room to catch

Tad in the jaw and tip him off. Just after, Matt's fist exploded onto Quinn's crotch hard, stunning him. Matt took advantage by grabbing Quinn's right arm and jamming it tight behind his back, pinning the patient's midsection against the table as he did. Tad slipped up behind them and jabbed a hypodermic into Quinn's thigh and depressed the plunger.

"Stay on him," Tad yelled, as he rolled over to tend to Donna, who had fallen off the table onto the floor. She gasped several times and pushed her final heartbeats of blood past his would-be staunching fingers.

When he was sure the heavy sedative had taken effect, Matt came off Quinn and once again regarded Jose, who was still frothing and trembling on the floor behind the slaughter. The other nurses and attendants broke through in time to do little that was constructive.

***

The buzzer sounded on Dr. Johnson's desk, and his secretary's voice came over the intercom. "Tad Panopoulous is here to see you, Dr. Johnson."

He clicked the button and answered. "Thanks, Grace. Send him in."

He watched as Tad entered his office, and took the chair that Johnson indicated with a motion. Tad looked a mess, Johnson saw. Heavy tape on his obviously broken-then-reset nose, black eyes, and jaw that was reddish and swollen. Johnson broke off his brief study. "What's on your mind, Tad?"

"I'll get right to the point, Dr. Johnson. I was talking about Quinn with some of the other doctors and nurses, and they mentioned that you had changed his treatment. I wanted to talk to you about that." Tad's speech was slightly altered by his injured jaw, but still understandable.

"Well, Tad, I think Mr. Utz has killed quite enough people, don't you? Dr. Brison's intentions were good, but her methods were clearly misguided. I can't risk more lives. I can't believe I let her do something that dangerous; I feel responsible. I guess I assumed that security would be extra tight around such a dangerous patient, and that her dubious theories couldn't do much harm."

Tad grew visibly angry, but he managed to control his tone. "With all due respect, Doctor, Brison's theories were correct. In the beginning they sounded a little out there, but I was there, observing first hand while she worked with Quinn. She'd broken through! He was learning to communicate. As for the security, it wasn't lax; it was a collection of freak episodes. First, Jose had his seizure, even though he has no history of them, no epilepsy or anything. Then, Matt forgot to remove his cologne bottle, and in going to help Jose he happened to bump it out of his pocket, where it happened to open and splash on Donna's arm at the precise moment when she was within Quinn's reach. And I slipped on the same bottle, which delayed me a few precious seconds. It was a million-to-one shot, easy. I…"

"Excuse me, Tad, but I'm familiar with what happened. The point is, it did happen, and personally I don't think it was as unlikely as you maintain. But that's not important. Donna saw what she wanted to see, and overlooked what she didn't want to. Quinn's a sociopath. Sympathetic in some ways, because he's deaf, and had those serious brain injuries, but still a killer. He was playing you, waiting for just such a mistake to murder someone else."

"That's not true! You had to be there, Doctor. You could see it in his face! He's terrified of people, and can't recognize them usually. And then the smell idea enabled him to do that, and he started to relax, and trust us, and then learn to sign. But then his trusted liaison changed before him, her smell altered, which to him would be like me pulling my face off to reveal a different one underneath. He freaked, and not surprisingly lashed out at this apparent betrayer. Look, just please read Donna's notes, look at the tapes, before you change anything. The best way to honor Donna is by continuing her work, and successfully treating Quinn. Otherwise she really did die for nothing."

"Tad, I'm sorry, but it was Donna who was tragically wrong. But fine, even though I already have gone through all the data, I'll review it again. But I'm going to have to cut this meeting short. I have other things to deal with." He stood up and began walking to the door.

Tad also stood, and he began talking quickly. "At least let me stay in Quinn's section, be in on any treatment you decide to do with him, please, Dr. Johnson."

Johnson reached the door and opened it. "I don't think that's a good idea, Tad. I'm concerned that you are too emotionally involved with this patient. You saw a close friend, a very close friend, murdered, it's natural you would feel this way. What you need is to be away from Quinn for a long while, maybe forever. Take a week or two of vacation, and then I'm transferring you to another wing."

"No, Doctor, that's…"

"Sorry, but that's the way it's going to be. Goodbye Tad," he patted him on the back, and pushed him lightly through the doorway. "Get healthy again. Do your mourning, get on with your life. Don't obsess over past events." He ignored Tad's further blustering and closed the door behind the nurse. Back in his chair, he stared at his doctorate certificate and considered Quinn Utz once more. Read Donna's notes again (or once)? Not likely. Typical young, woman doctor, sensitive to a big fault. Prosopagnosia! A freak condition, one that made for a fascinating read in a journal, sure, but something a regular doctor would probably never see. Donna reminded him of a hypochondriac with a little spider bite thinking that they had the flesh-eating virus after seeing a sensationalized account of it on television. She'd forgotten Occam's Razor. Besides, even if she was right about the agnosia, a big if, what did it matter? Quinn still murdered, and wasn't insane. Other people who definitely did have prosopagnosia didn't go around slaying anyone. Quinn was responsible. It was time to hold him accountable. Enough was enough.

Johnson sighed. Despite his disagreements with Donna, he would miss her. If she'd only been a bit more practical, more healthily cynical, she might have survived and made a good psychiatrist. She had been smart, and dedicated. That nurse, though, Tad, might be a problem. He seemed quite stubborn. Johnson grabbed a pen and began a memo, the meat of which was a directive banning Tad from Quinn's wing, explaining why it was healthier for Quinn and Tad both, their physical and mental health. It didn't hurt to be prepared for all eventualities, as the debacle of three days ago had certainly proven.

***

He'd forgotten how satisfying it felt to kill a demon. But the feeling had returned, one of the few friends he had here. He was relaxing on his mattress, hands clasped behind his head. Replaying the incident in his mind. He kept remembering the feel of the demon's flesh in his teeth, the hot coppery taste of her blood in his mouth. She'd been so surprised.

His jaws now ground together involuntarily. As shocked as she'd been, she was not more so than he had been. Or should he say, "Quinn Utz," and she was, "Dr. Donna Brison," and they were in the, "Orange County Psychiatric Hospital." Shit. Those fucking demons, you had to hand it to them. They'd worn him down, managed to trick him. He'd actually started to believe them, to believe that he wasn't in Hell. Plus, it was nice to actually talk with someone, even if they were demons. It had been something different, interesting. The tortures had ceased, too, and the benefits had also been nice.

But it had all been a diabolical ruse. They'd strung him along, probably laughing at him behind his back the whole time, reading his mind, observing his hatred and doubt waning almost completely away. And then, just as he was getting used to thinking of them as being people, their true nature had resurfaced. The memory of the change was also sharp in his mind. "Donna," had switched suddenly, becoming another. Demon switching to demon, all the same, like before.

But he had showed them. He'd gotten back at them, at least by a little bit. Another demon dead. How many was that? He couldn't remember.

So now it was punishment time. Back to stepped down meals, more torture sessions. And what then? More strange, hidden extended tricks like the last one? He'd have to wait and see.

They'd gotten him, though. It was shameful, galling. But still, overall, he felt mostly proud of himself. He was no sniveling coward soul, passively accepting punishment, not trying to battle his tormentors. They were beating him, as was inevitable given all their overwhelming advantages, but he was scoring some too. It was no blowout.

He felt a twinge in his bladder, so he got up to relieve himself. Today was the first day he'd gotten his commode back since the attack. He'd been restrained and put in diapers. This was much better.

After he was done, and was getting ready to lie down again, he happened to catch a glimpse of something shiny sticking just out of the bottom of his mattress. He picked the object up, and turned it over in his hand. It was a piece of a mirror, broken off from a compact. "Donna's," apparently. He held it up to his face and peered into it intently.

He stood like that, entranced, for over fifteen minutes, angling the mirror this way and that, catching different glimpses of himself. Then he collapsed, half on, half off his bed, and lay there, barely blinking, barely breathing. But with mind racing.

***

I'm a murderer, he thought. I'm Quinn Utz, and I've killed many fellow living human beings, the most recent one being a woman named Dr. Donna Brison. I'm in a mental hospital on Earth. And there's something wrong with me. Something very wrong with my eyes, or brain. I can't see people for who they are. I can't recognize them visually.

It was all so simple, and explained everything. All his musings on why "the demons" did things this way, or that way, all made sense now. They weren't punishing him at all. They'd been trying to help him. The harsh conditions had been due to his reactions to them. *My god, how many did I kill?* He still couldn't remember, and now it was very important to him.

And why couldn't he remember most other things? Who he was, really. Who he'd known, been related to, everything. Only ghosts and little memory shreds remained. Before he'd figured this was just a factor of being damned, another trick. Now, he knew, it was something physiological, accidental.

Wait, he thought, *is this really an even more elaborate trick? They're demons, capable of anything. This roller-coaster of ideas and emotions must be particularly sweet to them.*

But no. He wasn't dead. They were people. He knew it was true. The demons and Hell opinion were paranoid delusions. The only dangerous monster here was him. Even if he had been completely confused, and hadn't meant to do anything evil, a monster he had been.

So how to ensure that he didn't remain a monster? Quinn thought this over for a while, and then he leapt up and got as close as he could to the camera. As its unblinking eye stared, he made the hand signals that Donna had taught him. There had been others with them while he learned. Tad, he remembered. And Jose, and some other guy. They could talk all of this out.

About an hour later, the nurse at the console noticed the psychopath, Quinn, gesturing at the camera. She shivered as she looked at him. She'd heard the stories of what he'd done to that doctor. It looked like he was trying to entice in some more victims.

Not her. She turned back to her magazine. Every so often she checked the monitors of the other patients in the ward, but she skipped Mr. Utz's from then on. *Shit,* she thought, *why'd I agree to the transfer from pediatrics? She wasn't cut out for this. These people were really sick, and untreatable, apparently. Not to mention dangerous. The raise had been good, but she didn't think it was worth it, despite what Johnson had told her. She checked the clock again, and then, similar to wanting/not wanting to look at a car wreck, she glanced quickly at Quinn's scene again. He was still at it, waving his arms and hands around. She went back to reading about The Fifty Most Beautiful People.

***

Sam checked the twin hypodermics nestled in his shirt pocket once more. Still there. He looked over at Ricky and grinned slightly. "Ready man?" he asked.

Ricky nodded and tightened his grip on his baton. Sam slid the key into the lock. Remember, he thought to himself, he's like a rabid dog. Sick, confused, and very dangerous. He's all screwed up and scared, Johnson had assured him. Ending his life would be more of a kindness than a punishment. He turned the key and pushed the door inward, silently. The noise wasn't a danger, of course, but the vibration could be. He and Ricky ducked inside, and Sam relocked the door behind them.

There Quinn was, sleeping on his mattress, his back facing them. Remember John, too, Sam thought. Your best friend, brutally killed by this maniac. Not quickly, either; he'd died in agony, screaming. If Quinn didn't deserve execution, who did? And don't forget about Dr. Brison, and all the others. The guy's wife even. This one contributed nothing to nobody, and took so much.

Sam looked over at Ricky, saw his partner self-consciously looking at the overhead camera. When Ricky looked up and saw that Sam was watching, his lips twisted into a sheepish smile. No problem there. Johnson would take care of the camera. And everything else. They'd be suspended, of course, but nothing further. Nothing from the law, either, as long as they stuck to the plan. The cash prize, half of which had already been delivered, would more than get them through the rough patch.

They approached their prey. Ricky towards Quinn's head, Sam by his feet. Quinn had turned over and was facing them now, snoring away. Sam's heart was pounding in his ears. He'd seen what this guy could do to people. Johnson had assured him that Quinn would be dazed, partly sedated. Enough to slow him down enough that they could take care of him, but not enough to preclude a bit of a scuffle. It had to look somewhat realistic, after all. Ah, sedatives—drugs. The good Doctor's insurance. He had evidence of Sam's appropriation of some, and surely he had dirt on this Ricky, too. Sam doubted that Johnson took a crap without everything being planned out to the finest detail.

Well, no more wasted time. "Now," he said to Ricky. Ricky's baton rose and Sam's leg reared back at the same instant.

Suddenly Quinn was out of his bed, rolling rapidly toward Ricky. The baton swing struck through air, uselessly. Quinn knifed through Ricky's legs, and pushed against the attendant's knees, sending him crashing against Sam. As they lay tangled, Quinn kicked Ricky's hand, and seconds later the baton was in his hand instead. Quinn retreated until his back was nearly against the far wall. He kept switching the baton from hand to hand, watching his attackers get off of each other.

Shit, thought Quinn, and his vision blurred, then went sharp again. He'd been dozing when he'd abruptly sensed their presence. By now he'd easily and convincingly learned how to feign sleep, like a champ. It had been easy to wait until they approached, then make his own preemptive attack. Fucking demons, they never gave him any credit.

Suddenly he shook his head, even slapped it. What? He must be a bit punchy from a drug they must have given him. Jesus. You're Quinn Utz, alive, on Earth, in a hospital, he reminded himself bitterly. Not demons attacking him, just nurses and medical personnel treating him.

They were looking at him now, he saw. Unlike the others from before, this pair didn't reek of anything. They seemed very hesitant. Jeez, can you blame them, he thought. You're a goddamn murderer, and now you're armed. Gonna kill some more innocents, are we?

No. He would not. He threw the baton at their feet and held his hands out submissively. After a moment he remembered more, and began making signs with them.

The one who'd been by his feet grabbed the club and rushed him. Quinn forced himself not to fight back, or even ward him off, as blows rained on his shoulders, chest, and legs. After a moment he fell, but the blows continued to fall. The other one, he managed to see, was holding a hypodermic at the ready.

Why were they doing this? This wasn't right. They'd never beat him like this before. It was always three or four attendants, with cuffs, who quickly sedated him. Not like this at all. Whack! A blow exploded on his face, clipping his brow. Blood quickly pooled in his left eye, blocking his vision. Still more blows impacted his body. Finally, his attacker paused, his breath heaving from his exertion.

Despite himself, Quinn nearly lashed out with his legs. No, no! Don't fight back. God he hurt bad. He could feel several broken limbs, and enormous cuts. They were killing him; it was obvious. He didn't understand why, or why in this way, or why now in particular, but it was undeniable.

Here came the hypo. He let it come, didn't even flinch, not at the needle prick, or the gratuitous punch in the face that followed. He had it coming. Boy did he. It was only fair, really, after all the violence he'd dealt out. He slumped forward, feeling the sedative take hold. Surprised, he felt another hypo entering him. Two? That was unnecessary. Unless…. Oh, of course.

I'm sorry, Quinn thought. I didn't know. It was all a big misunderstanding. Will I soon be seeing demons again, real ones this time? And with this last thought, Quinn's brain shut down.

Ricky and Sam sat and waited another two minutes before speaking. "I guess that's it," said Sam. The fist in his face caught him completely off guard. The two or three others in his gut knocked him to the floor.

"What the fuck, asshole? What are you doing?" His hand searched his mouth. He'd lost a tooth!

"Our little play, remember? We look way too good in comparison to him. By the way, you hit him too many times. We were fighting for our lives, defending ourselves, until we could sedate him, remember? Double the dose, since I didn't see that you had already done him? Not beating him almost to death!"

"Fuck off! You didn't lose a friend to that psycho. Besides, our sponsor will fix everything. No worries."

"I just hope your overacting didn't kill this story. Now rough me up a little." Sam enthusiastically pounded on Rick for a while, until they were both properly wounded and bloody. Then after a shared glance they started yelling and opened the door. Sam spared a look behind them to regard their quarry once more. He was a pulpy mess. Maybe he had overdone it a little.

The door swung shut behind them. Left behind was the corpse. Its right hand, despite several broken fingers, was still arranged in a deliberate manner. Dr. Brison, Tad, Jose, or Matt would have recognized it as the symbol for "Quinn."

65

My Son, the Afterbirth

Craig Stewart

He walked in the door that day with a handful of tulips and a grin to match. They were my favourite flowers and he knew it. He wanted something. That schoolboy mischief living behind his smile was no coincidence.

I put my trashy romance novel to rest and rose from the squishy comfort of the love seat to greet him and receive his offering. I took them, smelled them and planted them into a vase, all the while keeping my trepidation safely tucked away where he couldn't see.

"Thanks, they're great," I assured him. "Is there a reason for your sweetness today?"

He was still a little out of breath and smelled hot from his bike ride home. I liked that. I liked that a lot.

Before he answered me, he brought his lips to mine for a quick meet and greet. They met and then parted, but not before a few of his laboured breaths titillated my lips and neck. I liked that too.

"You're reason enough." Doug was certainly a romantic man, the kind of man who would earnestly tilt his head and swoon over a mass-produced card from the dollar store about the healing power of kindness.

theI, on the other hand, was not that kind of man. Not that I didn't have my own weaknesses, sentimentality just wasn't one of them.

"So, you carefully balanced an array of tulips on your handlebars, dodging traffic all across town, just for little old me and nothing more?" I allowed for a little skepticism to seep through.

"Yes sir! That's right," Doug replied slipping off his spring coat and sneakers.

"There's no agenda in the gesture?"

"None."

"They're just for me for being me. Right?"

"That's it, babe."

"So you're not going to bring something up that I've repeatedly and explicitly forbid you from ever bringing up again? You're not planning on upsetting me?" I asked this all while nodding and smiling, waiting for the trap to fall.

"Travis," his use of my name was a clear sign of danger ahead. "I have some news."

"No." I was abrupt.

"No?"

"No. I won't hear it no matter how many flowers you offer."

"But, I have news. You can't just refuse news."

"I can. Observe, I'm doing it right now." With that, I pivoted and walked away. I had told him last week that we weren't going to discuss his delusion any further and if he tried to bring it up, well, I did exactly what I said I'd do. I ignored him.

Once my anger had carried me into the kitchen, I cursed myself for having already put away all the clean dishes. The counters were already wiped, the wood table already greased, the tiled floor already mopped. I had no practical reason for being in the room. Damn my efficiency. Why couldn't I have stormed upstairs where there was laundry to busy me? Then again, could I really be blamed? What else was I to do with my time other than tend to the house? I remembered when I wasn't such a homebody, but that memory had become corroded from years of cleaning products.

"Are you angry?" Doug asked innocently enough. He had smoothed out his voice, probably afraid he might ignite me again. It didn't really make a difference - I was already ablaze.

"I'm disappointed more than anything."

"I don't mean to upset you, babe."

"Fuck that. If you didn't want to upset me, you wouldn't keep bringing it up."

"I'm sorry. But I can't stop wanting it."

He stepped toward me and added a gentle touch to compliment his gentle tone. His large hands eased into the sleeves of my t-shirt and held my shoulders. The contact was intoxicatingly tender. I had weaknesses. I certainly did.

"Why?" I asked.

"'Cause I need us to be a family," Doug whispered next to my ear.

"We are a family. We love each other, so we're a family. What else is there?"

"Children."

"Fuck, Doug. We can't keep circling around this. I feel like I'm stuck in a vortex with you. We just keep repeating ourselves, over and over, and we get nowhere."

"This is different."

"Why? What's different? So far, it feels like the same old shit to me."

"It's different cause of the news I have, if you let me say it."

As much as I hated to admit it, there was something fresh in the way he spoke. It intrigued me. The optimism in his face reminded me of when he was younger - when we were younger and everything was different. Through the years we had both faded into our respective roles. He started making enough money for both of us with his flooring business, so I quit my serving job. If I knew then that giving up my dream of being a greasy spoon waiter would gradually mutate me into a 1950s housewife, I never would have signed in blood. But, there I stood in the kitchen, fretting about silverware and babies.

"You want to use a surrogate?" I asked.

"No. Not that. It wouldn't be real."

"I don't know what you mean when you say that. You want a kid, but you don't want to use a surrogate and you don't want to adopt. What do you want?"

"I want a child that's part of both of us. Born from us, from the love we have. I want what every other normal couple has."

"Well, we can't. We can't make a child, Doug. We could have nothing but sex for a week, a month, a year, and we still wouldn't make a baby. That's gay sex 101. Please, just accept that. Unless you want to leave me for someone who can bear your brood, I don't know what else to say. And frankly, I'm tired of having this conversation."

Before I could escape from the room, Doug caught me by the arm.

"What if it was possible?" he asked with a stern composure. "What if we could make a baby that was as much a part of me as it was a part of you? What would you say then?"

"I would say keep dreaming doctor Frankenstein."

"But you would want it, wouldn't you?" His blue eyes wavered genuinely beneath his troubled brow. Yet still, I could not bring myself to answer such a preposterous question.

So I posed a question of my own, "Just me, Doug. Am I not enough?"

Either he couldn't answer, or I didn't stick around long enough. Either way, the question lingered.

***

Our silk sheets felt like wet dirt that night and were trying to suffocate me. Sleep was not an option.

I dug my way out of them and allowed my wanting hand to glide over to the other side of the bed. To my disappointment, my fingers found no bare skin to tickle. Doug was in the bathroom.

My thoughts filled the gaping shadows that stretched across the ceiling. It wasn't entirely Doug's fault I was dissatisfied with how my life had turned. After all, it was my choice to stick around and play homemaker. And if I'm being honest, for a while I even liked it. Sadly, that was no longer the case. Doug had a vision of a cheery family with a picket fence, but what he got was a boyfriend. We could have been a family, a great family, if only he let go of his Sunday afternoon fantasy.

Through the dark patterns above me, however, there were still slashes of light visible. Though I had never been a fan of children – pathetic, selfish little things as they were - I would have given him exactly what he wanted if I could, for that was love.

Shoot me in the head; I did love him.

Then the noises began.

Horrible, sickly gurgles spilled out from the edges of the bathroom door. The sloppy heaving was so severe, I couldn't tell at first which end it was coming out of. Perhaps both. It sounded as though Doug was retching his very stomach. I could almost see the pink sack bubble up from between his lips and slap against the floor.

No wonder. He had eaten twice his normal portions at dinner that evening. Poor thing had brought it on himself.

***

The morning was merciless. It found my sleeping form contorted in an almost impossible shape. Following my restless nights, I often awoke in a tight weave. I tie myself in a knot to put an end to the tossing and turning.

Well, as soon as I crawled out of bed, I felt an ache from every twist my body had settled on. I was not as dexterous as I once was.

Doug was still missing in action. Normally the house was empty by the time I got up, but today was Saturday. Doug didn't usually work on Saturdays.

The bathroom door where Doug had been hurling was still closed. I knocked. There was no answer.

A brief but powerful moment of terror sank through my body. Maybe Doug was hurt? Maybe he needed my help last night and I just closed my eyes.

I threw open the door as if I expected there to be resistance on the other side.

The bathroom was empty. Empty, but not clean. The glowing white of our bowl-shaped sink was besmirched by a thick smear of red that drooled all the way passed the countertop and down to the floor. I saw chunky remnants in the blood as if some flesh had been shed. It reminded me of an experimental film I had seen which included repetitive flashing images of a woman's afterbirth. The woman also happened to have been the filmmaker. I didn't like the film. I didn't like this either.

"Doug!" I yelled.

Waiting for a reply was agony and impatience got the better of me.

"Doug! Are you okay?"

I left the bathroom when I noticed faint red stains on the carpet. They led me downstairs to the main floor of the house.

If Doug was hurt and I did nothing, I would have never forgiven myself. Why didn't I just ask him if he needed help? Why didn't I say something?

"Doug, if you can answer me, please answer me!" I was approaching panic.

Then, from the kitchen came a subdued reply, "Shhhhhh," it demanded.

"Excuse me?"

"Travis, please keep it down." It was Doug's voice. I started to breathe again.

"Are you okay?" I asked at a slightly lower decibel.

"I'm great. Why don't you join me in here?"

I entered the kitchen where everything looked pretty much normal, except for Doug who was crouched next to some cupboards.

He waved me over.

"Come here," he said with a smile. He didn't look sick, only disheveled.

"I saw the blood. What happened upstairs?"

"Oh right, I guess that would seem a little odd."

"I thought you were hurt."

"Like I cut myself shaving?" Doug chuckled modestly.

"I'm serious," I interjected, "I really thought something awful happened. And why are we still whispering?"

"'Cause we don't want to wake him."

"Him? Him who?"

"Come here. I'll show you."

Though he seemed out of his mind like some kind of fanatical street person, I knelt by his side anyway. You could say it was because I was concerned for him, but I blame curiosity.

His hand wrapped around the edge of the cupboard below the sink where we kept the pots and pans. He burrowed his eyes into mine before he opened it.

"Travis, you have to promise me you'll stay calm, alright? Will you promise me that?"

I nodded, knowing fully well such a promise was impossible.

"Good," he continued, "'Cause I don't want you to freak out. Just stay calm and I'll explain everything."

"Did you buy a puppy?" I asked.

"Not exactly." The response was too vague for comfort.

Before I had a chance to press any further, he began to open the cupboard. The hinges turned at an excruciating pace. Things were not revealed all at once, but rather, one little tease at a time.

The pots all seemed to be accounted for. Indeed, nothing was out of place.

I noticed the edge of one of our bathroom towels hanging over the side the largest pot. I leaned in to see where the towel led.

The rest of the blue cloth was bunched into the bottom of the pot, creating a bed for the creature that slumbered inside.

At first, I thought I was looking at a hairless Chihuahua of some kind. No, not hairless. Skinless. Its thin flesh was almost translucent. It curled into itself like a snake would with its emaciated arms bent around its soft skull.

What the fuck had he done?

I pulled away from the cupboard too shocked to scream. Too shocked to do much of anything.

What the fuck had Doug done!

"Okay, remember your promise? You said you wouldn't freak out," Doug said calmly, gently closing the cupboard.

"What the fuck did you do?" There was no difference between my thoughts and my speech at that moment.

"Alright, I'm sorry I couldn't tell you earlier. I admit I should have. But, I was afraid you'd tell me not to do it."

"Do what? What did you do? What is that thing?"

"That's Roy. He's just sleeping. I think last night tuckered him out."

"That thing is alive?"

"Of course he is. He's going to be our son."

My mind frantically sorted through thoughts to try to make sense of what Doug had said. Had he lost his mind? Did he steal a half formed fetus from the hospital or something? Was I now living with Norman Bates but in reverse?

"Travis, I can see you're having a hard time with this. So, if you'd let me, I'd like to start from the beginning."

"Yes. I think you should, Doug. I think that sounds like an excellent plan. Tell me. Tell me why there's some kind of little monster living under our sink."

"First, he isn't a monster. He's Roy. And second, I think we should move into the other room before we continue. I don't want to wake him."

After ten minutes of sitting alone on the love seat, Doug joined me with some hot tea.

"You know how much I've wanted a child," Doug began.

"Yes, I'm aware." My shaking hand made ripples in the mug.

"I found this organization. They're really cutting edge. They started small by growing human organs, you know, for people who might need them. Things like new lungs, new hearts, new livers, that sort of thing. Anyway, they developed this technique that actually allows them to grow a full person. If they can grow the parts, why not the whole thing, right?"

"You're talking about cloning."

"No, not really. See, the unique thing about their technique is that it takes two hosts to complete the cycle. And at the end of the cycle, you get a perfectly natural, perfectly healthy little baby. Do you get what I'm saying?"

"Not really."

"They're giving us the ability to make a baby, Travis, a baby that's born from our bodies. Our blood. It'll be part of both of us."

"That thing is not a baby."

"Roy is only through stage one. That involved me. He just has to go through stage two to complete his cycle. Once that happens, he'll be just the same as any baby you see at the playground, or rolling by in a stroller."

"What's the name of this organization?"

"You wouldn't know them."

"It's illegal, isn't it?"

"What do you think? New procedures are always taboo. People don't like it when you try to fix nature." Doug looked away from me with this comment.

"So you think we need fixing? You think we're unnatural?" I retorted.

"Of course I don't think that. Anyway, that's not the point." Doug took a long breath before he continued, "Travis, I started this process without your knowledge. I accept responsibility for that and I'm sorry. But now I'm asking you to finish it."

"What does that mean?"

"I need you to help Roy through stage two. Without you, he won't last a week."

I had to fight the urge to toss my steaming mug into Doug's face. He was forcing my hand and seemed to have very little remorse for doing it.

"What was stage one?" I asked pointedly.

"Each stage is different."

"That's not what I asked, Doug. I asked what stage one was."

Again his eyes relocated to another spot in the room. He seemed focused on the peach curtains as if afraid they might try to strangle him.

"Three weeks ago I started taking a series of injections into my abdomen. That began Roy's life. He grew inside me. Then, last night, he was ready to come out."

"Come out?"

"Yeah," he shrugged, "Roy came out. That's all."

"Jesus Christ, Doug! What were you thinking?" I shot up from the seat. The mug fell from my hands, but neither of us noticed.

"I was thinking that I might have the life I dreamed of since I was ten."

"This is insane!"

"Why? What's so insane about it? It's unconventional, but Roy grew in my body the way any baby does."

"Our bodies weren't meant to grow life!"

"Our bodies weren't meant to do a lot of the things we do. We're both men for Christ's sake!"

Doug had always retained a bit of internalized homophobia, but I always forgave him for it because I knew it came from his father. Not this time. This was too far.

"I've had enough of this self-loathing shit! I'm not going to let that thing come near me. Period." I stomped up the stairs.

"He needs you!"

"Let the fucker shrivel and die. You can join him for all I care."

I slammed the bedroom door so hard I thought I cracked the wall.

***

Two days passed and Doug hadn't dared to come and talk to me. I had taken the bedroom and he had taken the kitchen with his precious Roy.

The creature sickened me, but how Doug obsessed over it sickened me even more. It was like cancer eating away at us, and the only cure was to carve it out.

There came a knock at the door. I didn't answer. A second knock came.

"Travis, I know you're still angry with me. I'm heading off to work now. Roy is downstairs. When I get home, maybe we can talk." Doug waited for my reply then added, "I love you." He waited again.

Once I was sure he had left the house, I bounded out of bed and ran downstairs.

In the kitchen, I found the largest knife I could and headed straight for the cupboard under the sink. Each step tightened my grip.

I tossed the doors open and pulled out the pot where Roy resided. I had to be quick about it for fear I might lose my nerve. With the blade of the knife resting against the creature's scrawny neck, I took a moment to consider. Doug would be furious with me, that was true, but it was the only way I could think of to be rid of this horror and bring Doug back to me. And I wanted him back.

Shoot me in the head; I still loved him.

Roy whimpered in his silver cradle. His tiny body trembled as thin breaths sustained what I could only assume was an agonizing existence.

My hands protested what my mind demanded. I couldn't slaughter this pitiful creature. Such viciousness just wasn't in my nature. But, I thought if I distanced myself from the act, perhaps by the time my hands had figured out what my mind had plotted, it would be too late.

I found the appropriate lid for Roy's pot and sealed him inside. I placed the pot onto the front burner of the stove and clicked the dial to High.

I waited.

In a matter of minutes, the lid began to pop as the creature inside writhed against the heat. I had to hold the lid closed. It was surprisingly easy.

Then, Roy began to cry. The sound wasn't quite that of a baby, but I still recognized it, even sympathized with it. It was calling for help. The kind of sound a piglet might make if it knew what was coming.

My hands instinctively took over. They tossed the lid aside and without even a hint of revulsion, picked up the hysterical creature and rested it against my chest. It seemed to be soothed almost instantly.

It was then I realized I was only wearing a bathrobe. The creature's warm flesh felt curiously soft against mine, almost familiar. Its weak hand, which was about the size of a cat's paw, rested against the base of my neck. This spot on my body was a particular favourite of Doug's. Most of his kisses found a home there. Did it somehow know?

As I held Roy against me, I could understand why this little life was so important to Doug. It brought him joy, comfort and purpose. Though to me it was still just a creature, to Doug it was much, much more.

Maybe I had acted harshly.

Roy shivered again.

"It's okay," I said, "You're safe now."

* * *

I stood in our modest backyard watching the sun bleed through the sky as the day came to an end.

Right on time, I heard the patio door slide open as Doug stepped onto the grass to meet me. I chose not to turn around.

"Travis, I've been thinking about how unfair I've been," he began, "I'm sorry for how hard I pushed you. This has to be a decision we both make. I can't force you. I want you to know that I understand your anger. I'd be angry too if..."

"What's stage two?" I interrupted.

"Sorry?"

"What's the second stage Roy needs to become human?"

"He has to attach to you."

"What does that mean specifically?"

"To be honest babe, I'm not completely sure. It's a new process, like I said."

"But, he'll die if I don't?"

"Yes."

"And you want him to live."

"Yes, very much."

The decision came to me suddenly, though I wasn't really sure from where. It felt like the right choice, so why was it so hard to say?

"Again, I don't want to pressure you," Doug blabbered on. "You have to make up your own mind. So don't rush it. Take your time and we can discuss…"

"I'll do it." There it was.

"Are you sure?"

"Yes, Doug. I said I'd do it. Tonight."

"Really? Tonight?"

"Right after supper. I made mushroom chicken."

I finally turned to meet his flabbergasted face. I placed a kiss on it and went inside.

***

After a hearty meal of which I partook twice my usual serving as Doug had requested, all three of us headed upstairs.

The lights were dimmed to emulate the comforting glow of a flame. The bed was pristine, every wrinkle had been banished.

The air chilled my body as I disrobed. Goosebumps rose over every inch of my naked skin. Doug saw this and immediately warmed me. He was tender that way.

I leaned back on the bed, delivering onto it its first of many impurities.

Doug unbuttoned his shirt and then slipped out of his pants and underwear.

I stared at him. I stared at his body and was reminded of the handsome gentleman I served breakfast to twelve years ago. When he was finished his meal, he asked me when my shift was over. I ignored him. He left without another word, but there, written on the back of his receipt was his name, his number and the hope he would get a chance to see me again.

Now here we were, trying to make a baby. Who would have guessed?

He crawled on top of me, pressing his body to mine the way I liked. Of course, he also kissed the base of my neck. It had been so long since we enjoyed each other. I was electric.

Then he pulled away and placed Roy's pot between my legs. The metal was cold on my thighs.

"Are you ready?" Doug asked.

I nodded, afraid that if I spoke, he'd be able to tell just how unready I really was.

Roy was lifted out of the pot. He looked like a newborn pup. His eyes and mouth closed tight, but not for long.

My presence excited him and he came to life in Doug's hands. Suddenly, Roy's oversized eyelids opened wide, yet revealed no eyes beneath. Just two slurping craters that seemed focused on me. His mouth was the same, a toothless cavern of pulsing flesh.

"What's he doing?" I asked.

"I don't know."

Tendrils protruded from Roy's orifices like flapping blood vessels. They sprayed from his face, tumbling over themselves as they hungrily approached my skin.

At first, they licked at my body like wisps of tissue paper. I dare say the experience was almost pleasurable. They entwined with my own tendril and slipped into places not even Doug had gone.

Then they took hold.

The digging began on my right leg as they pushed their way into my calf muscle and behind my knee. A hundred needles began drilling through the layers of my body, mining for bone. They weren't gentle - they were ravenous.

The bed felt wet.

My quivering hands confirmed what I feared. It was indeed wet, steeped in my blood.

I didn't dare look, but when I placed my hand against my leg, it felt like I had been dragged through a shredder. I eased into the pain as the tendrils ate me away, sucking in whatever there was to suck.

They became thicker, like worms. And they carved out new trails all they way up to my nipples. I felt them snaking through my intestines and into my stomach. They hugged my lungs, constricting them, forcing me to take rapid, short breaths. Finally, they found my heart and explored all the secret caverns within.

My eyes begged for help. Doug saw everything, my carnage, and my desperation. He stepped toward me, that man, that man from the restaurant.

He rested his arm across my chest. I didn't bother pushing against him. I didn't need to. I knew he wouldn't let me up. We were both too deeply in love. I loved him, and he loved his family.

Before I drained to nothing, I heard Roy start to cry. This time, he sounded just like a baby.

Our baby.

I was so proud.

Advertising Eyes

Shaun Avery

I get fired from my job at the fried chicken joint when they find me out back at the bins, running leftover food all across my face. I try to explain to them that what I'm doing is normal – that the food was spat from the mouth of a famous person – but it does no good with my manager.

So I tell him what I think of him, and then I head home.

Where I find Suzie having a seizure on the floor.

She's naked, too.

Naturally.

But, after a few minutes of rolling and thrashing around on the floor, she comes to a stop and looks up at me.

"Don't worry, Ryan," she says. "It's just some guy whacking it to me somewhere."

I knew that, of course. This has happened a few times before.

"You're back early," she adds, standing up, dusting herself down.

"I know." I walk into the kitchen, plonk myself down at the table that has become our usual meeting point. And I'm about to give her the bad news, tell her I've been let go from yet another job, when I decide to lead with something pleasant first, and say, "hey, you'll never guess who I had in the restaurant tonight."

She sits down across from me, rubbing bare shoulders. "Who?"

"Roger Burke-Hart."

Her eyes go wide. "No way!"

"Yep," I tell her, beaming.

"What's he like?"

"Famous." I speak that word to mean all the other things it expresses, like wonderful, fantastic, superior to normal people. "But not too nice otherwise." My eyes meet hers. "He spat his food back onto the plate."

"Wow," Suzie says. Then asks the obvious question: "did you bring any back?"

"I tried," I say. "Manager wouldn't let me. That's why I'm home so early." I lean back in my chair. "He fired me, Suzie."

"God," she says. "The bastard."

Then a brief silence falls.

Until she says:

"Did you do anything with the food after he spat it out?"

"Rubbed it on my face a little," I reply, proud of this fact.

"Great!" she says. "Mind if I have a little lick?"

I don't.

And that's what we're doing when an eight-year-old boy enters the house shouting "fuck!"

"Oh, hi, Chris," I say to this newcomer, pleased at the opportunity to pull myself away from Suzie's breath, which I'm only now realising is slightly cheese-like. "How'd the audition go?"

I could probably have guessed the answer from his entering outburst, I have to admit. But I liked to needle the kid.

"I thought it was going sweet," he says. "They told me I had it in the bag." He walks into the kitchen, face twisting up with hatred as he stops before us. "Then who should turn up for the role but fucking Carlton Meyer."

Suzie winces at the name.

"That action movie guy?" I say. "The one from the Tomb Titanic films?"

Chris nods.

"Shit," I say, feeling genuine remorse for the kid. "Tough break, man."

"Tough indeed," comes a voice from up the stairs, and we all turn towards it. Towards him – the Mentor. "But you shouldn't be surprised. That's quite the in-thing, these days."

He walks down to join us.

"Big stars, doing commercials," he adds.

"Yeah," Suzie says, nodding her head, like the rest of us completely unfazed by the fact that she is sitting there completely naked. "Some bitch from a superhero movie got this advert role I was up for last week."

"Sure," Chris says to her, sounding bitter far beyond his years. "But at least you got that catalogue work."

"Yeah," she shoots back, "but look what happens to me every time someone decides to jerk it to my photos."

I guess she has a point there.

"That happens," says the Mentor, now standing in the kitchen before us. "You need to break into a higher level of fame to get past that." He looks over us all, a sage wise man giving council. "You need to make it onto TV."

Yep, I think, agreeing with him. But that's a lot easier said than done.

It used to be a whole lot simpler.

See, once we would-be types would break into the celebrity world via adverts. The more humiliating and degrading the better – it would be good practice for when our careers hit the skids and we ended up drinking rhino sperm just to keep ourselves on TV. But now, like the Mentor had just said, there was a new breed of ad star – the type that was already famous. How could we ever hope to compete with those?

The Mentor must be reading my thoughts.

"I think I know someone that can help," he says. "But first…"

And he spreads his arms wide, offering himself to us.

I look to Suzie.

"You want to do the honours?" I ask.

"Sure," she says. "Best put some clothes on first, though. Don't want to get blood all over my skin."

I'm sure that should be the other way round.

She's a little quirky sometimes, is Suzie.

But she's true to her word, and it's not until she's fully clad in a nice-looking suit – her audition clothes – that she grabs a knife from the kitchen draw and she starts cutting.

Not too long later, we're walking down the street, the Mentor and I, and now he's put on some clothes, too, lest people see the wounds Suzie just inflicted and we all drank from.

See, the Mentor's been with famous people. He's let them enter his body with their penises, their fingers, their blood and their spit. So whenever we drink his blood, we're letting celebrities enter our bodies, too. And we all get off on it. Though I somehow don't think Chris's parents would approve.

But I'm digressing.

Back to the here and now. Which happens to be a dingy house, no lights switched on inside, the whole place swathed in darkness.

"There you go," the Mentor says, pointing towards the front door of the house.

I look over at him.

He hasn't said who we're coming to see. Just that it's someone who can help us with our ad star problem.

And that it's a "she."

Which is always a good start.

"Aren't you coming in?" I ask.

He grins. "I think you'll want to be alone when you first meet her."

"Is that why Chris and Suzie couldn't come?"

He nods.

And I'm suddenly nervous.

"Go on." He motions towards the front door. "It should be open."

It is.

I step inside.

Plunged further into darkness.

Dust, too.

The walls are cobwebbed, the floor filthy. If I didn't know better, I'd say that no one had set foot inside this place in months.

But that's not true.

It can't be.

Because I hear somebody moving upstairs.

I look back to the door, closed now. Imagine the Mentor standing just on the other side of it. Outside. Where it's safe.

And I want to go there.

But fame beckons me on.

So I cut through the gloom and dirt and I find the stairs.

Walk slowly up them.

Reaching the next floor, I see an open door.

Opening up to the only room that seems to be lit from within.

I walk towards it.

And lay my fingers upon the door frame.

"Come in," says a voice. A woman's voice. "I can tell you're out there."

"Okay," I say, stepping inside the room.

Where finally I see her.

The woman that the Mentor said could help. The woman he called Deborah.

Though the room is light she sits in the gloom of the corner, only the outline of her body visible to me.

And what a body it is!

I mean, you may have thought that I was gay, considering my lack of reaction to Suzie's nakedness earlier. But we had been living together in the Mentor's program for so many months that she now seemed more like my sister. And I would probably never have sex with my sister. Unless she was famous.

Deborah, on the other hand…

"Enter, Ryan," she says. "Come closer."

Shadows still cutting across her face. Obscuring her features to me. But who cares about a face when you have a body that good? When you have those lush long legs, clad in tights with no shoes upon the feet, just the way I like a girl to look before I bed her?

I want to see more.

But then I'm close enough to see the face.

That's pretty, too.

But something about them makes me frown.

Her eyes.

They're clamped shut. Tightly shut.

But she still sees.

Sort of.

"Ryan Carver," she says, looking towards where I stand. "Appeared in a couple of plays whilst at school. Auditioned for a number of movies – no call-backs from any of them. Until recently working in a restaurant and trying to break into adverts." She sniffs. "And you had some sort of… contact with someone more famous than yourself recently?"

"That's right," I say, remembering the feel of Roger Burke-Hart's sacred celebrity saliva on my cheeks and chin. "But how can you tell all of that without looking at me?"

She smiles. "I can read auras. And I can tell how famous a person is from it."

I'm shocked by this.

But impressed, too.

And, if I'm being honest here, a little horny, too.

It's just that body… those lips…

And the lips then curl up into a smile.

As if she knows exactly what I'm thinking.

"So what can I do for you, Ryan Carver?" she asks. Eyes still closed, refusing to open them.

And this is where I throw caution to the wind, where I do the thing I always used to do in those school plays she just mentioned, the thing that stopped the bastards casting me in the end: I go completely off-script.

"How about a kiss?" I say.

***

The next morning, I'm heading home alone – I stepped back outside to find the Mentor gone, so I guess he got fed up waiting for me.

I'm expecting to find him in the living room when I get back to the house – sprawled out on the couch, feet up on the coffee table, expecting a report.

But he's nowhere to be seen.

Chris is, though.

He's in his pyjamas, sitting sulking at the TV screen, eating ice cream.

And what's he watching on the screen?

Why, ads, of course!

He keeps flicking between the channels whenever the advertisement break comes to its end and an actual show starts.

"Should have been in that one," he says. "Should have been in that one." I'm too pumped up from my meeting with Deborah to tell him that he's now watching the same advert over and over again, constantly pausing and rewinding to the start of its thirty-second run time. "But you know who keeps getting in the way?" He looks back over his shoulder at me. "People who are already big movie stars!"

Then he presses "play" on the ad break, and we look upon a sea of faces we know so well and hate so much:

Buff action star William Marcus – here advertising washing up liquid.

Gruff gangster type Harvey Thurston – peddling car and home insurance.

Hot indie movie darling Alicia Carruthers – promoting local holidays.

"Yeah, well," I say, almost choking on my disgust for those who would keep fame for themselves. "I might be able to do something about that." I look around the house. "Where's the Mentor?"

"Came back ages ago. Said he was going to bed."

"And Suzie?"

"Audition."

"Cool. You got much on today?"

Chris shrugs.

And I realise that I've probably had all the interaction I'm going to get from him, strange kid that he is.

When I'd first answered the Mentor's online ad – "Fully Immersive Fame Experience," it had read, "Six Months Living with Other Aspirational People, at the End of which You Will Leave your Shared Home a 100% Guaranteed Celebrity" – I'd been pretty happy about sharing a place with Suzie (back before the whole brother/sister dynamic came into play) but less so with Chris. I mean, I was a young, sexy, carefree guy – what the fuck would I want with a kid in the house? But his parents were playing the Mentor a big fee for his tutorage, so it made sense from that point of view. Plus, you know, the kid had kind of grown on me.

"So how did it go?" Chris asks, cutting into my thoughts.

I blink, amazed that he's chosen to start speaking once more.

"Not bad," I say.

Chris nods.

Then he finally switches off the ads, cutting off our torment. And in the sudden darkness of the screen, you can see his reflection. But that could never be enough for people like us.

"So what did this chick say?" he asks, standing, stretching. "This Deborah?"

"A couple of things," I reply. "Let's talk about it when Suzie gets back."

***

She does so a few hours later, arriving back mid-afternoon.

Seeing the look on her face, we don't have to ask her how it went.

She tells us, anyway.

"Fucking Alicia Carruthers," she says, throwing her handbag down on the couch. She starts peeling off her huge-heeled shoes. "Saw her in the casting room."

"But you still auditioned anyway?" Chris says.

"Of course." She sinks down onto the couch beside her handbag, tosses the shoes over her shoulders, narrowly missing my head with them. "You have to try, don't you?"

"Well," I say, "maybe not for much longer."

They both look at me.

Suzie on the couch, Chris over by the window.

"What do you mean?" the latter says. "Is this about that woman the Mentor took you to see?"

I nod.

I'm leaning against the living room door like someone giving a big important speech, loving the feel of their eyes upon me.

"Who is she?" Suzie asks. Eyes narrowing suspiciously – jealously?

I'm not sure. But I play it safe regardless, saying, "no one we know."

"Is she famous?" Chris asks.

I shrug. "She should be."

I sense them growing irritated with my vague replies. But I can't help it. I should have spent more time talking, planning, with Deborah earlier. Instead of doing… the stuff that we did.

Luckily, though, Suzie is patient, and she's nice, and the eyes return to their normal width and dimensions as she asks, "but she can help us, right?"

"Yep."

Chris wonders, "how?"

"I'll let you know," I reply. "I'm seeing her again tonight."

But the second meeting's not at all like the first one.

For a start, we're not in that creepy, dingy house of hers.

No, we're in a car – me in the driver seat, her sat beside me.

The vehicle was waiting for me when I got there. Deborah standing at the front door, waiting for me. Eyes still shut.

"You can drive, right?" she'd asked.

"Yeah," I replied, though I didn't tell her it had been a while. "Where we going, though?"

"Around," she said.

Try making sense of that one.

I didn't.

I felt a little scared of her, to be honest. Not to mention a little queasy about the first thing we had done with each other last night.

But I got in the car anyway.

And now here we are.

Cruising through the city.

Deborah's logic was that the actors must be staying somewhere around here, since there were so many of them suddenly popping up and taking all of our roles. Which probably meant a hotel. But since there were so many hotels in the city, all of them built with fancy VIP areas for the stars, how would we know where our advertising competition were?

Deborah was sure that she could find out.

Using that sense of hers.

She sits beside me now.

Wearing sunglasses to cover up the fact that her eyes are closed.

I'd asked her about that earlier, just before we got into the car.

"I was thirteen," she said, "the first time we captured and then ate a celebrity. That was when it happened – their eyes became mine when I swallowed them."

I looked over at her.

"That was when I realised they see things differently to us," she went on. "The famous, I mean. Everything's brighter, more vibrant. After that, I never wanted to see things as a normal person again. But it only lasts a certain amount of time before my own vision returns. Which means always eating more eyes."

"Right," I said, nodding, the whole thing making perfect sense to me. "So what happened?"

She sighed.

"My parents got too old to help me snatch them," she said. "I got tired of seeing things normally a few years ago. I haven't opened my eyes since."

"What?" I said. "Never?"

"Well, not never," she'd replied. "Sometimes it hurts too much, and I have to open them. Plus, when I wake up, you know. But that's why I keep it so dark in the house. So when my eyes are open, I still don't have to see much."

"Wow," I said. Then zoned in on something else she'd just said. "So where are your parents now?"

"Dead," she said, speaking the word matter-of-factly, no emotion there at all. "They left me the house."

I shook my head, amazed as we got into the car.

She got into the passenger seat beside me.

And I was about to get us going when she reached over, clutched my hand.

"You understand, don't you?" she said. "You see why I need to keep my eyes closed. Why I just can't stand to see things like a normal person does."

"Of course," I said, and I did. But I had to ask the obvious question, which was, "why not just become famous yourself?"

"No talent," she said.

Like that ever stopped anyone.

"I'd really like to see your eyes," I told her.

"So drive," she replied.

So I did.

It was her car, by the way.

Well, she said someone had given it to her. Though considering what she had just told me about some of her tastes, I wasn't sure I wanted to know who. Or why.

But the vehicle does the trick.

And soon she's buzzing beside me, saying, "there, there!"

I pull the car to a stop, look to where she's pointing.

A huge hotel.

"I can smell them," she says. "Dozens of stars." She turns her head towards me. "That must be where they're staying."

"Great!" I say. "Now all I have to do is figure out how to get inside."

"Don't worry," she says, and smiles. "I'm sure you'll think of something."

***

A few hours later I'm walking back out of her house, feeling tired but happy. The tiredness because Deborah had to be rewarded for helping me out, which meant sex – lots and lots of sex. The happiness because I'm sure that Suzie, Chris and I can come up with a plan between us.

That's where I think I'm going, back home to them.

But instead my feet take me past my old place of work.

The Chicken Shack.

I don't know why – I mean, for me a job has only ever been what I've done in-between attempts to get famous. But I worked at the Shack longer than I did at any other place – about four, five months – and I guess I can't help but feel a little nostalgic towards what I just lost.

When I take a look through the window, though…

I see none other than Roger Burke-Hart.

The bastard that got me fired.

And he's not throwing a tantrum now. Oh, no. Tonight the food is to his taste, it seems, and the staff are fawning over him. A couple of girls, too, one on each side of him as he eats. His arms around them both, sitting there like a king.

The sight makes me angry. So much so that I'm toying with the idea of smashing through the window, taking out my vengeance on him. But although that would no doubt get me in the papers, it's not the type of fame I'm after.

So instead I wait for Roger to leave the Shack.

Which he does about half an hour later, the two girls still in tow, one to his left and one at his right.

I'm on the other side of the road, my eyes on him. And when he starts walking, I follow.

He builds up a nice little entourage along the way, fans falling in step with him. I keep to the back of this group, fearing he'll recognise me from the other night. But he speaks so loudly that I still hear him say, "come on, everybody – the more the merrier!"

And where does he lead this ever-expanding crowd?

Well, it's a familiar sight.

It's the hotel that Deborah pointed out earlier.

But he takes us away from the brightly-lit entrance area, through a car park and down a dingy sort of side alley to the place.

"This is the Secret Door!" Roger tells us all, pointing to the item in question. "Where all the mistresses and hookers go – where the journalists aren't allowed!"

A huge cheer goes up from the crowd at these words.

And then, grinning wildly, groping various body parts of his two lady friends, he pushes open the door, leads the group inside.

But not me.

I've already seen all I need to see.

Satisfied, I head home.

Where Suzie is waiting up for me.

She's sitting at the kitchen table in a slinky dressing gown, legs crossed, one bare foot jiggling.

"Hey," I say, walking into the room. "Can't sleep?"

"Was," she says. "Had another seizure."

I switch the kettle on. "Damn wankers."

"Yeah." She smiles. "How'd it go with Deborah?"

She speaks the words innocently enough, but something in her tone, her body language as she says them, makes me think she might be jealous. I remember the way she narrowed her eyes when addressing me last night, and I wonder if I could have misjudged our whole brother/sister dynamic.

"Pretty good."

"You been with her all night?"

"Nah." I take a seat across from her, waiting for the kettle to boil. "Took a walk past where I used to work."

"Oh?" She seems intrigued. "Why?"

I shrug. "Not sure."

She nods as if I actually provided an answer. "It sucks, getting fired."

"Yeah? It happen to you?"

"Ages ago," she says. "I was working at a bakery. The family that owned it used to let me run the place, left me on my own there."

Now I was jealous. Marvin, the manager at Chicken Shack, would have never trusted me that much. The bastard.

"Anyway, one day I read that Craig Simpson – you remember Craig Simpson, don't you?"

"Yeah," I say. "R and B singer, wasn't he?"

"That's him," she says. "Anyway, he was in our town doing a gig. And I read that he absolutely loved freshly-baked bread. So I closed the shop down, took a pair of loaves to him."

"Wow," I say. "Did he like them?"

"Maybe." She shrugs. "I passed them on to his security team."

"So you didn't even get to see him?"

"No," she says, sounding sad about this fact even now.

"So they fired you?"

"Yeah. We lost a whole day's trade. Which they weren't too happy about."

I shake my head as the kettle comes to a boil.

Sometime it's hard, being a fame fan.

But now I have the answer.

"Well, you can forget all about Craig Simpson," I go on, standing to make us both a cup of tea. "We'll be meeting some much more famous people soon…"

I tell her about the hotel, about Deborah's ability, before we go to our separate beds.

But when I wake up the next morning, I'm still not sure what we'll do when we get to the place where they're all staying.

So I ask the Mentor for advice before we go.

It's early evening by that point, and we've all pretty much kept to ourselves the rest of the day. The silence has disturbed me a couple of times. But we seemed to need it. To prepare ourselves for what tonight's trip to the star hotel will bring.

Our Mentor included.

"Take care of the competition," he now tells me. He's standing there bleeding as he speaks, my lips still wet with his blood. "Take that how you will."

But his eyes flick down to the bloody knife in my hand when he says this.

I put it in the inside pocket of my coat.

Then I ask, "how do you know Deborah?"

"Friends with her parents," he says, pulling on his shirt. "Helped them get a few of their old meals."

Meals meaning famous people, of course.

I think of her eyes.

Remember that first time…

***

"Rub it," she said. "Unzip your trousers and pull it out and rub it on my eyelids until it gets hard."

I did so.

I wasn't sure that I would get hard. But the heat of her flesh, the hotness of her body right there in front of me, it all had the required effect. Until –

"Now take my clothes off," she said. "And –"

Well. You can guess what follows the "and," right?

***

I snap back to the present, pressing down on my sudden erection as Chris and Suzie enter the living room.

She's done up in a tight dress and the same huge-heeled pair of shoes she wore for her audition yesterday.

He's wearing a suit.

"You ready?" he says.

I nod.

And off we go.

Just the three of us.

The Mentor – older, less fit than us – is sitting this one out.

Which I guess puts me in charge as we head out. But it's only the most nominal of leaderships, since Chris is acting like the excited kid he is, hopping and bopping about, whilst Suzie is uncharacteristically silent. Or just concentrating on not falling over in her massive shoes. It's hard to tell which.

Whatever, though. It's only me that knows where we're going.

And soon we're there.

No crowd around the Secret Door this time.

Is my old friend Roger Burke-Hart inside?

Only one way to find out.

I wonder which way we'll go, when we get in there. But when we push through the door, we see there's only one way.

It leads directly to a lift.

Inside of which there's just a single button. Three letters written on it.

V-I-P.

Behind me, Suzie takes a deep breath.

At my side, even Chris seems subdued. "Are we…?" he says.

I touch the knife in my pocket.

"Yes," I say.

Then I press the VIP button.

It moves upwards with agonising slowness.

As it does so, I look around.

It's a pretty big lift, pretty wide. Even so, it must have taken Roger's crowd a couple of journeys last night. Was it worth the wait, I wonder, for those who'd had to remain downstairs until the lift returned? And what did they see when they got up there, to the lift's sole destination? Who was waiting for them when they emerged?

Stars, I guess.

Celebrities.

And soon I'll be amongst them.

But first I need an advert role.

Time to make that happen.

And eventually the doors slide open to show…

Debauchery.

It's a vast penthouse suite, the VIP area, and dotted all around it is beds. Dozens and dozens of beds. And on each bed is a star getting busy with someone – and in some cases, with a couple of people. All out in the open, in front of each other. But that's fine, as each celebrity seems to only have eyes for what is happening in front of them.

Except for one.

A man who slowly walks towards us.

Oh shit, I think, getting a closer look at him.

It's Carlton Meyer.

The guy who beat Chris to the ad role a few days ago.

"Oh wow," he's saying now, pointing to my young friend. "Who called for the Midget-O-Gram?"

I sense Chris's agitation at this remark, and I expect him to leap at Meyer, taking him down. But it seems that Suzie senses this, too, as she steps forward, laying a hand on the action actor's shoulder.

"I love that last advert you did," she tells him. "The one you did for cat food."

"Oh yes," Meyer smiles. "I'm very proud of that one."

"Then why don't you take me somewhere," she suggests, "and tell me how you made it?"

He does so, leading her through a side door marked Conference Room.

I watch her go, trying to work out what she's playing at, what her plan is.

Then I turn back to where to Chris, saying, "looks like it's just us, buddy."

He winks. "Not for long."

And he's right.

For that's when sultry country music singer – and star of a series of adverts for room deodorizer – Doreen Darwin comes towards us, a bulging make-up bag in hand.

"Oh, wow," she says, pinching Chris's cheek. "Are you my model? I just love giving little kids a makeover!"

I'm not sure what to say to this.

But Chris is, replying, "sure, yeah, I'm your model."

"Great!" she says. And pulls a nail file from her bag. "I'm going to give you the manicure first, and –"

But the rest of it gets cut off as she leads him away, off into another Conference Room.

I wonder what is with all those things.

I mean, what the hell are these guys conferring so much about?

I go to ask a writhing mass of flash atop the nearest bed. Some of which I recognise as wrestler turned actor turned spokesman for crisps Vince Brady.

"Hey, Vince," I say. "What's up?"

But Vince is not at home.

Just one look at his hugely spaced-out eyes suggests he has been pounding some illicit substances.

"Are you… the moon?" he asks me.

Not another question I can't answer.

But the sight of his wide eyes has made me think of Deborah.

I found this photograph in her house, last night. It was taken just after she ate her first star, eyes huge and pretty within her head. And I realise that's the look I want to see in her once more. I want her to look at me, to see how famous I am rather than just feel it. But how?

As I'm wondering, a hand falls upon my shoulder.

And I look back to see a panic-stricken, wide-eyed Carlton Meyer.

"It's your friend," he tells me. "Something is happening to her."

He's right.

She's convulsing on the Conference Room floor.

"What did you do?" I say to Meyer, the two of us standing over her.

"Nothing," he explains. "She just suggested we…"

But then he trails off.

"What?" I prompt him.

"That we play with ourselves a little," he says. "To get us in the mood."

So that's what her plan is, I think.

She knew what effect it had when men masturbated over her photos. She must have guessed the same thing would happen face to face. But why? What end result did she have in mind?

I'm not sure.

But whatever it is, I know she wants it to happen to Meyer, not to me. So I say to him, "get a closer look at her. Make sure she's not choking."

He looks queasy at the thought of doing so.

But he does what I asked.

He bends down over Suzie's wildly thrashing body.

And suddenly she stops throwing herself around the ground and kicks up with one high-heeled foot.

And that huge heel sinks into Carlton Meyer's eye.

We both hear the squelch as it meets something in his brain it probably should not be meeting.

He slumps forward, held up only by her outstretched foot.

I stand there, shocked.

Which seems to infuriate Suzie.

"Come on, Ryan," she says. "Pull him off my shoe. I have to walk out of here in these things."

I'm still too stunned to react.

"Ryan," she prompts. "Move!"

Her tone finally puts me in motion, and I come up behind Meyer's jerking body, grab him beneath the armpits and start pulling.

He comes free from her shoe with a plop!

I lay him down on the floor.

"Nice," Suzie says. She rubs a jelly-like bit of brain matter from her shoe onto the carpet. "Let's go find Chris. He should be done by now, too."

I look at her. "Done?"

"We had a plan," she explains. "For what we would do, when we got in here."

I push open the door. "So why didn't you tell me?"

She rolls her eyes. "We were going to. But we knew you were too busy with this Deborah business."

Fair point, I suppose.

But I'm still miffed to hear her say it.

"Where'd Chris go?" she asks as we leave the room.

"Went off with some chick," I tell her.

"Who?"

"That singer – you know, Doreen Darwin?"

"The deodorant girl?"

"That's her."

We're back out in the main meat of the VIP area now. So many stars, so much competition for advertising space. But why are they all here? I wonder.

"Did you talk with Meyer any?" I ask Suzie. "Before you started… you know?"

"A little," she says. "I let him lick me a bit, too. Wanted to see how that felt."

I remember the feel of Roger Burke-Hart's saliva on my skin a few days ago. "And?" We reach the door of the room where Chris is. "And?"

"It was fucking great."

I nod. Place my hand upon the door.

"But did he tell you why they were all here?" I ask her.

"Yeah." She nods. "Some seminar thing they're doing. Since it's such big business stars acting in adverts, they all want to get a bit of it."

Us, too, I suppose.

Which thought prompts me to push open the Conference Room door.

Where I see that Chris has been pretty busy.

I step around the pool of blood. Around Doreen Darwin's body – nail file jutting up out of her throat.

Chris stands over.

Make-up on his face.

Looks like he let her do a little of her make-over on him.

Without a word he turns to face the wall.

And the sight of all the blood wakes something up in me. Makes me want to do a little killing of my own.

I touch the handle of the knife that's in my pocket.

"Is it my turn now?" I ask, looking to Suzie. "Can I kill someone?"

But she shakes her head sadly.

"We don't want to outstay our welcome," she says.

Disheartened, I turn back to Chris.

Who now stands back from the wall, saying, "there."

We look at what he has done.

The words he had written there. In the blood of Doreen Darwin. And why the hell not? It's not like she'll be needing it again.

And I have to say it – it's great work, what he's put on the wall.

A simple, stark message:

We kill ad stars – keep off of the TV!

Looking at it, I feel that bloodlust once again. But Suzie is right. Once the two bodies are discovered, people will start screaming. And what the hell, right? I mean, I have Deborah to go back to. These two just have the Mentor.

So I'm not too disappointed as we walk back through the suite.

The sex-crazed stars are still ignoring us. All of them wide-eyed, just like Vince Brady, off in some whole other place.

But I know we'll be them soon.

And I'm smiling as we step into the lift.

We all are. All happy and gleeful, exchanging grins as we head back to the secret entrance. Knowing that we've struck a blow. Knowing that if just one person is too scared to audition for an advert role after this, then that's once more chance for us.

Still, the knife in my pocket brings some regret. I never got to use it.

But then the lift hits the ground floor, and the door slides open, and I look out to see...

Roger Burke-Hart standing there. Waiting.

I look around to Suzie, hand reaching for my knife.

She nods.

"Hey," Burke-Hart says, squinting at me. "Don't I know you?"

"Not yet," I tell him. "But you will."

Then my hand emerges with the knife.

***

A few weeks later, we're all standing at the bottom of the stairs at Deborah's house.

We're clad in graduation wear – jackets, mortarboard hats.

The Mentor has a tear in his eye.

"Guys," he says. "I'm so proud of you."

As well he might be.

We've all had our first advert acceptances.

There wasn't some massive drought. The actors didn't just up and leave – no, you still see them out and about in the city. But a few of them must have thought twice, must have decided they had enough fame and they didn't want to risk their lives by pissing off a bunch of murderers offended by adverts. And that was all we needed.

So, now I don't know what the future will bring. Don't know how much longer we'll all be living together. But we're probably sharing the house on borrowed time – I mean, Chris's parents have already been over to see him for the first time in months, and I've got the feeling they want him back now he's starting to make a little money for them.

But, you know, I think we'll all still be friends.

I hope so, anyway.

Suzie looks across at me, looking pretty as a picture. The envy I thought I'd saw in her a thing of the past now. And now that she knows she's going to be on TV, the seizures have stopped, too. Something else to celebrate.

I flash her a grin.

Then hear a sound from upstairs.

Chris nudges me.

"Hey," he says. "Here she comes."

We exchange easy smiles.

The kid's a lot calmer now that he's getting somewhere.

We all are.

The thought makes me reach inside my pocket. To touch what lies there.

"Come on down, baby," I say.

"We couldn't have done any of this without you," Suzie adds.

Chris says nothing, but nods at Suzie's sentiments.

And then she's walking down towards us.

Deborah.

My love.

Moving with such ease – and did I mention the house in which she lives has changed now, too? Yes, indeed… we've tidied it up, the three of us, got rid of all the dust and cobwebs, replaced all the old light bulbs, brought the whole place to life again. Not that Deborah has seen it yet. But she will. She will.

"I've got something here for you," I say.

She walks with eyes still closed, sensing where we all are from the fame she sees in her auras. We're all standing in the hallway, waiting for her. Me in the middle. A present now waiting in my hands, removed from my pocket.

She stops in front of us.

"What is it?" she asks.

"You'll see," I reply, "Hold out your hand."

She does so.

I place them in it.

"Oh, Ryan," she says. "Are these what I think they are?"

"Sure are," I say, grinning. "Why don't you try them?"

And that's just what she does.

She pops them into her mouth. Roger Burke-Hart's eyes. The ones I carved out for her whilst Chris and Suzie held him down. A real time effort. A loving affair.

We smile as Deborah crunches.

And then, a few seconds later…

She opens her eyes.

Every Body Dies

Jeff Meyers

"If he pops," the man behind the desk tells me, "don't let any of it get on you."

"Why?"

"Because six hours later you'll pop."

"How will I know if he's going to pop?"

"Oh, you'll know," he answers. "He'll heat up like a motherfucker. But not everyone is the same. The harder the worms work, the more likely you are to pop."

I can see that he sees that I don't understand. "He's in a wheelchair, right?"

"Right."

"Which means he can't walk. Which means the worms are going to have to work their asses off. So, yeah, he's gonna pop. If it were you or me, there'd be a fifty-fifty chance."

The apartment-turned-makeshift office is dark, thick with cigarette smoke, and cold. Too cold for the tip of a Los Angeles September. I listen for the hum of an air conditioner but only hear the large, bearded man standing by the door; short, congested intakes of breath that are spaced six or seven seconds apart. I shift from foot to foot as a hedge against the chill. There is nowhere to sit. The only chair is behind the desk, which doesn't seem so much placed as dropped from a height and left where it landed. The desk's surface is chipped and water stained, bare except for a small gold lucky cat statue. It's plastic paw waves at me.

The man behind the desk holds out his hand. At first, I think that he wants me to shake it. Then I realize I'm an idiot and give him the envelope. Eight thousand dollars. The last of my brother's insurance settlement. The man counts the bills then pulls on a pair of latex gloves. From a desk drawer, he takes out a small dropper bottle and an even smaller clear glass vial. He squeezes two dropper's full of yellowish liquid, half filling the vial. He then seals it into a small Ziploc bag.

"Contact is okay ten seconds after the pop," he says. "The worms can't survive the exposure to air. You're responsible for containing him. Ten to twelve feet of clearance is best. Most people shove them into a bathroom or closet. Bathroom's easier to clean up."

He hands me the bag and a second pair of latex gloves. "You'll want to wear those whenever handling the vial."

"Anything else I should know?"

"You watch the news?"

"Yeah."

"People are pretty bad at following directions. Don't be one of those assholes."

1:43 PM

Our apartment is the rear unit in a squat two-story building with a small, shabby courtyard. Squared into a "U," the heavily shadowed common area is a jumble of cracked green plastic Adirondack chairs, a long-dead fig tree and a wobbly birdbath that functions as the community ash tray. It's as depressing as it sounds.

Eighteen months ago I lived in a sleek, some might say skinny, condo in Silver Lake. A little more than two years ago my brother Tyler lived in a tidy, two bedroom bungalow in Los Feliz, a trio of five-foot sunflowers craning their necks away from his red front door. Now, the two of us share this ground-floor corner unit in Van Nuys, with ash-pocked carpets, windows that face a cluster of dumpsters, and a bathroom that long ago had its door removed to give Tyler's wheelchair access. Propped up by milk crates, it is now our coffee table.

Tyler doesn't hear me when I come in. His chair is turned away from the door, purple headphones crowning his untidy thicket of sweaty, unwashed hair. The volume is set beyond anything I could bear, as his head bobs to the angry thump of Eminem. A pair of dumb bells rests on the floor, just within reach. He doesn't realize I'm back.

I set the baggie with the vial on an end table then settle onto the couch that, in the small hours of the morning, becomes my bed. I listen to Tyler huff rap lyrics in a rage-filled whisper as I tilt my head back and close my eyes. I try to pretend that I am back in my old Silver Lake condo. I try to will into being the calm loneliness that use to embrace me after I left work, after I had eaten yet another frozen meal, after I had surfed the web one last time. But before I slept. I push the buzzing spillover of Tyler's music and creak of his wheelchair and furious cadence of his breath into a dark, dark hole that stretches into a well, that becomes a tunnel with just a pin prick echo of presence.

The peace doesn't last long. Tyler grips my thigh, hard, and shakes me.

"You got it?"

"Jesus. Yes. Shit. I got it."

I point to the end table and Tyler wheels over and snatches up the baggie.

"Leave it in the bag until you're ready," I tell him.

"What if I'm ready?" he says.

"You're not. And once you do the clock starts."

"Okay," he answers. There is disappointment in his voice. But also, maybe, fear. In his eyes. The barest hint. It's been a long time since I've seen that look.

***

I was twelve, he was fifteen. When we talk about it, and we do talk about it from time to time (especially if Tyler's been drinking), I claim not to remember what set me off. And to this day, he is as baffled by my behavior then as he is by his own. But, really, I remember everything. It was Thanksgiving. And he cheated. At chess. A game he hated and I loved. A game I always won.

"The king is dethroned," my drunken father crowed. "Long live the king!" And he clapped Tyler's back, a bit too hard, a bit too happily.

And when the cheers subsided and a dramatic fumble by the Patriots drew everyone to the living room television and my mother gave me a quick kiss on the cheek before returning to the kitchen, I retreated to our bedroom, closed the door and, one by one, snapped off the tops of the numerous trophies that adorned the shelf above Tyler's bed.

Most were plastic, easily broken. Soccer, track, swimming, basketball, a mother-fucking spelling bee. A few were made of metal so I slammed them against his desk's edge, gouging the wood with each frantic blow. Some fractured and broke, others bent at odd angles. Tyler had to have cheated.

I laid on my bed and waited, anticipating the satisfaction I would feel when he lost his shit. But after twenty minutes I grew restless. There was a small stack of library books on Tyler's bed side table. I can't remember which one I chose, but as I finished each page I carefully tore it from the binding and let it slip to the floor. Eventually, I drifted asleep, half of a book tented across my chest.

The first blow didn't hurt but it woke me up. Tyler stood above me, eyes bugged and lips tight.

It was a pillow. He had hit me with his pillow. And I almost laughed. I'm sure I smirked. It was ridiculous. So much rage and such a stupid, ineffective weapon. Then his face slackened. His eyes made a decision then flashed with doubt, maybe fear, then softened their focus. And his body became very still and he cocked his head ever so slightly.

I exhaled. "Tyler, I'm--"

It was fast. Light then absolute darkness. The pillow wrapped around my face, tucking behind my head to form a hot, muffled seal. At first, I palsied, became fixed in place, the internal circuitry of my senses disconnected from their power source. I tried to breathe and a wet crease of cotton pillowcase filled my mouth. Panic jolted me into action. I frog kicked and dug into Tyler's wrists and desperately tried to snap my neck back and forth, to create enough of a gap to break the seal, to find air. But my brother increased his downward push, the ridged, unyielding grip of his fingers pressing past foam and fabric to touch my face. I flailed and punched and even clipped his mouth, hot spit slicking my knuckles. But the pillow did not budge.

It didn't fully register that I was dying, just that it hurt and I wanted it to please, please stop. My lungs ached as they tightened and scratched. A strange hard pressure pushed against my face from the inside, and blood thrummed at my temples.

I can't say what it looked like to Tyler as my body lost the ability to fight back, but even as I felt the edges of consciousness constrict inward, and my awareness fuzz into a dizzy ache, I never stopped screaming.

And then, just like that, there was the rough punch of air and sound and light. I gasped a gushing inward breath, gripped the edges of my mattress, and tried to hold myself in place as my body violently jerked and shook.

Tyler had been thrown to the floor by my father, who stood above me with a distorted look on his face. I flinched, raised my arms to shield my face, thinking he intended to fit the pillow, once again, into place. Instead, he scooped me into his arms and pulled me against his chest, sighing, "You're okay. You're okay now. You're okay."

4:06 PM

Tyler wheels around the living room sweeping papers and takeout containers and crumpled napkins into a small white garbage bag. There's something touching about his desire to make our shitty apartment presentable.

And I marvel at his face, the hard jawline and sharp jut of cheek bone. The narrowed, bottomless brown eyes that don't blink enough and his short, creaseless forehead. His hair, the color of burnt cork, is too long, wrong for his face, but a long overdue shower flatters its complex color and texture. Even his chipped front tooth, the way it slants sharply away from its twin, is just the right amount of imperfection. It humanizes him, suggests there are stories about him you'd like to know.

"They're late," he says, with a hint of worry.

I check my watch. "Not exactly a profession known for its punctuality."

His mouth dimples into a quick smile. People used to wait for that smile. Then the accident.

Tyler pulls on the latex gloves, opens the baggie, removes the vial and holds it up to the light. "Looks like piss," he says. "How long does it last?"

"The guy said six hours," I answer. "It's not exact."

Then we sit. And wait. Without speaking. Which happens more often than you'd think. Until--

"Thank you," he says. Suddenly and softly. "I know I'm asking a lot."

4:31 PM

When the hookers show up I usher them into my brother's bedroom and tell them to make themselves comfortable, it'll be a few minutes. There's champagne on the night stand and, of course, the plain white envelope with crisp one hundred dollar bills.

The women are far more attractive, and younger, than I imagined. One has thick blonde hair, toned biceps, thin lips and hard eyes. The other is a pretty brunette, with chipmunk cheeks and a prime-time TV smile. Her breasts are enormous. Tyler spent hours reviewing websites and 'hobby' discussion boards before selecting them. Seeing them here, dressed in high heels and tight, not-quite-revealing dresses, I realize his bedroom is about to become the kind of porn set he obsessively watches on his laptop. It wouldn't surprise me to learn that one or both have been in such videos.

Tyler waits in the kitchen, out of view.

"All set," I tell him.

And I can see that he's already drunk from the vial. It lies on the floor, by his front right wheel. His teeth are clenched in a violent smile that is stretched too wide. His head is shaking, vibrating really, as if electricity were coursing through his body. Tears stream from his eyes and gummy rivulets of snot dribble past his lips, then chin then onto his freshly pressed shirt. Tyler grips the armrests of his wheelchair with such force, the seams on the pads split. A wet stain spreads across his crotch and I think that his catheter is leaking but then notice that he has an enormous erection.

It's his skin, however, that keeps me from getting closer. It ripples. Not in any particular pattern, just constant movement. His arms and neck and face dimple and undulate as if swarms of insects are burrowing beneath. It happens with such force that I worry they'll split his flesh like over-ripe fruit.

"Fucking hurts," Tyler spits, each syllable forced out between his lips. But behind the agony, there is something else. It's the way his eyes roll back in their sockets and the corners of his mouth quiver into a grin. A kind of ecstasy. As the worms eat, they excrete, and as they excrete, the unique narcotic they produce floods his senses. And I think about the stories of firefighters overcome by the flames, how their bodies, as they died, surged with endorphins, sending them into a state of bliss.

"Are you okay?" I whisper.

And it stops. And Tyler goes slack, his head hanging low and loose, a single thread of spittle dangling from his lower lip.

"Fuck," he growls. "I want to fuck."

Bracing himself on the chair, he rises from his seat and steps, holy shit, steps clear of the foot rests. His mouth cracks into a toothy smile. He takes another step. Then another. He's toe-to-toe with me now, his face filled with crazed delight. "Watch the clock. In 60 minutes, I want you to knock on the door. I have a lot to do."

I've never sat in our apartment courtyard... common area... whatever the hell you call this, before. The air is stale, ashy and bitter, an exile for smokers. God, I hate smokers, with their fidgety fingers and squinting eyes and the small wrinkles that crease their mouths like a puckered asshole. I can't stand breathing in their weakness. Sometimes my mother would smoke, at parties or when she was angry at my father. I mostly thought she was beautiful.

I check my phone. Fifteen minutes have passed. I close my eyes and listen to birds argue in a nearby tree. Upstairs, from the third floor, there is music. It has a Latin beat and hip hop vocals I don't understand. Behind that there is L.A. traffic. Always the traffic. The shush of the freeway and the start-stop growl of vehicles pausing, never quite stopping, at the intersection in front of our building. It's comforting, the metal and rubber and pavement equivalent of ocean waves lapping at the shore.

This is how I get by. I find a rhythm then get lost in it. I empty myself of everything but the steadiness of sound, the broken wash of traffic. Some people would call it meditation. But that would suggest purpose or intent.

When Tyler and the hookers first started making noises, I panicked. The worms. What if he passed them into the women? What if he created two more time bombs. And then they created that many more, turning clients into raging bags of infection. Calculating the exponential rate of transmission made my head swim. But then I remembered that the worms can only live in the blood. Saliva, semen, snot, it's all safe. Only the blood is dangerous.

And this is how I lose track of time. Thinking about the blood and the way there are highways of it running through our bodies. More traffic. I can't hear it, can't feel it, but it's as busy as the I-5 between the 710 and 605. I press my finger against my carotid artery, and the pulse is strong. I try to trace the flow, pushing my middle three fingers into the crevice of my collar bone then slowly working them toward the underside of my jaw. Thrum-thrum-thrum-thrum.

Tyler's hand on my shoulder jolts me into the now.

"You forgot to knock," he says. He's freshly showered and dressed in a linen shirt and jeans. I am still having trouble getting used to him standing, shit, walking. I remind myself that this is the reality now. And for the next four or so hours.

"Sorry," I say. And I mean it. "Where are the girls?"

"I told them to take their time, use the shower to freshen up," he says. "Let's go."

"We're just going to leave them in our apartment?"

"What are they going to steal, my wheelchair?"

"I have shit in there too."

"They don't care about your shit." He flashes that he's palmed the key fob to my car. "Come on, tick-tock."

5:53 PM

There is a curl of mad glee at the corner of Tyler's mouth as he zig-zags through street traffic on Valley Glen. The aggressive lane changes and sudden acceleration jerks me left then right then left again. What if we hit someone? What if we get into an accident? What if Tyler bleeds on me? I should be worried. And for a split second I'm tempted to say something. Instead, I sit quietly, grip the groove between my door and the window. Once I agreed to buy the worms for him, watched him swallow them, I made a commitment. Developing a fear of flight is pointless after the cabin door closes.

When we finally reach the 170, I pull out the gold lucky cat I stole from the man behind the desk. I place it on the dashboard.

"What's that?" Tyler asks.

"Just something for luck."

"Today, I make my own luck." He then swats the plastic cat to the floor and concentrates on the road ahead.

I study my brother's profile, how it is hard and angular where mine is soft and round. I wonder why angles denote strength but curves suggest weakness? Don't buildings topple? Can't they be knocked down? Spheres are strong, solid, difficult to break. They defy strategy because their very shape renders all attacks equal.

Then I notice the flecks of dried blood below Tyler's right ear.

"There's blood," I say. "By your ear."

"Cut myself shaving," he answers, as the car slows to a stop. Tyler grips the steering wheel and tries to keep his impatience in check.

I survey his jaw line, his cheek. I don't see a nick or a cut. Only the three specs – one large, two small - of blood. And there's a small itch in my brain that tells me Tyler is lying.

I reach over and let my fingers hover about an inch from his bicep. I can feel the heat, coming off his skin. Not quite a fever, more like a rash. But it will grow hotter with time. I check my watch. It's been almost two hours. So strange to be measuring my brother's life this way.

6:32 PM

Tyler changes in the parking lot of Pan Pacific Park. He then grabs a small gym bag from the trunk and tosses it at me. Inside is a t-shirt, shorts and a brand new pair of sneakers.

"I don't play basketball, Tyler."

"You do today."

He's planned this day more carefully than I realized.

It's always been like this for us, living in parallel lives, mine watching his, one step behind. Even when he was with Em, in the house in Los Feliz, when they would invite me to one of their dinner parties, I was more a witness than a guest. The bait was that Em wanted me to meet one of her single friends or that I was owed dinner for feeding the cats while they were on vacation. The hook was an announcement -another promotion or award or engagement- that could now be made public. Tyler confided with others, but he needed me, watching from the sidelines, to officially register his achievements. And I would clap and smile and give my compliments or blessings like a good brother should, then return to the condo Tyler has never seen. Still hasn't. I think he would like it.

My brother is happy. I would even say joyful, which is a word I think I have only ever used when singing Christmas carols. It's in his eyes, which are hungry and alert. And it makes me uncomfortable. I've become accustomed to the flat distracted gaze Tyler has cultivated since the accident, as if he were watching highlight reels of his youth on the other side of his eyeballs. I liked the muted awkwardness of our interactions, the way there was no pressure to connect, to manufacture shared moments.

But now, his eyes are filled with want and expectation, confrontational in the way they devour everything they see. And I think of the infants I've met, the way every muscle in their face brightens when something delights them. Tyler has that same look as he dribbles the basketball, tempts me to steal it, then shifts his weight and rotates past me to shoot. The ball drops cleanly through the hoop and he smiles. It's the kind of smile that used to be rewarded with annual raises and phone numbers from anonymous women. And I should be happy for him, glad that these last hours are giving him what he wants. But mostly I feel pity. And, if I am honest, a kind of contempt. Tick, tock. Tick, tock.

Tyler sinks a three-point shot then tosses me the ball. Too hard.

"Come on, you can do better than that."

Of course, I can't. I take three steps and he steals, feints right and lands a sky hook. When he turns back, the smile is gone from his face.

"Are you even trying?"

"I told you, I don't play basketball."

"Bullshit," he spits. "You've always acted like sports were beneath you. You just don't like taking risks. And that's a pussy move."

"Thanks for the pep talk, coach."

For a moment, it looks as if Tyler is going to hit me. He grips the basketball hard enough that its roundness starts to deform. Then his fingers relax and he gently hands me the ball.

"Ok, I'm the asshole," he says. He then walks over to his bag, pulls out a water bottle and drinks deeply. "Let's see if those guys over there are up for a little two-on-two."

Risk averse? The term makes the skin behind my ears hot. My brother has no concept of risk. He's just another boy with a ball who thinks that not winning is the same as loss. Financial ruin, public humiliation, incarceration, death--you have to be in danger of losing something for it to be an actual risk. And unlike Tyler, I have always embraced the threat of ruin, the chance that my actions might actually cost me something

I first started shoplifting when I was ten. Mostly candy bars slipped into the waist band of my pants or slipped into a sock. Within a year I had graduated to video games, DVDs, and books. By thirteen I was pocketing small electronics and even jewelry. For years my mother wore the pearl pendant I lifted from a mall display case and gave to her for her birthday. I approached every theft like puzzle, what and how much could I get away with? Could I slip a box of lighters from the front counter into my coat as the cashier rang up my pack of gum? Could I snatch a copy of Grand Theft Auto from the locked case as the clerk, standing right next me, showed me Halo 2?

My acts of larceny weren't limited to stores. I swiped cash from the purses of my mother's friends while they chatted over coffee, sometimes even taking photos and keepsakes. One afternoon, in eleventh grade, I took the thick stack of wallet-sized pictures I had accumulated and inserted them into our family photo albums. I was tempting fate. Or maybe God. Certainly my family. Would they notice the stiff smiles of kids we barely knew sharing the pages of vacation snapshots and black and white photographs of long dead relatives? I suspect they are still there today, the photo albums stashed in some long-forgotten box in Tyler's storage unit.

Tyler chats up a skinny Latino guy with a smudge of a mustache and a large black man with tied back dreadlocks, too wide eyes and a gap between his front two teeth. Together, they glance my way, and the man with the dreadlocks smiles broadly and nods his head.

"The big guy's name is Calvin. The other one is Rafael," Tyler tells me when he returns. "You don't have to do much. Just pass me the ball or, if you can't do that, lob it into the air."

"Tyler, this is a bad idea. I'm--"

"--Don't ruin this, okay?" he says. "At least, not anymore than you already have."

I have the ball. The skinny latino guy—Rafael—charges me and I lose control of my dribble. It bounces off my ankle and Calvin scoops it up. He pivots toward the basket but is surprised to find Tyler between him and the net. A full head shorter, my brother blocks the shot, stops the ball at the line, spins then launches the ball into the air. The backboard rattles as he scores.

Tyler doesn't see it, or maybe he doesn't care, but Calvin gives Rafael a dark look as he hands him the ball. Something is wrong, but they're not sure what. I offer Rafael the check. On the return he shoots from the foul line, and sinks the basket. Then he and Calvin swap coverage. I can't see past the big man's waving arms and fumble my pass. Still, Tyler is there to intercept the ball before Rafael can grab it and he lands an easy lay-up.

"Shit, where'd you come from?" Rafael snarls.

Another swap. Calvin fakes a shot at the line and rockets the ball to Rafael, who loses it, once again, to Tyler. The next four possessions go much the same. No matter how our opponents shift their game, my brother holds them to that single basket as he widens our lead.

And the friendly banter of dares and trash talk fade. There is only the sound of the ball bouncing against the cracked concrete of the court, the shuffles of shoes, and the bark of frustrated commands.

"Motherfucker," Calvin growls as he takes a moment to catch his breath.

A small crowd gathers at the side lines. They know Calvin, mock him for letting a pair of white boys get the better of him. And I can feel his frustration boil into something dangerous. His elbows jut higher and wider, his body makes contact more often. I'm knocked to the ground a couple of times but Tyler holds steady, even bumps backs. He is fucking loving this. His face is flushed with elation, his eyes are wide and wild, his mouth is cracked into an infuriating grin.

I know Calvin is going to hurt me three baskets before he actually does. I can see it in the way his eyes narrow as I check him the ball. He's calibrating where and how hard he'll hit me. It makes sense. I am clumsy and unpredictable. Maybe it's an intentional foul. Maybe it's because I play like shit. But when it finally comes, when Calvin plants his feet and pivots at the waist and his elbow catches me full in the face, I am unprepared for just how hard he can hit.

My nose makes a sound like wrapping paper being crumpled. Then something grabs my ankles and yanks them forward, sending me to the concrete. As I land on my tailbone, the impact sends waves of agony up into my bowels as my head whips backward. All I can think before the blackness comes is: please, don't let me shit myself.

"What the fuck, man?"

When I open my eyes, Tyler is standing above me, his feet inches from my face, his shoulders squared with Calvin's.

"You elbowed my brother in the face."

"Not my fault your boy can't play."

"You hit him on purpose."

"The fuck I did. Besides, it was just a love tap. He don't want love from Calvin, he should go play with the little people." Calvin gestures to a nearby playground.

"Say you're sorry," Tyler demands.

"Fuck you, mothafucker."

And my brother smiles. I can't actually see his mouth from the ground, but his jaw lifts and points forward. He takes a step closer to Calvin, close enough that his mouth pulls up beside the big man's ear. And then he says, too quietly for anyone but Calvin and me to hear, "Say, you're sorry, you ugly, piece-of-shit nigger."

The response is immediate and completely predictable. Calvin steps back and rounds on Tyler, hits him solidly across the jaw, snapping his head back and to the side. It's the kind of holy shit punch that sends men to jail for manslaughter.

Tyler lists, his right foot lifting from the ground. Then it reasserts itself. It's an action movie moment and I have to stifle a laugh at the clichéd absurdity of Tyler's head popping back into place. He then grabs the big man's left arm and in one clean move, snaps it half way down the forearm.

The sound is horrible. And so is everything else. Splintered bone juts from ragged skin and gristle, as the muscles below the elbow spasm like fish pulled from the water. The lower half of Calvin's arm, the wrist and hand, dangle and flop, threaten to detach. Blood is everywhere. And Calvin is on his knees screaming. And the men on the sidelines are screaming. Everyone is screaming. Everyone but me. And Tyler. Who pulls me roughly to my feet and grabs me under the armpit and escorts me toward the parking lot.

"Stop! Somebody stop them!"

But nobody does. Tyler pushes me into the passenger's seat and drops behind the wheel and guns the engine and pulls out of our parking spot then the lot then onto Beverly Boulevard.

"Tyler," I garble with a voice I don't quite recognize as my own, "that man could die."

"Oh, grow up," he growls. "Everybody fucking dies."

7:58 PM

We take Western Avenue to Los Feliz Boulevard onto I-5 North in silence. Traffic is thick. Tyler's lane changes are rougher and more sudden. As we careen left, my hand brushes against his arm, feels the feverish heat that emanates from his skin. The veins along his forearm are as blue as I've ever seen them.

I check myself in the makeup mirror. My nose is broken and bloodied. Black and purple circles are forming beneath my eyes. Two of my teeth are missing. No matter how I position myself in the seat, the point where my spine meets my ass throbs with unbearable pain.

"Where are we going, Tyler?" I gasp.

He doesn't answer, as he steers us onto the highway shoulder, blowing past the slowing lane of cars. Angry horns blare and Tyler purses his lips into satisfied smile. He's feeding off their outrage.

"Where are we going?" I ask again.

Again, no answer.

I watch through the windshield as the low autumn sun casts long shadows across the highway embankments. Above, the clouds are stretched like pinkish orange gauze. In the distance is the sign for the San Fernando Blvd exit. And I feel a dropping sensation in my stomach.

"Why are we going to Burbank, Tyler?"

He doesn't answer, but the smile is gone. I know why we are going to Burbank.

8:41 PM

The address is 736 North Lima Street. The house is a small white Spanish hacienda with a red tile roof. Water rationing has turned the once green lawn into a brittle yellow, but the small flowering bushes that line the walls are in bloom, dark reds and fragile pinks and paper whites. It is the home of David I-forget-his-last-name and Emma Cafferty. Tyler's ex-fiance.

We've been parked at the corner of Clark and Lima for nearly twenty minutes. At least, I think it's twenty minutes. Everything outside my body is muffled and muddy. Inside, the back of my skull screams and my nose stings and dried blood is tightening the skin above my lip. I shift in my seat for the ten thousandth time, try to find a position that doesn't hurt. I compulsively run my tongue over a broken tooth, taste the blood that pools in its socket.

"What are we doing here, Tyler?" I slur.

My brother is now radiating so much heat that small beads of sweat are forming at the collar at the back of my neck and along my hairline. His skin is flushed but also kind of glowing, the color deepening the definition of his muscles. My God, Tyler has never looked so beautiful.

"It's been nearly five hours," I say.

He doesn't respond. Maybe he can't make out my words. He is a statue. So I try something different, break the rhythm.

"Tyler, did you kill those women?"

And the question gets through. He turns his head. Stares at me for a long time. "No," he finally answers.

128

"Did you hurt them?"

He unbuckles his seat belt, opens the door, leaves the car running. "Go home," he says.

I'd like to tell you I try to stop Tyler as he gets out of the car, walks down the street and heads up the walkway to Emma's front door. But I don't. I sit in the car and, with my head hung at an angle, watch. Because I know it's pointless. I can't stop him. Not with words and certainly not with force.

David I-forget-his-last-name answers the door. He's dressed in a white polo, blue shorts and dark boat shoes. He's handsome, disarming even. And as the smile melts from his face, Tyler's hands reach for his throat, thumbs digging into the soft flesh beneath his jaw, piercing the skin, spraying gouts of blood onto the clean white canvass of his shirt.

I watch David's body crumple onto the front stoop, beside the blue planter with the orange and yellow mums. His face is locked in a surprised expression, a stream of red flowing from beneath his chin, over the lip of the stoop, and drip-drip-dripping onto the stair below. Did you know that mum is short for chrysanthemum? I didn't.

At my feet, on the car's floor, the gold lucky cat smiles up at me. I reach down, grab it, place it back on the dashboard. I touch its chipped paw, which starts it waving at me. Hello. Goodbye.

I shuffle across the street. It's so fucking quiet here. I try to find a rhythm, something to distract me from the pain, but hear only kids, in the distance, screaming, which is really laughter but sounds like screaming. I try humming but worry Tyler will hear me. So I make a list instead.

I have never seen the Atlantic Ocean. I have never tasted anchovy pizza. I have never had sex with two women in one day. I have never seen a movie by Akira Kurosawa. Or Jean Luc Godard. Or Ingmar Bergman. I have never driven a stick shift. I have never participated in a "fun run" or a 3K run or 5K run. I have never fired a gun. I have never been on a cruise. I have never gotten straight A's. I have never bought the perfect gift for anyone.

I step over David's body and walk into Emma's house. There is shouting, I think. Other than my body. And crying. It's far away.

I have never babysat. I have never gone snowboarding. Or para-sailing. Or skydiving. I have never visited a cancer ward. I have never ridden in an ambulance. I have never been arrested. I have never told someone they were my soul mate. I have never looked through a telescope. I have never believed in God.

I pass through Emma's kitchen, take a knife from the knife the rack. There are many to choose from but I pick the small one, the paring knife. In old black and white army movies, the funny ones, it's the knife they'd peel potatoes with.

I have never been in the army. I have never played Mahjong. I have never had a cavity. Or a root canal. Or braces. I have never held a newborn. I have never refinanced a loan. Or ridden a horse. I have never seen the Grand Canyon. Or kissed the Blarney Stone. Or walked on Bourbon Street. I have never told someone, "I am on your side."

Tyler is standing in the living room, a small tidy room with white carpet and off-white furniture and black and white photographs on white walls. The air around his body ripples with heat. Em is on the ground, at his feet, crying.

What to say about Em? I like her. She is kind. She used to ask me questions about what I was thinking. Like she really wanted to know what I was thinking.

I reposition the knife in my hand. I have to do this right. Not lose my grip. Which is hard, because I keep steadying myself as I lose balance. Is this what a concussion feels like?

Tyler doesn't seem to notice me. Not until I slash, flail really, the short blade opening a short red line above his bicep. Barely turning, he backhands me, like swatting a fly. And the force of the blow sends me careening backwards, crashing into a standing lamp and then the wall.

My God it hurts. And I think about just going to sleep. But I still have the knife. And I bring it to my mouth and lick the blade, too quickly, nicking my tongue.

It takes only seconds for me to feel them, attaching to my gums, and onto the soft pallet behind my teeth, and along the underside of my tongue. First it's a tingle, like electricity, then there's pain. Sharp and hot, like a lit match. Then the itching. Oh my fucking God the itching. I want to reach my hands inside my mouth and rip chunks of myself away from the bone. The sensation ripples through me, shakes me violently as my jaw locks shut and burning nausea churns in my gut. I can feel my stomach tightening, threatening to erupt, and I fear bile and acid will fill my sealed mouth and drown me in its stinging heat.

The worms dig deeper, their angry bristles wrapping around my nerve endings, giving them a perch from which to feast, and a cascade of agonies stab my mouth, set it on fire, scorch it with acid, and salt the wounds. The feeling intensifies as the wash of parasites spirals down my throat, each latching onto and burrowing into the soft tissue. And just as the pain rolls my eyes back into their sockets and bludgeons against my consciousness, there is a surge, and it comes with a force that is both orgasmic and euphoric. For the next six hours I will be motherfucking Superman. And then? I'll lock myself in the bathroom and let the worms decide.

Devil's Lane

Marc DeWit

This part of the city is a faded and cracking portrait of metropolitan death. Its inhabitants, encased in rows of broken-down brick buildings three to four stories high, are an industrious yet impoverished lot. They worship the streets, hanging half-way out of their windows, bellowing into the winter's air their exaggerated tales of toil while the dregs scatter about under the night's sky below. Night after night, these scum stumble, trudge through pools of filth, patronizing the neon-illuminated, sinfully-suggestive storefronts. Illuminated hair, lips, and breasts, flashed against the snow. The wind-muffled wailings of scraggly, disfigured streetwalkers, these diplomats of despair, signal the onset of night and invite the tired and disconsolate to find release in their shadows, comfort in their alleys, salvation in their sin.

An isolated district, Bishop's Hill is roughly four square city blocks of densely-populated brick buildings blockaded by a river to the west and north, a railway hub to the south, and an abandoned industrial complex to the east. St. Hippolytus Cathedral, a large, black-stone structure, towers above the three- and four-story tenements, a testament to the neighborhood's once sacred solidarity and shared commitment to their faith. The vibrant, diverse river neighborhood of factory workers and shipping laborers for years lived in a content closeness. Localized deindustrialization, however, forced thousands into poverty. Bishop's Hill, a lively district of ethnic marketplaces, clothing stores, libraries, and other innocuous enterprises, almost transformed overnight into a closed-off cesspool of deserted buildings and lurid advertisements. A stench of productive sweetness turned sinfully sour.

The main artery, 15th Street, cuts directly through the neighborhood, starting north at the river and ending south at the railroad near St. Hippolytus. Recently referred to as "Devil's Lane," 15th Street serves as a concrete representative of the town's decline and fall into urban depravity. Adult bookstores and seedy strip clubs line the road, punctuated by take-away food joints reeking of burnt grease and unidentifiable meats. The streetlights, tall, thick, red antique-like beams, once prominently and beautifully adorned the sides of the avenue. Now, the red is gone, leaving an unromantic patina peeking through years of neglect.

When viewed during the day from the rooftop at St. Hippolytus, 15th Street is reminiscent of an abandoned ghost town in some arctic frontier. Garbage occupies the sidewalks. Boarded-up windows and chain-locked and barred walkway establishments await the night. Darkened signs dangle over the urban landfill. Come nighttime, the living dead emerge from their crummy urban cocoons to explore the cold realities of the street.

Emaciated addicts with sunken eye sockets and trembling joints lurk in the murkiness. Bitter penniless mothers dragging their crying, babbling brood about, sniffling, misshapen little reminders of the hopelessness of their situation. Loquacious hustlers of all shapes, sizes, and smells, swindle their needy neighbors. Hoards of nameless, soulless, and downtrodden men and women, and whatever, exhaling clouds of frosty forlornness into the urban December blackness. Most horrifically, another sickly subgroup festered. A concentrated collective of the hyper-sexual - the creep.

In open yet quiet defiance of decency, these men flood nightly Bishop's Hill and filter directly, in a prurient procession, onto 15th Street. Penetrating deep its sensual superficiality, these creeps with a calculated curiosity peruse and patronize the sordid establishments and bask in the raunchy radiance of their signage. Representing the gutter of man, they embody industrial waste. They are the manifestation of suppression; engaging in the self-dehumanization of submission, they forever dwell in the deepest recesses of the foreskin of existence. They drip, oozing into the bookstores, strip clubs, and peepshows, begging to be chosen, to be wanted, to be used, disposed of, forgotten.

One establishment in particular attracts the lowest of these creeps. A den for the desperately despondent. A few hundred feet to the north of St. Hippolytus, adjacent to the adult book store, whose uncharacteristically large sign box of successively-illuminating red bulbs light the street corner, and across the street from an abandoned metal recycling center, rests a nondescript storefront. Its dark red bricks, aged and cracked, exposing black steel beams behind, are piled precariously up to a large black and red-striped awning. Extending far over the walkway to the street, the awning provides shade for the shadows. The door, a solid ebony slab, stands within an arched entrance. Next to the door, a shabby, dimly-lit sign, reads - XXX Theater.

Once inside the theater, one is overtaken by the smell of cheap perfume, stale popcorn and flickering lights. A thin hallway lined with graffiti and half-torn porn advertisements leads directly to the ticket booth.

An oblong, poorly-constructed box with a cheap plastic window. An elderly man, the manager, Abner, rests inside. A laid-off dockworker, Abner once served as a charity coordinator for St. Hippolytus. However, after years of bad luck and bad dreams, Abner, like many others, opened the door for the dark. He now greets his ghoulish guests. "Welcome to my theater. I'm Abner. Five dollars for movie. One dollar for soda."

The theater itself is disgusting. Dark red walls, peeling away, like the bent, phallic light posts outside. A crusty and cracked cement floor supports ten rows of decades-old fake leather theater seats. Exposed seat stuffing exploding out of the brittle and discolored cushions. The room is dark, stuffy. The screen, a moldy, sagging white sheet hangs like white make-up dripping from a clown's face on a hot day. And stains. Stains of all colors and textures. Dark stains, bright stains, filth spatters, coat the room. Like a large, maroon garbage can turned on its side with seats and a screen, the theater moans, an infernal invitation to the creeps outside. A tight, warm retreat for the wretched recluse. But, as one may imagine by its underground popularity, it isn't just extreme vintage pornography on display at Abner's theater.

Three years ago, Will lost his position at the processing plant at the east side of the city. Dejected and drawn into episodes of violent depression, he found himself alone. His wife, having grown intolerant of his melancholic outbursts, left Bishop's Hill. Will, committed to the impossible ideal of an economic resurgence, remained, moving onto 15th Street into a relatively clean one-bedroom apartment. His optimism soon faded though, with what seemed to be an endless night suppressing any figurative sunrise in his life. With the state providing just enough for his subsistence, he glided in a pitiful dance on top of the widening poverty line, abandoning his hopes, his aspirations, instead refocusing his energies on the corrosively consuming street below.

Will spent hours at his window, in his small, simple wooden chair at his small, simple wooden table. Despite the weather, for whatever reason, the windows of the tenements remained open. Whether it was the temperature of the elevated temperaments of the poor inside, or the boiling onslaught of bright, loud, neon sex outside, the inhabitants of those especially broken-down brick buildings three to four stories high on 15th Street insisted on paying witness to the disreputable dealings of the street below; or, as some people have said, it is the street itself that wanted to permeate the buildings, the homes, and the minds of the inhabitants themselves.

From Will's window were sights typical of 15th Street. Odorous outcasts yelling back and forth; their cheap brown slush-soaked boots and shoes sliding and slipping on the yellow rinks of frozen piss hidden beneath the snow. The signs, circus-like, of all shapes and sizes and colors, electrified sex, showcase foulness of all tastes. Will found himself at the window, every night, lost in a drunken, dream-like daze, ogling at the people, the signs, the sex. His mind sometimes reverted back to happier thoughts, of his wife, their goals, their life. And in these thoughts, he found temporary respite.

What Will missed most of all was the warmth of his wife. His tears sometimes froze upon his face as he remembered her body, how it fit against his own. Her kiss, the comforting caressing of her soft hands against his skin as they lay under the sheets at night. Her eyes, a summery blue that warmed his heart and mind as he washed away into their depths. It was these thoughts, at the window, that filled Will's mind one fateful night.

Thoughts compelling him to seek again this warmth. Thoughts compelling him to walk the street.

Will rarely ventured out at night. Preferring the safety of his apartment window, he resisted from a distance partaking in the devilish delights of 15th Street. Curious, for sure, but Will fought the urge to indulge, instead invoking thoughts of his wife amidst the festival-like orgy of lights outside. But that night was different. His loneliness, that cancer of the soul, pushed him to the gutter. In his jeans, frayed at the foot, resting high against his flimsy brown boots and his faded black leather jacket, he walked. He walked past a group of transients playing dice near an alley, a drug dealer whispering the day's specials to a skeletal-faced woman holding an equally skeletal toddler, a cadre of cross-dressers cackling on the corner, and a multitude of creeps, men in ones and twos, wandering back and forth like a perverted metronome, from one side of 15th to the other. Among this human pollution, Will thought to himself, "I am one of them now, alone, purposeless." And he continued to walk, pondering his loneliness, his fear, his longing…his death.

Lost in the morbid thoughts of his macabre mind, Will found himself blinded by a large sign with successively-blinking red bulbs atop an adult book store named, fitting enough, ADULT BOOK STORE. Outside of the store, a scantily-clad elderly man held a large sign, screaming in a maniacal monologue: "In St. Hippolytus's name, condemn them! These sinners! You! You sinners! You abandoners of God! You sleep with them and you become them! Do you not see? Evil is here! Evil is now! You must remain in your homes, find solace elsewhere! I warn you!"

Will stopped to listen, acknowledging the lowly and shoddy condition of his old neighborhood. He saw first-hand his part of the city's decline into a third-rate cellar of sin. Violence ran rampant under the grittiness of the tenements, with juvenile crime rates increasing at an alarming rate. Recent reports of increased birth defects in the area also helped solidify amongst the other districts in the city Bishop's Hill's position at the bottom rung, submerged in the muck of the hierarchy of the city's living conditions. Will observed this eerie deterioration from his window and struggled with the demise of both the neighborhood and his own happiness. He listened for a few more minutes to the old man before noticing the unremarkable, large-awninged establishment next door.

There appeared to be a steady line of men, alone, streaming in and out of the building. With hands in their pockets and heads down, they moved in a trance-like determination unlike the usual hesitancy of the perverted upon entering a sex shop. The solid, heavy-looking black door reminded Will of a dungeon's entrance - equipped with the large metal handle and arching entranceway. No flashing sign, no kicking leg illuminating the windows. Just a simple "XXX Theater" plaque attached to the rickety bricks near the door. Will leaned against the tilted and flickering streetlight post across the street and watched. Each man, each creep, entered and exited glossy-eyed, empty. Will became unsettled with the noticeably vacant expressions on their faces. Shaking his head and spitting into the oncoming rush of frigid wind into the street, Will said to himself, "They must be showing a depressing movie."

"Actually, it's a classic tonight," responded a soft voice from behind, startling Will as he stumbled off the walkway into the street. "I'm sorry, I didn't mean to scare you," she laughed, shoving her hands into the pockets of her short, tight jacket. "Are you thinking of going to the theater?"

Will, still startled, laughed and looked over at the large awning sprawled over the walkway over the theater. "I wasn't, no. I see everyone else is"

She laughed, looking down 15th Street. "Yes. They are. We're different."

"And how is that?" Will asked, blowing into his cupped hands.

"We don't rely on flashing flesh and neon lights to heat the bones," she responded, with a coy smirk, turning her eyes towards Will's.

Will looked away again toward the theater and let out another nervous laugh. "And on what do you rely at the XXX Theater, miss?"

"We turn the heat on," laughed the girl. "Why don't you pop in for a few, see what's playing."

Will now began to notice the girl. Her long, dark-black hair, waving delicately over her perfectly symmetrical face, past her shoulders, and onto her jacket, resting on her chest. Her eyes, bright blue, like his wife's, opened wide as he looked her over. Her lips, glossy, glistened under the flickering streetlight. Her skirt, not remarkably short or prudishly long, hugged her body. "Your boots look warm," Will joked, noticing the excessive fur exploding out of them from just above her calves.

The girl laughed, kicked a bottle, smiled at Will, and began walking across the street towards the theater. "I'll see you inside!" she yelled, in an exaggerated strut as if mocking a runway model.

Although he did not follow her into the XXX Theater that night, the image of her remained indelibly impressed upon his mind as he tried to sleep. Her lips, her laugh, her whimsical humor, her hair, her long black hair, and her eyes, her perfect blue eyes, staring at him with a warm smile. He slept that night, better than ever, and woke up with the girl in his mind.

Will entered the XXX Theater at about five in the evening the following day. The moon freshly risen, the December wind whistling, he walked through the solid ebony door into the theater. Nobody was in the lobby, if that's what it can be called. He walked down the darkened corridor of advertisements to the ticket booth.

"Welcome to my theater, good man. I'm Abner. Five dollars for movie. One dollar for soda," Abner the owner said, welcoming Will.

"No thank you. I'm actually looking for a girl that might work here, or at least comes here often. She has long black hair, blue eyes; she was wearing a tight coat with a skirt and boots. I ran into her outside on the street last night, probably around midnight." Will enunciated, projecting his voice through the small cracked plastic speech-hole in the ticket booth window.

"She works here," the old man mumbled.

"I was hoping to have her name, or be able to come back when she's working." Will tried peeking around the wall into the theater, but couldn't see.

"Buy a ticket and you'll see her," Abner responded, smirking. Will immediately removed his wallet from his back pocket.

"Deal. Five dollars, right? No pop necessary."

"Five dollars. It's right around the corner." Abner lifted his skinny, blotched arm up inside of the window and pointed in the rough direction of the hallway leading to the theater.

Will walked down the hallway, darker than the one near the entrance. Like a cheap haunted house, the corridor appeared to be framed with plywood painted black. A single lightbulb swung in the airless passage.

The theater itself was dark, with a 1920s or 1930s-era pornographic movie projected onto a wrinkled, shabby off-white screen. A grainy video of vintage sleaze. Grime from an older time, a hapless flapper floozy in action, flaunting her sexuality almost a century later. Will sat down in the last row, scared to move any further. About five other men, or what appeared to be men, squatted near the outer edges of the theater.

Will was uncomfortable. The seediness of the establishment disturbed him, yet he was determined to find the girl from the street. He sat in his seat, careful not to touch anything directly, as the seats themselves reeked of sweat and bargain fragrances. A large, sticky-looking black splatter adorned the wall next to his seat, just under a large, hanging patch of old red paint. The seats were torn and worn, sunken cushions that probably supported thousands of creeps. A new vintage porn started promptly, with no notice. An unknown, scratchy 30s or 40s-sounding record playing in the background. And then, a girl walked in from behind the screen.

She was younger than the girl from the street, and blond, but equally as beautiful. As she entered the room, the men sat upright, their breathing audibly heavy. She sashayed in between the aisles, smiling, greeting each man individually, before taking a seat next to one a few rows ahead of Will. He watched intently, curious as to their interactions. Was she a prostitute of some kind? Was she there promoting the movie? Will pondered a number of questions in the warm, dark theater. How can this seemingly cheap and dilapidated theater employ such attractive and well-groomed women? The younger blond moved closer to the man, whispering in his ear. This movie was brighter than the last, illuminating the room periodically, allowing Will to see better what was happening.

The movie continued, the scenes growing louder and more intense, even for today's standards. The blond then crawled onto the lap of the man, forcing herself upon him. Will sat shocked, wanting to leave. Surely, he thought to himself, this must be a working girl of some kind. The blond removed her shirt and, from what he could tell, began having sex with the man. The others in the theater, creeps, observed from afar, engaged in their own lewd acts of self-pleasure. Despite his repulsion, Will felt himself compelled to remain seated, to watch, to observe, to submit to this scummy display of underground sexuality. When they concluded their act, she whispered into the man's ear and looked directly at Will. Will stiffened in shock, watching her whispering to the man while she stared at him, her eyes widening and, to Will's horror, reddening in the shadowy glow of the movie. She then lifted her head and, with her blood-red eyes, smiled at Will.

Will fled the theater in a panicked frenzy, exploding past Abner resting in his rickety ticket booth, pushing through a quiet, expressionless procession of silent creeps and out the large, solid ebony door. A frigidly cold wall of fetid air welcomed him back to 15th Street, Devil's Lane, with the usual scum shuffling about. He hastened home when, past the adult bookstore, he was stopped in the shadow of the bright red lights.

"I warned you! They are the servants of the devil, I warned you!" The old man screamed, pushing Will into the alley adjacent to the bookstore.

"Warned me of what?" Will replied, backing against the wall next to a large abandoned crate. The old man quieted down, took a breath, and spoke calmly.

"This town has been plagued by these...by these...agents of the devil, these succubi, unwelcome denizens of our dreams. Have you not seen? Have you not heard? Their remnants are everywhere. The signs, the drugs, the malformed children, products of human intercourse with these creatures." The old man sat down against the crate and rested his hands against his forehead.

"What do you mean?" Will asked, shaking his head in confused and frightened disbelief. "I need to go." Will began walking away, dismissing the old man's ramblings as some absurd expression of his religious fundamentalism and still shaken by what he thought he saw inside of the theater.

"The succubi are alive and well in Bishop's Hill, William," the old man yelled from inside of the alley, stopping Will in his tracks. "The men are held in sexual captivity, serving their purpose as frequently as needed, emptied forever of any purpose, of any hope, of any individuality. Sperm donors for the infernal one for eternity."

William stood motionless. Overwhelmed with horrifying confusion, he took small steps across the street and gained a determined momentum to return as quickly as possible to the safety of his apartment.

Once home, William sat at the window on his small, simple wooden chair. The buzzing of the signs below drilled into his mind; the cold, the endless darkness, the endless December, deadened his thoughts. He was again alone. His despair, thick as the urine-soaked trash accumulating in the stuffed sewers below, rendered him unconscious right there at the table. His dreams that night brought him no relief, as he was haunted by the vision of the theater, its mysteriously-large awning extended far from the door over the walkway below, like death himself with outstretched arms; the door, that blackened portal to some subterranean coven of witch-sluts, opening easily at its blood-lubed hinges; the old man in the hall in the ticket booth, that obscurely oblong old box with the cloudy, cracked plastic window, welcoming the patrons with his century-aged physical decrepitude; and the theater, that filthy, dark, cauldron of fiendish activity so devilishly hidden from view, with its fluid-splattered walls, seats, and floor, projected for the creeps what they longed for in life. Love, compassion, warmth, a woman's warmth. Nonstop woman's warmth.

Will awakened, trembling in a cold sweat, shielding himself from his own dreams with as many blankets as he could find, and cried. His nightmarish visions of the theater and the tragic reality of its patrons crystallized in his mind, he curled up against himself, alone, in the unlit safety of his bedroom. A deep, brooding realization of his own inevitable surrender to the darkness overcame him as he reflected on his mounting debt, declining physical health, unseen relatives, forgotten friends, and his wife. Will thought longest of his wife, to whom he for so long pledged his obedience and undying devotion. The woman with whom he would have children, the woman with whom he would share his final breath. But, like the broken, vermin-ridden bricks of the theater, these longings stacked strongly, encasing him in his current life like a fortress of futility. Will remained hidden, shielded, consumed in his own mind; standing on a spiritual precipice, accepting his fate, he prepared for his fall.

That night Will found himself outside of the theater. The street was unusually quiet. St. Hippolytus, in its abandoned grandeur, kept silent witness to the December nothingness under its watch. An eerie stillness to the otherwise heartbreakingly hectic highway of wretchedness. Defeated and devoid of any more tears, Will opened the large, black door and lumbered inside.

The welcoming hallway was crowded. Men mashed together in a noiseless mass of disregarded flesh. Will meandered through them, turning his head from the offensive odors that hung like a thick, swampy fog through the hall. At the ticket booth waited Abner, with the same welcoming smile.

"Welcome back, Will. Five dollars for a movie, one dollar for soda," Abner whispered, as if not to disturb the silence of the foyer. Will unfolded a ripped and crumpled five dollar bill from his jeans pocket and slid it softly under the ticket window to Abner.

Abner's blotchy, pale, bony hand took the five dollar bill and placed it ever-so-gently into his rusty cashbox beside his can of soda. "Enjoy the show," he said, in a much deeper register, with an uncharacteristically long-faced frown.

Will found himself again pushing through a musty mob of creeps, rubbing against their unwashed and flea-ridden clothes in the dark, single lightbulb-lit hallway. The theater itself was filled to capacity, save one seat near the back corner. Navigating through a row of unkempt and odorous men, Will found his seat and descended into its cracked and wrinkled cushion. The arm rest, broken and hanging limp towards the floor, offered no barrier to the man next to him who, as Will believed, was pleasuring himself to the scratchy black-and-white pornographic feature illuminated onto the sack-like, saggy screen.

The fan at the front of the theater offered a slow and steady buzz, with its oscillating head circulating the acrid air around the room. Gasping, Will took notice of the walls, the same dark-red walls, peeled and dripped like devil's sweat from their frames. The floor, covered in an unearthly grime, was sticky in some spots, slippery in others. The movie, another distasteful vintage film of unspeakably odd sexual scenes in a spooky, aged black-and-white format, projected onto the empty faces of the creeps, with a musical and voice-over background out of sync with the choppy film itself.

Will then looked out at the audience. Their faces and bodies half-visible in the half-light of the theater, Will took them all in. Rows and rows of men, all disheveled, leering at the screen. Their eyes, unblinking, fixated upon the depraved acts of the actors. Their tongues, sliding against their cracking lips, wetted their appetite for debauchery. They sighed with short grunts, abandoning efforts to conceal their masturbatory exertions. Desperate hands bobbing in their sweat-filled laps. A cacophony of groans, whispers, hacks, grotesque inhalations and nauseating exhalations filled the room. Will noticed their faced appeared bent and saggy in the darkness, like miniature extensions of the depressingly-droopy screen above. Sorrowful frowning, the creeps' faces spoke volumes - buried stories of loves lost, jobs lost, families lost, hope lost. Depressed facial diaries of the living dead.

Engrossed in the foul air of the theater, Will felt a profound sense of solidarity with the other men. Useless and alone in an unforgiving and uncompromising world, they sat together, united in their purpose, offering themselves to the enchanting allure of this neon-lit, depravity-infested underworld. He watched the film, its timeless perversions, and smiled. Finding comfort among them, the theater, its isolation. Will laughed to himself, squeezing his leg in fiendish delight as he consciously abandoned his concerns, his hopes, his thoughts of love and life. And, at the apex of his satisfaction, he turned to the creep next to him, hoping to engage a new-found friend in polite conversation.

"Hey there, great film tonight," Will whispered.

"The best is yet to start," replied the creep, pushing the words through his sweat-filled beard.

And at that moment the room went black. His face, dried in the parched air, remained motionless as the flickering of the projector worked to resume.

The film, silent, again black-and-white, showed a still image of an urban alley. A thin fire-escape stairway lay in the center of the shaky frame. A large dumpster, empty, open, sat near the stairway, welcoming the company of whatever refuse the city had to offer. The building, a solid-brick tenement-like structure of similar design as the ones found throughout Bishop's Hill. Noticing this strange likeness, Will leaned into the creep again.

"That looks a lot like 15th Street."

The creep, maintaining his glance on the screen, responded. "It is."

Will sat back in his seat, in disbelief, when another film began. This one of his wife and him, happy, wrestling in their bedroom. Their laughs filling the theater, the crispness of the image improved from the other films. Will sunk in his bug-infested seat and attempted to cry. His eyes were dried, however, and he felt all love and hope still lost. The image quality of the film, declining before his eyes from a sharp, colored memory to that of a grainy, black-and-white, dreary and choppy silent film. And then blackness.

Sitting in the dark, Will then felt hair, long hair, tickling against his face. A sweetness filled his nose. He felt lips, soft, wet, softly kissing his neck; hands, gentle, feminine, running up his legs. His pants, pulled down, he knew it was the long black-haired girl from the other night. Her tongue, sliding against his body; his erection standing tall like a rusted light-post on a forgotten, dirty street. And she appeared as beautiful as ever, hovering over him in the darkness of the theater, moving to the rhythm of the breathing of the creeps; her eyes shined red in a hazy nocturnal luminescence.

"You're mine, now," she whispered, as he succumbed. She was cold and cavernous. Will dazed into her red eyes as her fiendish grinding continued, sitting corpse-like in his rotted seat until the hellish harlot evacuated every ounce of love from his body.

Ten years later, Bishop's Hill continued to stink. 15th Street's garbage continued to pile, and the creeps continued to cram inside of the porn theater with the unnecessarily large awning next to the adult bookstore and across from the closed-down metal recycling center. Inside, vintage smut shone across the same saggy screen. The seats stunk and the walls peeled. The halls were dark. In the ticket booth, that malformed box now ten-years more dilapidated, stood a man. His hollowed face, cadaverous and cold, twitched like a fresh corpse in the dimly-lit entryway as he greeted his patrons. "Welcome to my theater. I'm Will. Five dollars for movie. One dollar for soda."

Sweet Meat

Timothy Wilkie

I walked the silent, sacred ground yanking the boots off the dead. The ones that were flat on their backs were easy. You just lifted their legs and yanked them off. I didn't like it but Pa would blister my backside if I gave him any sass about it. "They just Federals," he'd say. "Our boys done kicked their collective Yankee asses again."

I respected the dead sometimes I could even feel their ghost right beside me. I always asked their permission and thanked them when I was done it was only right.

Pa was a share cropper and we were poor as dirt. I was only eleven years old when the War of Northern Aggression started. Pa always said. "We take what the good lord provides."

The crows were already picking at the remains of the soldiers. They were the first to come and the last to leave. For most of the morning I had been so full of doom and gloom that I might well have taken a lesson from the crows and got about what needed to be done before the Cherokees showed up and took all the good stuff. The Federal's boots and jackets would fetch a good price with Mister Mac at the trading post.

In a vast sea of death I found a rock outcrop and sat down. The day was grey and cold the snow no longer poured down out of the sky like yesterday instead it came down soft and fine like white flour. The kind mama used to bake with.

I rubbed my palms together and then tucked them in between my thighs to warm them up and took a deep breath letting it out slowly. It hung there for a moment and then disappeared in thin air as if by magic. I took my hands that were still cold as ice and put them under my shirt flat on my stomach to warm them up. One crow had feathers missing on the back of his neck. He turned and eyed me he seemed older and wiser than the rest. He looked at me with disdain as if to say there's work to be done.

It seemed I had been out there forever. It was cold and my butthole itched like crazy. Pa told me it was pinworms and he'd pour me a cup of shine. "If this doesn't cure ya nothing will." He'd say.

I took my load of jackets and boots over to where I had started a heap and piled them on top, when I was done Pa would come by with the wagon and pick them up. He and my baby sister Iona were up on the ridge tending the fire. "It was gonna be a cold night, and if we lose the coals" Pa said. "We'll freeze plum to death."

The truth was he was sick like mamma had been. He had this cough and sometimes he'd keel right over and see Jesus and then straighten up again and go back to working. The angels came and got mamma just last year they took her while she was sleeping. Pa said. "It weren't a bad way to go." We dressed her up in her Sunday go to meeting clothes and chucked her on the bonfire. Pa said. "We do what we gotta do the ground's too frozen to burry her proper." Then he lay drunk for two whole days. It was okay he had a broken heart I tended to Iona. Pa says, "that's what it's like for us poor white trash we can't afford to die. God don't want us no-how."

So it was a gloomy process in the morning going up and down the seemingly endless rows of the dead. Some of them I patted down their pockets for valuables just like the highway men that Pa told stories about. The grass they were laying on was tan and brittle like straw. It had a light coating of snow and ice, but it was as dead as the blue coats that lay on top of it.

At noon I walked across the field and down to the creek. I was hungry so I reached in my pocket and pulled out a biscuit I had stashed there. It was mostly crumbs now. When I was done I knelt down and took a long cold drink of icy water from the creek. It did more to fill my empty belly then the biscuit.

I made my way back up to The Field taking my own sweet time. The snow had changed to a slow mizzling rain. Even the crows were discouraged and hung to the tree-line. I found a place in the thick brush to huddle and wait it out. That's when I saw him he was making his way slowly across the field occasionally bending down to pick something up. The man wore a big grey slouch hat pulled down low on his brow and his head was tipped down like he was looking for something. I could tell even in the rain that he wasn't from around these parts.

He walked on past me and then turned around and smiled and said. "These are sad times my boy," and then walked on and into the trees. The rain got harder and fell slantwise stinging my face and hands bitter cold it was. I dug deeper into the bramble trying to stay dry. Pa always said. "The wet will kill you boy."

As I sat there brooding all wet and cold I could see The Field was awash in blood and it soaked deep into the soil turning the clay red. I looked over to where the little man had entered the woods but he was gone. I hoped and prayed that my pa would come soon with the wagon I was frightened and very hungry ill-prepared to spend the night out here while he lay drunk somewhere. My will to do for him was almost gone. I was growing up.

Then suddenly out of nowhere a voice said. "I see you wait for the very cord of your deliverance from this hell spawn place. I too am forced to come here by my father." I spun around and the little man was standing there. He looked too old to have a father making him do anything. His slouch hat was off now and the rain spattered off his bald head. He made a sweeping gesture at the field, "may I offer you something to eat? Nature's bounty you know."

I stared at him having no shame in examining him from head to foot he was such an odd looking little fellow. He was short and fat his body completely devoid of hair. His lack of eyebrows and lashes made his eyes almost appear square and demonic.

Suddenly I heard the voice of an angel singing.

"Swing low sweet chariot,
Coming for to carry me home,
Swing low sweet chariot,
Coming for to carry me home."

A big black woman was walking across the field towards us. She was as big and thick as a man and carried a jug of corn squeezing in one hand it looked exactly like my pa's jug. She wore a black leather apron and a white cotton dress that was soaking wet and clung to her exposing her huge breast. The rain didn't seem to bother her at all and she abruptly stopped singing when she saw me looking at her. "You just gonna sit there in the rain waiting for your drunken papa? You gonna die of exposure boy." She declared her huge beefy hands on her hips.

Her question took me by surprise how did she know pa? I just sat there staring up at her. "This war is something else," the little man said from where he was kneeling next to a body going through the pockets. He rubbed his hands and stood up and shifted his feet in a little dance to find a better grip on the muddy ground.

The woman gave me a sharp look. "Are you not well?" She asked me. I was too frightened and shocked to speak and before I could answer her she just turned and walked away. Over her shoulder she said. "Follow me." For some reason that I couldn't explain I did.

We walked across the field with the little man following close behind stopping from time to time to pick something up or go through someone's pockets. At the other end of the field there was a footpath going through the woods. It was dark and scary and like no path I had ever been on. Huge creatures seemed to be all around us hidden by the thick brush just watching us. I could feels their eyes watching us. I drew back in horror as the woods got darker and thick brush seemed to close in on us. I looked at the woman as she stopped and turned around facing me. Her face changed for and instant and it took on the appearance of a skull her brown skin like parchment over bone. Her movements were frenzied as she motioned me on.

The little man came suddenly up behind me and put his hands on my shoulders. They looked like monkey hands and I shivered at his touch. "Move along boy."

A few moments later I smelled the hint of a heavenly aroma in the air. I was so hungry and it was the smell of cooking meat. Snuffing my nose and blinking my eyes with my head cocked to the side like an old hound dog. "Hurry, hurry, my boy a feast awaits," the little man whispered in my ear. I was so, so, hungry I followed along obediently. We soon arrived at a camp on a stream with a covered wagon and a number of horses. There were several large gray pyramidal tents and a large crackling fire. Strips of meat were hanging down over it and they smelled delicious. My mouth watered at the very sight of it. "Are you hungry?" She asked with a faint smile.

I nodded my head yes. "Pa says not to take food from strangers though." I muttered.

Her smile broadened. "I am Lucinda," she said. "See we're not strangers anymore." As she spoke the little man circled her on his hands and knees." I stared at him as he sniffed her legs like a dog. "He has no name he hasn't earned one." With that she kicked him and he scurried away. "All men are dogs," she said. I hurried over and took a large chunk of meat off the spit and ate it hungrily. It was so good and I was starving. It had been a long time since I had tasted meat.

Later with twilight setting in they built up the fire and Lucinda began to sing.

"When I fall on my knees,
With my face to the rising sun,
Oh Lord, have mercy on me."

We heard gunshots in the distance like sticks snapping under foot. "My pa," I said.

"Naw sir," Lucinda said sofly. It's the savages. "Your daddy is in heaven with your mother." She reached over and picked up the jug she'd been carrying. "This here was your daddy's," she said holding it up. "He was laying there drunk when I slit his throat. "He was going to leave you out there to freeze to death and Iona your baby sister?"

The little man looked over at me and held up a piece of meat he was devouring. "Sweet meat, sweet meat," he hissed.

Lucinda laughed out loud. "Well, she saved your life. How'd she taste?"

Rebecca's Story

Quinn Cunningham

Rebecca was driving home from work, reaching over to change the radio, when the cold metal of the gun barrel pressed against her temple.

"We're gonna make us a little turn at the next mile-marker up here, alright?" a voice which sounded as if it had seen one-too-many years of smoking, chuckled.

Rebecca's asthma kicked in and she hyperventilated like a fish out of water.

"Hey," the man hiding in the backseat said in a falsely-soothing voice. "Just do what I say and you'll be alright." A hand the color of chocolate reached up and stroked her blonde curls. She cringed away from it like an abused puppy from the boot of its owner. Tears spilled down her cheeks. Mascara stung her eyes.

"Duh-duh-duh-don't tuh-touch me," she managed.

"It wouldn't be wise of you to tell me what to do. I'm in charge now, miss. What would be wise of you is turnin the goddam car around like I told you to." Now there was coldness in that gravelly voice.

She did what she was told, and turned her silver Malibu onto that ominous-looking back road. She followed it another half-mile, and turned onto an overgrown dirt trail which led into the woods. She drove until the man said he was sure they wouldn't be seen, and then forced herself to do what she had been purposefully avoiding.

She looked into the rearview, staring into the face that would haunt her nightmares for the rest of her life. The man was black, about fortyish, with a giant nose that's nostrils flared up at the ends. His muscles bulged from his Metallica T-shirt.

The worst thing about him was his eyes. The brown iris was such a dark shade that it appeared black. Not just black. Obsidian. She couldn't tell where his pupils began because the eyes were so dark.

In her shocked state, she could distantly hear him talking. His mouth appeared to be moving, but no words seemed to be emanating from it.

"Rebecca!" He clapped his hands together. That brought her back. Not the clap, which was very undramatic since the pistol grip had gotten in the way; it was the use of her name. It made it clear that he'd been stalking her.

"Get out of the fuckin car." He smiled. A single gold tooth gleamed. But his black eyes didn't. No light ever seemed to show in them.

They opened their doors and stepped out into the dark forest. Above them, wind sifted through towering trees like sand through an hourglass.

"What are you gonna do to me?"

"Look over there. I bet you can figger it out for yourself." With a nicotine-stained finger, he pointed to a little pocket where the underbrush was cleared away. A yellowed mattress lay there.

"Okay, Becky – "

"Don't call me that."

"Okay, Bitch. Are you gonna fight, or are you gonna let me get it over with?"

She knew what was coming and decided she'd get it over with as quickly as possible. She promised herself, no matter what, she wouldn't scream or cry. That would give the sick bastard satisfaction.

"Well, what happens to me afterwards?"

"I'll letcha live, and the first cop that comes a-knockin on my door'll get a bullet in his brain. But I'll still letcha live. I don't know if you'll want to, though, after everyone close to you dies. You'll just have to remember what I tell you: Keep your mouth shut."

She didn't know what to say.

She sure as hell wasn't gonna spread her legs and holler, 'Stick it in me, big boy!' The whole act was just going to be so awkward. Sudden rage boiled inside her. She meant to show the bastard that she was not going to put up with it. The whole time there had been this feeling over her that was saying, 'No. This can't be happening. It's all okay. It will get better.' That same voice had told her not to put up a fight. That same voice had assured her that he would let her go afterwards, and not kill her.

That voice was a liar.

"Go to hell," she said through gritted teeth, and sprinted down the trail like Roadrunner, deathly sure that Wile E. Coyote was right behind her.

"Bitch! If you know what's good for you, you'll get back here RIGHT NOW!" He was already close enough to reach out and touch her.

His long, dark fingers reached out and touched the sail of blonde hair that was billowing out behind her. His fingers snapped closed over a snatch of it, and he yanked back.

Rebecca's head whiplashed backward like the head of a crash-test dummy.

"Jesus! Let go of my hair!" She kicked his legs, and beat her small fists on his sides. She clawed at his throat, and felt her fingernails rip their way through his flesh. They left scratch marks that instantly beaded up with dark red blood. He seemed to not even feel it.

The sudden impulse came upon Rebecca to cry out for help. She screamed at the top of her lungs, "HELP! RAPE! OHMYGOD! SOMEBODY PLEAAASE!"

"Shut up Bitch! Don't you get it? No one can help you now! No one can even hear you out here! THIS LITTLE BITCH IS GETTIN WHAT SHE DESERVES, WON'T SOMEBODY PLEAAASE HELP HER?! See Bitch? No one! You're just makin it worse!"

Rebecca flinched back at every word until she felt like she was being driven into the ground with a hammer. When he was done shouting at her she felt one feeling dominant above all others.

Hopelessness.

"Okay, Bitch. We're gonna do this my way now."

She struggled in his grip. He had his huge brown hands locked tightly over her pale white arm in a death grip. He twisted her arm behind her back. Her mouth opened in a grimace of pain, but she remembered her half-assed promise, and refused to scream.

"Fuck, stop twisting my arm! You're breaking it!"

His grip loosened, and she tried to pull away. It was no use. He was in control. She squirmed, and just as his grip started to tighten back up to twist her arm, she brought her foot up hard.

Right into his crotch.

His eyes bugged. He made an Ooo! noise, and Rebecca almost laughed. She remembered the circumstances, and bit down on her tongue to keep from it.

He grabbed his balls with his gun-hand, but made sure to maintain his grip on Rebecca with the other. He took a deep breath, shivered as if to shake the pain away, and snarled, "You little cunt. You get back there, and you open your legs, and you take it." He bit off each word with stunning clarity.

"No."

He punched her in the temple. Grayness washed over her vision, fuzzing in and out like a TV with bad reception. He dragged her back to the mattress and threw her down. He jumped on top of her with his knees on either side of her waist, and wrapped his hands around her throat. She was forced to look into those terrible black eyes. He squeezed tighter until she thought for sure her neck would snap like a Popsicle stick.

Mercifully, he released his grip. She foolishly sucked in deep lungsful of air that felt like inhaling metal shavings. He delivered several bone-rattling blows to her chin that crunched her teeth together. She tasted blood.

And, horrifically, she could already feel his erection poking her in the belly.

"Bitch, I expect you to lay there when I get up. Don't think about movin." She lay back, defeated. She didn't have the energy to get up.

"You're just a fucking pussy, you know that? You're no man at all."

He got up, knowing she was too exhausted to move. He smiled his gold-toothed smile, pulled the pistol out of his pocket and set it on the hood of her Malibu, far out of reach. He came back, removing his shirt on the way, and sat on her again.

"Now, you get what you deserve, you dirty Bitch." He unbuckled his belt and pulled down his pants. What lay beneath looked like a snake ready to strike.

He slid off his shoes, flicked off his socks, and pulled off her shirt, sitting her up and arching her back to get the right angle. He unhooked her bra after a few seconds of fumbling around with the strap. Her breasts bounced as they were released from the mold of the bra. A milky stream of premature ejaculate shot out of his iron bar of a penis, and onto Rebecca's naked chest.

"You're just a thirsty little boy who never got any, aren't you? You can't even take a bra off without pre-cumming!" She wiped some of the semen off of her bare chest with her index finger, as if to underline her point.

"Fuck you, Bitch!"

"I bet you can't last thirty seconds inside me. If that." She flung the cum in his now-sweaty face, and he scraped it off. He elbowed her in the stomach, knocking the wind out of her. He yanked off her jeans and set his finger at the top of her Hello Kitty panties.

"Underwear, underwear, I wanna see what's under there!" he sang, and pulled them off. "Well, hel-lo, kitty! Too bad all the girls are shavin' 'em these days, I like a good bush!"

He grabbed his cock and guided it into her vagina. She sucked in a little gasp of air as he entered, and bit into her lower lip. He felt so big. And it hurt. She imagined that she could feel her hymen snapping, but didn't know if you'd actually be able to feel such a thin layer of skin breaking open.

He began the thrusting until he was panting above her, dripping sweat, forcefully driving his giant cock deeper within her, until it felt like her vagina was literally ripping.

He flinched upwards as if he was goosed, and suddenly there was a warm, wet feeling spreading inside her. He pulled out, panting like a dog during a sweltering summer day. She was disgusted to see that his genitals were steaming in the chilly November air.

Rebecca numbly realized her virginity was gone. She'd been raped. She really had. Rebecca Dianne Ellison had just been raped.

She felt some nasty fluid oozing out of her. She wondered if it was blood or cum, then decided she didn't want to know. And she didn't dare look. She felt dirty, she felt violated, she felt tired. But Rebecca stayed strong, kept her promise, and refused to cry in front of him.

She didn't know what to do next, and if she really was free to go now, did he expect a fucking ride home after what he'd done to her?

What happened next made her think she'd never be taking rides with anyone ever again. He plucked the gun off the hood of the car, and crunched through the dead leaves back to her. He raised his weapon, and insanity bloomed in his eyes like a million spring flowers. "Dumb Bitch. You liked it, didn't you? You actually liked it, didn't you?! You liked it!" He shook the gun at her to emphasize his point.

"Go to hell, you sick bastard," she spit at him. Then she tried to literally spit at him, but when she hocked back, she started choking on her own blood.

He pulled the trigger. The gunshot rang throughout the entire forest.

Oh my God, she thought, that was loud. I remember hunting with dad, and even the rifle shots weren't that loud. It didn't sound like a shot, it sounded like an explosion.

Then she thought, Wait, how am I still thinking? All she saw was darkness, so she wondered, Am I dead? She realized that her eyes were closed, and that's why it was all black. She felt exquisitely stupid that she had mistaken death for closed eyelids, and burst out laughing.

She forced herself to stop, because that's what crazy people did. They laughed in the face of danger. She had no interest in believing that she was losing her mind. That was rock bottom. That was losing all hope.

She sat up in spite of her aching body, and the miracle she saw made her think twice every time someone told her they didn't believe in God.

The rapist was lying dead on the ground, both arms reduced to bloody stumps. The gun had exploded when he pulled the trigger. Now a smoking piece of metal was lodged in his skull.

There was a God.

Rebecca saw his leg twitch, and his mouth opening… and closing.

Scrambling to her feet, her crotch sang with extravagant pain. She picked up her pants, and was about to look for her shirt, but a wounded mumble from the man made her think otherwise. The idea occurred to her that she should go bash his sadistic brains in, but she did not want to touch him.

So instead, she hurried to the Malibu. She turned the keys in the ignition with zero hesitation.

Rebecca drove out of there at roughly the speed of light. All the way home, she checked her rearview, sure that she would see the gleam of a gold tooth from the back seat.

When Rebecca pulled into her sorority, she prayed no one would see her. She'd checked the car for something to cover up with, but found nothing. She slipped on her jeans, and a dime-sized pool of blood began to spread from the crotch.

So half-naked, scared, and seeping unknown fluids from her privates, Rebecca Ellison got out of her car, and limped up to the door. She'd broken her self-promise now; she was sobbing.

***

Something almost worse than the rape itself had haunted her back then: humiliation.

She remembered how all the girls just knew. They didn't know exactly what, but they knew there was something. And they preyed on it like cheetahs on a cornered zebra.

Rebecca became an outsider.

Pregnancy hadn't even reared its ugly head in her mind yet until two weeks later when her period was late. She didn't need the pregnancy test to tell her what she already knew. After waiting the couple minutes that lasted at least an eternity, she picked up the thin white stick with shaky hands, and glanced down to see whether it had declared her pee + or -.

+

Of course.

After very careful consideration, she decided she wanted an abortion. She didn't want to live with the daily reminder of what had happened to her. Yes, she could set him/her up for adoption, but she didn't want people to know she was pregnant. Rumors would spread like plagues, and once the truth finally came out, she'd never be able to show her face again. She could feel part of the rapist growing inside of her like a nasty tumor. She wanted an abortion. She needed it. Maybe to save what was left of her dwindling sanity.

A bit of studying told her that the procedure would cost $650. She phoned her mother and asked for a loan, not having to pretend when she tried to sound helpless. Her story was that she was falling behind on costs, and could really use the extra $300. Abigail, her mother, accused her of snorting cocaine, and reluctantly sent the money. Rebecca scraped together the rest of the money, and had the abortion.

And to this day she distinctly remembered how freaked out she'd been in the operating room when she had it. She'd been so sure something would go wrong. Embarrassing the hell out of herself, she had an asthma attack, and instead of just numbing the lower portion of her body, they were forced to clamp restraints on her wrists and put her under. She felt so suffocated in that room by the no-nonsense look of the abortionist that seemed to seemed to say, Go ahead, Becca. Tell me your fears. Confide in me. I'll take one look at them and crush them with logic.

***

All that shit seemed like a fantasy to her now. Ten years ago, by God, and it felt like a lifetime. She was thirty-three now, with a family. And she actually had a son. One that she hadn't aborted. She had a husband, too. Thank God he was the father, and not that man. LeRoy Johnson, his name had been. She remembered seeing his obituary in the paper, back in college, and crying hot tears of joy and relief. That misfire had killed him after all, his opening and closing mouth and twitches either figments of her imagination, or last minute reflexes of a dying body. He wasn't going to come back for revenge after all.

And let's get one thing straight, Rebecca had never told a single soul about those terrible college days, about rape and abortion, about any of that shit. The past was the past. It was behind her and forgotten.

Or almost forgotten.

Until just lately, all of those experiences were bundled up like bales of hay, and stuffed way back in the back of her mind with God knew what other things she had willed herself to forget. But one day, all those memories came flooding back like a hurricane. Ten whole entire years ago, back when Rebecca Warner had been Rebecca Ellison.

Most rape victims are quite stereotypically sketchy about the idea of relationships and marriage. Rebecca wasn't. Instead of rejecting the idea, she welcomed it. It was an opportunity for change. An opportunity for the past to finally become the past; a new beginning.

So Rebecca had sprung on the opportunity, and married Dave Warner, mostly for freedom, partly for love. The freedom he provided made her love him all the more. And she especially loved the idea of having her name changed. Not having her old last name was great; it made her a new Rebecca. Rebecca Dianne Warner, to be exact.

Dave Warner never had a clue that his wife was not technically a virgin when he had supposedly "broken her in" on the night he proposed. That he would find out later.

*****

It all started again about a week before everything really hit home, and it probably saved her mind from breaking when it all hit home again. She was sitting in her room reading some love story that she couldn't get into when the baby monitor crackled. She looked at it with curiosity and love. It was sweet hearing Ashton's baby coos, letting her know he was alright. But what she heard… wasn't Ashton. It was some other voice. Maybe that of a child. It was distorted but she could make out a child's voice for sure. The voice seemed to be saying –

BAM!

The door crashed open and a scream leaped into Rebecca's throat like a frog being eaten alive who doesn't want to die.

Dave. It was just Dave.

"Honey I'm home!" he said with a stupid smile on his face.

"Shut up and come here!" she scolded him in a harsh whisper as if any noise would make the strange voice stop. But it did. Now there was no noise coming from the other end. Just the same silence as before.

"Dammit Dave! There was another voice on here! Not Ashton! And don't you say you don't believe me, because there was! And now it's not on there because you barged in!"

Dave laughed and sat on the edge of the bed. "Honey, don't you know that happens all the time? It freaks a lot of people out, but sometimes they pick up signals from other houses and you hear what's on theirs. I bet you picked the signal up from the Ramirez's."

You son of a bitch, she thought with true malice in her voice. Don't you try to rationalize what just happened. But he did, making her feel stupid, until eventually she gave up on the subject.

***

Rebecca Warner made her way downstairs with one towel put up in her hair, and another one around her body. She stopped dead in her tracks in the kitchen doorway when she saw what was on the counter.

The sugar was tipped over, and in a child's shaky script was the word:

HI

We've got a little ghost, she started to think, but the second word told her it was much more than that. The second word was:

MOM

Hi mom.

Rebecca felt dizzy, and gripped the wood paneling of the doorway to keep from tumbling over like a top that can't keep spinning any longer.

Eventually the lightheadedness passed, and with less than a second of consideration, she wiped the mystic message off of the counter and into the sink, then capped the overturned sugar jar, and stood it upright. Dave could not know about this.

Questions would lead to

(I was raped)

…something else.

Asthma that had remained dormant for years flared up once again, and she had to will herself to stop. She'd reopened that mental scar, and the loathsome bastard was bleeding out grotesque memories.

Rebecca pulled herself together like a schoolboy who has dropped his papers, and has to collect them before the wind blows them away. She made a visible effort to keep herself under control, and went upstairs to feed Ashton his formula.

It was crazy, that kid seemed to be getting more and more tan by the day. At the time, Rebecca thought nothing of it.

She stepped in the room, peered lovingly down at Ashton's chubby face. His brownish-blonde hair was getting longer

(darker?)

and needed cut. She brushed it out of his closed eyes, not wanting to wake him, because she thought she'd never seen anything so sweet in her life.

He's precio – she began thinking, but stopped. Her eye had happened upon the dresser in the corner of the room. The baby powder canister had been tipped over, and all the white powder was laying on top of the dresser. Written in it was a single symbol:

David was a very logical man, and in the middle of the night, when the crying baby woke them up, he pushed the idea, *That doesn't sound like Ashton*, out of his head. There was no other baby in the house, how could it not be Ashton?

Normally, Becca would have mumbled in a sleepy voice that he found incredibly sexy, "Will you get him?"

Tonight, however, that was not the case. She was already up and out of bed. Her face told David she knew something, but was very reluctant to say what.

"I'll get him," she said immediately. No sleepy seduction in that voice. She was wide awake.

"I've been in and out of sleep, I'll come with you."

Rebecca started to hesitate, and then simply said, "Okay." Dave noticed that she was sure to flick on the hallway light, as if she was afraid of the dark… or something in it.

Dave pushed the thought away.

They opened Ashton's nursery-room door, and saw something strange. Ashton was asleep. That continuous *Weaahhh* was coming from the crib. But not Ashton.

He was asleep.

Becca's face looked as pale as a vampire.

"Becca – he's, he's probably just… I don't know, crying in his sleep or something."

He knew that Becca knew of his aversion for the paranormal, and also knew that she hated it. She'd once told him that he had no consideration for the truth. This time she was different, as if she had something to hide. She looked like a kid who was about to be punished.

"Um, yeah, probably," Becca said. David was shocked. Usually, Becca would have protested, pointing out the flaws in his idea. The major two being that Ashton's mouth wasn't moving, and he didn't even look restless in his slumber. He looked peaceful, and he was dead still.

"Or maybe the pipes. That seems a little more realistic. I mean, his mouth's not moving an inch," David said.

"That's what it is, I bet."

Neither of them dared to admit that they saw a suspiciously baby-sized dent weighing down the mattress right next to Ashton.

***

Later that night, Rebecca lay awake. She knew that she might not be able to hold off on it any longer. She needed to tell David what was going on. She'd be forced to revisit those dreadful college days, when she'd been at her very worst. She'd have to –

Suddenly, a little extra weight seemed to materialize itself next to her in the bed. Ice cold, invisible arms clutched her for support. They felt similar to mist. That cold feeling pressed itself against the small of her back. She was cuddling with her dead child that she had aborted ten years before.

It took every ounce of willpower not to scream.

***

Knowing that she would be forced to tell Dave sooner or later, Rebecca pushed open Ashton's door. She hadn't slept a wink last night due to the clutches of those ice-cold hands. She tried to tell herself it was a dream, but deep down she knew the truth. She peered over the edge of Ashton's crib, and shook her head in confusion and fear. He was three months old today, and had become exponentially more tan overnight.

She registered this now, and accepted that something was wrong about it. It danced on the tip of her tongue like a name you can't quite remember. She let it go for now, because she didn't know what it meant.

Rebecca changed Ashton's diaper, kicked a toy elephant out of the way on the messy, toy-raddled floor, and left. As the door clicked closed behind her, she heard a baby rattle shaking on the other side of it. She flung the door open like a soldier breaching a room full of terrorists, hoping to catch the possibly paranormal occurrence in the act. Instead, Ashton (with no rattle in his hand) had his head cocked to the ceiling, and was staring at something Rebecca's eye couldn't see. His head moved around, seeming to trace the path of whatever he was watching. A chill rolled down

Rebecca's spine. Ashton clapped and giggled, his chubby arms jiggling.

His toys, which had only a few seconds before been strewn carelessly across the room, were now tucked neatly into the overflowing toy box. The toy elephant she had scooted out of the way stared at her, taunting her with its beady black eyes. It was on top of the pile, and now it tumbled off. Rebecca jumped.

She closed the door again. Behind it, she heard a baby laugh. And it wasn't Ashton.

***

Dave had nearly forgotten about the crying incident from a few nights before (once again, he was a very rational man), until he started to leave for work.

He opened the door, and was about to leave, but something made him halt. Three words were scribbled on the wall in blue crayon:

YOUR NEW DADA

He stopped in his tracks. Rebecca must be playing some stupid joke on him. Either that, or Ashton was one of those child geniuses that could write and read in even the earliest stages of infancy.

He assumed the former and hoped for the latter. He marched to the car, thinking about the right time to confront Rebecca about this.

***

Rebecca entered Ashton's nursery once again, and a gust of, wind?, rocked her backwards. Thoughts rushed through her mind. They were pictorial thoughts with very little vocabulary. Mostly, they were just general understandings of certain topics. But the knowledge seemed to be growing, and fast. Getting older, maybe? That sounded crazy but true.

Ashton was borderline black with his "tan" now, and she knew why.

The baby she had aborted ten years ago was black. And he was trying to possess her son.

She believed the baby had found a way to broadcast thoughts into her mind, a telepathic bond only mothers and their unborn children must share She almost laughed at the absurd stupidity of this idea, and then stifled herself. It wasn't funny. It was the truth.

Somehow, her dead child had filled the room with his thoughts like an overstuffed suitcase that you have to sit on to pack. The room had become his brain, which she could look into and see the swell of thoughts (mostly pictorial, but growing) flowing around her like a soft breeze. She could actually feel them. In return, he could also see into her while she was in this room. She had discovered a telepathic link to her long-dead baby through her son's bedroom.

The only problem was that her living son was most likely the broadcasting system as he became slowly possessed by her "failed" abortion, as he came back from beyond the grave to reclaim his rightful place as her child.

See now mama? the voice which was a mix between that of a fetus and a ten year old (ten years was how long ago her abortion was, oh yes this did make terrible, perfect sense), but much closer to the fetus end, asked. The idea of that alone, a halfway grown up fetus voice, hurt her head.

No! she screamed not out-loud at it. Get away from my son!

Letter blocks on the floor which she hadn't noticed before burst apart like a popped blister and hit the walls, leaving several dents. They'd been spelling ASHY BUBBA before; now some of them rearranged themselves (and a few others) into BABY MAD. That ghostly but audible crying started again. Now it was almost shrieking.

***

That night at the dinner table, David asked in a misleadingly casual voice with undertones of anger, "So, I don't suppose you've seen what Ashton left for us on the wall, did you, hon?"

In fact, she had. But she knew it wasn't Ashton.

"Honey, I need to tell you something. I don't quite know how to, and you probably won't believe me at first, but you have to. You have to."

"What does this have to do with what 'Ashton'" – he made air quotes around his son's name – "wrote on the wall?"

The fact that Dave accused her pissed her off, but she didn't have time to argue. She needed to tell Dave before it was too late.

She took a deep breath, and did exactly that. All the repressed memories that she had never breathed a word of to anyone, before now, spilled from her.

***

When Rebecca finished her story, Dave had tears in his eyes. He had not spoken a single word the entire time. Even when Rebecca said, "What really scared me about being raped was that I never saw it coming," something in his wife's eyes told him not to. He sat quiet for about thirty seconds when she was finished, hand propped under his chin, soaking up the story like a sponge. Then he finally spoke.

"So, you're not joking? I hope with all my heart that all that was not some kind of joke."

"I'm not joking. I've never been more serious."

"Well, I honestly am speechless. I don't know what to say."

"Do you believe me?"

"I don't know honey. It's just– " he sighed. "It's a lot to swallow. I mean, how can it be true? It's not like we live in the movies. This is real life."

"Dave, I'm sorry but it just really rubs me the wrong way when people deny everything, like you insist on doing. People that have this need for some kind of grounded reality where the only thing they believe is what they want. You can say I'm wrong. You can say 'I'll believe it wrhen I see it' or that you need some scientific proof to believe in a paranormal occurrence, but what you really mean is not that you can't believe in it. It's that you won't. You refuse to accept the truth because it screws up your closed-minded, perfect little world, and you're scared. You say there's no proof of

God or ghosts or aliens but you're wrong. Look around you. The truth is everywhere. It's like you—"

"I never said I didn't believe you."

"Well do you?"

He seemed to consider this for a while, then nodded.

"I believe you, Becca. There's a ghost-baby trying to become our son by hollowing out our own to make a home for himself, and that's just about the most impossible damn thing I ever heard, but I believe you." Rebecca's heart warmed at the fact that Dave actually believed in something that he could hardly believe in, just for her.

"Is there anything I can do? Can I help? Can we save our son? What can we do, damn it!?" he asked shakily.

"There is something we can do. Believe it or not, we'll have fun doing it." Dave looked shocked at this statement. "Just for tonight, of course; the next nine months will be hell."

***

When they were done, Dave rolled over, out of breath, dilated pupils slowly returning to normal size. He wrapped his arm around his wife to cuddle like they usually did after making love, bet Rebecca sat up.

"Davey, I feel bad about this, but I really have to go. I promise I'll be back real quick."

"Where are you going?" He twirled a strand of her hair through his fingertips, and then let his hand drop back to the bed.

"To save Ashton," she replied, and walked out the door, still as naked as the day she was born.

As she walked down the hallway, she wondered. *What if this doesn't get me pregnant?* She figured they would just keep trying until little baby – *Oh my God we still haven't named him!* – was announced in the form of a plus sign on a department-store pregnancy test stick.

But, somehow, she had a feeling this would work. That maybe the baby had willed it to work. Because it craved living, even though it never had lived, in the same way a pregnant lady (ironic, huh?) craved things she had never eaten before.

The fact that she was already pregnant struck her like a sucker punch. It seemed impossible since her egg certainly hadn't had time to even be fertilized yet, but that was just the way it was.

When she opened the door this time, there was no gust of wind to signify that the telepathic link had been opened.

What she realized was that during intercourse, the reason her orgasm was so brief was because it wasn't an orgasm. It was the telepathic link opening again, only instead of feeling it around her in the room like she had earlier, this time it was inside her. And growing ever so much faster and stronger by the minute.

Hey, listen! She thought at the baby. *You're gonna leave my son alone! Have we got that clear? I set up the chance for you to –*

She was cut off. *Know already! I sleep-a now, mom.*

I am not your mother, she thought at it. *You tried killing my real son. How c –*

She stopped. It was useless. He was already gone. "Asleep," if you prefer. The mental link was closed. She had a feeling she would be hearing from that voice in about nine months. By then it will be very strong, she thought.

She stepped over to Ashton's crib to confirm her belief. She saw what she was expecting. His complexion was once again very pale. He no longer had his tan.

***

The next nine-ish months were kind of hectic, but not too bad. Although there was a lot of bad, there were some good times. Dave got promoted to corporate manager and Ashton took his first steps on the same day. Ashton started being able to string together short sentences, and there was a lot of joy in that.

Those were the smoother times, but of course there were a lot of obstacles to face. Like Rebecca's pregnancy hormones. And they also didn't know whether or not to see a doctor. With the whole supernatural thing, drawing in unwanted attention just seemed asinine. What if some unusual sonogram caught the doctor's eyes (for example, what if instead of portraying a baby, it instead said, HI MOM), and led them down a path that neither Rebecca nor Dave wanted to go down.

Other obstacles included nosy people asking their nosy questions and poking their nosy noses in where they didn't belong. They tried to cover the large umbrella of questions, and struggled with some of them. They were going to name him Gregory if he was a boy, and Julia if she was a girl. The doctor they were supposedly seeing was a man they invented named Doctor Ronald Stephens. They also told people that Rebecca was carrying the child for an infertile family up north, so they wouldn't be keeping the baby. Gregory – or Julia – would only make occasional visits to his or her birth mother. In reality, they planned to set him up for adoption and hoped he never found his way home. But that was a worry for another day.

One day, while Rebecca was pouring tea, she felt the mental link reopen inside her. It was so much bigger now. This shocked her, and she spilled her tea all over the floor, narrowly avoiding a scalding of her left leg.

Birfdayyyyy! the voice cried in splendor.

It was November 23rd, the eleven-year anniversary of the night she had been raped.

She prayed that the voice wouldn't pop back up sometime in December or January, the day of her "failed" abortion, and proclaim, Defdayyyyy!

She tried to beg her unborn son not to say deathday, but the mental link was already closed. He needed to sleep. She knew that whatever potential son may have lain underneath Greg's (yes, he was beginning to be Greg to her now) new fetus body was completely destroyed now. The fetus was hollowed out for Greg to wear. Thank God this hadn't happened to Ashton, and she had an idea of why it hadn't. A person's will can change a lot of things. People are much stronger than they realize. Rebecca's love for Ashton had protected him from Greg. It had taken a long, long time for Greg to hollow out Ashton, because Rebecca wouldn't allow that to happen. Greg's will to live had allowed him to break through her will and almost destroy her son. Now she was allowing Greg to manifest easily inside her uterus. He didn't have to break through defenses this time; this time it was a free ride. This time she actually wanted it to happen, in order to save Ashton. That was why the potential son had been eliminated by Greg much quicker than Ashton almost had. Willpower.

***

On March 2nd, Rebecca woke up to the voice calling her name. It sounded full now. That mental link was stronger than ever. *I coming, mom,* it said. Then the link snapped shut like a crocodile's mouth.

Rebecca frantically shook Dave awake. "Dear God, Dave! He's coming now!"

Rebecca went into labor. From the next room, she heard Ashton crying his much less baby-like cry in his bed; He had been promoted to a bed in place of his crib for his first birthday. The crying wasn't necessarily sad, though. Maybe Greg and his brother shared a telepathic link, too. Maybe Ashton knew he was getting a little brother today.

The mental link briefly opened. *No adopta, mom!* Greg cried. *You kee-me!*

No adoption, mom. You keep me.

***

"Shit! Dave!" Rebecca howled. "He's coming now! Tell me to push and all that shit you're supposed to do!"

"Becky, I–" She made a half-grunt half-scream, interrupting him. "Heyyy," he soothed. "Becca, it's okay, come on. You've been through this before. You know what to do. Just take a deep breath, and when you feel the contraction coming on just blow out your air and push. I'm here with you."

Rebecca sucked in her breath and let it out, flexing the muscles down there as she did so. "Damn you men. You have no idea."

Dave understandingly tapped her hand with his free one.

"Get down there and check. He's got to be coming out now. I can feel it." And it hurts like a bitch, she thought but didn't add.

Dave released his grip on her hand, and ducked below the swell of her belly, staring into that pink chamber that was her vagina, refusing to vomit.

Rebecca could no longer see Dave, and she panicked. "Is he down there? Is he out yet? Damn it, Dave, tell me! He's gotta be, I can feel him! Do you see him Dave, do you–"

"No!" He realized he'd raised his voice, and knew that was a terrible idea. He was dealing with a pregnant woman here. "No." Softer. "Not yet, keep pu– Holy crap, there he is."

Dave could see the emerging head. He hadn't been expecting the baby to be black, although it made sense because of the whole Ashton tan thing, and it came as a great surprise to him. Neither Rebecca nor Dave was black, yet they had given birth to a black baby. This supernatural thing really was happening, whether he liked it or not.

"Push, Bec!"

"What in the name of Cuh-rist does it look like I'm doing?"

"It looks like you're doing good. Just keep on."

Eventually the baby was forced out, and he plopped into Dave's outstretched arms.

"Son of a–" He remembered there was a baby in the room and rephrased his wording. "Shoot! What do we cut the umbilical cord with? More importantly, what do we get the placenta out with?"

"Never mind the goddamn placenta! Smack him before he dies!"

At first, Dave was startled. Smack him? Was she crazy? Smack a baby? What the –

Then he realized why Greg wasn't crying. He was still used to the amniotic fluid, and hadn't learned to adjust to the air yet.

Dave slapped the baby on the right buttock hard enough to hurt, forcing him to draw in his first breath. Coughing up phlegmy amniotic fluid, Greg sucked in his first breath. He wasn't crying. Dave was puzzled by this, but Becca thought she knew why. Greg wasn't scared, he was happy; he knew he was finally alive.

Dave handed Rebecca the still-slimy baby. "I'm gonna go get scissors," he said, and ran out of the room.

Rebecca took her first real look at her second (or was he really the first, since he had halfway-existed long before Ashton) child. She smiled at first. Then Greg stopped blinking to adapt to the light, and looked up at her.

"Dear Jesus Christ," she whispered.

His irises were completely black. It appeared to be just a single pupil.

Just like his father.

Rage exploded inside her like an overcooked frag, and she flipped off her back and onto her stomach with the baby underneath her. Excruciating daggers of pain screamed throughout her entire body in protest.

You are your father, she screamed at it through the telepathic link that she forced open. She had a feeling that as soon as the umbilical cord was cut, that eleven-year-old baby voice would lose all its memory and become just a baby, and the link would cease to exist. *It's just your father back for revenge and I opened the gateway to let him through by having you, didn't I?*

She saw surprise and fear on Greg's end of the link. She welcomed it.

Well you won't have me and neither will your father! She wrapped her hands around Greg's throat and squeezed. She dug in with both her thumbs and shook violently. *Yeah, Johnson! I hope you can feel this all the way down in hell! It's not so good on the other side of the hands, is it, you sick f—*

She stopped in mid-thought, because Greg – not Johnson, Johnson was dead, and she had been wrong to think that Greg was some diabolical reincarnation of him – cut her off. His voice was now much closer to the eleven side, simply from being born, although she knew a simple snip of the scissors would change that. *Mom! Stop! I just wanted a chance to live! I never wanted to hurt anyone!*

She pulled her hands away. What in the hell was she doing?! She was strangling an innocent infant to death with her bare hands. How crazy she must have looked to David, who had just stepped through the door. He stopped in his tracks, dropping the scissors, mortified surprise spreading across his face. He'd been carrying Ashton to show him his new brother, but now he set him down, telling him to go on back to his room and daddy would be in to see him later. He could walk pretty good on his own now, and David hoped he would get back to his room before any more crazy stuff happened. *Wow,* he thought somewhere in the back of his mind. *I'm protecting my son from his mother.*

He shut the door and yelled something at her, but she didn't hear it. She was too lost in her own sick action.

Rebecca realized what'd happened. She'd assumed from the beginning that Greg was evil, just like his father, since her first impression of Greg was that he was trying to possess Ashton.

All he ever wanted was a chance to live like everyone else. A chance that Rebecca had ripped away from him just like LeRoy Johnson had ripped her virginity away from her. She'd just assumed something, and so she strangled him to death. She was sick.

Dave tugged at her arm and screamed at her.

Greg, she thought, but she was also speaking aloud. "My God, Greg, I'm so sorry. I didn't know – I – " But it was no use. She quit talking and started crying. The link was broken. Greg was gone.

And with even more horror she thought, *This would probably be what LeRoy would have wanted all along. It's like in the end he won, because he has brought more horror into my life than I've ever thought possible.*

"I killed him twice!" she wailed hysterically.

Years ago, she'd aborted him, ending any chance of life he may have had. She'd delivered him into life today, only to rip it away from him once again, in less than a minute. She'd taken his life twice. She was a murderer. Worse, she was a fucking serial killer, because she'd done it twice.

Greg's eyes were opaque and lifeless. His head lolled unresponsively in her arms.

What had she believed he was? Some new, evil manifestation of his father, hellbent on murdering her family? That was far from the truth. He was absolutely nothing like his father. He was a sweet little boy who wanted a chance to live. If she was in his shoes, she probably would've done the same thing. Desperate times call for desperate measures, after all, and what more of a desperate measure than life? She couldn't think of one.

Also, had Greg ever actually done anything besides trying to possess Ashton that would lead her to believe he was some diabolic devil-baby? Besides the BABY MAD blocks, which weren't evil, but just Greg's feelings when Rebecca yelled at him, he really hadn't done anything bad. No. He'd left her sweet messages around the house, played with his brother, and created a mental link so he could talk to his mommy. Shit, he'd even cuddled with her.

In return, she'd murdered him.

"I killed him," she said to David through tears.

"Why? Why Becca? What the hell happened?"

There was not a worse sin she could think of committing than what she'd just done. She'd killed a baby. Twice. Infanticide.

Some things, she decided, were worse than mere words can describe.

Even worse than rape.

Skin

Melanie Waghorne

Twenty-first century medical science had seen many advances, from whole face transplants to the mapping of the human genome. By the end of the century many fields had been seemingly conquered, rendering many diseases a thing of the past much like polio had been in the century before. With so many achievements made, scientists of the twenty-second century turned from the altruistic to the egocentric. There was big money to be made from cosmetic surgery, in assisting the affluent to stay wrinkle free and perky bottomed well into their centenaries and beyond.

As was the case with any new trend and certainly one enjoyed by the very rich, the compunction was to be better, bigger and bolder than the person before you. The glossy, gossip magazines were filled with the lording of fresh faced looking octogenarians and the derision of those whose face-lifts looked held together with a bulldog clip and double sided tape. Funerals became the social events to be seen at. No one wanted to spend hundreds of thousands on sculpting the perfect body to just stick it in the ground with no pomp or ceremony.

Open caskets became *de rigeur*. Funeral homes became booked up months and years in advance. They offered lavish packages; award winning make up artists, flattering lighting and champagne receptions. Each funeral was more opulent than the last but it did not stop ravishing geriatrics passing judgement on the affair, standing around the coffin like a high school clique. The elderly took great pleasure in clucking and tutting their disappointment; no centrepieces? A buffet? You know Margery had waiter service! What a shame she went for the cheaper surgery, look one of them is lower than the other! God rest her soul.

It was at one of these fashionable galas for the deceased that Dr Martin Plebble envisaged the concept for his Levicute 5000 machine. Martin had started his medical training as a surgical resident but found that the sight of a cadaver always ensured that his breakfast made a reappearance. He had found that an analytical mind paired with the propensity to daydream could solidify a career in inventing handy dermatological machinery. He'd enjoyed some mild success with his motorized tweezing machine for the excessively hairy and the FootScrubDelux; a machine that burnt off dead foot skin with a mild but pleasantly scented acid solution that left healthy skin intact. He'd even had a day devoted to his inventions on one of the televised shopping channels, never realizing lavender scented acid would be so popular.

Although he was happy with these achievements, in his heart he had always wished he would become the kind of inventor who had a blue plaque on their house, who was well knowkn to generations to come. He knew he wouldn't obtain this by ensuring that the prosperous ladies of the world stayed well plucked. Little did he know that the Levicute 5000 would make him famous. Not like he had hoped, like Pasteur or Graham Bell but more like Fritz Haber or Arthur Galston.

As it became Martin's turn to pay his respects, he looked into the silk lined, under-lighted coffin and marvelled at how well Great Aunt Jeanie looked, not a day over thirty-five although she was easily pushing ninety. She looked resplendent, nubile enough to make Martin uncomfortable. The only thing spoiling the illusion of an excellent Marilyn Monroe impersonator was her terrible skin, as badly pitted by childhood acne as the skin of a strawberry. Martin thought what a shame it was for such beautiful work to have been ruined by bad luck and blocked pores.

He mused on Jeanie's skin for the rest of the festivities. He knew a lot about skin, he could tell solar keratosis from a basal cell carcinoma from scurvy. He thought he had seen every erythemic, reticulated, pedunculated lesion that skin had to offer but he had never really turned his hand to the treatment of acne. He knew that its main cause was the blockage of hair follicles with sebum which then became infected. There was no way to stop the blockage of the follicles but he wondered if there was a way to treat the scar once it was formed. Non-ablative laser treatment for acne scars already existed, the laser being used to stimulate the growth of collagen but this only helped the scar and did not remove it. What if he could create a laser which removed the scar completely? Electrocautery caused damage to the skin as it coagulated the end of vessels, causing trauma but if he could get the laser hot enough it would eliminate this problem. It could be used not just for the dermatologically challenged but for burn victims, the disfigured. He could be famous after all.

Doodles, sketches and blueprints littered the floor of Martin's office like fallen snow. He had decided that the machine would allow a patient to lay within a small housing that would hold a laser. The laser would be trained on each lesion independently and minutely cut out each scar. Then a 3D printed, skin coloured graft would be stretched over each wound and the collagen stimulated to assimilate it into the skin. After healing the patient would be left with perfect, blemish free skin, free to nip, tuck or lift as they saw fit. Finally naming, Martin wanted something grand, something that fit what a pioneer this machine would be. The Latin for smooth skin was *levi cutem* but why not shorten it to cute, that's what he was trying to make these women wasn't he? 5000 made it sound like it had been through rigorous testing, subsequent models and as such the Levicute 5000 was born. Martin could practically feel the weight of the Nobel Prize in his hands.

Nearly every penny of Martin's savings went into the construction of his prototype. He couldn't afford to rent a lab so made do with the basement in his house. The soldering was a little shoddy in places but Martin thought he might very well be in love. The theory of it worked so beautifully and he was so eager to get started that he decided to skip the animal trials and move straight to human. He didn't think he had ever seen a pimply creature and soothed himself that it would be fine, prudent even to skip this part of the trial. If he advertised locally no one would be any the wiser.

He advertised for participants in the local paper, requesting a picture along with the application. He was almost ghoulishly looking forward to some frightful looking faces, something that would make an astounding before and after picture. Legions of pustulated boy and girls mostly afflicted with childhood acne that would likely clear up on its own answered but none of them really inspired Martin, not until he found Marie. Marie was a thirty year old woman with active acne so severe that it looked like erupting volcanoes on the pitted surface of the moon. She was perfect. Martin burst out laughing, kissing her picture and spinning it around like a ballroom partner. This was the face that would make him famous.

Marie's lesions were even more impressive in person. She sat in Martin's kitchen, the early autumn light slanting through the windows, illuminating her puckered skin. Martin examined her face carefully; turning it this way and that, feeling the pustules move underneath is fingers like a water bed. He ran through the formalities, trying to blind her with the science of it, skimming over the risks before moving in for the really hard sell. He used his most grandiose pitch, medical pioneering, changing the fate of the unfortunate, anything he could think of to lock her in. He was comfortable stooping to emotional blackmail.

"You know the machine is just downstairs, we could begin this afternoon" he cajoled.

"Umm well I don't know. Shouldn't I have some time to think about it?" Marie stammered, hiding the worst of her scabs behind a veil of hair.

"Well of course you must be sure my dear but if you take too long I can not guarantee that you will be the first test subject. Well that you will be a subject at all in fact"

Martin swept his arm towards the loaded counter, scattered with applications.

"It's a very popular proposal you see. It's a pricey procedure but being in this study allows you to have revolutionary, never before attempted work done. For free" Martin had to stop himself from wiggling his eyebrows enticingly. He could see the panic he had elicited in her, he kept quiet hoping the hook would hold, that he could reel her in.

"Lord's no I don't want that, let's get started!" she cried.

He led her down into the basement, trying to ignore the extinguishing of excitement on her face. The prototype wasn't very sleek but Martin bustled around importantly, installing Marie onto the modified dentist's chair, securing safety goggles over her eyes. Patting her arm reassuringly. Scar tissue was still skin but the fibre composition of the collagen had been altered at the time of injury. The machine would scan the skin and be able to point out the different collagen. It effectively only had two settings, the depth of the scar that needed to be removed and the fineness of the scar. The graft would be added once the scar had been removed and required a second programme. Martin was so engrossed with looking busy and professional that he did not feel his elbow brush against one of the laser's dials. He did not see it move.

Sliding himself behind a solid steel plate, Martin called to Marie to stay still and pushed the remote control of the laser with gusto. A violet light scanned the length of Marie's body, interpreting data back to the machine. That was curious, thought Martin, I thought I had set it for just her face. He had no time to act on his confusion. The first zap of the laser sounded like a fly hitting a fluorescent bulb, a pop with the smoky smell of sizzled flesh. He watched Marie's body jerk. She hissed an intake of breath.

"It's okay, that's norma...." Martin's cry was cut short but the second strike of the laser, the third and fourth until it became a continuous volley.

Marie's body was sent into a tonic clonic seizure of activity. Martin cried out, huddling to the steel plate for safety. He clamped his hands to his ears to drown the cacophony of noise, like a thousand angry wasps but underneath it he could hear Marie screaming.

The laser opened every scar on Marie's body. Every healed paper-cut, childhood scabbed knee, shaving knick or old graze burst open. The skin over her knees and shins tore away like a cheap suit, her hands were eviscerated, each metacarpal standing out starkly, jumping and jiving like the rest of her body. Martin gawped as Marie's Caesarean scar, yawned open from hip to hip like a gaping maw, spilling a cascade of gore and viscera across the floor. Marie had stopped screaming. The laser fizzled and stopped. The only sound in the room was Martin's panicked breath and the rhythmic plink, plink, plink of Marie's blood dripping from her once covered fingertips, off of her shoes, over the side of the drenched dentist's chair.

Martin stood, swaying slightly, his legs felt wobbly, almost gelatinous. A thin layer of heavily charred meat scented smoke hung in the air. He rushed forward, towards the machine, skidding a spastic cha-cha through pools of blood and chunks of skin. Marie's body was deflated, her intestines hung from their cavity, blue and cyanosed. They looped to the basement floor like Rapunzel's hair. But her face. Her face was unrecognisable, as split and mashed as a rotten peach. Like a somnambulist, Martin tried to shake her awake, tried to end the nightmare. Her mangled body sloshed from side to side in the chair, spilling more gore from every inch. The last sound he heard as he slumped to the floor in a dead faint was the crack of sinew and bone separating from butchered meat, slithering to the floor.

The neighbours called the police. They would later tell the police they thought it had been someone playing a movie too loud, they'd grown concerned after hearing Martin's gibbering, panicked wailing after he'd regained consciousness. For his part Martin barely remembered the swam of emergency services in the room, did not see their pallid, clammy faces or hear their heaving at the sight the gory piñata that had once been a person. He continued to scream until a young officer gave him a resounding slap across the face, hard enough for Martin's jowls to wobble and the officer's hand to sing for a good hour. He told his commanding officer it was to stop the hysterics but part of him wanted to hurt the snivelling little man covered in his own butchery.

Martin was held on remand without bail awaiting a trial for murder. His lawyer assured him it was perfectly normal for bail to not be set in cases of murder. He tried to smile soothingly but the woeful little man, silently shredding a tissue in-front of him did not elicit any of his sympathy. He wondered if the judge had set no bail for the benefit of Martin's own safety. The lawyer had seen the papers, Martin was front page news. The press had taken pictures of Martin being led from what the papers had now dubbed 'A Mad Scientist's Lair". He had been caked in Marie's blood, glutinous blobs hanging from his hair and clothes. His shell shocked expression had made him look devoid of any emotion, apathetic, monstrous even. The lawyer shuddered involuntarily thinking about it. Some of the more insalubrious online news outlets had even published pictures of the removal of Marie's body from the house. They had not been able to carry her body out whole in their normal body bag, instead she had been removed in three crimson streaked buckets. There was out-roar.

Martin was oblivious to all of the news hype. He at first felt glad that no bail had been set. He was badly shaken and could not fathom how he would have gone about his normal life. He didn't know how he could have taken a bath, watched television or made a cup of tea without seeing the image of Marie flayed and gaping underneath his hands. At first he found it easier to be malleable, completely under the control of the prison service. He was guided from court room, to holding cell, to prison van and through the hire wire gates of the prison. He waited in line, trying to drown out the whispers of his fellow prisoners, waiting for his strip search, the image of Marie pumping behind his eyelids like a heartbeat. After what felt like an eternity he was led to his cell and unceremoniously shoved inside. Martin sat on the bottom bunk and listened to the nocturnal cacophony of the prison, men shouting, shouting to each other, calling out for their mothers, wailing in pleasure or pain. His heart skipped and stuttered in his chest as the coils from the bunk above squealed and moaned. A hulking shape dropped from the mattress and extended its hand to Martin. His cell mate was a behemoth.

"Hello" Martin whispered.

"Ahoj" came a gravelly voice.

"I…I'm sorry I..I..don't understand" The figure snorted, viscously at the back of his throat.

"Je to v pořádku" The big man rumbled, patting the top of Martin's head clumsily and climbing back into his own bed.

Martin did not, could not sleep. The next morning he wobbled at the entrance of the cell as he was called. He looked to his cell mate who started an elaborate mime, trying to explain to Martin what was going to happen. Martin was too tired to process the meaning of the charades. He followed a line of men to the dining hall, robotically shuffling down the line to take his various pieces of food. Unthinking he followed his cell mate to a table and sat. He didn't understand a word any other prisoner said but found the droning of their conversation comforting. His head started to nod.

"Give us your cereal mate" came a voice with a sharp elbow to his shoulder. Martin roused enough to see a small wiry man, missing most of his teeth leaning into Martin's space.

"Are you stupid?" the man whistled and waved his hands in-front of Martin's face, his own screwed up in scrutiny.

Martin struggled to understand, his senses felt whisked by the unfamiliarity of the situation. The interrupter moved closer, Martin could smell the cloying smell of his pomade and bad breath enveloping him. He suddenly was not hungry. He limply passed the small box of cornflakes, dropping them onto the other man's tray. The rat-like man scurried back to his own table, whispering gleefully to his comrades. He was marked, a soft touch. Martin would not eat well for his entire stay, most of his rations going to Ratty and his friends. His food was picked over like vultures at a carcass at every sitting. He only felt lucky that no-one had taken that kind of interest in him. Yet.

When he wasn't forced to be outside of his cell he lay on the thin plastic mattress and ran calculations through his head. It would be another couple of weeks before he got his canteen money and was able to buy paper so he ran them through and through over and under and round in his head. He designed, broke down and built the laser over and over again in his mind. He checked the dials twice, re-adjusted them and came out of the scenario a medical genius. He jumped in-front of Marie as the laser started to react, emerging a hero or what if, what if, what if. He was exhausted. Exhausted and hungry.

Visitation day was always on a Wednesday and as such Martin was confused as to why he was being delivered to the visitation room on a Thursday morning. He'd had no visitors since he'd got here, none of his friends or colleagues wanted a paparazzi picture of them visiting the heavily press vilified 'mad' scientist. He wondered unemotionally if his being taken to the visitation room was just a ploy to get him shivved, jumped in an orchestrated prison riot. His overtaxed brain did not know whether to be relieved or apprehensive at the single figure seated at the badly scarred Formica table. The figure did not rise to greet him but sat with a posture ramrod straight, up to the tip of his buzz cut hair. The man regarded Martin as he dropped into the opposite chair with almost girlish blue eyes, delicately almond sloped and framed with heavy lashes.

"I want to talk to you about your invention." No introductions, his voice was clipped and gruff.

Martin groaned. All he had done was think about, dream about, worry about this damn invention ever since they had put Great Aunt Jeanie in the ground.

"Are you a lawyer or from the papers?" Martin sighed.

"Neither." came the curt response "I wish to buy it"

Martin began to laugh, high pitched and manic. He had expected another interrogation tinged with disgust, the only interactions he had experienced in this place so far, certainly not a business meeting.

"You can't be serious" Martin spluttered "It's not ready, I have to fix.., the calculations..."

The man raised a calloused hand to cut him off.

" I don't want you to fix it. I want to buy it as it is" The guest's eyes twinkled with amusement. He leaned back in the cracked, plastic chair, waiting for Martin's reaction.

All of Martin's laughter was gone, panic sat solid and immobile in his guts.

"You..You can't. Jesus Christ you didn't see what it did to her?! She looked as though someone had dropped a pumpkin in December. SHE WAS EVERYWHERE! HOW COULD YOU WANT THAT?!" Martin screeched slobberingly, bile hot and sour in the back of his mouth. He retched noisily, sloppily, saliva dripping down his chin.

"Understand me, I personally not offering to buy it. It is your Government who wishes to acquire your machine Plebble"

Martin put his head between his knees, letting a thin trail of drool puddle onto his prison issue shoes. His head was spinning. The man in-front of him didn't seem to mind that Martin had slipped below the table, he carried on, talking into the space Martin had previously occupied.

" The Government is wishing to do an exchange of sorts. Your machine for your freedom with a caveat of course. You will be released from this prison without charge as long as you accompany me to work further on the invention, under the supervision of the Government. Otherwise you will be left to rot, not in this place of course, somewhere much worse I'm sure" Martin gurgled under the table.

"She didn't just die did she Dr Plebble? From what I have read the paramedics had to practically scoop her from the floor, she went to the morgue in a bucket" Martin's gurgles turned to renewed retching. "Inadvertently you have created a fantastic machine of war and we want to harness this apparatus before our opposition does. Harnessed properly your prototype could obliterate any army it is pitted against making your country a super power. You are a patriot I'm sure"

The man smiled, almost to himself and stood. He walked past Martin's huddled figure, clasping his shoulder as he went.

"I realise you will need some time to decide but think very carefully Dr Plebble, you can either die in prison or your name could go down in history as creating the greatest military weapon in the history of war. His hand clamped down a little harder "You should be proud". Martin snivelled as he watched the man depart, his face a mayhem of tears, snot and saliva.

###

Captain Absylin waited outside one of the aircraft hangers on the edge of the base, desperately trying not to sway in the 104° heat. The baked desert wind hurled sand into his face, he could feel it crusting there, trapped in the sheen of sweat that covered not only his face but his entire body under his fatigues. He desperately wanted to return to barracks, to be out of his oppressive heat. Honestly what he really wanted was to lay naked in a bath tub of ice cubes while a similarly naked, voluptuous waitress spoon fed him ice cream but he had been charged to wait for a very special shipment and presentation by his CO. Absylin sighed, he didn't want to see any crack pot inventions. He'd seen pictures of the rocket scooters given to the French during the Vietnam war. What he really needed was more gas masks, more tanks and more grunts.

Thankfully he could see a Ridgeback 4x4 and a Bedford truck with a large item covered by tarpaulin in the flat bed, trundling up to the camp. Absylin covered his eyes from the astringent incoming wind but saw his

Colonel; Martin's prison visitor and a small mousy man make their way towards him.

"Sir," Absylin snapped to attention.

"At ease Captain," The colonel replied, looking pristine and decidedly dry in his dress uniform. Absylin was jealous.

" Absylin this is our new consultant Dr Martin Plebble. He will be assisting me in showing you this new piece of equipment you have been briefed about"

Martin shuffled up to the Captain, eyes averted and flopped his limp hand into the Captain's sweaty grasp. Absylin could not shake the feeling of wanting to wipe his moist feeling hand down the leg of his trousers, Martin's grip had been like a fish that had stopped flopping on the dock, resigned and slick.

"You may have read about him in the papers I'll grant" the Colonel said, bustling the small group towards the corrugated aircraft hangar.

"We don't get the papers delivered very often Sir" Absylin muttered. The heat was getting to him and Martin's strangeness had unnerved him. Thankfully the Colonel didn't seem to have heard him, he was already striding towards the door, Martin loitering behind him.

"Coming master" Absylin whispered under his breath. Martin had struck him as the cloying, pitiful Igor, two steps behind his master with no free will of his own. He followed the small group up a soft incline to the hanger, they hadn't used it for aircraft in several months, it had become a dumping ground for broken machinery and old pieces of kit, a junk graveyard.

As the Colonel rolled back the heavy sliding doors of the hanger, the stink of unwashed bodies was so ripe that it made Absylin flinch. The space was no longer filled with detritus but had been emptied out and covered in clear plastic. At the far wall a holding cell had been constructed. Within it huddled twenty or so prisoners that had been captured on manoeuvres and were awaiting transport to trial. Absylin wondered when this had all been constructed and why as highest ranking officer on base no one had bothered to tell him. He turned to ask the Colonel but found him too busy directing the pallet from the back of the Bedford into the hanger. He noticed a row of chairs had been set up. A viewing gallery.

The Colonel pulled back the tarpaulin. The Levicute 5000 machine had undergone a drastic makeover after its acquisition by the military. The old dentist's chair had been replaced by an adjustable gurney, complete with restraints for singular usage if required. The brittle plastic lid had been replaced with a gantry similar to that of a CAT scanner. It now looked as sleek and streamlined as a bullet.

"Now Captain" the Colonel turned and beamed at Absylin "What you are about to see is not quite Geneva approved if you understand me correctly" he winked " But you and I both know that war is a dirty game and I think this machine could really turn the tide for us. Please sit, sit." He gestured to the other soldiers to do the same. "Plebble, will you do the honours?"

Martin shuffled up to the machine and stroked its slick casing. This was no longer the machine he had dreamed about, a machine that he had constructed with his bare hands to make people happy. To garner his Nobel Peace Prize. He knew he was now an architect of mass genocide. He began to push the numerous buttons, to program in what he wanted the machine to do. With a whir a rotating arm rose out of the hard shell of the roofing, the head of the laser tilting this way and that like a consternated animal.

Absylin realised what the Colonel had meant about not quite Geneva improved. These men were going to have their trials here and now and not in-front of twelve good men and true. The prisoners had caught on faster, they had started to panic on the raising of the laser's head, pulling desperately at their bonds, shouting out to the small group of soldiers watching them, begging for mercy. The laser stopped its tilting and began to hum and jiggle. A noise started to generate from the bowels of the machine until a beam erupted from the nozzle of the laser, lengthening and widening until it encapsulated the whole line of prisoners. There was nothing more Plebble could do, he sank to his knees, the hard gurney digging into his back and covered his ears with his hands.

The first beam hit a forearm, opening an old cooking burn, the second a scar from a playground injury, the third the site of previous stitches until the volleys came too fast to pin down. Like a violet mist of mosquitoes the beam swarmed over the men, opening every imperfection in their skin. Absylin watched as the men began to disintegrate in front of him, each small wound blossoming open like a flower in bloom until most of the skin had peeled, flayed and melted away. Screams wrapped around him, pushing against his ear drums, fading quickly to gurgles and yelps. The air hung heavy with the stench of cooking flesh. The floor began to swim in offal and entrails. Absylin watched as a solitary eye weaved through the bars, buoyant on the small lake of viscera that was running across the plastic-lined floor. He could see other small offerings bobbing in the mire, a single toe or finger like fruit in a punch bowl. His stomach heaved.

The laser stopped, buzzing slightly before crouching back down into the machine. A fan whirred somewhere within, cooling the machine. Blood had seeped across most of the hangar, lapping at the boots of the viewing gallery. The Colonel squelched out into the mire, turning to face his small audience. His face was stretched and rictus in its joy. The face of a serial killer before the victim draws their final breath. Absylin put his head between his knees, clenching his eyes shut when he saw the splatter across his boots. He could hear the panic and revulsion of his men.

"Gentlemen, I have presented to you just a taste of what this machine can do. Today it is twenty men, tomorrow it could be a whole army. Our troops will no longer have to go into close proximity combat with our enemies, no more being blown up at the roadside or gunned down in small arms fire. With this machine we can be the masters of war!" His voice rose, quivering in its excitement, his arms raised in punctuation. The Colonel looked around the room of grey, stupefied faces. "Don't you see you idiots, instead of these men trying to kill you in these god awful dust bowls you'll be at home with your families with lasers like this do the dirty work. We'll man them remotely like drones and wipe everyone out who opposes us. Gentleman today you are privy to the revolution of war and it thanks to this man here" He gestured at Martin.

Martin felt himself pulled to his feet by the Colonel, his feet sliding in the cruor. He looked over the small gathered crowd, saw fear and repugnance on all faces by the Colonel. He felt this abhorrence as a palpable thing and knew he would have to get used to this feeling. There was nothing more he could do, the machine had been bought and mass production must not be too far behind. He knew his hands would be stained with the blood of millions. Like all mass murderers his name would be notorious, there would be books written about him, textbooks bearing his visage for decades. He was going to be famous. A watery smile touched the corners of his mouth. He was going to be famous.

Nameless

Marc E. Fitch

For Geoff, the beauty of the Internet lied not just in the anonymity of sitting alone in a room while simultaneously being a part of millions, if not billions around the world; rather it was in the namelessness. He had four separate online identities, complete with false profile information, pictures, and marital status. None were true; none even came close to him. He was out there like the Invisible Man, that old movie, which had spurred his fantasies through adolescence, and which now had come true. Of course, he did what any man who was invisible would do; he watched women undress, fornicate and defile themselves in any number of ways before his unblinking electronic eye. The Internet was a vast sea of Invisible Man delights; everyday there were new girls, women, hags and bitches doing anything that the human mind could imagine. And there were so many, so very many, videos, secret bedroom films where the women were caught unaware in the throws of carnality, private pictures sent to ex-boyfriends now shared with the world and web-cams. He knew, undoubtedly, that at some point during his rare forays into public, he must interact unknowingly with one of these online vixens. The idea let him feel a strange connection to those girls on the screen. It was like he had secretly fucked every girl he had ever met because there they were all there in their naked defeat or glory – depending on which way you looked at it.

This world of the nameless had been good to him financially as well. He had managed to invest early in an adult site based out of California and it had performed marvelously, bringing in large amounts of money that were funneled directly to the investors. The film sets were cheap, the girls cheaper, the men practically free and their willingness to do anything, priceless. But Geoff did not monitor the business side of things. He received his quarterly reports and watched what he wanted for free and did most of his shopping, grocery and otherwise, from the comfort of his living room. The money was there and it kept him happy with his sedentary life.

Naturally, his tastes had mutated through the years. The truth of the matter was that in front of his computer – his window to namelessness – the prospect of a man and woman having normal, run-of-the-mill sex on video was simply not enough to satisfy his urges anymore. A real woman hadn't touched him in years and he had given up on them. Several years ago, before he had invested in the company and still had to work for a living, he had been a measly clerk at Staples, working the copy machine, stocking shelves, and, when he had the opportunity, sneaking into the store room with some of the new computers and programs to give them a try. It was while he was working there that he met Samantha, whom everyone called Sam. Sam was oddly attractive for having any interest whatsoever in Geoff and he knew it. So he met her early advances with embarrassment and skepticism, not accepting them for what they were – honest-to-goodness come-ons and flirts. She finally goaded Geoff into attending a party at one of the managers' houses and he agreed. While there she got drunk and fell all over him and pulled him into a bedroom and began to take off her clothes. When he tried to speak she said "Shut up" and for a moment he almost burst with the vision of her body; like that of some forgotten goddess – she stirred the deepest well of compulsion and feeling in him that he had ever known. It was almost a religious experience. She took him and used him and she was tender with him and, in that moment, he felt truly human. She said his name over and over and he was overcome with the intimacy. It occurred to him, afterward, how odd it is that people would invite a camera into the room with them, when he could barely comprehend the many workings and subtle feelings that were so vast in number that the room felt crowded with just the two of them.

After that night, she was gone and there were rumors of her stealing from the store. Geoff never saw her again. Geoff found himself more and more online trying to find it – trying to find that moment that he had with her. And on screen they all appeared to be sexual goddesses; larger than life, they occupied the screen like a pixilated force; commanded the presence and attention of the beholder; they sacrificed themselves and others; they took control in one moment and gave themselves over completely in the other. It occurred to him that everyday, boring life was guided by some kind of morality that oppressed the people, a religion that did not allow for this kind of worship – but that worship stirred beneath the surface. He realized that there existed a deep chasm between men and women; women probably enjoyed sex and they found the occasional man attractive but they did not worship; a woman would not be found at 2pm in a dingy, dark strip club feeding money to a goddess that danced on a stage, looking up with a sense of wonder and awe and lust the way that a man would. Those women, their bodies and beings, were things to be worshipped; their ability to sacrifice for and sacrifice to made them all Christ-like in the eyes of man… but then, it was man that whipped Christ nearly to death and then nailed his arms and legs to a cross.

And as Geoff's fascination, his worship, progressed so did his need to view a new kind of intimacy. He watched couples fuck but, after a time, they all looked the same. They became boring and could not steal him to another world the way Sam had. So he began to seek out that which most fear; the kind of sexuality that replaces intimacy with a brutality that had only been known in ancient times of inquisition and sadomasochistic, religious statism. The love, lust, or attraction was gone, but Geoff stood witness to acts that most women would never know. Now Geoff knew them and had experienced it with them and, therefore, was more intimate with those women than any other man could ever be with a woman in the context of normal, society approved sex. Everyone has normal sex – not everyone can experience the torturous rape of another individual.

Geoff wasn't dumb. He knew to stay away from the kiddie porn sites with all their twisted uncles and cousins and stepfathers speaking in code and probably jerking off while chatting with an FBI agent in the nameless guise of a 12 year old girl. But the small, intimate world of rape and torture had its own little innuendos and codes and secret sites that a novice would never find. For the most part, no one cared about rape porn. Most of the women were whores from Bangkok or some Midwest runaway that no one missed and who would never say anything. So no one really cared and even if they did, there was really nothing that could be done, so it worked.

The sites Geoff now frequented were nebulous; ever changing, rearranging and morphing into different amalgams of legitimate enterprise. Now, it was a site for Mazda Miata enthusiasts and then, a month later, that site was dead and it was now an oceanographic charity organization. If you didn't know where to look – the code words specifically – you would never know you were there. The sites were often frequented by the clueless who were seeking their sexual pleasure in some mundane aspect of existence like cars or charity organizations; people who would cringe if they knew the reality behind their virtual fantasy world. They didn't know the true meaning of intimacy – knowing someone in their most desperate moment.

The nameless had nameless friends: TommyT54 was like a wizard with the web and he used his magic to shuffle around the videos that would normally land one in jail. TommyT54 was adept at hiding in the namelessness of the web. Every site he developed had so many different names, links, pop-up windows to work and slog through that most people would give up after five minutes… unless they had the code that TommyT54 would distribute to only his best clients. Geoff had never met TommyT54 but they were, in effect, partners, the way that a seller and his customer are partners. Once a month a new code would be sent to Geoff with a link that would bring him to new snuff videos; Geoff knew that they weren't all real, it was impossible that he could procure this amount of product. For the most part it was ginned up snuff films, poorly acted at best. Geoff was pretty sure that he could tell when it wasn't real – no runaway wannabe actress could fake the real terror, the real helplessness, the real victimization, the real intimacy. Geoff told TommyT54 what he wanted and Tommy occasionally acknowledged him, but, he had a lot of customers, a lot of product to produce and post and, therefore, sometimes actresses had to be used; it couldn't always be real.

But real is what Geoff wanted and this time TommyT54 sent a quick message with the new link saying "You're gonna like this…"

The video was shot in night vision with the grainy digital flickering of green and white dots, human eyes lit and shining like a cat's at night. She could see nothing. She sat in the middle of an empty room, naked, her arms wrapped around her chest to cover her breasts, her legs crossed over each other, only revealing the beautiful curve of her thighs. Her hair was pulled back into a pony-tail and her glowing eyes darted back and forth across the room, her body shifted uncomfortably, she whimpered slightly. There was sound in the video. The two men were talking, laughing back and forth to each other, each with night vision goggles on; the hairy forearm of a big man appeared in the camera's eye for a moment and then disappeared again. Geoff knew this wasn't a fake or fraud. The camera trained in on her face. She was beautiful. She had a slender face and what he guessed was auburn hair and elfish ears that stuck out just a bit too far but gave her that beautiful quality of everyday, ordinary, girl-next-door imperfection. This was no runaway, he thought. This was no prostitute. This was something different. She had been taken. She was the named, relegated to the nameless. As she heard the men's voices and the shifting of their bodies as they moved toward her she began to whimper loudly and push herself back across the concrete floor until she was against the corner of the room. The black of the room was pitch – she could not see them, only hear them, smell them and feel them.

Then, in an instant, the man with the big, hairy forearms reached out and grabbed her ankles. She shrieked and began to kick but he caught both of her legs and dragged her across the floor to the middle of the room. She instantly lost all pretense of covering her naked body; her arms and hands grasped at nothing but bare walls and dirty concrete ground. Her perfect breasts, her tight little body, were on display for the camera, caught in the throws of action that so few men would ever see or know. He watched the motion of her parts and she kicked and screamed; he paused and slowed down the video at various moments to truly capture the motion of her body and the intimacy of the moment. The big man was on top of her now and he could see the look of pain on her face as she quietly and tearfully gave up, knowing that there was no stopping it now, knowing that the damage had been done and now there was only the hate and power to be absorbed until it was over. She seemed to momentarily hug her attacker as if she were looking for any human contact whatsoever. The cameraman came in close onto her face watching the little movements and emotions as she rhythmically received the big man. "Let's see those beautiful brown eyes, girl," he said and she flashed a look at the camera.

The big man climaxed on top of her and suddenly she looked at Geoff. Through the lenses, wires, satellite signals, cables, fiber optics, electricity, and machinery, she looked directly at him, her eyes pouring into him a rage and despair that he had never seen before. And yet, in that rage and despair, a certain sensuality of doom, as if the joke were on him. And in that moment Geoff felt himself aroused to the point of explosion. He paused the video and played that moment again and again, her moment of simultaneous despair and overwhelming power.

"You're gonna like this..." he had said. Whoever she was, she was now burned into Geoff's world. It was the single finest video he had ever seen and when it was over he felt a strange and sudden relief – not just a sexual relief – but a greater relief that he had been desperate to rid himself of for so long. He felt a sudden weight lifted off his shoulders. He imagined it was probably the same feeling born again Christians describe when they first find Christ. He smiled with release and relief. *Gods unto ourselves,* he thought, *and we all require a sacrifice of some kind.*

In the following days, Geoff felt lighter, happier, and more energetic. It was as if some great burden had been taken off his shoulders, although he could not quite say what the burden had ever been. He returned to the video again and again and each time the penetrating, direct look that the beautiful young victim bore through his body, his mind, his very being and he felt reinvigorated. She was like a drug. Geoff found himself leaving the comfort of his apartment, walking through the dull corridors of the complex and out into the bright light of day. He began to walk through the city in the light of day, no longer feeling oppressed by the wonders of human interaction. He began a routine of walking down to a coffee shop in the morning and getting a coffee while obtaining the news from its most traditional and dying source – the daily paper. The mornings became something of a ritual for him and he found himself spending more and more time at the coffee shop, not just reading the paper, but watching the people pass by, watching their faces. He realized that he was looking for that connection – that look which he found in the video, the intimate eye contact that could bore through your soul – with someone, anyone else.

He noticed the women and girls that surrounded him every day; the cute punk chick that served the coffee and looked at everyone like she might just snap and shoot the place up, or the business woman in a skirt suit with bulging hips that buried herself in her business laptop, hair pulled back tight in a bun, trying her best to look 10 years younger and important. He watched them and imagined them with their clothes off, stripped of the pretense they projected to the world and, like the girl in the video, sacrificed to the gods of electronics and base animal desire. He tried to picture them frightened, receiving it from the big man with hairy forearms; he tried to imagine that very same look in their eyes but it wasn't quite there. There was only one way to capture it and he would then return to his apartment and watch the video again. He tried to contact TommyT54 and ask him to send more like that, but there was no response back.

Geoff felt good, as if the longing in him had finally been quenched. He was losing weight and the sun and the walks were helping his complexion. Regulars at the coffee shop would casually wave hello to him and engage in banal conversation. Geoff enjoyed his departures into the "real" world. But at night he couldn't help but returning to his digital world which was, at the same time, more and less real than his coffee shop world; more real in that it showed humanity in its stark and stinking reality and less in that there was no communication, no interaction that could be called in any real way human. He was feeding his dual personality and feeling satisfied and satiated, his body and spirit in good health.

Then he began seeing her. At first, she seemed only a figment of his imagination, a quick glimpse as she walked by the coffee shop window; out of the corner of his eye on the street; a glimpse of her long brown hair flipping in the breeze as she stepped aboard a bus or into a taxi. Suddenly it seemed as if she were a struggling actress working as an extra in the background of every scene. But he recognized her – at least he was pretty sure he did. He thought it was impossible and yet he couldn't deny that he recognized in her the duality of her essence, she was both worlds blended as one – the digital world of carnal fantasy and the everyday world of a girl on the street that drew the attention of every man she passed. In his mind, Geoff tried to calculate the odds of the girl from the video that saved his soul actually being in the same town, the same street, on a regular basis as himself, and he determined that it was an illusion; an oasis in the desert of the nameless. But still, he would see her and race home with her image fresh in his mind and compare it to the girl in the grainy, night-vision video and he was sure that he recognized her beauty, her tragedy, her violent sensuality. He didn't believe it himself but he was forced to, at least for now, admit it.

He began watching for her – actively looking for her rather than just allowing her to appear out of the corner of his eye. But when he looked, he couldn't find her. And when he wasn't looking she would appear again, seemingly from the spaces between material and digital reality. Then he began to follow her. She would pass on the sidewalk outside the café and Geoff would quickly leave money on the table and rush out the door. Her long, straight hair disappeared around the corner of a brick building and Geoff would jog – for the first time in many years – to the same corner only to find that she was again gone. He would search the alleyways, search the windows of parked buses but still she was not there.

He began to think of her constantly and return to the video again and again, but the video was no longer sufficient. He was sure that it was the girl from the video at this point. He spent hours a day reflecting, meditating, offering silent prayers to this mystery goddess of the digital world, hoping that he would find her and follow her and truly know her the way he wanted to. She became, in his mind, the most beautiful creature he had ever seen; she became the subject of his thoughts and dreams. He began to wonder if she was real. He began to wonder if he was sane. The stark light of day in the city was not a place for ghosts, he thought. But then, in the namelessness of the city there can also be false identities, people who don't exist or are actually four people in one – just like himself; how can you tell among the throngs?

Geoff began to find himself getting closer and closer to her - or was it that she was getting closer to him, he wondered. One day while sitting at the window of the coffee shop scanning the passersby for her, he turned saw that she was sitting only a few tables away, coffee cup in hand, reading the paper, seemingly at peace with the world and never knowing a day of tragedy in her life. He was able to study her more closely in the shop and he was more certain than ever that it was the girl from the video. Her hair was silk-straight brown down to the center of her back and hid her elfish ears that were probably the subject of teasing in middle school but now made her so much more perfect. Her eyes were big and green and seemingly innocent and her face was a symmetry of sharp lines; she seemed to hide some greater power, as if the very core of her were an unfolding glory. He watched her in the shop, gently sipping her drink and he pictured the video – the image of her nakedness, which he had found in an online wilderness – was now before him, clothed, spectacular and hiding. He felt aroused toward her; his heart quickened, the adrenaline rushed to his limbs as if her were about to run for his life or confront an attacker.

Then, one day, she was there, sitting at his table, smiling sheepishly at him. He could now see with striking clarity how beautiful she was and how cutting her lines. He was silent for a moment, staring in disbelief, and then she spoke; "I've seen you looking at me…"

Geoff sputtered for a moment and began to say, "I'm sorry…"

"It's okay," she smiled. "I've noticed you here, too. I thought it was sweet."

This was the first woman who had looked at him in such a flirtatious manner in more than three years and he suddenly suspected some kind of con.

"I was just… interested, I guess," he said. He heard the sound of his own voice trying to participate in human communication and hated it. Even his words sounded like keystrokes in her presence.

"Interested in what?" she said.

He immediately felt the guilt overtake him. "I'm not, like, stalking you…" he forced a laugh. "I just thought I recognized you from somewhere else."

"You look kind of familiar to me too," she said. "Do you have any idea from where?'

"No," he said.

She reached her slender hand across the table. "I'm Diana," she said.

He took her perfectly molded hand in his, "Geoff."

She smiled at him quietly for a moment. "Have you ever done speed dating, Geoff?"

"Uh, no. What is it?"

"It's where a bunch of singles gather together in a café – like this one – and they play a round robin type game, where each man has five minutes to talk with a girl before moving onto the next table and the next girl, and in that five minutes they decide if they want to see each other again. Most of these kind of decisions are made within the first five minutes of meeting someone anyway so it just makes sense to give several people five minutes rather than one single person several hours like a traditional first date. What do you think?"

"What do I think about which part?" he said.

"Do you want to play?"

"Right now?"

"Sure. I have about five minutes before I have to leave, so why don't we use it?"

"Okay…"

"You are interested in meeting me, aren't you?"

Geoff stumbled a bit; "Yes," he said.

She set her digital watch. "Okay… we have five minutes, Geoff. Better make them count. So, Geoff, what do you do for a living?"

"I'm… uh… into investments in online companies."

"You're an investor?"

"Mostly in online media and computer technology," he said, trying his best to sound like professional Wall Street exec rather than a chronic masturbator to online fetish porn.

"Have you been very successful?" she asked.

"Yes," he said. "I don't have to work, really."

"So, you're a playboy, Geoff?"

Again, his nerves seized up at the mention of playboy. "No… I just keep a quiet life."

"And you must live in the uptown area somewhere?"

"Just a block down the street. I don't travel far but I'm interested in trying to get out more."

"Are you lonely, Geoff? Do you have a girlfriend?"

"No, I don't have a girlfriend," he said.

"But are you lonely?"

Geoff thought for a moment looking into her deep green eyes as her sculpted face leaned toward him across the coffee table. "Yes," he said.

She smiled. "Me too," she said. "It's funny that in a city with millions of people around you constantly, I still feel alone like a nameless nobody. You would think that one would feel less lonely in the crowds, but sometimes it's just worse."

"I know," said Geoff.

"I'm glad you know that feeling, Geoff," she said. "Sometimes I feel like I'm the only one."

"You're not," he said. "I've felt it for a long time."

"But then there are moments like these..." she said. She reached across the table and squeezed his soft hands with her own. She glanced at her watch. "You're good," she said. "Four minutes and fifteen seconds and I think you might have hooked me."

Geoff felt suddenly proud and nervous like a teenager that just received his first kiss; as if he had done something wrong and right at the same time and his life would never be the same. A hurdle had been jumped, a boundary crossed.

"Will you see me, tonight?" she asked. "I don't feel like being alone again and I want some company."

"Okay," he said.

"Meet me here at seven," she said. "You're five minutes are up and I have to go. Good work Geoff the Internet investor. I bet you're better at this than you thought." She smiled, squeezed his hand one more time, stood up from the table and walked out the door. Geoff watched her go down the sidewalk and then disappear among the crowd. He was suddenly scared. He had a date with a beautiful girl and once again wondered in all his human paranoia whether or not he was the subject of some con or joke, that a woman of her beauty would be interested in him. But, even if it was a joke, he knew that he would walk willingly, if not robotically, into it just to be near her, just to experience her. He knew, now, that it was the girl from the video. He had seen her eyes up close, the curve of her face. He no longer had a doubt and now he wanted her all the more.

At seven, at the coffee shop, she took him by the hand and they went walking through the city, except, with Diana on his arm, the city seemed more like a vast forest, as if the bricks and concrete disappeared and instead the land existed as if man had never set foot on it. It was only him and her and he could not believe that she was touching his hand, letting him curve his arm around her slender waist, feeling the loose waist line of her jeans and occasionally letting a finger slip down the small of her back. She laughed like a little girl. She liked it and she let him. He was amazed at how beautiful she was and still unsure as to what she wanted with him but he continued to let her lead him through his new-found forest. She was like a dream to him – sweet and smiling – a free spirit with a checkered past. "I have bad history with men," she told him while they sat eating ice cream cones and sitting on the edge of a fountain spraying water into the air. "But I thought that you seemed nice because you were shy. Shy guys are usually nice," she said. Then, in the moment, she pulled off her jeans and danced in the fountain in only her underwear. Passersby watched and laughed or shook their head with disdain. Geoff didn't know how to react, he was both amused and aroused; in love and in awe and there were no words that would express such a complex of emotions so he only smiled and watched her glorious semi-naked body in the fountain and stared in wild wonder.

She walked in her underwear through the city with Geoff until she was dry and then she dressed again. They stopped at a bar and had a couple drinks and they talked; mostly she told him about her life and it was exactly the type of life he had imagined for her when he saw her being taken in the video. It was a typical mid-western American dream childhood. There was even a farm with lots of sisters and pond in the back. She grew up and moved to the city because she wanted the bright lights and the fast nights but all she found was that things were kind of lonely. She had the face – the "girl next door" quality that so much pornographic video was dedicated to – the elusive and mythical. But she was here and she was with him and she was more real than he had ever known another person to be. He saw her and he saw her face on the video in his mind and they were the same.

At the end of the night she kissed him and it felt electric. Then she asked if they would see each other again and Geoff said that he would like to. He rushed home and immediately watched the video and began to imagine himself with her, analyzing every curve of her naked body and mentally stripping her in his mind. They saw each other again seven days later and she said that she wanted to see a movie. She took him to see a film he had never heard of before, a small, independent film about a woman living alone in the city whose landlord spies on her through hidden security cameras. Geoff felt uncomfortable and guilty sitting next to her but she clutched his arm and merely believed that the tension in his muscles was the result of the taut filmmaking.

"Isn't it a strange thought," she said after the theater had released.

"What is?"

"The idea of being watched when you don't realize it?" she said. "That someone could be so interested, so obsessed that you become their whole world? Its like you have to unknowingly give a piece of your life to everyone who looks at you."

"Maybe it was a kind of worship," Geoff offered and hoped that maybe she would realize that he, in his own sick way, worshipped her.

"Maybe," she said. "But when you're worshipped you have to be dead or sacrificed. I don't think that being worshipped is all that it's cracked up to be. You have to give everything to receive."

Then she took his hand and kissed him hard. She pulled him into an alleyway and pushed him against the brick wall of a nameless building and took him as if she were trying to envelop him whole. Her hands found his way to the crotch of his jeans and Geoff stopped for a moment, almost not believing it. She pulled away and looked at him with a smile that seemed almost predatory and sensual at the same time; as if she would rip him in half and orgasm in the blood. He was hard and of single mind and she said, "Take me to your apartment." He kissed her long and deep and she pushed her glorious hips against his and it was as if all the city had disappeared and he was once again in the magical forest with her alone, naked and pushed up against the mossy trees with an animal passion. She took him by his hand and seemingly led him to his own apartment.

They pushed through the door and she stayed on him, pushing into him and not letting up. Considering the money that he had, Geoff's apartment was a modest studio and she led him from the door to his bed and then pushed him down onto it. She crawled sensually onto the bed and straddled him with her clothes on, her long brown hair hanging down wild and shinning. She smiled for a moment as if she had finally come back to her senses. Geoff's hands were on her ass and she seemed to consider this fact for a moment. She turned around as if she were bored, scanning the studio apartment.

"Is everything okay?" Geoff asked.

She turned and looked at him with a naughty smile. "Do you have a digital video recorder?" she asked.

Geoff was dumbstruck for a moment. "Uh, yes. On my computer."

"You wanna set it up?" She smiled again as if trying to conceal her true desire. She wanted it, he thought. She wanted it out in that other world, that digital kingdom of namelessness.

She didn't wait for him to answer. She walked over to his computer and tapped a few keys to wake it up, as if she used it every, day. "Wait..." he started. There were links and images on the screen when it blinked to life. She looked at them and then looked back at him and winked and shook her ass slightly. "I know what you like," she said.

She expertly worked her way around his computer and positioned the camera so that it had a full view of the bed on which he lay. He could see their images in the screen, digitized and surreal. She stood and turned to look at him. She walked toward Geoff slowly, removing her shirt and revealing her tanned and taut body. She slid her jeans to the floor and let her bra and panties drop. She stood before him naked, glorious, tight and beautiful; every inch of her seemed perfect, her long hair hiding her elfish ears and her eyes narrowing with a sudden look of despair on her face.

"Do you want me?" she said.

"More than anything," he said.

"Do you think about me at night?"

"Yes. Constantly."

"I'll give you exactly what you want," she said and she moved slowly, cat-like toward him. She took off his clothes piece by piece until he was naked and laying beneath her. Diana straddled him once again and slid his cock into her. She winced at first and then released a sigh of relief and began to ride him as if she were completely alone, barely looking at Geoff. She kept her eyes closed. She moved her hands over her own body, squeezing her breasts and moving rhythmically as if she were doing a private dance, wild and alone. She seemed a separate being, gliding back and forth on him until he felt that he could no longer hold back. But she kept moving, twisting her body in a dance he had never seen; it was something truly intimate, truly holy, and private; it seemed to be between her and some unseen force and Geoff only the tool, a means to an end.

She moved faster and faster, her eyes closed, biting her own lip in ecstasy until Geoff could no longer control his urge to explode. And, just at the moment of his climax, she leaned over his face, her hair enveloping them both in a tunnel of thick, brown radiance and she opened her eyes, big, wide, green and endless and suddenly he saw it there, deep in her irises; it was the same haunting glare that had pierced his computer screen and driven right to his being. She stared at him with those same eyes, calling forth all the emotion that had ever been known into a perfect, penetrating stare.

He came inside her, convulsing and groaning in release and, at that very moment, he lost himself in her green gaze. It suddenly seemed like he could not only feel her, but feel everything, as if his body were spreading out like a pool of water, reaching into the fibers of the world. Suddenly he could feel his computer. He could feel himself digitized, recorded, interconnected to the world. He looked further into her eyes and he could see and feel the circuit boards, the wires, the satellite signals, the ones and zeros and tiny electrical impulses sparking between ions and eons and continents and time and space and suddenly he was everywhere, in everything, a sentient being digitized into the ethereal realm of the Nameless.

Then he was in a cold, metal room with fluorescent lights swinging overhead that flickered in and out from total darkness to pale, lifeless light. He felt changed physically. He felt his body and it was not his own. On the far wall of the room was a two-way mirror and he could see himself in it – or rather – he could see Diana in it. Geoff ran his hands over his body feeling a thin, smooth, foreign skin. He touched breasts that were suddenly a part of him and, terrified, he realized that he was no longer in his own skin. He could see in the mirror an image of her – him – naked and trembling with cold horror in the corner of the room. He stood for a moment and walked slowly toward the speculum, not believing what was before his eyes; alienated from his own body, he felt the horror of a place and person so foreign to him and feeling. Suddenly his entire life was only a dream from which he was now waking, dawning with the deep terror of his new reality.

A door opened and two men walked in. One held a video camera and the other he recognized – the big hairy man from Diana's video. They walked toward him/her slowly with a swagger of perverse, redneck malice. The camera was up and filming. Then the lights were out and it was total darkness and all he could feel was his new body and the wall against which he cowered and struggled and cried knowing what was coming.

The big, hairy man was on top of him now and thrusting himself inside and there was pain and burning and fear and loathing. And then he felt it again and again and again –repeating in an endless cycle of perverse violation - and with every thrust it felt like a knife plunged into his core, killing him. Every view from every anonymous voyeur, every download, every click of a computer mouse anywhere in the vast world of seven billion people and his terror was repeated and the big, hairy man would thrust into him again and again. He looked for help but knew there was none. He strained against the pain but it was impossible. He fought and screamed and looked into the lens of the camera with his new big, beautiful green eyes hoping to see someone, anyone, who could possibly save him. But all he could see was Diana and all he could feel was the terror.

Somewhere in Germany a young man sat watching a video - grainy, digital night vision - a beautiful nude girl in the corner of the room, a big, hairy man walking toward her as she cried. He linked it to a new website and an email list that stretched around the world. A mouse was clicked, a link exchanged and the dark grainy video was sent to a million twisted, nameless deviants and Geoff felt every electronic impulse and every painful thrust of the hairy man's big digital cock. He stayed in Diana's eyes, in Hell, for an eternity, feeling the deep brutality of violence and hate rammed into his core. He knew her now. He knew her intimate secret and now he was lost. Relegated to the Nameless – merely a body to be used, abused, stabbed, and tossed into the forgotten heap of lost souls.

Coils of Love

Stanley B. Webb

Zeke roamed the benighted quay, tempting himself with suicide.

The river slithered along with him, glistening in starlight, and smelling of open sewers.

A crocodile bellowed on the opposite bank, where the Westerners ruled. The town's citadel confronted the borderland. From atop the stone wall rose the voices of the garrison men, who played Ruff and Honours around their watch fires.

His brother Esau boomed, "I've got the king of trump, and you can kiss my donkey!"

Esau, who bedded many women while loving none, would not comprehend Zeke's broken heart.

Life goes on, for those with still reason to live. Laugh, cruel Jardia, for tonight I wed Death instead of thee!

Zeke disrobed, neatly folded his attire, then stepped down the boat ramp into the turgid current. The flagstones, treacherous with algae, betrayed his footing. Zeke staggered off the ramp's low end, into deep, warm ooze. Fecal gas bubbled up. He wrinkled his nose, and waded out. The river climbed to his neck, then lifted him. Zeke struck out toward mid-stream, swimming poorly.

Commotion arose on the river's west bank, lanterns flickering through the trees, and hunting dogs braying. Harsh, Western accents cried out, furious with excitement. The Eastern garrison men interrupted their cards to catcall at their foemen. The Westerners ignored the challenge, and put canoes into the river.

Zeke felt annoyed at this distraction from his pathos.

He stopped at mid river, muscles a-tremble with fatigue. His feet plumbed the depths for support, but found none. Zeke's heart beat rapidly, frightened of his intentions.

Quickly shall it end, with a crushing bite, then sweet oblivion.

A crocodile as long as a skiff appeared from the night.

Your teeth shall be kinder than Jardia's tongue.

His body still quaked, desperate to flee, but he constrained himself to await death.

Suddenly, a larger crocodile appeared, and attacked the first. Teeth and claws flashed, and their tails beat the river to brown foam.

Zeke's fear began to erode his romantic despair, but he held himself firm.

The smaller crocodile retreated. The victorious monster turned upon Zeke, its protuberant eyes streaming with false tears as it yawned him welcome.

A powerful blow shoved him aside, and a giant snake rushed past, its body as thick as a hogshead. The serpent attacked the crocodile, wrapped it in powerful coils, and dragged it under.

The northern frontier bred tales of such horrors. Death by crocodile seemed hideous enough, but a serpent fed differently, ingesting its victim inch by living inch. Zeke's endurance broke. He struck out toward the Westerner's canoes.

"Help!" The river engulfed him

Zeke struggled upward, desperate to escape the snake. He raised his arms.

"Help!"

A man's glottal voice responded, "There she is, Kaleb!"

Kaleb, in the lead canoe, aimed his shotgun and fired.

The pellets splashed around Zeke. He sank, then struggled back to the surface, and turned to the east. His legs cramped, and he sank for the third time.

He sensed the monster's pressure in the water. The serpent's coil embraced him. He fought, but it lifted him to the surface, where a fair voice cried in his ear.

"Help me, they seek my life!"

Not a serpent's coil, but a woman's arms embraced him, and by her touch, she swam as naked as himself.

Suddenly, one of the citadel's mortars thumped, and the bursting shell overturned Kaleb. Esau's men hooted with glee. More shells followed. Spray and smoke obscured the Westerners.

The woman struck out to the east, towing Zeke with her. He kept a terrified watch for the serpent, but saw it not, and hoped that the explosions had killed it. The woman helped him up the ramp, and they collapsed in each other's arms.

Kaleb rose behind them, his western garb drenched, and his expression rabid. He stalked up onto the quay, and aimed his gun.

"To hell, demon!"

The sodden cartridge failed. Kaleb dropped the gun, drew a kris dagger, and charged.

Zeke thrust his leg between Kaleb's feet. The Westerner fell, losing his knife. Kaleb snarled, and clawed for the woman's throat. Zeke grappled with him.

They rolled over the hard flags. Kaleb thrust an expert blow, and Zeke's kidney exploded with pain. The Westerner crawled over him, intent upon the woman.

Esau and his squad arrived, their carbines ready. Esau held a lantern high.

"Surrender or die, Westerner!"

For a moment, it seemed that Kaleb would continue his assault toward the woman. Then, he swore, and raised his hands.

"Take him in, boys!" The squad hesitated in distraction. Esau followed their line of sight. "Oh!"

Zeke, for the first time, had a look at the woman who had saved him, and this vision made him forget his pain. She lay belly-flat on the quay, her luminous eyes darting from man to man. Her color marked her as an aborigine, but she had not the coarse features of the local natives, indeed, despite her excessive gauntness, she looked more beautiful than any woman of the town. Zeke felt his broken heart mend.

The woman's hunted eyes met his. As if reading Zeke's mood, her expression softened. She smiled.

Esau crossed the flags, gave Kaleb a passing kick, and hoisted Zeke upright. Esau's gaze remained on the woman. "Who are you?"

Kaleb said, "She's infernal!"

Feeling protective, Zeke stepped before her.

Esau indicated the Westerner with another kick. "Take him in, I said!"

The men shackled Kaleb, then dragged him off, casting lust-filled glances back at the naked woman. Kaleb also looked back, but his desire looked murderous.

When they were gone, Esau resumed. "You're not Eastern or Western, who are you?"

She replied with a sibilant accent. "Tanith," and cast an entreating eye to Zeke.

He said, "Tanith's my friend."

Esau leered. "Well done! Didn't I promise that you'd forget Jardia?"

Zeke remembered the serpent. "Did you see anything monstrous in the river?"

"Yeah: my brother's bare donkey."

"No giant snake?"

"You'll not impress the lady with such an idle boast! I, on the other hand…" With a final leer, Esau returned to his duties.

Tanith offered her hand. Rings glittered on each finger. "Would you help me up?"

She wrung out her long, dark hair, then stroked the lingering water from her body. Zeke watched, unaware of his erection until Tanith smiled and said,

"I'm flattered."

Zeke blushed, and wrestled himself into his trousers. "You can have my tunic."

"I'm comfortable naked. May I ask why you swam so late?"

"I wanted to die, or thought that I did."

"Because of this Jardia?" Tanith's eyes narrowed. "Is she your wife?"

"I asked her to be."

"And, her reply?"

"She took my ring, but then I discovered her at play with the ruffians and soldiers on Rowdy Street. I confronted her, and she laughed at me, said that she had pawned my 'Worthless bauble'." Zeke wiped his eyes. "Look at my tears! She's right, I'm not a man, just a boy."

Tanith held his hand. "Jardia's a fool. Tis a noble man indeed who will express his tears, and nobler still one who would sacrifice himself to love. However, you must save yourself for a woman who's worthy of you. I've long yearned for such a man."

He met her direct gaze, and his pulse beat harder. "This is sudden."

"It is my way."

Tanith seized him, her mouth engulfing his, her tongue intruding between his lips. She pressed him against the citadel's wall. Zeke's thoughts whirled into anxious lust. His hands wavered, uncertain what to do. Tanith displayed no uncertainty. She yanked his trousers back down, and grasped his stiff manhood. That organ became a spike of sensation. With a strangled cry, Zeke thrust at her, and his manhood spurted its contents across her belly.

From down the quay, there arose catcalls, where a crew of stevedores paused unloading a river ship.

His manhood shriveled. Zeke hung his head, his cheeks burning with sudden shame.

Tanith looked down at what he had done, then scooped his ejaculate into her hand. Semen-threads depended between her fingers. "So much, and so ready. Are you a virgin?"

He could not meet her eyes. "Yes, I'm sorry."

"I'm pleased. You shall be mine, and never another's."

She transferred his seed into her mouth, and swallowed.

\#

Esau descended the stone ramp to the citadel's detention level. His knee-high leather boots splashed through the dungeon's leech-infested sump. Kaleb hung naked from wrist manacles, his feet in the water. Leeches had already fastened on his calves, and more crawled higher.

Esau asked, "What's your mission?"

Kaleb remained stoic.

"You're plainly a military man, and experienced to judge from your scars. You understand your situation. Tell me as I ask, and avoid the worst of this." Esau gestured around the dungeon.

Still, Kaleb refused to answer. A leech attached itself to his throat.

"So then, I must leave you to the affections of your new admirers." Esau turned to go.

"Your brother's in peril."

He tried to deflect the Westerner's ruse. "I have no brother."

"The boy with Tanith is half your twin."

Dread jolted Esau's spine, so much that he barely maintained his professional composure. "You know her?"

Said Kaleb, "Last year, I led a penetration to the north, through the river marshes, attempting to circumvent Eastern territory. My brother Henry, a language specialist, accompanied us to deal with the aborigines.

"We discovered Tanith a captive in an aborigine village, imprisoned from a country much farther north. They had her caged in an animal pit. Henry found the natives on tenterhooks, wanting to kill the woman, but fearing her father's revenge.

"Tanith's appearance, more civilized than aboriginal, gained my sympathy, and I decided to rescue her." Kaleb snickered. "The natives gladly foisted her upon us. "We continued north. I planned on returning the woman to her village, and seeking alliance with her people."

"Tanith's refusal to dress caused immediate disruption. I gave her into Henry's charge. He kept her out of sight, and taught her our tongue, but at the same time, she vigorously seduced herself to him. Without a constant chaperone, she'd have stolen my brother's chastity on that first night. I lacked the manpower to keep them decent, so I did what I had to. The company's chaplain married them. This was only meant as an expediency, and the union would have been annulled upon our return, but…" Kaleb's face drained ashen.

Esau waited.

"They both disappeared on their wedding night," said Kaleb. "My trackers found signs that a gigantic serpent had entered their tent."

Esau controlled his reaction: Zeke had talked of a serpent in the river.

"Of course," said Kaleb. "I had never believed in such things, but there was the monster's spoor. Evidence suggested that the monster had swallowed both newlyweds. We followed its trail back to the south, determined to kill it, and recover the remains."

Kaleb spent a moment in grim silence, then continued his tale.

"The aborigines told me what had really occurred. The woman Tanith is a Yig-child, spawn of an ancient God-creature: The Father of Serpents. She had transformed herself into her father's image, and swallowed my brother.

"We lost her trail in the fens. I've tracked her ever since. Now, I've finally failed my brother's vengeance. Beware lest yours succumbs to Tanith's fascination."

Esau said, "You're daft or drunk," but his voice cracked.

Kaleb looked him in the eye. "You are a military man, plainly skilled with interrogation. You perceive when a prisoner lies."

Esau departed, determined to regain control. The Westerner's story could not be true, and yet Esau believed it. He returned to the river, hoping to find Zeke and Tanith still present.

He found naught but a broken-backed crocodile, which drifted beside the quay.

#

Zeke led Tanith home to his tenement cell.

She looked about at the spare furnishings, then pointed. "That is your bed?"

She crossed the cell, a shadow among shadows, and lay herself down.

"Join me, Zeke, I promise that I will control my enthusiasm this time."

He disrobed, and lay beside her. His manhood stood as ready as before, but still he dithered, inexperienced.

"Do this." She took his hands, and placed them upon her breasts. Tanith's nipples stiffened. "And this." She lifted a teat, put her other hand to the back of his head, and pulled him to her. Tanith's nipple thrust in between his lips. "Suckle me."

She moaned and writhed as he did so. A heady, estrus scent rose from her, clinging to his skin, and entering his pores. Zeke's heartbeat pulsed in his ears. She moved one of his hands downward across her belly, over her thick groin hair, and to her open womanhood. Zeke's fingers bumped across a stiff protuberance - Tanith gasped – then sank into her. Zeke massaged her sex, its lubricant as hot and thick as blood, and pushed a finger into her hole. Her passage gripped him.

Tanith rolled, sliding her trembling knee over his legs, then rose, and crouched astraddle him. Her bosoms lay on his neck, and her hair sway around his face. Her womanhood dripped on his manhood.

Zeke took her by the waist, and lifted his hips. His organ bumped into her rear cleavage. Tanith moved her crotch against him, and they sought together until Zeke's organ nudged her entrance.

She whispered, "It has been so long."

Tanith lowered herself. Her hole opened, engulfing Zeke to his hilt. Zeke seized her buttocks, and thrust in and out, his instincts compensating for his inexperience. Tanith responded in kind, riding hard against him, her hole slurping his organ, and her breasts pummeling his face. Zeke felt united with her beyond their physical joining, as if they had become two creatures with a single will. His sensations exploded. He pulled her to him, seeking her depths, and with a shout he released inside her.

She answered his passion, crying out in a strange tongue. Her knees clamped around his hips, and her inner passage rhythmically gripped his manhood, as if to milk the last drop of semen from him. Then, they went limp in each other's sweaty embrace. Zeke's organ twitched inside her, and Tanith shuddered. He twitched again as his organ softened, and slid out of her hole. Zeke drifted toward sleep, caressing Tanith, who remained atop him.

He murmured, "I love you."

She murmured back, "Thank you, you have given me what I've so long sought."

Her breathing settled into a somnolent rhythm. Zeke remained half aware, gazing up at this stranger who had become his wife in all but the ceremony. He had never felt so happy.

Moonlight crept in through his cell's lone window, and glowed on Tanith's face. Her lips curved with satiation, and her eyes, wide and blank, stared down into his.

Zeke cried out in alarm.

Tanith startled awake. Her blank gaze opened, revealing her true, warm eyes. "What's wrong?"

Zeke laughed in relief. "I was frightened. Your eyelids are tattooed!"

She paused before replying. "It's a family custom."

Her tattoos reminded him of a serpent's lidless stare. "I saw a giant snake in the river."

Tanith closed her eyes. "That was me."

"Oh. An illusion, then, produced by starlight shadows: but, the crocodile—"

"No, I am the snake. Darling, I will explain my nature, and what I must now ask of you."

Before she could explain, however, someone knocked at the door.

\#

Their watch shift ended, and Esau took his men to a Rowdy Street tavern. The men expressed high spirits, but Esau felt troubled. The tavern's queans gathered, luring his men to the upstairs rooms. The last girl backed up to Esau, and hoisted her valentine skirt. She wore nothing beneath.

"Not tonight," he said.

The quean wiggled her plump behind. "Is she too much for you?"

"Not by half, but I'm preoccupied."

He sent her off with a friendly swat.

Esau dwelt on his brother's new woman, if woman she truly was. Esau had searched his memory, but never recalled seeing Tanith around the town. He also had searched the citadel's intelligence archives, and found Kaleb listed among the West's most honored veterans. Esau felt concerned, for such a man would not go hunting legendary monsters. Either Kaleb had fallen mad, or…

Esau felt himself in a quandary. His martial instincts demanded that he arrest and interrogate Tanith, but doing so would estrange his brother.

A girl sidled up to him. "Here's a handsome sergeant."

"Not tonight, I said."

Jardia giggled.

Esau looked up sharply. "You're dressed like a quean!"

"And, acting like one." She lifted her skirt. Jardia wore nothing beneath except a garter knife.

Esau's fist clenched beneath the table, but he forced it to open. He would never strike a woman, not even Jardia. "You betrayed my brother, stupid slut."

She dropped her skirt, and scowled. "I gave him no vow, and did you see the pauper's ring he offered me? Even the pawnbroker laughed!"

Then, Esau had an idea. "That's irrelevant now, for Zeke's found a prettier woman."

Jardia scowled. "There are none prettier!"

Esau shrugged.

Jardia strutted to the door, cast him a doubting glance, then departed.

Esau beckoned his quean, satisfied that Jardia was off to interrogate Tanith for him.

***

Zeke stepped into his trousers, and opened the door.

"Have you missed me?" asked Jardia.

"What do you want?"

"A polite 'Hello', at least." She tried to peer around him. "I've been worried about you. May I come in?"

"I have a guest."

"At this hour?" She pushed her way in, then stopped short.

Tanith lay naked on Zeke's bed. "You must be Jardia."

Jardia cried, "Get out, you brazen tramp!"

"You get out, for Zeke is mine now."

Jardia turned to Zeke. "You betray me so, after I retrieved this?" She hurled the ring at him. "The pawnbroker laughed at me!"

She charged Tanith, clawing to blind. Tanith caught Jardia's wrist, then countered with a powerful slap. Jardia reeled across the cell, then wiped her lips. She screamed at the sight of blood, drew her garter knife, and sprang for Tanith.

Tanith blocked. The blade pierced her arm. Her cry of pain changed into a furious hiss. She transformed into a green and pink serpent, forty feet long. The bed collapsed under her increased bulk. Tanith reared to strike.

Jardia screamed again, scrambled backward through the door, and fled down the hall.

Zeke fled behind her.

***

Shortly afterward, he followed Esau back to the tenement. Esau thrust the door open with his carbine's barrel, then reconnoitered the entryway before proceeding.

Zeke's door stood closed.

"I left that open."

Esau kicked the door in, and backed to the opposite wall. Zeke's ruined bed lay empty. "Where's the snake?"

Tanith replied, "I'm here."

She sat on Zeke's chair. A bandage wrapped her arm.

Esau sidled into the room, keeping his aim at Tanith. His trigger finger tensed, but then he hesitated. "Are you sure it really happened, Zeke?"

"Yes."

Again, Esau aimed; and again he paused.

"I can't shoot a woman! Become a snake."

She placed her hand on her belly. "Would you murder your brother's child?"

The men exchanged a glance.

Zeke said, "But, we've only just…"

She replied, "It is my way."

Zeke's fear melted away. He stepped forward, hand extended.

Esau asked, "What of Kaleb's brother, your husband?"

Zeke froze, eyeing Tanith's rings, and suddenly felt appalled.

She lowered her gazes. "He's my husband no more."

Esau said, "Because you ate him."

She flashed anger at Esau. "Should I have starved to death? I am a Daughter of Yig, a demigoddess, constrained by our Father to take only willing prey. At home, covens of men and women vie for the honor of feeding me. But here in the south I starved, until my husband gave himself." Tanith wept.

A lump formed in Zeke's his throat, but after all that he had seen and heard, he could not offer Tanith his comfort. He backed away.

Esau asked, "Why are you here?"

"To get with child," Tanith replied. "My lineage balances on the cusp between squamous and human. My mother, a serpent who becomes a woman, mated properly with our Father Yig. I, a woman who becomes a serpent, required a man."

"You have what you came for." Esau gestured with his carbine toward the door. "Go home."

"We will starve on the journey."

Zeke felt the intensity of her gaze, but his heart had turned cold and shivery. He would not look at her.

She implored him, "Have you no pity for your child?"

"That's enough!" Esau aimed his weapon at her. "Go now, or I will shoot you, woman or not!"

Zeke listened as her bare steps faded down the passage. Then, he collapsed into his chair, with his face in his hands.

"Why me?" Zeke wept. "First Jardia, now this! Am I cursed?"

Esau patted his shoulder. "You'll come around."

"I'm hopeless, I lack even the courage to die!"

Esau remained silent for a while.

"I know what you need," he finally said, and hoisted Zeke by the arm. "Come along."

Esau propelled him from the tenement, then across town to a Rowdy Street tavern. Esau dropped him onto a bar stool, and beckoned the serving maid. She accepted Esau's coin with a saucy wink.

"Drink up, Brother!"

Distraught as he felt, Zeke paid little attention to his surroundings, but the whiskey offered oblivion. He seized the cup, and drained it. The spirits burned a path down his gullet, then spread warmth to his limbs.

Esau poured again, and beckoned a quean who wore a valentine skirt. "Show my brother what you showed me."

She turned, then lifted her skirt.

Zeke stared at her naked rump, feeling no interest.

Esau dropped two coins into the quean's pocket. "Give him your best."

She took Zeke by the hand, and led him up the tavern's narrow stairs, to a corridor of narrow doors. In the cubicle behind one of those doors, she deftly lowered his trousers, sat him on a hard bed, and knelt at his feet.

The quean took his soft manhood in hand. "Poor thing, we'll have him happy in no time."

She bent into his lap, and sucked his organ into her mouth. The quean worked at him with lips and tongue, making noises as if his manhood tasted of ambrosia.

He experienced a moment of sexual pleasure, then grieving shame descended. He had fallen in love with Tanith, upon first sight, upon first touch, and neither her nature nor her needs had altered his heart. He had betrayed her by fleeing his cell, and by allowing Esau to drive her off, and he betrayed her still in this cubicle, with his unresponsive penis in a stranger's mouth.

Zeke sobbed with self-loathing.

The quean spat him out. "What's wrong with you?"

Zeke stood, and restored his trousers. "I shouldn't be here."

He walked out the door, turned toward the rear exit, away from his smug brother, and away from life.

The quean followed him into the hall. "Hey!"

Zeke paused.

She tossed Esau's coins after him. "I don't take money for doing nothing, I'm an honest businesswoman."

The back stair delivered him into an alleyway, from where he wandered toward the river. His fingers idled with the cheap gold ring in his pocket.

What use is life, if love hath fled?

The commercial wharf had become silent, the stevedores finished with their chores. A crew worked on the loaded ship's deck, preparing for departure. Then, fog hid the ship, isolating Zeke in a personal realm.

He looked down into the river. A crocodile floated below, its spine broken.

She saved my life, and I shall let her die. I should not be here.

Zeke leaned over the edge.

Tanith stepped from the mist, and took his hand. "I knew that you would follow." She smiled.

Tanith's belly had swelled to a small, round bump, and the rest of her body turned gaunt.

"What's become of you?" Zeke asked.

She placed his hand upon her bump. "Our child demands much nourishment, but now you are here. I knew that you loved me as I love you, and would not let us die."

Zeke choked up. "I could not live while you perished. I give myself to your need."

"I accept your gift."

A trembling fit seized him.

She folded him into her arms. "Please don't be frightened."

"Will it be horrible for me?"

"No, it is the ultimate act of love!"

Suddenly, Esau's voice cried out from the turgid distance. "Zeke, where have you gone?"

"We must flee!" Zeke clutched the quean's coin in his palm, and led Tanith onto the waiting ship.

****

The quean directed Esau down the back stairs.

He cried from the alleyway, "Zeke, where have you gone?"

No answer returned.

He considered checking at Zeke's room, but then his instinct sent him toward the river, where the misadventure had begun.

The wharf master approached. "Are you looking for someone?"

"My brother."

"Was he in company with a naked foreign girl?"

Esau's throat went dry. "I hope not."

The wharf master nodded vigorously. "They're on the Intrigue."

The riverboat's foghorn sounded from upstream.

Esau grabbed the man. "I need a skiff!"

The river master shrugged him off. "Sorry, but we're closed until dawn."

Esau could have used his martial authority to commandeer a vessel, but in truth he feared tackling a being such as Tanith alone. He needed an ally, and he knew of only one possibility.

Esau returned to the citadel, and masked his anxiety while plying the detention master with spirit. The jailor's capacity finally eroded his patience.

Esau pointed downward. "Your boot's come unbuckled."

The drunken jailer bent to investigate. Esau knocked him out, then took his keying, and descended to the flooded dungeon. Kaleb hung stupefied. Esau released his chains. Kaleb dropped into the stagnant water, then arose sputtering.

He eyed Esau for a moment, then fell to ripping the leeches from his skin. "Has she ingested you brother?"

"They've eloped

Kaleb chuckled.

"This isn't funny!"

"I laugh not in mirth, for she led my brother on the same damned course."

They went upstairs. Esau returned Kaleb's garments from the intelligence stores.

Kaleb said, "I want my shotgun."

"No."

"Don't be a fool, you have already forsaken your duties, and even now Tanith might be charming your brother down her throat."

Esau allowed that Kaleb was right, and fetched the Western shotgun. He took a carbine for himself, and plenty of ammunition. They hurried along the river, arriving at the wharf master's darkened hut. Esau banged upon the door until the man appeared.

"I said we open at dawn!"

Esau displayed his carbine.

***

The Intrigue made her living on frontier cargo, but rough passenger accommodations were available. A crewman led Zeke and Tanith deep into the hold, where a dank straw pallet lay on the deck boards. Rats crept around in the ticking, but froze when Tanith arrived. A moment later, the rats fled, squealing.

The crewman sniggered. "It's a cozy nook."

She said, "Please see that we're not disturbed."

When their guide had departed, she turned to Zeke, and smiled. "Now, my love, become mine forever!" A thread of saliva escaped her lips.

"After—" Zeke swallowed hard. "Afterward, will you be safe?"

"Fear not, I will slip unobserved into the river, and seek a place where… we can rest together."

A place to digest me.

Zeke began to shudder.

She took him into her arms, her mouth open.

Zeke held her off. "First, will you marry me?"

"Of course!"

They climbed to the fog-bound deck.

The grizzled captain eyed Tanith's rings, then asked, "Are you both eligible for matrimony?"

"I am a bachelor."

"And, I'm a widow."

"My condolences, Miss. So, then, do you both take each other, flesh of flesh and blood of blood, forsaking all others until the Reaper himself parts you?"

Tanith gazed into Zeke's eyes. "I do."

He choked, then replied, "I do."

"And," the captain recited, "Are there any here to give reason why this union should not occur?"

From astern of the ship there came a yell: "Heave to, Intrigue!"

The mist parted to reveal a skiff in pursuit, with two men rowing furiously. One was Esau.

Fatalistic urgency surged through Zeke. "If you would finish, Captain?"

"Right. Have you the ring?"

Zeke slipped his ring onto her finger, where it sat atop her others.

"By the power vested in me through the River Guild, I pronounce you Man and Wife."

The captain hurried aft.

They watched the approaching skiff.

"Kaleb is with him," said Tanith.

"We'll steal a lifeboat."

Zeke ushered his bride forward, and they absconded on the river. The Intrigue's lanterns dematerialized in the fog. The captain's voice became indistinct, then faded to silence.

Several minutes later, Esau's desperate cry echoed between the shores:

"Zeke!"

***

The Intrigue's captain released the skiff's line. Esau and Kaleb grabbed their oars.

"There's an outpost nearby."

"And, if they're not there?"

Esau cursed.

***

Zeke rowed until his arms felt as heavy as logs. The mist blew away. The moon's light revealed a little village, where a sentinel guarded the small, log citadel. Zeke rowed to shore.

"I think he's asleep, wait here for a moment."

Zeke mounted the riverbank. The sentinel remained still. Zeke motioned Tanith to follow. They slipped into the village's barn, and climbed to the hayloft. Tanith lay down, breathing heavily in the darkness. Zeke's heart struggled within his ribs. He pulled off his tunic, but his fingers shook so that he was unable to manage the buttons of his trousers. Tanith assisted him. He joined her in their marriage bed. She stroked his naked body. Zeke reciprocated, but his fingers trembled violently. She took his hand, and kissed it, drooling on him.

"You are so frightened."

"No, I'm-I'm—" His protest stuttered to a halt.

"I will release you," she said. "If you wish. I take no one against their will."

"I made you my promise," he replied. "You need me."

"I love you, father of my child."

She embraced him. Zeke trembled, awaiting her transformation, but she kissed his mouth instead. Her tongue pressed between his lips, and roved within. Despite his fear, his manhood rose. Indeed, his passion grew firmer than ever before. He cupped her breast. Tanith pressed his hand, then returned it to his side.

"Lie still, Darling," Her mouth dripped as she spoke. "And allow me to savor you."

She kissed his face all over, leaving him wet, then kissed his throat, his shoulder, and traveled down his arm. Jolts rang up his nerves. Tanith nibbled his first finger, then sucked it in, moaning. She took the second digit, then the third, and then the fourth.

He said, "You feel good inside."

Then, she spat him out. Lonely chills traveled up his arm. He reached again for her mouth, but she transferred her kisses to his belly. Zeke quivered with anticipation, his organ twitching at its roots. He tangled his fingers in her hair, urging her toward it.

Tanith paused her ministrations. "Relax your hands."

"But, I want—"

"Shhh."

Zeke obeyed.

She slithered across to his opposite hand, her teats stiff against his skin. She sucked in his first four fingers, then took his thumb as well. Her jaws stretched, and with a groaning shiver, Tanith engulfed his hand. Her lips encircled his wrist, while her throat pulled at his fingers.

Tanith slowly disgorged him. "Once more, my love, I offer yourself back to you."

All of his fear had transformed into passion. "I'm yours, swallow me!"

In a moment, her embrace became strong coils. Zeke's body revolted instinctively, fighting against the predator's grasp. Tanith constricted gently, her serpent fleshes warm and smooth. His physical terror peaked, then surrendered, and he lay quiescent in her hold. She turned, rolling him belly-down, and touched her snout against his crown. Her tongue flickered, kissing his face.

Zeke took a deep breath.

She engulfed his head. His crown pressed her esophageal ringing, which gaped to admit him to her throat. Her passage filled with lubricant, flooding his ears with her deep heartbeat. Her jaws nudged his shoulders, and he folded himself into her. Tanith's throat stretched wider, encasing him snugly. Her slanted teeth walked side to side down his back, tearing his skin like passionate fingernails. Zeke shuddered at the sensations.

Her mouth stretched over his hips. His manhood nudged its way into her distended jaws, then his legs followed rapidly. Her mouth closed. His toes entered her esophagus, which pinched shut afterward.

Tanith's throat expanded before him, and tightened behind, pushing him deeper. Her vertebrae stroked his back. Her ribs clutched him. His pulse throbbed in tune with hers. Zeke's lungs strained for air, but he held on until her peristalsis thrust him into her stomach's fluid heat.

His mouth opened, blindly seeking air, and sucked in her fluids. He experienced his final orgasm as he drowned inside her.

***

At dawn, Esau and Kaleb found their way into the outpost's barn.

Esau muttered, "Zeke's a fool, but he's not such a fool."

Kaleb remained grim.

They climbed to the loft. As Esau's vision adjusted to the dusty gloom, he discerned a gigantic, striped serpent, its middle swollen full. He saw no one else, and his mind reeled.

"Where's my brother?"

Kaleb indicated the serpent's bulge. "There."

With a strangled cry, Esau raised his carbine.

Tanith reared up, and dodged either way, but she found no escape.

Kaleb chuckled, "You're mine at last, you bitch!" and aimed his shotgun.

Below Tanith's sated belly, Esau noted another, smaller bulge. With a strange chill, he realized that small bulge was her womb. A tumult of emotion struck him.

Kaleb said, "This is for Harry!"

Esau swiveled, and shot him. Then he lowered the carbine, and collapsed against a beam.

Tanith froze, gazing between Esau and the dead man, then she slithered over, and looked into his eyes.

Esau said, "My brother gave you his child, and loved you enough to give his life. I won't mock his sacrifice. Now, go back where you belong!"

She hurried away down the ladder. Esau followed, in case the local guard had awakened to his duty, but the man still slept. Tanith submerged into the river.

Esau viciously kicked the sentinel.

The man leaped to his feet. "I'll blacken your eye, you donkey-hole!"

"Will you, private?"

The sentinel blinked, then went to attention. "Apologies, sergeant!"

"Fetch your commander, I just shot an escaped prisoner."

The sentinel ran off.

Esau sat down to cry.

The Night They Closed the Last Dirty Bookstore

Tim J. Finn

Owen Barnaby stared through the barred windows of Lamplight Adult Books. He recalled the days when dark and semi-deserted Washington Street teemed with neon, perverts, hookers, and easy money. The area designated as Boston's adult entertainment district looked so respectable he wanted to puke. Barnaby winced when a trio of female voices interrupted his reverie with a shrill imitation of Danny DeVito's mother in Throw Momma from the Train.

"Owen!"

Barnaby grimaced and he turned to the group of women gathered around the lounging security guard at the store's front counter.

"Those voices killed my rap booth business. And your saggy ass bodies didn't help either."

Libby and Carol flipped him a quadruple bird. Stella stuck out her grape juice coated tongue.

"We've been closing early all month, boss," the guard said. "Nobody's coming to give us Auld Lang Syne."

A pair of men browsed through the store's magazine racks. The less bald one looked up from his perusal of Lesbian Love Nest.

"Screw you, Paul, we showed, we're loyal. Right, Ernie?"

The second man ignored him in favor of a continued scrutiny of Fisting Fashionistas. His buddy whacked him on the shoulder.

"Get your head out of those chicks' asses and support me here. Paul just insulted our dedicated patronage."

"Fuck you, Wayne. Fuck you, Paul. Fuck everybody."

"No swearing," Barnaby said. "It's doesn't fit the neighborhood's new fucking image. Okay, that's it. Good bye, Beantown."

Owen locked the Lamplight's door and lowered the shades over it and the adjacent windows. Libby and Carol hummed an atonal rendition of taps. Stella grabbed a tissue and wiped imaginary tears from her eyes. Wayne shifted his attention back to the display racks. He stared at a boxed blow up sex doll at the end of the row.

"Still got it."

"I named it," Barnaby said. "Dorian Dingus, the amazing interchangeable fuck toy. My only special order for a customer. Remember him, Paul?"

"I tossed him out often enough," the guard said. "Dr. Dirty. He did everyone, including himself, a favor when he ran into traffic the last time I chased him out. He was pawing that box and mumbling horseshit. He did fly pretty high before he splattered all over the street."

"Dr. Dirty?" Libby said.

"Dr. Monroe Davidson," Barnaby replied. "Before your time. An egghead professor who pretended coming here was a cultural exercise. He wanted a fuck doll with interchangeable gender parts so he and his wife could do it together."

"Kinky," Carol said. "And, ewwww."

"I found it for him," Barnaby said. "When he took it home to surprise his wife, she'd run off with the neighbor couple they'd been swinging with. Good thing I made him pay upfront. He loved her, though, because it drove him shithouse crazy."

"He'd come in here spouting some crazy ass quantum philosophy bullshit," Paul said. "Embedded sexual energy possessed the place, waiting to do what, I don't know."

"I heard the whole spiel when he'd hit my booth," Stella said. "The whole Zone was filled with the implanted sexual energy of the doofus customers. Who could never really get off, since it's just titillation you get down, and not true, lasting release. Christ, I remember it. The whatever energy just twists around the area endlessly, doing the hokey pokey, I guess."

"It recycled around what used to be here," Carol said. "I heard his dumb ass theory, too. He claimed since it was the energy from the jerk offs who never really got off, it was angry energy. If these was ever nowhere for it to go, I guess it would blow a hole in stratosphere or some BS. He started talking directing ion particles, some spacey stuff. I left the booth when he came in. You put up with him for a time, too."

"I'm a sympathetic S.O.B.," Barnaby said. "Especially while he had money. He got to be a real pain when everything started closing. Where would all the frigging energy go next. That's what happens when you're real smart. You're already mostly screwy."

A couple strolled in holding hands.

"Virgin alert," Stella said.

"Jealous skank," Carol said. "Your snatch has seen enough clap to have a permanent standing ovation."

"We're not offended," the male said. "Jaimie and I have heard it all since we decided to work in the Combat Zone and test our celibacy till marriage commitment."

"Mostly from my parents," Jaimie said. "I thought my father's insensitivity would drive Sammy away."

"I'd only go away if you wanted me to, sweetheart," Sammy said.

The rap booth operators cooed in mocking unison.

"The spread is all, spread, Owen," Sammy said.

"Last supper in the Combat Zone."

Wayne motioned Barnaby aside when the others herded up the staircase tucked in the corner.

"I know you got Chinese food," he said.

"We are in Chinatown."

"It gives me wicked gas," Wayne said. "I was thinking of another way I could celebrate the last night."

Barnaby clapped him on the shoulder.

"I know my customers."

Owen tugged a three-inch length of string from his jacket. He dangled its attached silver dollar size coin in Wayne's face. The words 'Heads I Win' encircled the engraving of the buxom top of a naked woman. The opposite side featured the female's bubble-butted lower body and the phrase 'Tails You Lose.'

"The reusable strokin' token," Barnaby said. "Use it, abuse it, just don't lose it. Good for one night only."

Wayne snatched the coin and marched towards the aisle of video booths.

"I'm glad I'm getting out this business," Barnaby muttered. "Wanker."

He flicked the wall switches, leaving the room lighted by four recessed domes in each corner of the ceiling. Barnaby paused mid-step and listened for a repeat of the crinkled rustling he thought he heard. He shrugged and trudged up the stairs.

The Dorian Dingus box wriggled and its cellophane window ripped open on the grated edge of the display rack. The deflated pleasure doll unfolded with accordion styled contractions and catapulted onto the floor. Dorian squealed air and expanded into a willowy blonde with cherry nipples protruding from her crescent shaped breasts. Fine strands of synthetic hair curled around the slotted opening below her trim waist. Dorian shimmered and shimmied in place. The breasts flattened and remerged as muscled pectorals. The blonde mane receded to neck length and the crotch sealed. A ribbed dildo pinged from the closure and inflated to a rock-solid eight inches. Two conjoined gonads the size of golf balls dropped from it and sprouted a layer of fuzz.

The doll rippled. Dorian's right half regained its feminine features while its left side retained the male characteristics. The contrasting cobalt and indigo eyes sparkled as the doll surveyed its surroundings. Dorian shuffled herky-jerky steps to a wall display containing sex toys and marital aides. The doll's mouth writhed into a drooped combination of lustful grin and sadistic leer.

***

Wayne hunched forward in the plastic chair and drooled spittle onto the booth's floor. He stared while the climactic scenes of Aerobi-sex Girls played on the video screen. Nubile young ladies clad in sweat bands and leggings thrashed their oiled bodies around slippery gym mats. The women moaned and squealed as they fingered and slobbered any and all orifices on each other's bodies. One girl tried to stand. Wayne chuckled when she slid and fell, enjoying the plop of her ass hitting the mat.

Wayne unzipped his pants and stroked his penis to erectness. He giggled at the thought of leaving his own final mark on the Lamplight. Wayne started when a thump rattled the booth. He scowled and his penis drooped. A second strike snapped the door's lock.

"I'll kick your ass, making me lose it, with all it takes to make it. I'm not young…"

Wayne heard moist suction from the figure silhouetted in the booth's doorway.

"No way."

Dorian Dingus pressed a finger against her lips and her circular mouth formed a salacious grin. Wayne shivered at the rekindled tingle in his testicles. Dorian crooked her finger and Wayne felt compelled to follow her towards the front of the shop. Dorian snagged a vacuum pump from the wall display. She pointed at Wayne and pantomimed a downward gesture. He broke the snap on his slacks in his haste to unfasten it. Wayne slid down the pants and his yellowed boxers and laid on top of them. Dorian squatted beside him and inserted his organ into the vacuum tube.

"I never had much luck with those. I guess we can have fun trying."

Dorian squeezed the pressure ball attached to the pump. Wayne gasped at his dick's instantaneous stiffening. Dorian pumped the ball again. Wayne stifled a scream when the skin on his cock stretched to near breakage. He stared at the purple mushroomed tip of his penis.

"Shit, it's bigger."

Dorian lifted the pump. She poised her butt above his crotch and slid Wayne's prick into the hole in the center of her ass.

"A back-door girl."

Dorian bucked and rode Wayne's throbbing cock. He grunted at the warm friction generated by her frenetic up and down movement. Wayne grinned and he felt his scrotum tighten.

"Get ready for a special delivery. Mega wad!"

Dorian shook her head. She boosted her ass from his crotch. Wayne's cock shriveled until it resembled a gnarled twig. He screamed when she snapped it and the jagged stem spurted bloody sap. Dorian slammed the vacuum tube over his nose and mouth and crushed the pressure ball again and again. Wayne's face colored to a reddish shade of purple as he spewed up pink tissue. The doll's form reshaped. Wayne recalled an Aerosmith song while he lost consciousness.

Dude looked like a lady.

***

Owen Barnaby gnawed the remaining meat scrap from the spare rib. He guzzled the rest of his Budweiser and belched with gusto. Libby, Stella and Carol frowned from the opposite end of the table.

"What, it's carbonated."

"So is champagne," Carol said. "That's what someone with class serves at a celebration."

"In a nice restaurant," Stella said.

"Cheapskate," Libby told him.

"Blow it out all your asses," Barnaby said. "I'm not getting any part of the sweetheart deal the city gave the building owners."

Paul swallowed his mouthful of fried rice.

"You could've bought the whole damn block, boss, if not for all those trips to Foxwoods."

Ernie laughed and spat chicken chow mien

"It wasn't the trips. It was the losing he did on them."

"Eat me on rye," Owen said. "I'll cut off all the alcohol, you comedians. Jaimie and Sammy aren't busting me, probably because… What the hell are you drinking, seltzer water?"

"Spring water," Sammy replied.

"With a little sugar free, low-cal peppermint," Jaimie said. "We're boring."

Sammy clasped her open hand.

"Not to each other."

"I don't know what you're made of," Barnaby said. "But I wish I… No, I don't."

Libby pushed her chair back from the table.

"Time to go and flow. And no talking about me, I'll know."

She walked past the pair of makeshift offices at the end of the floor and skipped down the staircase. Libby paused on the first floor landing, shook her head and continued to the basement. She clicked on the bank of bug flecked fluorescent lights and winced at the frenzied rustling in the room's shadowed edges. Libby slipped into the bathroom and emptied her bladder. She blotted her crotch with the hanging roll of Charmin and recalled the customer who liked to see her pubes wet when he visited. He pretended to be her father and scolded her for wetting herself. She called upon Paul to roust him the night he insisted she pee in front of him.

Libby stepped from the bathroom. She recoiled with a shriek when a rat half the size of a Chihuahua scampered over her feet and ran across the floor. Libby heard a wet rippling in the shadows, followed by a strangled squeak. Libby gasped when the fully male Dorian Dingus shuffled into the light. She admired the chiseled features, the muscled chest and ripped abs. Her eyes widened to take in the entire length of his wagging penis. Dorian held the cleaved rat impaled on a bondage pinwheel. He smirked and flicked the rodent at Libby. The rodent landed in two furry chunks at her feet. Libby backed against one of the ceiling's utility pipes and placed her hands on it.

"I can't help myself. Come and get it, my hero."

Dorian sidled against her and lashed her hands to the pipe with a leather strap. He spun the pinwheel and shredded Libby's clothes. She moaned when the tatters caressed her body on their slide to the floor. Dorian clamped his elongating arm around Libby and steadied her squirming body. Libby whimpered and rubbed her crotch against his hard plastic genitalia. Dorian retracted his arm and stepped from back her. Libby whined and strained against the strap.

"Don't!"

Dorian flicked the pinwheel into a blurred spin. The doll shimmered and its female side reformed. Dorian slashed Libby's larynx. The doll carved an X in Libby running from shoulder to thigh. Libby croaked an attempt at a scream. Dorian grasped the loose folds of skin and ripped it free in triangular patches. Libby gaped at her bared, squishy insides. Dorian pared through exposed veins, capillaries and arteries. Libby slumped against the pipe. Her body gushed blood, water and flayed guts while it swayed as the leather strap twisted and unfurled.

Dorian flashed sparkling eyes in response to the clump of footfalls on the first floor. The doll shifted to full female form and lumbered towards the stairs.

***

Ernie plodded down the staircase and stepped into the front store. He gazed at its displays and waved a dismissive hand at the flight leading to the basement. He volunteered to check on the rap booth broad in order to gain unfettered access to the stack of fisting magazines. His dedicated loyalty to the Lamplight warranted a few gratis parting gifts.

"No, they didn't."

Ernie gawked at the empty space where his sought after magazines once resided.

"That touch hole Wayne. He took them, the bastard."

Random lights flickered on in the store. A magazine smacked him in the back. Dorian Dingus grabbed another publication from the stack on the front counter. She threw it at Ernie and barraged him with the rest of pile. He bleated and covered his face with his arms. Dorian reached under the counter and flaunted a rubber arm that tapered into a pointing index finger. She pointed to the picture imprinted on the limb's plastic cover.

"Belladonna," Ernie said. "I shut off her Diane Sawyer interview when she got all weepy. She's a hot ass chickie."

Dorian tossed another magazine at Ernie. He stared at the glossy cover photo depicting a latex clad woman with her fist jammed in a restrained man's butt. Ernie studied the man's ecstatic look. Dorian unwrapped the replica Belladonna arm. She lathered it with a bottle of personal lube and pointed it at Ernie. He gulped as Dorian strode towards him and he dropped the magazine. She snapped open his jeans with the pointing finger and ripped apart his underpants. Ernie dropped to the floor on his hands and knees and arched his bare ass. He shivered when Dorian rubbed the Belladonna finger up and down his butt crack. She tickled his testicles with it for a couple of minutes. Ernie groaned and drizzled semen down his leg. Dorian traced a line from his genitals to his anus and fingered his butt hole until it reddened and puckered. Ernie shrieked when she slid the Belladonna hand into his ass.

"Butt peggers are really onto something, shit"

He heard a wet ripple behind him. Ernie experienced stabbing cramps as the hand skidded up his alimentary canal.

"Back it up, too much. Shit, it opened!"

Ernie turned his head. He tried to scream when he saw the doll's half and half appearance. Dorian shoved the arm up his ass all the way to its elbow. Plastic fingers erupted through his heaving stomach and waved. Dorian yanked back on the arm. The limb tore deep rents in Ernie's butt as it ripped free. The hand emerged from his ass clutching a mixture of mushed internal organs and noodles encrusted with bean sprouts. Ernie collapsed in the bloody slop that gushed form his perforated belly and ruptured anus. Dorian threw the arm in the corner and snatched a bag from the counter. Ernie formed a final thought as Dorian walked past him to the stairs.

I just got ripped a new asshole.

***

Barnaby nibbled a chicken wing and watched Jaimie and Sammy combine the remaining food onto paper dishes. They swept the empty containers into a Hefty trash bag.

"You're domesticated already," he said. "Just jump in the sack, never mind the paper."

"You have no romance, Owen," Carol said. "It's not just sex. There's more."

"Yeah, we're selling romance down here. Bite me, Miss Lonely Hearts."

Jaimie and Sammy secured the filled bag. They laced hands around its ties and carted the sack towards the stairs. Stella's attempt at a mocking gag ended in a panicked scream when a blood streaked half and half Dorian Dingus strode from the stairwell. The trash toting couple backed away from the sex doll. Dorian followed and trapped the slower running Jaimie against the wall. The doll stumbled when it neared her. The mismatched eyes flashed confusion and Dorian hiccupped a fizzle of latex scented breath. Sammy scrambled back to Jaimie and stepped between her and the doll. Dorian sagged as air hissed from its cavities.

The other store employees scattered from the table. Paul unhooked the stun gun from his belt and crackled it as he walked towards Dorian. Paul waved Jaimie and Sammy away from the wall. He jabbed the gun against Dorian's oversized breast.

"Go down, you she him freak."

Dorian's rubber skin unwrinkled and regained its hardened elasticity. The doll grasped Paul's throat and wrenched the stun gun from his hand. Paul flinched in anticipation of the weapon's charge when the sex toy brandished it in his face. Dorian patted his cheek and tossed the gun down the stairs. The doll pulled a thick anal plug from the bag it carried. Dorian switched it to maximum vibrate and crunched the tapered point into the guard's forehead. Dorian dropped him and the plug drilled through Paul's skull. He thrashed on the floor as the butt plug burrowed through his brain. Red, pink and gray goop seeped from his head.

"The offices," Sammy said.

He and Jaimie led Barnaby and the rap booth ladies towards the closest office. Dorian slung a strand of anal beads at them. The whirling cord wrapped around Carol's neck. The beads sliced her skin. Dorian yanked on the string's trailing ends. Carol's decapitated head cracked loose from her eviscerated neck stump. Dorian nabbed it and hurled the still gasping head at the closed office door. The cranium ricocheted and spun across the floor. Dorian pulled a studded leather paddle from the bag and stomped towards the office.

Sammy jammed a folded chair under doorknob. He and Jaimie wrapped their arms around each other and hugged.

"What the fuck?" Stella said. "What the fuck?"

"The area is embedded with powerful and angry sexual energy," Sammy said.

"And where does it go once its containment regular area is gone," Jaimie said.

"Dr. Dirty knew something, really?" Stella said.

"His pissed off spirit could be running that thing," Barnaby told her. "He's got enough reasons to come after us. Does it really matter?"

The door shook and splintered. A second blow punched a hole in it and Dorian stared in. The sex doll hammered the door with the paddle and broke apart the top half. Dorian pushed the chair aside and stormed the office. The Lamplight employees ran to the connecting room. Barnaby and Stella exited it as Dorian strode in. The doll barred the doorway with the paddle when Jaimie and Sammy ran towards it. The doll's faces formed a quizzical expression and it wobbled. Dorian lost its grip on the paddle and dropped it. The doll staggered backwards and propped itself against the table. Barnaby and Stella stopped a couple of inches shy of colliding with it. Dorian chased them as they ran around the opposite side. Jaimie grabbed Sammy's arm and restrained him from going to them.

"We got to try to help them."

Jaimie traced his lips with her fingertip.

"We need to stop it completely," she said. "Just think if it gets loose in the city."

"How do we do that? The stun gun didn't work and we don't…"

Jaimie placed her hands on his groin and her crotch.

"It only seemed to weaken when it got near us."

Sammy gazed in her eyes ad nodded.

"Ultimate absorption. I guess we've seen enough working here to figure out the how. And we won't be doing it to each other, not really."

Jaimie steered him back into the office.

Barnaby and Stella gasped and paused at one end of the table. Dorian perched on the opposite side and synched both faces into a smirk.

"We can't keep running, it can," Barnaby said. "We split up. One of us should get loose."

"If you were a real man, you'd take the hit so I could get away."

"Chivalry's dead, toots. Ready. Steady. Go!"

Dorian wriggled her arms and stretched them the length of the table. The doll snared Barnaby and Stella around their waists as they poised to run. The arms retracted and dragged them through the food laden take out plates and unopened beer bottles.

"Yoo-hoo. Dorian."

The doll's arms uncurled from their captives and snapped back to normal length. Dorian belched an extended wisp of air. The doll's posture slumped as it turned.

Jaimie and Sammy stood naked in the doorway of the second office. Jaimie parted her lips and licked them with a flick of her wet tongue. She cupped her pert breasts and slavered them to spit trickling moistness.

Sammy smiled and fondled his hairy scrotum. He formed a circle around the base of his penis with his thumb and forefinger. He flailed it against his hips.

Dorian cringed when the bare couple sashayed from the offices. Jaimie inserted her finger in her vagina and moaned a theatrical groan. She popped her probing digit free and swabbed Dorian's male lips. A choking hiss slipped from the doll's mouth. Jaimie jumped on Dorian and wrapped her legs around the sex doll's waist and ass. She leaned back and her weight dragged Dorian on top of her as they sprawled on the floor. Jaimie trapped the doll's bouncing pecker in her vagina. She writhed and performed energetic reverse pushups.

Sammy knelt behind Dorian's bobbing ass. He slapped the doll's female butt cheek. Air squealed from Dorian's lips. Sammy pushed against Dorian's knees and forced apart the doll's legs. He milked his member and dribbled a slippery gob onto the doll's fake pussy hole. A moan escaped from the quivering sex toy. Sammy jammed his hardened penis into Dorian's wet pouch. He linked hands with Jaimie and they engaged in a frenzied seesaw momentum.

Dorian's synthetic skin crimped and lost its solidity. Jaimie licked the male half of Dorian's mouth. She twisted its head, allowing Sammy access to lap the female side. Dorian's noggin bopped side to side and the doll squeaked a long, drawn out whistle.

The sex doll shriveled, deflated and folded in on itself. The flattened slab of rubber and plastic covered Jaimie as Sammy flopped on top of her.

"It worked, baby," he said. "We motherfu... ah, we rule."

"Honey, even though there is rubber separating us, let's not push things, okay."

"Oh, right."

Sammy sprang to his feet. He pulled the collapsed sex doll off Jaimie and helped his girlfriend to her feet. He noticed the stares from Barnaby and Stella. Sammy covered Jaimie's vagina with a soggy plate of chow mien remains and plastered a Styrofoam carton over her breasts. He emptied a container of pork fried rice and draped it over his cock.

"You guys could make a mint doing Jack and Jill stuff," Owen said. "I know a few guys that run webcam sites. We could shoot some test stuff, have a little bid war…"

Stella punched his arm.

"I know you kids want to get dressed. The butthead is right, though, you put on a good show."

Jaimie and Sammy scuttled backwards into the office. Barnaby walked over to the crumpled Dorian doll and poked it with his toe.

"Now to explain this cluster fuck. I should've just set the place on fire like my bookie told me. Except, I'd be the first suspect."

Jaime and Sammy returned from the office clothed.

"You look puzzled, Owen," Sammy said. "We just found a way to drain its energy."

Stella whistled and she stepped over from the table.

"Everybody's a bit of a horn ball before their cherry gets popped. You two must have mega sex drives. All that embedded energy…"

Stella laughed when the couple blushed.

"We'll sort out everybody's sex drives later," Owen said. "Some druggies went nuts when we didn't have much cash for them to rob. They took off when they started to sober up. No cameras, no contradictions. The Zone will be good for one last crime headline. I'll even pay for the funerals. Copacetic?"

The others held a whispered consultation.

"It's lying," Sammy said. "But I guess, well…"

Jaimie squeezed his hand.

"It's better that people not know stuff like this happens, baby."

"You ain't shitting," Barnaby said. "A big n-f-w to that."

***

Police sergeant Garvin listened to the report from the uniformed officer in charge of the search of the area surrounding the Lamplight Adult Bookstore. He issued further instructions to him and strode back to the surviving store employees sequestered at the front counter.

"No sign of them," he said. "I'm widening the scope, but unless they surface somewhere else, I don't know. With the Pike right there, they could be halfway to New York by now."

"Speaking of being somewhere, Sergeant," Owen said. "It's been a fuck of a long night for us."

"Mine's just starting. Yeah, I guess we're done. Sure none of you want to go to the hospital, or a counselor, or something?"

"You're sweet, Sergeant," Stella said. "I think we just want to be with our own thoughts right now. Can I have your card, in case something else comes to mind?"

Garvin fished a business card from his jacket and handed it to her. Stella brushed his hand with her thumb as she took the card from him.

"Oh, maybe I should ask, any of the rest of you want…"

"We're good, Sergeant," Barnaby said.

"Okay. You realize this is an off-limits crime scene, so everything in here is impounded."

"Keep it," Owen told the policeman. "I think I've seen enough of this shit for a while. A long while."

The Lamplight employees exited the store and walked up Washington Street towards Downtown Crossing.

"Want to turn around and try for breakfast at the Blue Diner?" Owen said.

Jaimie and Sammy looked at each other.

"We have something else in mind," she said.

"Like where and how can we get married fast," Sammy said. "After what we felt in there, well, we want to feel it again. With each other. Big time."

"Congratulations and welcome to the real world," Stella said.

"Vegas," Barnaby said.

"You just want go gamble," Stella said.

"Hey, I need some way to get the money to give our departed friends good funerals."

"We have some money saved up," Sammy said. "We were going to look for a bigger apartment."

"But we can live in your studio, baby," Jaimie said. "We'll be nice and close and cozy."

"I'll take care of it all," Stella said. "I can finally use all the extra bonus miles on my credit card. I never go anywhere."

"Casinos take credit cards, too," Barnaby said.

"We're going as witnesses only," Stella told him. "Unless you want to get hitched, too, while we're there."

"Even I wouldn't take that gamble. Wouldn't you rather hook up with sergeant sweetie anyway."

"Hey, it never hurts to be in good with a cop."

Jaimie and Sammy paused to hug. Their embrace turned to a simultaneous grope. The couple shared a lust-tinged look of fear and broke apart. They walked half a dozen paces in opposite directions.

"Not to be impolite, but can we get headed to Logan," Sammy said. "Like, quick."

"We better book way separated seats," Jaimie said. "And neither of us should be allowed to go to the bathroom alone, or at all."

***

Crime scene tech Miller turned over the squashed Dorian Dingus doll and snapped a picture of its blood-stained front. Sergeant Garvin joined him as he set up another shot.

"Strange ass thing," Miller said. "They must've been real freakazoids to fuck with this after what they did. I wonder how the developers will like having this shit tied to their plans."

"Some weirdo will probably buy it because it was a killing site," Garvin told him. "I used to think no matter how much they gussied up the neighborhood and made it look respectable, down here would never outlive its history. I feel something different now. Something is missing, some energy or attitude."

"This is, or I guess was, the last smutty business down here," Miller said.

"Maybe that's it. After all years I've worked down here, I finally feel like the Combat Zone is actually gone. Who knew that could happen."

Feeding the Beast

Ken Goldman

On their first date, he told her she was the most beautiful woman he had ever seen. Blushing, she managed to feign modesty. One evening over wine she told him she loved him. Later in bed he told her he loved her.

For the wedding, she insisted on writing their own vows.

During the ceremony, she said she looked forward to growing old with him, adding a cute remark about keeping adjoining 'his' and 'hers' jars in the bathroom for their teeth. That one got a few laughs.

Then her pledge turned serious, and she promised to remain by his side no matter what obstacles life threw into their path. Many present cried.

When his turn arrived, he told friends and family that his world had been empty before she came into it. He vowed he would die for her, and at the time he meant it.

On their wedding day, he didn't have to actually do it.

***

Wesley and his young bride would make Honolulu International in another two hours, plenty of time for what he had in mind. He focused his attention from the Piper's control panel to where it really mattered.

" 'A`ohe lokomaika`i i nele i ke pâna`i. ' How's that for a Harvard man?"

"Another of your legal terms, Counselor?"

"It's Hawaiian for 'No kind deed ever lacks its reward.' Sort of like 'quid pro quo,' but it sounds prettier."

Charlotte smiled. "Is this your way of asking for a blow job?"

Wesley smiled too. "See how easy it is to master the ancient tongues?"

He snapped on the auto pilot and unzipped his jeans, a guy who had the world by the balls. As one of Seattle's select divorce lawyers, Wesley had managed that trick one gonad at a time.

Charlotte examined the goods, grinning even as she went down on him. The woman's tongue became hotwired, and Wesley leaned back in his seat to savor the moment. Once started, Charlotte could probably bob her head straight into Waikiki.

The manbeast within responded.

Eat it, babe. That's it, bitch. That's real good. Eat it all up ...

Although Wesley had never met a blow job he did not like, there was a serious downside to his bride's initiation into his mile high club. Getting sucked off at three thousand feet had taken his attention from the Piper's fuel gauge whose indicator had accelerated its movement towards 'E'.

Spuk-Spukka-SpukSpuk ...

"What the-?"

"Sorry, baby. Got a little bicuspid into my work."

"Shh ...!"

The Super Cub's engine burped again, and Wesley stared at the blinking red fuel light unable to do more than gape like an idiot while his bone-on quickly shriveled. Somehow gasoline from the Cub's tank was not making it through to the single engine, and he was rapidly dropping fuel. Considering the plane's altitude, the whys and what-fors didn't matter much once the needle fell to 'Empty' and the front propeller turned arthritic.

Pulling herself upright Charlotte saw the warning light too, and for one terrible instant the couple exchanged glances with a dim comprehension that they had shared the all-time mother of bad timing.

Spukka-Spukka ...

"Wes, is everything all ...?"

...SpukSpukSpuk ...

"Put your belt on."

"What?"

"Just do it. Okay?"

Her groom's eyes said it all. One thousand miles from the mainland his rebuilt Piper was coughing fumes like a consumptive hag. Wesley flicked his thumb at the fuel gauge because he could think of nothing else to do. He tried telling himself that maybe the indicator was damaged, maybe the vortex generator was on the fritz and the sputtering didn't really mean any--

The engine choked and the Cub took a mean dip as the bottom dropped out of the world.

Wesley had enough time only to mutter "Oh, Jesus-" before the small plane dipped again, pulling the steering column from his hands. The engine managed one powerful fart before it went dead. The law of inertia kept the Piper airborne for an uncertain moment, long enough for Wesley to swap a last uneasy stare with his wife.

"Shit ..."

The plane plummeted like a sack towards the Pacific. Wesley's stomach and heart mashed into one organ as the horizon became vertical and spun wildly, the entire vista of heaven and earth unraveling as if on a huge spool. The Piper corkscrewed while some distant part of Wesley's brain registered Charlotte's screams.

"Omigod, Wes! OhGodOhGod!!"

God wasn't listening. The plane tumbled into a dizzying death spiral. A man plunging several hundred feet per second has little time to weigh alternatives. He has time only to scream his throat raw for his own sorry ass, time only to hope that death, when it comes, will be quick.

The Piper struck the water balls-to-the-sky, catching a huge cresting wave at the peak of its swell. Its bizarre angle of impact made for an intriguing lesson in physics that defied the laws of probability. Both seats tore through the cabin doors just before the floor and ceiling of the fuselage crunched into a chunk of tangled metal. The twin cushions skittered along the water's surface like skimming stones, catapulting the couple yards from the Piper's debris. Surrounded by open sea the plane's explosion seemed more of a loud thud. What remained of the cabin burst into flames.

A large area of metal detritus heaved among the waves, the misshapen globs of tortured steel gradually sinking piecemeal. A gnarled section of the plane's extended flap briefly stayed afloat, and a hundred feet from that a twenty-six inch Tundra tire and some Gucci luggage bobbed alongside the swells. One bag had sprung open and women's clothing rode the waves like a floating yard sale.

The primitive manbeast caged inside Wesley's brain kicked into action, although later he would remember little of what he did. Charlotte remained buckled to her seat, and both had somehow been thrown clear of the wreckage. Now his wife's seat rolled on the waves maybe a good hundred feet from her husband. Somewhere out there was a float kit, but that might just as well have been back in Seattle now. The Piper's cushion was no flotation device, and the plush leather pad could not remain adrift for very long. Strapped in, Charlotte would soon be going under with it.

If his legs were still working it wouldn't be a difficult swim to recover her. On his own automatic pilot, Wesley didn't consider that when he reached his woman he might be unbuckling a corpse. He knew only that he did not want to die alone.

He swam towards the red leather seat cushions, but Charlotte was not moving. Her forehead's nasty gash was bleeding badly, and he ripped his sleeve to apply a makeshift tourniquet to the wound. Exhausted and shivering Wesley pulled himself alongside her, draping his arms around his wife with no idea what to do next. Already the leather pad had taken on too much water, and it would be going under any minute. He had managed to escape the plunge from three thousand feet only to come to this. The Pacific owned both of them now, and he could do nothing as he waited for the ocean to claim what belonged to her.

A remnant of the Piper's wreckage floated among the rainbow of Charlotte's strewn wardrobe. It thumped against the side of the padded seat, and at first Wesley saw only a blur in the sunlight reflected off the waves. He reached for the large box as if to assure himself it was real.

Three Person Sea Cloud Model #417-B
Max Weight 510 lb
Pull Cord to Inflate

USE CAUTION WHEN INFLATING

Part of the flotation kit had broken free. Maybe God had one good ear after all. Wesley tore at the Styrofoam and found the cord, tugging at it like a madman. The heavy duty blue and yellow vinyl inside did its thing and with a hiss the box fell apart.

The life raft fully inflated the same moment the saturated red leather cushion slipped below the surface. Charlotte had gone as limp as a rag doll, but Wesley managed to unbuckle her and pulled the two of them on board. He tried mouth-to-mouth, managing to get her to spit up a bellyful of seawater. Exhausted, he had enough strength to yarf his own breakfast before passing out.

The sun already had headed West, and the air developed a cold bite. It was 5:37, and regaining consciousness Wesley had the disjointed thought that Rolex made one hell of a watch. The timepiece was still kicking, but he didn't feel as certain about himself. When reason returned another thought occurred, this one unsettling. Soon darkness would come.

He held Charlotte close. Her pulse was weak but she was breathing. The long gash had stopped bleeding, but a grotesque Rorschach of dried blood still caked most of her face. Splashing some seawater on her, he could manage only a whisper.

"Charlotte? Can you hear me?"

Nothing.

"You okay?"

Her eyes opened. "Are we dead?"

"Not yet."

She took a moment to consider that.

"Then we're all right?"

"Not yet."

She considered that too.

"Jesus, Wes. What happened?"

"Must've ruptured the fuel line somehow, maybe during take-off. It's a moot point now."

She moved closer. "I'm cold. And I could use a drink."

"Room service is about five hundred miles that way."

Charlotte watched the bleeding sunset and managed a weak moan.

"What happens now?"

"We survive," he told her, trying to believe it. The Pacific was a monotonous heaving mass, and if land were anywhere near, the ocean gave no hint where to find it. Help would come, he told her, someone would realize the Piper never arrived at its destination. But the plane had sunk too far at sea for wreckage to wash on shore. Worse, from the air the bobbing Sea Cloud raft would appear a speck to anyone searching for them, even with optimal weather conditions.

"Maybe we should've fished some of your things from those Guccis," Wesley suggested. "Might've kept you from the whole 'Lord of The Flies' fashion statement. And it's going to get damned cold."

Charlotte managed a twitching smile. "A girl wants to look her best when she's eaten by barracuda." She warmed herself against Wesley's chest and watched the sun drift below the horizon. "Ordinarily I'd think this is one beautiful sunset."

"It still is. Someone will find us. I'm sure of it. It just won't happen tonight." He offered a wet stick of gum and took the last one for himself. Wesley spent the next minute wondering if their final meal would be a salt watered wad of Juicy Fruit.

They waited in silence for over an hour until full darkness came. Near the raft some invisible thing went splunk! Maybe another section of the plane's wreckage had popped back to the surface to say howdy. Wesley hoped that's all it was. He was in no mood for surprises.

Beneath a pale moon, a dorsal fin sliced the water's surface about thirty feet from the raft. Wesley spotted it circling like a shadowy scout, and a moment later half a dozen more closed in. He pointed for Charlotte to see. Each time the couple turned there were others, some drifting along the waves in tandem until fins appeared on all sides. They slid closer, tightening their orbit like an advancing war party, dark floating lumps dissecting the water. Wesley slid a paddle from its neoprene sheath, holding it before him like a battering ram.

"Wes, there's too many of--"

One bumped against the life raft. Charlotte almost toppled over the side, but Wesley managed to pull her back. He felt something churning the water just below the surface.

"They're under us..."

In dark committees, the sharks were maneuvering for position. Murky clusters surged toward the raft, hammering it from all sides as if one might fling itself on board like a dead weight. Sprays of seawater rained on the couple while they performed a lunatic balancing act to keep the raft from capsizing. Charlotte clung to her husband as he poked the paddle at the invading snouts. Winking in and out of the moonlight the fins kept coming. Charlotte's fingers tore twisted tracks into Wesley's chest so she would not be pulled from him, but she lost her grip and tumbled over the side into the dark waters. Mouths open, the sharks were waiting.

"Wes-!!!"

Her shrieks filled the night. From the agitated seawater, Wesley heard what sounded like a crunch of dried wood. He dropped the paddle, slamming fists to his ears, but Charlotte's screams wouldn't stop.

I would die for you, Charlotte...

He crouched in a fetal position.

"Wesley! Oh God, Wesley! Help--!"

"Jesus, no! Charlotte, I can't! I can't!"

...Die for you...

He mashed his ears, but the shrieks went on.

"...can't..."

"Wessss-leeeeee ...!"

The manbeast heard. Wesley grabbed the oar again, battering the dark thrashing forms, blindly smashing at whatever moved. One of the sharks sank its teeth into the thick paddle, and Wesley played a useless tug-of-war with the fish. He stared dumbly at the worthless stump of plastic he pulled from the water.

"Motherfuckers! Shit eating cocksuckers!!"

And then it ended. Charlotte's cries stopped as if an electric cord had been pulled from its plug. Their hunger sated, the sharks disappeared, gone like a magician's trick beneath the surface with their catch of the day. The ocean lapped at the raft's side as if the incident never happened. Wesley crouched waiting for an encore, but it didn't come.

The whole thing had lasted maybe six minutes, but it proved time enough to total his life with Charlotte. Wesley needed significantly more time for clear thinking to return. Assessing his circumstances, he came up empty. Even if the sharks didn't reappear, he knew he remained in ten thousand fathoms of deep shit. Maybe Charlotte had been the lucky one.

Charlotte was somewhere down there now.

Or what was left of her.

Charlotte...

"Sorry... I'm so sorry..."

The gum had lost its flavor and he spit it out. It was an absurd thought to occur at this moment, but easier than recalling his woman's final cries for help before the sharks took her down, cries he could not find inside himself to answer. And easier than contemplating what might come next.

Plenty of water, but not a drop to drink.

Water water everyfuckingwhere…

Charlotte was dead. He could do nothing about that. But he had to consider his survival now, and he knew that in forty-eight hours, dehydration would turn his insides to wood shavings. Wesley remembered some Discovery Channel program about castaways who wound up drinking their own piss. In another day swilling pee would be like polishing off a daiquiri. Right about now, his bride and he should have been dining on Kalua pork and sipping Mai Tais at The Royal Hawaiian. But it didn't appear he would be chowing down on solid food anytime soon.

The wind kicked up. Wesley was cold and wet. Worse, he was scared.

He slapped himself hard.

"Can't lose it… can't lose it…"

And then he almost did.

A weak pounding came from against the side of the raft. Some object had tangled itself in the mooring line, but darkness made it difficult to see the shape clearly. Wesley tugged the rope until a thin pale mass emerged, dripping of seawater and cold to his touch as he pulled it on board. Holding it to the moonlight he noticed the large pear-shaped diamond ring first. The realization took a moment. He had hauled Charlotte's arm from the ocean, gnawed clean above the elbow.

He dropped the slab of shorn flesh and bone, backing off from it as from some diseased thing.

Sobbing like a child, shivering and moaning, he crouched in the corner of the raft, swearing to himself that he would not move until rescuers or death found him. He didn't give a shit which might arrive first.

At night, a shivering sleep came only with complete exhaustion. During the following day his flesh seared in the heat like over-fried bacon.

Searching for a plane he saw nothing but a burning sun. Inside himself he felt a burning too. This was hunger, but it was also fear.

He was alone, more alone than any man could be.

Throughout the second night he shivered but did not sleep much.

When day again arrived, he knew it would be his last.

Hunger hammered Wesley's gut in dull thunderbolts, and he did not feel like opening his eyes. Instead he lay with the morning sun warming his face. In another hour, the sun would not be so hospitable.

The sharks had not returned, but there had been no rescue party either. He didn't have much fluid left inside to pull off that piss-drinking stratagem much longer. The Discovery Channel hadn't covered that part.

So many thoughts. Too many. Better to clear his head. Better not to think at all if he wanted to stay sane.

"Wesley…?"

"Unghh…"

"Wake up, Wesley. Talk to me."

In the brilliant sunlight, he squinted. Someone - it was a woman - came into focus, but he was seeing her through gauze. He recognized the voice before he saw her face clearly. Clumps of sopping hair lay in mottled ringlets. The woman stank of sea water.

"Charlotte?"

Wesley no longer trusted his own senses. His bride's corpse rested on the ocean floor with the local marine life, that much he knew. The sharks had done one bitchin' job on her, and she wasn't coming back.

Try to keep an open mind. Take a good look before you decide what's true. Just hold on... hold on...

It certainly looked like Charlotte, although much of her was gone. The stub of what remained of her upper arm dangled like a fleshy wind sock, and tattered skin hung from her face in thick lunch meat shavings. A portion of her skull had split, and tufts of blood-spattered curls spilled over a spongy mass that must have been the woman's brain. Sunlight peeking through an empty eye socket made her resemble a rotted jack-o'-lantern. Not much remained of her face, or her torso.

She held the severed arm Wesley had fished from the water.

"I didn't want you to see me like this, but I had no choice when you broke your vow. We have to set this right, Wesley. For both of us."

She wasn't there. She couldn't be there. It was too soon for this lunatic horseshit to be happening.

"You're dead!"

"I'm not certain, but I think so."

She tugged the tatters of silk that had been her blouse, trying to conceal the exposed flap of breast sagging from her chest like a torn sleeve. Thick strands of cheeze-like goo hung from it.

"I'm sorry, Wes. I know how bad I look."

The saltwater crazies had finally arrived. It hadn't taken long.

If I close my eyes you'll go away...

She didn't go away, only smiled and moved closer.

"Touch me, Wesley. Feel for yourself."

He didn't have to. Her ear dropped into his lap. She tried cramming it back into its cavity, but it wouldn't hold.

"Oh, Christ, Charlotte. Don't do this to me."

"You're not crazy, Wes. But you're hungry, aren't you? You would do anything to eat. Anything."

She didn't need to tell him. The gnawing punishment inside his belly reminded him every second.

"I can help," she told him. "I think maybe we can help each other."

"You can get me out of this place?"

"No, I can't do that. But I can do this…"

She held her own severed arm out to him.

"Eat me," she said.

"What?"

"Start with my arm. It isn't a part of me anymore, so it won't be difficult. Eat me, Wesley. I know there isn't much left, but do it for us. I want you to."

He felt his innards kickbox, but there was nothing left inside his stomach to woof up.

"I can't do that!"

"Start with my ear, then. Maybe that will be easier."

"Oh Jesus! Go away! Just let me die!" Wesley's breathing became labored. "I tried to save you, Charlotte! You know I tried! There were too many—"

"—You broke your vow, Wesley. Help me keep mine."

If solid nourishment didn't get inside him soon Wesley would starve. This wasn't rocket science, and the babbling corpse was probably some guilt-soaked brain fart anyway, a figment of an encumbered mind baked to a crisp. He was sane enough to know he was probably losing it. But if he were hungry enough to believe himself talking to his dead wife, then maybe he could convince himself he was just scarfing down some fast food.

He took the ear and gnawed. It was more crunchy than he expected. The salt water helped a little, even added flavor, and he ate the whole thing. It wasn't all that bad, and it piqued his appetite.

"Tastes like chicken," he said, licking his fingers. He even smiled.

She handed him the severed arm, and he sank his teeth into the fleshiest part of the upper segment like a man working over a rack of ribs. Charlotte's daily weight training at the spa had paid off because the meat was firm and there was very little fat. Hell, this tasted too damned fine to be a concoction of his imagination. Wesley made certain to remove the engagement ring before he started on her fingers.

Waiting until he finished, the woman held out her remaining arm to him.

"That too? Are you sure?" he asked.

"But the ring means something to me Wesley. I'd like to keep it. I'm still your wife."

The thought had not really occurred to him, and he felt shamed that the idea sickened him. Maybe it was better not to go there, better not to let the revulsion show. Nothing out of line here, babe. Not a damned thing. Wesley slipped the diamond upon the third finger of the hand attached to Charlotte's remaining arm. She moved closer.

Charlotte's lips felt cold against his. Still, they were surprisingly sweet. She parted them a little as she always had done, and her tongue found its way into Wesley's mouth. There was no other manner to describe the sensation. He was not disgusted or repulsed. He was hungry.

And here was the corned beef special.

Too damned fine not to be real. Human flesh, the other white meat.

The manbeast couldn't help itself. It nibbled the fleshy gobbit and felt its appetite grow. She pulled herself from him. Wesley couldn't be positive with so much of Charlotte's face gone, but it appeared she was smiling.

"Quid pro quo?" she uttered, her uncertain expression still there.

She slid towards the shredded fabric remaining of Wesley's pants, unzipping his jeans with her teeth. First offering soft butterfly kisses with her tongue, with an audible gulp she took all of him into her throat. The feel of her mouth was waxy as if one lip might loosen and tear clear off, but she managed to get seriously down to business. His response amazed him as he felt himself grow erect.

Eat it, bitch. That's it, eat it all up...

The woman stopped cold, her one remaining eye seeming to look through him, seeming to accuse him.

Yes, she's got you where she wants you now...

Sensing danger, the beast stirred, but too late.

Charlotte sank her teeth into Wesley's cock, attaching herself like some rabid pit bull refusing to let go. She swung her head to strengthen her grip, and the pain ricocheted straight into his brain. He twitched and kicked like a man caught in a bear trap, the crotch of his jeans darkening in an expanding smear. When finally she released him, he felt the limp wad of his manhood slap low against his thigh as if roadkill dangled between his legs. He stared at the butchered member that seemed no longer to belong to him.

"Look at what you've done to me! Oh, Jesus, Charlotte ..."

"I eat flesh too, Wesley! What did you expect? It's what the dead do!" She lunged between his legs again to finish her work.

Now the manbeast awakened completely, commandeering Wesley's brain. The jagged paddle stump lay within reach and he went for it, ramming it through the soft flesh beneath the woman's cheekbone. He twisted until he felt the delicate bone inside splinter and crunch, grinding the plastic stub into her skull until he could force it no further. She turned to face him, her remaining eye dribbling from its orbit like a ruined puppet's.

"I don't think this marriage is working for me, Wesley!"

"You tried to bite off my dick!"

"The tribe has spoken! I'm voting you off this island!"

She was on him again, ripping flesh from his face with her nails and teeth, and she kept coming back. He pushed her away in time to see a sunbaked flap of his skin disappear into her mouth. But the struggles had weakened her. He grabbed the woman and twisted her in a half nelson against his chest. The easiest thing to go for was her nose, although he couldn't get a firm grip. Wesley tried three times before he managed to chew it off.

Charlotte writhed like a wounded animal and pulled herself free. She backed off from him, covering the gaping cavern in her face with her remaining hand.

The beast found a voice, and now it roared. "The new nose was nice to look at, babe, but for eating I would have preferred the old one!" Panting heavily, Wesley spat the thin proboscis bone at her. The rest he chewed into peanut-like fragments. He swallowed, sneering at his crippled adversary.

"Say 'goodbye' to your balls, Wesley!" Charlotte growled.

"Tit for tat, Charlotte! Now say 'goodbye' to your tit!" He swiped a haymaker at her, grabbing her limp breast. With one yank he tore it free. His tongue flicked the nipple he held, licking it on all sides. "Does this feel good, cunt? You used to love when I did this."

Shoving the fleshy sack into his mouth he chewed, smiling as meaty chunks of pulp spurt from it. Charlotte fingered the lumpy guano inside the deep crater of her chest. With her eyes gone her face revealed almost nothing, but her body shook in violent spasms. Wesley could not tell whether she felt despair or pain. Maybe she wasn't capable of either, but he didn't care. The battle had gone beyond self-serving survival. Now it was about betrayal and humiliation, and this was much worse.

"You're a bastard, Wesley, a real bastard!"

The beast and its host came together as one.

"I'm helping you keep your vow, babe. You're always going to be with me, Charlotte, just like you promised! Right here inside my belly!"

Rallying with renewed strength she threw herself on him, biting and chewing. Wesley slammed his Rolex against the plastic stub that protruded from Charlotte's face, removing a large jagged slab of crystal. He slashed the shard through the woman's neck, yanking a lengthy strip of meat from it and biting the rest free. In a frenzy of fresh assaults each clawed skin divots from the other, stuffing into mouths whatever shredded flesh they could snatch before going at it again. The stakes had been raised, and if there had been nothing fair in love, then perhaps the scales might balance in war.

Wesley had once vowed that he would die for Charlotte, but he had failed to live up to his promise the first time.

He wasn't going to let that happen again.

His beast would see to that.

****

Brothers Pete and Zack Mulraney were among the several rescue teams dispatched from Maui. The two usually shuttled tourists who flew among the islands, and the pilots knew a thing or two about the area and its surrounding waters. On their third day out, they located a small patch of yellow and blue that, on closer inspection, proved a life raft. Seen through a binocular lens from the low flying Cessna there wasn't anything moving on board. Pete brought the small sea plane down to have a look.

A week had passed since the Piper Cub carrying Wesley and Charlotte Donner had been overdue at Honolulu International. News stations ran the heartbreaking wedding video of the pair's moving exchange of vows, and many viewers around the nation had themselves a good cry. After the fifth day, the media issued the statement that all hope had been lost for the handsome attorney and his beautiful young bride. The couple's families needed closure, and in deference the search for the two continued.

From the Cessna, Pete watched as Zack boarded the raft. At first, he didn't quite understand his brother's bizarre signaling gesture that he viewed from the plane's cabin. The man was flailing his arms, beckoning the pilot to join him. Pete decided to check out what was going on.

He disembarked the small plane, climbing on board the life raft to discover that Zack was vomiting.

The Man Who Visited
- Or -
'Poor Brother Ed'

Ralph Greco, Jr.

As if a slightly drunk ballerina had entered the shed, The Wizard's two-inch heel boots kicked up dust off the wood floor as he spun from one shaft of light to the next. The ancient carnie lived and loved the fantasies and submerged disappointments in the boxes of this room; stuffed canvas bags of memories spilling over the bowing shelves above his head; casks and bottles of various perverted potions leaning up against the crinkly sepia stained walls. In this grimy rollaway shed were the reminders, remainders, and reenactments of all the years that The Wizard had lived among the ruins of 'the show.'

Just beyond this one room the taste of the Pacific mixed with the smells of thick, musty curtains and creosote from the boardwalk only a block away. If anyone among the pierced skateboarders and sun-addled, beachcombers could have even imagined in their wildest fever daydreams what was hidden here and why, The Wizard would be chased with torches, run-out-on-a-rail and peppered with garbage.

But no one regarded him or cared to know what was in the locked shed.

As the man shook his hands free of his pockets, the crane of his eighty years lifted off him as if he was shaking arthritic crumbs from his limbs. He stood fully then, all five feet seven of him, and decades flittered up and away from the muted sunlight spilling through the pair of crusty windows over his head. Like delicate birds alighting from a tree around him, The Wizard poked the air with his still nimble digits, reaching for the formidable casket standing upright at the eastern corner of the shed. His usually quiet penis engorged to erection, his high brow burned with a quick sweat; his tiny blue eyes opened wide, the old man opened the lid of the coffin to himself and kissed a somnambulist's breath.

"Brother Ed," The Wizard said to the 105-year-old petrified corpse, a mummy really, he faced.

The Wizard reached in and rolled out his star attraction, very much like-and with the requisite same sound-unraveling wrapping paper from a soft cardboard tube.

"Full moon once again," The Wizard said as he leaned the reed thin, papier-mâché-like body of the man once known as Joshua McKinney out and to the side of his coffin. Just outside the shed's door and three feet away, two ten-year-old boys execute tight circles on the bicycles round one another.

***

In life, Joshua 'Ed' McKinney had been a drunkard, semi-outlaw who had lived his final days on a cattle ranch in southern Oklahoma at the end of the nineteenth century. With Joshua's pappy not near in attendance any of the boy's formative years, his mother—a drunk, blind-in-one-eye and spit-evil with the other, a sister who had begun taking money for her ample worn favors at the age of thirteen, and a sadistic spinster aunt who visited her brother's brood every year or so, only to engage and investigate her young nephew's rumored unusually-sized appendage, there wasn't much else for poor Joshua to do except get out as far and as fast as he could and make the best of his days... short though they would be.

Joshua learned to rustle some, cheat at cards and to use his obvious street wit and his cold blue eyes (and that rumored ample body part) on as many and as young a woman as he could entice. That last year of his life, though, while he was working a real job on a kind cattle rancher's farm, the thirty-year-old man began to 'court' the only daughter of a half gypsy woman named Mama Lee.

'Dating' Mamma Lee's daughter would prove to be Joshua McKinney's undoing.

Mama's only daughter Beb, only fourteen at the time, began seeing Joshua as often as she could sneak. The man was as unwelcome around the young girl as Mama Lee could sternly warn, but the older woman realized there would be no stopping such a willful beauty as Beb. Knowing he was dancing in a fire pit, Joshua still took his opportunities with the dark-haired woman/child as often as he could; in backyards, farmyards, and sheds, the girl continually rent in vagina, anus, and mouth by the crude, yet filling 'lovemaking' of the man she fantasized would one day be her husband. Of course, all Joshua (or Ed, as his aunt had nicknamed that part of him) wanted was to continue his prodding and poking of such nubile willing beauties, so when Beb began making overtones of a more permanent arrangement, the man 'pulled out'... literally and figuratively.

Glad for the halting of their romance but hurt by her daughter's rejection, Mama Bell decided to get back at Joshua, 'Ed,' the only way she knew how. Relying on her Creole lineage and the magic supposedly still surging through her veins, Mama Bell met up with the unlucky Mr. McKinney one fine spring day, confronting him on the town's main street, of all places.

"Know for the rest of your days…" the stout woman shouted down the dusty, busy street as Joshua faced her wide-eyed, smirking… and drunk "…whether dead or alive, Joshua McKinney, you will always a-wander for the touch of feminine flesh."

The town people who reported witnessing the incident that day told of Mama Bell turning on her ample heels while Joshua called after her a choice few phrases no church-going woman could repeat, then stumbled back to the local tavern to continue his second favorite activity. This drinking soon killed Joshua, though, for not a full year later the man died from an imploded liver. His age notwithstanding, the pure rot gut potato whiskey the man could only ever afford, his less than nutritious eating habits, and the constant barrage of hard labor (when he did labor) killed young Joshua but quick to no one's grief.

Buried in a potters' field a week later, it was then that the true infamy of 'Brother Ed' began.

To the horror of a pair of gravediggers, Joshua McKinney split open the top of his coffin as it was being lowered! Puking the most horrific cry ever heard by the two shocked men, the suffering corpse sauntered off, flaying into the night, now following well the old Creole curse coursing through him. As most of the townsfolk remembered well that fateful day Mama Bell had confronted Joshua, it was simply assumed the dead man was up and walking to quench his never-to-be-satiated, cursed lust.

It was decided by those who decide such things that Joshua McKinney should be found and his body burned to avoid any further wandering by the unfortunate dead man.

A posse was assembled. But there was an enterprising duo, Hap Seasons and his only son Brady, who lit out a day before the search party. Hap and his son were about done with their time in this not-good-for-even-one-horse town and were looking for an opportunity to light out for pastures west. The older man had seen his time in circuses when he was younger and now, his wife dead, the motherless boy and widowed dad were aching to put dad's old carnie know-how to work. What could an honest-to-goodness zombie fetch on the tent-show circuit, Hap wondered?! Hap had a cousin who could probably help set-up the show and fetch the father and son team a pretty penny.

But first, the men had to find the suffering cursed corpse of Joshua Ed McKinney and do so in a day's time.

***

Although The Wizard was the age he was, he still managed to shimmy Ed's light, brittle body to the door of the shed. Just beyond, in the carnie's home trailer— the permanent one he kept here in California, not the one he used to drag behind his truck when his carnival was traveling the byways of America—a bright-eyed seventeen-year-old girl squirmed on The Wizard's immaculate bedspread. As The Wizard opened the single thin metal door of the shed, he didn't smell it. But he knew Brother Ed certainly could; the pheromone rush from that squirming scared girl wafting clear across the backyard lot to them.

"First one's on me ol' friend," The Wizard said holding both the single door wide and Brother Ed's left stretched bicep. If not for the red flannel shirt it might have been impossible for the old carnie to hold to, let alone find any muscle in the desiccated, leathery covering that was Brother Ed's skin.

"Go 'head," the man said and smiled across to the grimacing sunken face of the dead man in his arms. "Go 'head," he repeated releasing his hold on his ancient charge.

For a fleeting few seconds, The Wizard feared his old friend was going to teeter back into him, but then the slightest shimmer passed through that rail-thin reed of a corpse, and Brother Ed was standing on his own, all in for the game.

***

The Seasons men made Willard's Eve that very night. Although there were two towns on a direct path from the potter's field, Willard's had the distinction of being the only one to house a whorehouse. In fact, father Seasons had recently brought his son Brady to the red brick building only two doors down from the bank, to deflower the sixteen-year-old boy. It was possible that Joshua had simply fallen out, and was rotting someplace in the hilly and dry country between Willard's and that lonely potter's field or he could be laying down with a sow, not being able to distinguish species only gender. But the Seasons men, like the posse behind them, believed Mamma Lee's old curse was working well. If Joshua Ed McKinney were destined to seek female company he would have to be led right to the "Purple Parrot" and the fine ladies within.

As Brady would explain years after they had made their fortunes and sold 'Brother Ed': "My daddy said the man was being led by his Johnson, more than most. Those ugly old whores had him if anybody did!"

No sooner had the men arrived in town then they heard the screams from the house of ill repute. Luckily, the local sheriff was none too hurried to visit the local eyesore and the minutes it took for him to finally get his large self into his shirt sleeves and suspenders, Brady and his dad barged in, bid helloes to the Madame they had only just visited a month before and walked right down the hallway to room number four.

"Damnedest thing I'd ever seen…" Brady continued his account. "…there was Blue-Eyed Molly, nice and big boned as she was, half-dressed with Joshua pawing at her. She didn't seem as frightened—those ladies of the P.P. had seen their share—as she was simply humored! She screamed that the 'man' had snuck in through a window to simply lie down beside her as she was resting for what Molly assumed would be a busy Saturday night. Damn, she was busy a'right with that dead man rolling and huffin' next to her, the dirt from his grave staining her sheets more then what big Molly was used to them being stained with!"

The Seasons' men managed to spirit the zombie to their wagon, tying him tight in the back. It was a hell-ride Brady would later recall with unabashed horror mixed with glee; Joshua moaning and flapping as they drove west the entire night. Neither son nor father spoke about their prize until they were well over the state line and hiding out waiting for Hap's cousin to find them.

***

"She's the prettiest little thing," The Wizard was saying as he and Brother Ed executed the slow walk to the trailer.

The Wizard knew that as a man ages he needs more than just the sight and smell of a woman, he needs to consider her, pine for her a bit, anticipate her being there in a myriad of possible poses. Now no man was as old as old Brother Ed, so he needed this attention more than most, The Wizard reasoned. True, his old boss Preeson and those men who had kept Ed before him had probably not taken the time like this, but The Wizard had been Brother Ed's keeper longer than any of those men, and he had made a quiet fortune with the man: He owed him pure and simple, let the man have this walk now.

The Wizard didn't even especially mind disposing of the bodies as he had all these long years. Like giving Ed his 'walk,' The Wizard had come to see his part in all of this and was proud of what he provided. Shit, the stuff he had seen in the carnie life, a few dead bodies didn't pay him any mind at all. It was the least The Wizard could do for his best friend.

"I think she's Mexican if I'm not mistaken," the old carnie whispered. "You know how much fire they have."

It was at times like these, the heat finally waning under the full midnight moon of a July night that The Wizard felt, sensed even, telepathy from the man plodding next to him. He never had, nor would he ever expect a reply, that was simply too much to ask. Brother Ed was dead, after all, but the old carnie just knew his words were getting through, knew he was understood and somehow felt silent acknowledgment. Let's face it, there were very few folks left in 'the show' anymore, and certainly none as old as The Wizard or as odd as Brother Ed. If these two men couldn't have a kinship, and unspoken communication, who could, The Wizard wondered?

***

'The Wizard' was Arny Ullman when he first saw 'Brother Ed' enter the carnival he was working the summer of 1922. Ed had just come under the care of Arny's boss, an enterprising amateur magician and professional con artist named Robert Preeson. While not exactly sure what Ed was, the lanky Preeson did know a potential moneymaking opportunity when he saw one, 'buying' Ed from Hap and his cousin when their battered and broke tent-show carnival passed through the orange groves of a pre-Hollywood L.A. Robert had seen plenty gimmicks in his time-quite a few he perpetrated himself in his rusty stage act-so the weathered body was an oddity but not so much to dissuade the budding entrepreneur. But when he was told there was indeed no gimmick, that Ed was an honest-to-goodness animated dead man, Robert couldn't have been happier with his purchase. Furthermore, much to Robert's wonder and amusement, Ed's priapismic pride still seemed intact as he rolled, moaned, and walked to every pretty woman who passed by him to the horror of onlookers and delight to the man who owned him.

Dead men do not make the best of lovers, but they can grope, slobber and shuck themselves at legions of paying ladies and their titillated mates. Brother Ed would spend his days quiet, dead as he was, until nighttime when his coffin was opened to the full view of a tent-show audience who had paid well to view him. With the whiff of perfume

on the air, or the sound of light tittering laughter, Ed would begin to stutter and shake in his coffin and in no time would be lunging forward to the lip of the stage for the women in the audience he had been cursed to hunger for. Whether the audience knew exactly what they were witnessing—who knew and who cared—Brother Ed was an honest-to-goodness money maker!

Robert had learned from the Seasons' men and his own time with him that all Ed needed was to take a little 'taste' from time to time. If the poor man's lusts were satiated Brother, Ed could be counted on to never venture far even on his nights off. All that was ever needed, as Hap and his son had told an entranced Mr. Preeson, was for a willing lady to be procured from time to time. Nothing as perverse as copulation had to be even attempted, ol' Ed was content to just lie down next to a lady for a few minutes, maybe have a friction if possible.

It was a simple thing to ask, really.

Robert Preeson, as had the Season men before him, began to scour the local whorehouses wherever his carnival happened to stop, buying Ed local prostitutes or any woman really who could be convinced for a few pieces of silver to spend time with the man in the box. It was a creepy request to be sure, but as the Season men had, Preeson merely convinced the women that this was his particular fetish, which in a way it was. He had a dummy for his show that he liked to see bedded down with a real live lady. Most women agreed, especially for the handsome Preeson, but found they had allowed more than they could have ever bargained for when the dummy they lay next to began to rub himself against them! One lady even stayed long enough to have

Brother Ed reveal his now withered, yet still considerable cock to the side of her leg and begin humping her thigh like a Border collie!

***

The light from the trailer shone down on the ancient friends. To the uninitiated, out here in the wash of high moonlight, it would seem as though two very old men were standing, admiring the abundance of stars in the southern California night. It would take a closer inspection to realize the condition of the thinner man, the pallor of his face and his leathery sunken looks, the cobalt dead-fly stare of his open eyes.

Brother Ed had never really gone to rot. Sure, he was a 105-year-old corpse, his flagging skin had peeled pretty much to leather and what hair remained on the man's head, though unusually thick and shiny given the state he was in, grew to the consistency of straw. But his body was so well preserved one would believe the man was just recently deceased. True, Ed had been embalmed but still a body would never keep as well as Ed had if not for some other element in the mix… mainly the mojo of Mama Bell's spell those many years ago. The old half-gypsy woman truly was determined to have Joshua McKinney wander the backwoods and alleyways searching, so his body had stayed pretty much intact.

Less one ever doubt ancient Creole magic and the animus of a woman who has felt her daughter abused.

"Give a look," The Wizard said, standing then with Brother Ed at his bathroom window.

Through it, they could see the bathroom door, left ajar by The Wizard only a half hour before. Beyond the doorway, lying on the bed, tied and gagged, was a brown-skinned girl, naked save for the red bandana The Wizard had bidden her wear after he paid her the requisite hundred dollars for what the waitress assumed would be this old man's quick fun.

Jeanne was not a working girl, far from it, but she'd let an ancient harmless man have his way if he bought her dinner (which he had), drove her around all night to bars and friend's houses (which he had), and begged her enough, for one hundred dollars, to "just strip and let an old man feast his eyes on what he used to be able to put his hands on." Sure, she'd tie the bandana around her neck. Fuck, Jimmy had never been this polite or sweet and he had taken a lot more from her, that's for sure. Maybe this was even a way she could make some extra cash; the guy seemed to have enough of it and, truth be told, she had always fancied herself pretty enough to be a model. Christ, she had the tits for it, and hers were at least real!

What the seventeen-year-old girl did not count on, though, was the old man's agility and his damn quick way with ropes.

***

In the second decade of the new century, a carnival such as Preeson's never stayed in one place too long. The stories about the odd man in the box and the ladies who met him retreated like so much locomotive steam as the popular carnival jumped from town to town. Business was good. As good as could be expected with movies an all-too-new and all-too-present booming entertainment. People still came out for the brittle romance of a carnival passing through town.

Counting ragged receipts was one thing for the prematurely graying magician, but despite the good money, Preeson began to tire of procuring lovelies for Ed. Of all things, the carnie owner was jealous. Jealous that his once ashen, slightly mysterious looks had gone to seed with the tensions of running his enterprise and jealous of how women were now demanding more money for his odd 'request.' These ladies, some not even prostitutes, would barely ever even bat an eye his way unless more silver was forthcoming.

In his roiling rage, soon Preeson was allowing the unthinkable… the very thing the Seasons warned could never pass.

Preeson began to let Brother Ed out on his own.

While no lady was hurt during Ed's midnight wanderings and he'd usually be content to trawl only once or twice a week, Preeson still turned a mighty blind eye to the idea of a sex-cursed zombie walking into the latest town to steal some time with an underage lass or a budding bride-to-be. Rumors abounded, stories followed, there was even once a reporter who managed to catch up with them in Oregon, but Preeson managed to dissuade actual fact into innuendo so he could spend the few days with his carnival, bilk the marks for as much as possible, then be on his way as the story of 'the man who visited' became part of the folklore; a maybe-it-was, maybe-it-couldn't-be fright time story one would tell their children as they walked the midway or made their way back home.

This was how things flowed from Preeson's jaded black disposition and ennui until he sold the carnival and all its possessions to Arny "The Little Wizard" as his last bequeathed request to his best worker, in that dusty hellhole season of '48. Arny took to Brother Ed as he did the acquisition of the rest of his old boss's carnival, dropped the 'Little' from his name and Brother Ed soon had a new owner and friend.

The Wizard came to understand and subsequently sympathize with his new, most famous charge more then the men who had owned Brother Ed ever could. The Seasons' men had brought prostitutes and joked as Brother Ed took his need, Preeson grew resentful, too horny for his own good and let the zombie loose on his own, but The Wizard felt a kinship to Ed. He knew he owed it to this 'man,' his alter ego, to provide the best he could on the special nights when the moon was full, and The Wizard could take his time to find a lady.

And while prostitutes would suffice, 'real' women, not those in the show were what The Wizard wanted for his best friend.

Of course, there was simply no way a woman who had been tied down, forced to copulate with a zombie wouldn't tell her tale. But with his skill with ropes, his still flexible sinewy muscles, and carnie wit, The Wizard found he could procure women about as easily as he could dispose of them. Even with those who managed out of the bonds from time to time (usually after Brother Ed had had his way), The Wizard was there to dispose of a flailing, running girl before she got past his trailer door.

When The Wizard stopped to consider the amount of women he and Ed had procured and subsequently disposed of during their travels, he matched himself against some of the best serial killers this country had ever seen, though his reasons for killing were purely utilitarian.

With Brother Ed, satiated—at least for that month—Arny could sleep contentedly, knowing he had provided his cursed partner with the very best he could afford and allow. Sure, he would have loved to have done more for Brother Ed, but it seemed that as the years slowed The Wizard down they had also slowed the curse in Joshua

McKinney; one woman a month seemed enough for him now.

***

They came to the front door of the trailer, these two old men. One dead, one close enough he smelled of it. The Wizard opened the door for the zombie shuddering next to him, the single stone step challenging most of Brother Ed's brittle resolve. But for what lie within, scared and unknowing on The Wizard's bed, the zombie would muster the strength. He had done so all these decades on the nights of the first full moon as he would continue to do until no one came for him anymore, to open his box. The Wizard practically beamed as he stood in the doorway, watching the achingly slow progression of his friend, executing tight paper steps down the hallway to the woman-child who lay beyond.

This was truly the very best part of the anticipation The Wizard knew, as he stood there in the hall, unzipped his fly, and released his now raging member. As old as he was, The Wizard would still sport quite the erection as these scenes unfolded. The girl began to thrash as she saw the bedroom door open even wider and assumed the old man's game was now afoot. Then there was that quick squeaky sensation of the bed moving, then muffled squeals, the bed rutting against the wood floor once again and the sensation of utter horror seeping through the walls as the girl tied to that bed saw Brother Ed and realized she would not be indulging The Wizard's need this night, but something quite a bit more sinister.

What the Wizard would love to know, but would go to his grave not knowing, was whether these women knew they were going to die? Did they think Brother Ed was The Wizard playing dead-man dress-up? Did they even conceive what it was that was bending down there to roll next to them? Could they even imagine what the next few minutes would be like? What exactly did that horror smell like as their sanity ripped from them with the impossibility of what was happening and had any of them truly ever realized what Brother Ed was?

Did they even ever see the flash of The Wizard's blade after the zombie got off them?

The Wizard imagined Brother Ed's movements as he heard his old bed groan with the added weight of the dead man. The living man grabbed his purple stump-of-a-cock and began pumping his fist wildly to what he imagined was happening in that room beyond. But The Wizard wasn't by himself for more than a minute when he felt a clutch across his chest. His eyes tearing, his left arm thumped his side as he heard a soft intake of female breath from his bedroom… then the old carnie fell dead from a massive heart attack.

***

"And this is where…" Benny said to the wind as Teresa Riner turned to him. "…nah forget it. Just one of those urban legends."

"Where what?" the pretty oval-faced blonde said.

With blue eyes that lustrous, Benny was hard pressed to ignore any request this woman made. And truth be told he had purposely taken this moment, here in the buzz and scrape of the bulldozers below, to entice the lady architect with some horrific folklore.

"Benny, we go back a long way," Teresa said. "You got some good gossip; you just got to spill it."

Truth be told, although Teresa's architectural firm had hired Benny's builders (that was actually the name of his contracting company, "Benny's Builders") for this very expensive and expansive condo site, the flaxen-haired woman had yet to be out here at the site. Now that she was, Teresa felt a strange chill she was damn sure did not emanate from the breeze blowing off the near ocean. She pulled her arms tight to herself, silently reveling in the fact that her covered yet ample cleavage pushed up at the handsome foreman facing her.

"The way I heard it," Benny said, leaning in so close the heat between the pair was palatable. For simply too many years Benny and Teresa's firm had worked together, and an attraction had always bubbled, unrequited, "there was an old trailer here, shed too I think, that the locals burned after that night."

"That night? What night?"

"The night that girl came runnin' out. The night they found the two old guys raping her," Benny said.

Involuntarily leaning even closer, the couple spied the progress of the machines and men down the hill from them. Mixed with Teresa's undetectable pheromone secretion was the sweet Oliva Bath Perfume she had added to her bath the night before. But that odd chill, just what was it exactly that was gnawing at the deepest pinpoint of her belly?

This combination of the woman's scents and reactions worked its unique spectrum of brightness though the stale smelling development on this California shore and down to the unknown grave, not three feet from where the man and woman stood close enough to shiver. Below, eight feet down just to be sure, now covered in concrete and mesh and a new condo water pipe system, lay a man who could smell Teresa's welcoming scent, even though he was in a box that had been provided by a shocked yet sympathetic populace.

That sad and cursed ancient man smiled to the possibility of a visit sometime in the future.

The Whispers from our Secret Archeological Remains

Roger Leatherwood

The air was as thick as menstrual blood. Arianna leaned back against the paneled wall in the dark, closing her eyes to try to block out the sounds of her roommate fucking, just on the other side. The sound came through the dark wood like drumbeats, heavy fists on tight canvas, booming counterpoint to the thick rain outside.

The guy, whoever it was, probably not older but instead just a student, even an entering sophomore because Arianna knew Brit's tastes, for his energy pounding vibrated the thin paneling off its mounting glue, was pushing her with desperate grunts against the couch on the other side of the wall. Brit's face and head must be kissing the wall in oppressive thrusts. Whoever she had in there, Arianna dreamed, must be slamming into her not like an older experienced professor or husband of some clueless wife, not sliding his erection into the tender ripe love tunnel of a lithe pale coed over the break, but instead rutting like the mating ritual of two possessed rams, large pieces of hairy meat slapping against the rounded rumps of each other in rude violence, the mindless targets of each other's ardor.

Arianna closed her eyes tight and clenched her fists, her final paper still distracting her as her thoughts moved to more physical needs. Yet her ears were open and soon she couldn't control her hands. One pushed up on her heavy breasts constricting them and teasing the nerves firing in a spiral around her areolas, tightening and causing her nipples to erect. The other hand slipped down and pushed her cotton boy shorts, red and tattooed with an iron-on of ASM (for Alpha Sigma Mu) in Greek letters, down the top of her thighs, exposing the thick hair of her pussy to the smoky cool air.

It was late and not nearly quiet enough. Her back hardened against the grain of the paneling, as if she was trying to absorb the rhythm on the other side as that anonymous sophomore banged and bruised Brit's tender reproductive organs. Arianna's fingers split the lips freed from her panties and a thin red paste lubricated her fingers from her slit. She was still on her period, near the end and the flow waning, but it still made her inner cunt warm and wet and sliding against itself with each long-legged step. God she got so horny at the end of her period and once, just once wondered what it would be like to have some guy to fuck the shit out of her while she was still bleeding, horny and sloppy and rank. Leaking with her piss fluids overcome with abandon.

She always thought lovemaking would be like a whisper. The gentle brush of skin on skin. For now, the vibrations from the other room satisfied her lust. Some hairy nineteen-year-old humping against Brit's raised rear end. Red and swollen by now, certainly, for Arianna knew that Brit was also on her period. Everyone in the sorority had gotten their cycles synced month to month the way women did when they lived in close proximity to each other, their hormones sensitive and fluxing with the other throbbing ovaries as they dined and drank together, went to bed at the same time, woke up and shared the showers, watched late night movies and peed one after another and whispered secret confessions, even sometimes shared boyfriends.

God, sometimes the stink in the house was hair-raisingly ripe. Dripping. Brit was unaware of the noise she was making - or was she intentionally broadcasting her animalistic monthly ritual through the house as the clock passed 11 o'clock, passing towards minutes after? When the heat was settling in the floorboards and cupboards, the candles on the kitchen counters shone mandalas of light through the still cool air from the rain outside. Arianna saw her own swollen flesh in the candlelight slick with her sweat.

She raised her own temperature by stimulating her swollen clit with gentle jabs up and down. She had no sense of the minutes passing. She could be doing this for 5 minutes or kill the whole afternoon if something didn't distract her back to the real world. The candle smoke scented with hints of oaky merlot (the dark ones along the wet bar Sylvana had bought), or something called Rosemary Cicada along the outer window, filled the dark corners just off the kitchen. Arianna stood at the doorway, the only one else up this late; there were 3 or 4 other girls still there in the house over the Christmas break but they were in bed. Arianna had been working on her archeology project at the table near the sliding door that opened out into the hillside behind the sorority. The dark rain had kept her distracted until she heard the sounds of Brit's moaning and pounding.

The light flickered off the beaded leaded windows and splintered in sharp designs. Plastic red cups and wine glasses were stacked at the sink. Arianna smelled the thick smell of cum and menstruation on her fingers and sunk her fingers deeper in. The nub of her clitoris swelled and began to poke out as she twisted and squeezed the fleshy ball expertly between thumb and forefinger. A quiet splooshy *shrripa-shrripa-shrripa* sound whispered between her legs.

Outside the yard yawned and tilted with a groan that the rain blanketed in one last wash. As the water thinned and stopped falling suddenly a subterranean tremor below the topsoil, not reaching or quite cracking the surface, rumbled the lawn and shifted the dirt, burying roots with a vibration that echoed Brit's humping in the den, a spasm that didn't quite reach the house.

The rolling hills up into the black were pockmarked with the loose piers from a missing chain link fence that stuck rudely in concrete sockets. Water dripped from the corners of the eaves and knuckles of the branches of denuded trees. The air was thick with anticipation. A pause in the weather, of stalled activity, of time held in high tension. Her loins tingled and each spasm was a wet invitation to fill what was already evacuating the bloody remnants of last month's unappreciated fertility.

Arianna looked out at the wet yard, lit by the unseen moon and lights mounted on unreinforced posts. She spread her legs and looked down at her panties, wound in a cord and stretched across her thighs. Her pad was folded and damp with her red. She'd have to change it when she was done, once she made it to orgasm before midnight.

She liked writing at night. She welcomed the dark and the quiet introspection it evoked. It put her in the mood of fairy tales and ancient myths, and as a graduate student in anthropology studying regional splinters of certain religious practices she could sense the subconscious connection to the spiritual soul. It helped her chart and formulate her theories about ancient worships.

As elsewhere, the cults in the backwoods of Pennsylvania, here in the east of the Wilkes-Barre forests and north of the Shroudsburg coal region, remained isolated, sometimes for generations. A place cobwebbed with overgrown and uncharted paths, abandoned by the settlers when the area went too native to mine. No one wrote their practices down or filmed their ceremonies. Often technologically undeveloped, without phones or reading, even inbred and backwards in this day and age. And yet so close to civilized society. Arianna's thesis, "Regional Para-religious Rituals in the Appalachian Backwoods and New England at the Turn of the 19th Century And Undocumented Seismic Emanations of Natural Phenomena As it Relates to Increased or Altered Sexual Behavior, Social Oppression and Evidence - An Investigation" - what a mouth full of cock - had been a frustrating search for gossip, whispered evidence of feuds and long-dead leads. Mr. Madaba kept telling her, don't be like the other students; apply yourself!

No wonder Arianna needed to let off some frustration by masturbating, it seemed almost every night. People tried to find sense in a world that had no sense. Like all religious pursuits seemed to do. Create order from chaos.

Indeed, the people in these parts were truly alone. Arianne and the girls here in the house surrounded by heavy weather at the cusp of winter break, a dark wooden structure built as a canvas tanning shop decades before 1880, was little different. The candles gave it a dark wilderness feeling that Arianna always thought had a witchy Halloween vibe during the solstice.

As if that weren't enough to make people a little more primitive, when the periods kicked in at Alpha Sigma Mu the horniness was so thick it could be cut with a knife. It wasn't uncommon to turn the corner and find one of your sorority sisters leaning against the tub with a large glass dildo or the handle of her hairbrush up her cunt trying to give herself relief in the thick atmosphere of coeds, fertility and youthful sex drives. During Christmas break they'd all go home for the holidays and their cycles would drift and go out of sync, but by March all eight girls would be back menstruating at the same time. The smell in the rooms and the perfume coming from the ass of the girl right ahead of you, the randy conversations that were blurted in drunken secret, the single drips of blood on the porcelain floor, and a line of soaking hand-washed panties hanging on the shower rods in the morning were common occurrences.

Sometimes, as Brit demonstrated, it didn't matter if they were on their period - she had to get some cock. Guess that sophomore didn't care either. And there was no need to use birth control then, only to cover the couch with a towel or spend the next morning washing the cum and blood stains.

With winter solstice, it had been getting dark earlier. Arianna planned to stay over through the break to finish her anthro' paper. She was looking forward to being alone in the house for the month, staying in, staying dry. Well, dry in terms of the weather. She would be playing with herself in the front room, her legs open and completely nude in full view of the front windows that faced the street, visible to no one since foot traffic was so light during the holidays. (She remembered the time she'd been fingering her hairy pussy one morning after everyone left for class and the Mexican gardener had been standing out there the whole time with a week whacker in one hand and his cock in the other.)

The air filled with warm acrid smoke. She wanted to step out, get a breath of night air away from the hot sweaty grunts of Brit's infertile mating, the heathen coupling without chance of procreation. Her cries were more 'urrgggh' than 'ahhh!' Pain as much as pleasure. Arianna slid open the glass panel to the wild field behind them. The wet ground outside prevented her from going out but the rain had stopped, even as the storm could be felt in the air, lingering in the far distance. The air seemed supersaturated with warm electricity.

A large sinkhole on the hill oozed a black oily residue, worked on by the gardener and a construction crew last summer and they put some peat moss into it but the hole had seemed bottomless. Every winter it opened up again, like a recurring cycle, wider and slicker. The shifting earth pushed strange rotting pieces of green stiff kindling out of the bottom lips of the hole. When it got wet it made clicking noises, like a dead cat's frozen fur being pulled from ice it had gotten stuck into. A sharp tinkling like broken glass and fingernails.

They'd have to get the facilities guys from campus up here to Alpha Sigma Mu again in the spring.

The whole area was wilderness with only a sprinkling of civilization laid over. The settler tribes here, according to her research, disappeared without trace. Regional rituals, quaint and hidden and unknown, always seemed to end up being mirrored by someone else somewhere in the world. If all those people who believed in the same things ever found each other and joined together, what a revolution that could be.

As her orgasm built within her, her thoughts turned from her anthropology project to her anthropology teacher, from impressing him to fucking him. Thoughts of the handsome and dark-skinned Mr. Madaba - was he Egyptian or from somewhere in the ancient quadrant of humanity's birth? How fitting. She was still struggling with the class and he always corrected her when she misspoke embarrassing her in front of everyone. Once she said "anthropological dig" instead of "archeological dig" and Mr. Madaba shot back "Archeology and anthropology are two different things; one is about the earth's secrets and one is about yours!" She also tripped over the term "cranial cavity" and said "anal activity" - while all the others giggled Mr. Madaba merely glowered.

She got so tongue-tied, mostly fantasizing about getting bent over his desk after class to be taught how to apply herself, once and for all, to show her how hard his job was, how hard his cock was, ask her to become his assistant, do his dirty work, suck his cock under his desk, offer her asshole to his dark thick cock, grade his papers.

How his body must look as he pulled up his pressed cotton shirts and down his tight jockeys to expose his firm muscles and rippling skin - thoughts that fueled Arianna's fingers inside her love crevice, although it was impossible!

Her rhythm and the deepness of her slickened fingers, the wetness as her hand slide in and up, almost to her palm, got her off. She'd apply herself all right - to her clitoris, open and throbbing and framed by sopping pubic hair.

Sylvana came down just then, still dressed but looking ready for bed. Arianna saw that her camisole on over her breasts showed her nipples poking in the fabric indicating there was no bra underneath, and tight denim shorts that were cut off at her crotch. They showed off Sylvana's legs as high as they could, emphasizing her teasing thigh gap.

Arianna was too horny to move from her stance, and stayed against the wall with her hand halfway into her cunt, slimy and pink.

"I couldn't sleep either," Sylvana slurred, "but then I just woke up like I'd been sleeping for hours. Is it really after 11?" It was 11:11 exactly. She smiled at her, seeing her pussy open and swollen. A warm sensation overtook her, although the air was still and thick. Wanting to push into her and beg her to take her as well.

"Jesus, you're on your period too?" Sylvana went to the fridge to pour a drink. "I get some guy lined up and then when we're going out and fuck here comes the cardinal. I love getting the pussy licked but I just end up giving blowjobs."

Sylvana poured three fat fingers of wine and downed it in one gulp. Putting the glass down she knocked over one of the candles.

"Shit. Sorry."

"Don't worry, I'll be done in a minute."

Sylvana laughed at that. "Don't hurry on my account. You like the light?" Arianna spread her legs a little more widely, letting Sylvana's gaze whisper across the lurid display of her masturbated cunt.

Arianna sighed. "Too bad we're not alone." She nodded in the direction of Brit in the other room. "Who's she got in there? She picking them up from the high school now?"

"God only knows. She was out cruising gay bars tonight! Some thrill. It doesn't sound like she picked up a fag though." Arianna nodded. "Hell, maybe she went to Engineer's."

Engineer's was the local tranny bar. Arianna understood the attraction Brit would have to a transsexual, those deceptive creatures without sure identify, soft around the edges but hard in all the right places. Being able to mix her spilling blood with no risk, a ritual of physical need, divorced from biological result except dumb hormonal urgency. When the lesbian activities around here were not enough, it was an avenue for more exploration, a way to get off with new alien flesh without the bother of sperm, without the bother of a real boyfriend.

And sparks fell from sky, an emission from the passed storm, chemicals forming with the electricity of the weather, the moon passing over the sea and the salt mingled with the blood of a dog that has recently spilled in the furrows of the grass.

They fingered each other - Arianna and Sylvana rumbled their fingers in both bloody creases. The earth scent of eucalyptus rose from Arianna's gash; Sylvana tasted on her fingers the pungent wine like garlic and warm sardines. Pink foam lubricated her fingers as she rubbed them over the marble nub at the heart of Sylvana's shaved and carefully plucked inguinal crease, hidden under her jeans.

Drips and saliva mixed in the murky water along the oil outside. Lightening without rain. There was a noise in the bushes, and the trees withered.

"What's that?" Arianna grabbed Sylvana's wrist at her pussy, stilling it but not pushing her away - yet. The temperature raised 5 degrees, and the air sucked out of the kitchen. Lights flickered outside and then the ground came alive.

The movements of the wind in the low weeds, the waving switches with pale thin leaves, they swirled in a disembodied movement and Arianna saw it was not wind, it was things.

There was something out there! Little wet woody nymphs. Dozens of them! She could make out yellow pale creatures running without feet through the wet sod.

"The hell!"

"Are those - dogs... or...?"

"What are those?"

And they were upon them like velvet hands in a carwash. The things flowed through the open glass, more like snickering dust devils, blown willow fronds that surrounded Arianna and Sylvana at their ankles. Wet and they clung.

"Arrlll!" Sylvana fainted, gasping all the breath she could and falling against the counter.

Arianna pulled up her panties and ran to the window door. She was wet and still throbbing.

The slick things stayed just out of sight, could not quite be seen. She couldn't focus on them really, her mind feeling dulled like milky whiskey. It was the late hour; or it was the sex. All the blood had rushed to her vaginal walls and clit and she felt woozy. The yellow children blew through the hot smoke like scarves, supported by invisible wire frames. She felt fingers going up her thighs and she looked over at Sylvana, keeping her grip, keeping her cool.

"Sylvana you have to wake up!"

She was at the open window, being pulled out onto the grass.

Leaning just inside. Taken over. The children surrounding her, they were everywhere. The window was still open. The window was closed but it still felt open. Arianna felt like she was with a crowd. She felt surrounded.

There's so many of them! she said to no one. The smell of wet felt. Of burning hair. Not fingers so much as the heat of bodies nearby.

A crowded stadium. I'm not alone. She felt heavy.

This was normal, Arianna thought. I'm heady, it's late and I'm drunk, a kind of mass delusion. She watched Sylvana disappear in her own drunk delusion into the dark finger weeds outside. She knew this, in special circumstances, the bad weather, her blood pressure and what food she'd eaten. I just need to sleep.

Brit came out around the corner, stark naked. Her left breast was red, the outline of an open hand on it suggesting it had been the steel-grip handle for her fuckbuddy. A rope of cum dripped from her inner thigh.

"The fuck? You guys are up making so much noise--"

Arianna noticed her beautiful dark skin. She also had no hair on her pussy, being shaved as well as Sylvana. Her boobs sagged as if stretched from wear. She was sweating, seemingly exhausted.

"What…?"

And it hit her too. Her eyes rolled into her head. As if in the frenzy of orgasm, she began spasming. Oh, god, it's got her too. Where are they coming from? Candles fell, spilling sticky wax on the tiles. Her arms shook and she held her stomach.

"Brit! Don't let them get in!"

The minions, Arianna thought of them that way now for that was what they were, came out again and they were suddenly in the walls. Small ghosts surrounding them, passing through the doors, like ferns with teeth, wet and opening my legs. To take her. Take me, yes. To fall into the floor with them. It was winter and the ground was so warm.

The ground. Arianna suddenly understood. The creatures were serving something else. Out there. Something in the wet oily alien ground.

Something was hungry and needed to be fed. It had taken over Sylvana, the others, the back woods, the very air. What had awoken it? How had it been raised?

The wet creature Shub-Niggurath was older than the sorority house, older than the tanning business that stood there before it. Older than the hills although it came to live here after being driven out of eleven other countries. A whisper of dark prophesy, known variously as Shub-n'gurath in broken tongues in the southern continents, or the Black Goat with a Thousand Young in places that had no spoken learning, the slippery sentient mushroom creature lived between the creases of two worlds, in the fold between the inner thigh of a third dimension and the stubbly pubic mound of an alternate sex dream. She was not raised. She was always here. She had been here 999 thousand years and reached the outer boundary of all humanity's imagination.

The girls' imaginations saw things in the dark that were not there, saw beyond horse-hair plaster and fiberglass walls to see what waited with infinite patience and could reach through to their inner need and desire. Without words the inhabitants of the house walked from their rooms to the open glass at the edge of the porch.

The guy that had been banging Brit in the TV room in a rhythm of ceremonial sacrifice walked out as well, also nude and acting drunk. His thin form was lit by the candle flame, slowly spreading across the green fiesta tiles around the sink. Skating on wine and wax. His chest had no hair and he had small breasts that where mere handfuls.

But he was feminine. His hair was short and in a dusty shag; his hips were rounded, smooth, curving in at the top of his pelvis. Arianna would have assumed he was a girl on first glance in this light, but for the long piece of penis flesh hanging from the patch of pubic hair between his legs. He was still hard and slick, otherwise she might indeed have been fooled, and perhaps he really was, as well or both.

His eyes glowed in the shadow, catching some flicker from the candles. In the dark she saw no testicles at his crotch. Possibly already deballed if in transition.

"This is Chet," Brit half-smiled, holding up her hand in a closed fist. Or he was perfect in his state, halfway to everywhere. His eyes, they seemed to coalesce in his sockets then and become normal, except they were skewed sideways, twisting out of sync in their sockets. Like the inside of his head was twisted. It wasn't a glance, Arianna thought, but a possession.

She screamed!

"The fuck!"

"Don't look in his eyes!"

Brit was now convulsing, her skin shivering with small personal tremors. The comingling with his sperm kept her the same way a virgin, unsullied by other seed, not yet knowing the pleasure of adulthood, of true passion, untouched and uncorrupted, would be. Clean and untested. The tranny who couldn't father nor birth a child. The perfect open vessels for--

Some alien presence.

Some evil.

The house was not a safe place.

Outside Arianna felt her panties bunch in a wet knot at her cunt. The sinkhole formed flowed like water and she deepened the sense of something forming in the air, from above, from far off, from far ago. Deep in time deep in our unconscious.

Her hands opened. Wanting to let it in, to let it own me. But it already does.

Arianna might have been more susceptible. She knew how the power of suggestion, the power of night overtook people in isolated situations. You only knew what those around you told to you. Yet these other girls, the other ravaged ASM girls, had not participated in any intentional rituals or sacrifices, only in the mindless habits of the young and horny, unaware of and unconcerned with the darker consequences.

It had been ready for anything. The presence had just the right combination of lost souls, weather, opportunity and hunger.

The creature in the dark cloud above dropped closer, opening its tentacle'd wombs. It did not call itself by any name. It was known in darker histories far north as Shub-Niggurath. Iä! Shub-Niggurath! Arianna began to yell yet couldn't help watch as Sylvana's shape disappeared into the womb, into the dark wet endless singularity of fecund living earth.

Whispers. Clear as day and inside her head. You want me. She completely understood this was not a taking over, it was a homecoming.

Brit had gotten a rake or something - a sharp objects leaning against the patio concrete and was trying to rake it against the wind that filled her mind, the yellow horde that filled the air. "Bastards! Leave him alone!"

And Arianna saw, even as she blindly swung and clawed, blindly because her eyes were blue - and milky - and opaque like oysters - she was cumming. Her thighs shook in an open-mouthed orgasm. Chet, whatever he was, embraced her from behind holding her up, rubbing his cock/her cock against the lower opening of her naked ass crack. She received as she fought, fertile and mindless.

Shub-Niggurath drank of their souls

It subsumed their presence. She was not aggressive, it only waited to nurture, in hiding like a wet braying cow mother, knowing the children would eventually pass through the veil where they keep away from the dark side but constantly glanced over in teasing curiosity before finally coming back to the nest where they were freed and comforted at last.

Brit held the stiffening penis of Chet and stepped closer. He walked being led by his female cock, by Brit with pale thighs and purpose into the undulating vines and 1000 fingers. Chet's face cracked with a smile lined with small perfect teeth and a widening jaw. In the dark ahead smoky tentacles and a black fog of smoke, and blood, and a prick of singed hair clogged their noses like dull thumbs. Arianna pulled at Brit's arm, pulling her back from something that was not there. Something ahead but not reaching for her. Yet was already behind them.

Arianna looked past her but could not get her eye on anything. The slippery mother goat lay ahead but unseen, as if lurking in the periphery of her vision even though she was staring right at it.

It was sucking them in. Brit was the one who was most out of control, the one who brought trannies picked up in Hollywood home to fuck her while she was on the rag, fuck the risks or the possibility he/she'd been sucking off diseased faggots in alleys all year, been butt-raped in prison after being picked up for hustling on the streets of nearby Shroudsburg. Brit embraced the dark potential of her own immorality and reveled in it (and tried to talk the others into joining her more than once). Arianna had only let Brit finger her and give her a short hour of cunnilingus once one afternoon. She'd wanted to know what it would feel like, what a girl who knew how it worked down there could make her cum, just in case one day a guy had the nerve to go down on her. Arianna just wanted to know what she was missing by leaving those boys on the doorstep instead of joining them in the backseats of their cars, like Sylvana said. She'd never ask one to go down on her and never felt comfortable pulling off her pants in the dark parked somewhere.

It was barely enough when she pulled their members out of their unzipped pants and gave them only tentative licks. She was amazed at how quickly guys came with a little oral stimulation. She hadn't understood until Brit had given her a good licking and fingering that afternoon and she'd cum explosively onto her face and open hungry mouth.

Now Brit was the one to be sacrificed. Arianna tried to pull her back from her revelry as the wind flurried leaves and sharp nail points up and around her thighs and buttocks. "Brit, wake up! Resist!" Brit looked but her eyes now were as bland and milky as Chet's had been. It has her.

"You listened to the whispering! You were wide open! You invited her - that! - in!"

Shub-Niggurath owned her. Arianna knew that the balance of power was in her immortal hands, not in Brit's. Even as the minions surrounding them trashed her clit and fingered her cunt, entering with invisible sharp knobs and stiff wet ticklers Arianna knew Brit was gone, always the slut more into the cock than to her own morality and was leading them, looking, dripping and spreading in a night in which no time passed, her fingers at her wet bloody crease again that teased and winked and attracted them, a sluice of your fingers and to our eyes.

Arianna let her legs open. Take the tentacles, own them, the fingers of a faith that had already been accepted and only needed their admission. She had not technically been a virgin, fingers and dildos and the top of a Heineken and Brit's first two fingers and even that hairbrush handle had all been inside her cunt high and vigorous enough to make her experience close enough so she knew what she'd be feeling when a real cock finally entered her with throbbing promise.

Arianna realized that Brit was only the bait and that the Goat-thing, the wet slip that was Shub-Niggurath that slipped into and covered her brain was fucking her from the inside and Arianna could do nothing but let her and to fuck her back. Arianna melted in the helplessness of her own need.

And when she was taken she still felt it like it was the first time.

324

Graveyard Patrol

Vincent Treewell

I had been a deputy sheriff just over ten years when I ended up with the glamorous assignment of patrolling the county cemetery. That was not an accident. I was fresh off of a suspension for excessive force that had cost the county well more than they cared to pay in settling a lawsuit. On paper, I was guilty. But I didn't feel particularly guilty. I had responded to a fairly normal domestic violence complaint in the trailer park near the airport. I separated the couple and waited for back up to arrive. It was pretty obvious what had happened. The guy had broken his girlfriend's nose, blackened her eye, and left abrasions all over her face and neck. Once my partner got there, I arrested the suspect, but everything was by the book.

But then, as I was patting him down, he looked me right in the eye and sneered, "I'll be out tomorrow, the bitch wouldn't dare testify against me." I kind of lost it for a moment. I drove my knee into his groin as hard as I could. That folded him up, and I began punching him in the head and shoulders. I grabbed him by the throat and threw him down the small stairway at the front of the mobile home. He landed on his knees and I kicked a field-goal in his ass. He tumbled over and then started to get up. I swept his leg out from under him. He scrambled around to face me. I kicked him in the chin with my heavy-duty work boot, dislocating his jaw. Right at that moment, my partner grabbed me from behind in a full-nelson shouting, "Goddamn it, Witkowski, you're gonna kill him!"

The suspect had fallen back to the ground and was now whimpering in pain. That was when my supervisor showed up. I was sent back to the station and told to start writing a report, "and it better be good enough to help you keep your job!"

Apparently, it was. The suspect was a douchebag with a lengthy record, and he wasn't hurt that bad. Much as he predicted, the victim didn't show up to testify against him, but he was on probation, so his officer revoked him and he ended up doing about two months. Which is right about how long I sat on desk duty being investigated for excessive force. She did find the courage to testify against me for beating up her boyfriend. The official final result was that I had made bad decisions and needed to learn to relate to the public. I was suspended two weeks without pay and sent through remedial training. The unofficial decision was that I was a hazard and needed to be buried somewhere that I wouldn't cause trouble.

Well, the county cemetery sure as hell fit that description. It was vast, as the county had been burying indigents and John Does there since before the Civil War. Approximately five square miles, it was a labyrinth of mostly unmarked service roads built in different eras to allow maintenance workers access to the many crypts and tombs.

The first night, Lieutenant Rick Myles called me aside and gave me my orders. He was a tall, slim guy with a pencil moustache. He always seemed to me like he belonged on a country club tennis court instead of a police station, but whatever. He seemed somewhat uncomfortable around me. I get that a lot. Even though he was a few inches taller, I probably had eighty pounds on him, and that was mostly solid. Plus, I just kind of look like a caveman. Even with my shaven head and face, it's just how I look.

Anyway, Lieutenant Myles was clear. Every evening I was to report to third shift roll call at Patrol Bureau headquarters, then sign out a marked squad car from the county garage, and drive directly to the cemetery. I was to patrol the cemetery grounds for the next seven-and-some-odd hours and then sign the car back in. I could be outside the grounds for thirty minutes to get lunch, but, and I quote, "nothing better happen, okay? I mean nothing. It would be smarter if you just packed your lunch, y'know?" I was not to leave the grounds, even to back up other deputies or respond to emergencies or any other reason unless ordered to by a supervisor. I got the message.

Actually, graveyard patrol was not a bad gig. I soon found it to be quite comfortable. After the first couple of weeks, I developed a nice, easy routine. By the time I had two months in, my stress level was probably the lowest since I became a cop. Management considered it a punishment, so I was happy to let them think that. I'm a loner, and I don't really get bored very often. I'd just go out every night, with my brown bag lunch packed, listen to some music, and slowly cruise around the cemetery.

That's what I was doing when I met her. Understand, when I was graveyard patrolling, I never saw anybody. Ever. Not even homeless people want to hang around the county cemetery. There is just nothing there. Plus, it's totally dark, I'm driving in the middle of the night, and I'm usually at least a mile from the entrance. So when I saw a young woman standing in the road flagging me down about 3:00 AM one night, it came as quite a surprise. My first thought was that the county mental hospital is a couple of miles away, but there had been nothing on the radio about an escape. I pulled over and shined my spotlight on her.

She was black. Not just African-American, but like jet black. And she was beautiful, disarmingly, intensely attractive. She had her hair done in thick cornrows. She had two pairs of hoop earrings in one ear, only one in the other, and a nose ring. She was dressed in a tight white t-shirt and what seemed like the scrub pants nurses wear. She had on flip-flop shoes. Her finger and toe nails were close cut and unpainted.

"Can I help you, Ma'am?" I asked.

"Yes, I need to report a crime. Can I get in your car?"

"Uhm, yeah, sure, hop in the passenger seat." I admit to being tongue-tied. I had scarcely talked to anyone at work for months. Plus, she was strikingly, hypnotically beautiful. "A-are you o-okay?"

"No, I'm really not okay." She slid into the seat beside me.

"W-what are you doing out here?"

"I'm always out here. I've seen you before. I just never spoke to you until now."

"Do you live around here?"

She chuckled bitterly. "This is where I stay."

"W-what was the crime you wanted to report?"

"I need to report a murder-mine."

"What do you mean?" Then her eyes locked with mine. That instant was the most intense, realest moment of my life.

"I think you know exactly what I mean, out here in the graveyard, in the middle of the night. I think you get the picture." And I did.

"How can I help?"

"My name was Tasha Wright. I was a dancer, and yeah, I hooked on the side sometimes. I was no angel. But a pimp named Lawrence "Big Money" Henderson beat me to death when I wouldn't work for him. I didn't deserve to die, especially not like that. I never got to say my goodbyes. I never got a funeral. I ended up on a slab at the county morgue and then dumped in a mass grave with the other Jane Does. They never even investigated enough to find out my name. There was no obituary, no announcement, no nothing. How am I supposed to rest? Where is my peace while the one who did this is out living it up?"

"What can I do?"

"You're a cop, aren't you?"

"Well, yeah, but…." She put her finger to my lips.

"I should have known. You're looking for some motivation, aren't you?" I opened my mouth to reply and she leaned over and kissed me on the lips. Her tongue slid into my mouth as she climbed across the seat and straddled me. Her mouth was soft, wet… and, just for a second, as cold as the grave.

There were a lot of things I should have done at that point. I did not do any of them. Instead, I had sex with her, in the squad car, in several different ways. I climaxed insanely hard. Then I drifted off for a moment.

When I awoke, the sun was rising and I had just enough time to get back to the county garage and sign the car back in before someone started looking for me. Tasha was gone, and I was not certain she had ever been there. I didn't know what had really happened. Had I fell asleep and had a dream? Was I losing my mind from isolation?

When I started work the next night, I used my squad car computer to look up Tasha Wright. There were a couple of entries: one bust for prostitution, one for retail theft, one for misdemeanor marijuana. Just as she said, no angel, but no one who deserved to die. She had nothing after three years ago. I also looked up Lawrence Henderson. It was a very different story: seven arrests for domestic violence, two of which resulted in conviction; heavy felony case for human trafficking that got plea bargained down to pandering/pimping; felony substantial battery dropped due to lack of victim cooperation, and conviction for felon in possession of firearm- currently on parole. "Big Money" liked to hurt women and he usually got away with it.

Of course, getting that information was a complete mindfuck. Because here I had official confirmation that what "Tasha" had told me was real. I could only have gotten those names from this apparition that I encountered in the cemetery in the middle of the night. And had sex with.

I drove around that night in turmoil, trying to get it all clear in my head. Then, I rounded a corner and saw a figure leaned up against a light pole, one of the few in the area. She casually stuck out her thumb like she was hitchhiking. I pulled over and rolled down the window.

"You goin' my way, Cowboy?" I popped the front passenger door and let Tasha in. "You been working my case?" she asked, sliding over next to me.

"Uh-yeah."

"So, you've checked some facts so you know I'm for real?"

"Yes."

"So when are you going to arrest Big Money for my murder?"

"Well, that's the thing, I'm gonna need proof to get a conviction…."

"He beat me to death in the back room of the Golden Lounge at 2:15 AM, two years, seven months, and five days ago. The only witness might be an old-timer named Virgil who was tending bar that night." She put her hand on my thigh. "But you're the cop, you figure it out. I'll just provide you the motivation to keep taking this serious." She undid my belt.

An hour later, I was in perfect peace, my arm slung around Tasha as I wove in and out of consciousness. But I had a plan.

That morning, I left the cemetery early. It's not like anyone was going to check. I drove to listed residence of Lawrence Henderson. I had called up his mug shots on the computer, so I could identify him. I parked the squad in front of his house and turned the flashers on. Then I walked up to the front door and knocked. Hard. "Yeah?" a groggy voice called out.

"Sheriff's department, open up!"

The door slowly unlocked and creaked open. A red-eyed and unhappy Lawrence Henderson stood in the entrance. He was a big dude, easily six' three plus, maybe 285 and solid. He stank of marijuana and booze. "Yeah?" he grunted.

"I'm doing parole compliance checks today, I'll need to look through your residence."

"Bullshit, cop. Where's my P.O., Mr. Fulton? You can't do no compliance check without the agent present." He was an experienced criminal, and he was technically right.

"Lawrence Henderson, I can personally observe the evidence of alcohol and marijuana use on your person. You are under arrest for violating the conditions of your parole. Turn around and place your hands behind your back."

"Man- fuck you! This is bullshit!" He was pissed, but he slowly turned and put his hands together. I cuffed him and walked him out to the car. As I drove him to jail, he calmed down and stared at me in the rear-view mirror with a calculating look. "Ok, Deputy? Can we cut the shit? I know damn well you ain't at my house at five AM to see if I've been drinking or smoking blunts. What is this really about? If you're looking for a pay-off, shit, maybe we can work something out."

"You beat Tasha Wright to death at the Golden Lounge two, almost three years ago."

Henderson froze. He averted his eyes. He went silent for a long moment. "Hey, fuck you. I don't know shit about any murder. And I want a lawyer, like now, before I say another goddamn thing."

I dumped Henderson off at the jail, made a quick call to his P.O.'s voicemail saying I arrested him for violating his conditions due to an anonymous civilian complaint, and lead-footed it over to the county garage to turn the car back in. I was late, but nobody really cared.

That night was my night off. But I did something I had never done before. I got in my own car, in jeans and a t-shirt, but with my gun and badge on just in case, and I drove into the county cemetery. There was no rational reason my actions. It was official. I was now acting crazy.

I didn't have to drive that far. There she was, leaning against the tall stone of one of the marked graves, smoking a cigarette. Tasha looked absolutely beautiful. "Beautiful" is too generic. She looked intoxicating, in every sense of the word. I could feel myself being drawn in, and there was not a damn thing I could, or even wanted, to do about it.

"Well, well, well, if isn't my hero," she said, leaning into my car window and exhaling a cloud of smoke onto me. Her full lips were half smile and half sneer. "Can I get in?" She registered my surprise. "No, really, I have to ask."

"Yes, of course, Tasha."

She climbed in the passenger side and slid over to me. Caressing my thigh, she extinguished her cigarette in my pristine ashtray. She nuzzled my neck. "So, how's my case going?"

"I arrested Lawrence Henderson on probation violations this morning. He's in a cell in the county jail."

Her fingers touched my chest. "That is so good." She slid further over onto my lap. "but you know he'll only do a couple weeks unless someone can connect him to my case. I'm on nobody's radar. Nobody except you. Isn't there somebody you can call, drop a dime to, get things going?"

"Yeah, I'll make some calls tomorrow, no problem."

"So whatever are you doing out here in the cemetery at midnight, when you're off-duty?" she smirked. Before I could answer, she kissed me. Her hands went to my groin.

When I awoke, it was the predawn hours of the morning. I was alone. My ashtray appeared unused.

I knew the detectives came in at 7:00 AM. So I went back to my apartment, showered and shaved, and put on my one suit. Then I went and drank coffee at the greasy spoon next to headquarters, trying to put my statement into some form that wouldn't sound as crazy as it was.

At 7:15, I knocked on Detective Mike Frasier's office door. Detective Frasier was not far from retirement. He had done my background investigation when I got hired. I had worked with him a few times in the ensuing years. He was a wizened, chain-smoking black man with a pencil moustache.

When I came in, Frasier was sitting at his desk with his obese, bespectacled partner Detective Dan "Boomer" Castanello drinking black coffee. "What can I do for you , kid?" asked Frasier.

"Well, sir, I've received an anonymous report of a homicide."

"From where, a fuckin' Ouija board?" piped up Castanello, "Everybody knows all you is drive around the cemetery all night." I blushed and fell silent. "C'mon, I'm just busting your balls. What you really got?"

"Well, I've been told that a woman named Tasha Wright was beaten to death by a pimp named Lawrence Henderson about two years and seven or eight months ago."

Frasier nodded. "Did you look into any of this, Witkowski?"

I nodded. "I verified that there was such a person as Tasha Wright. She had a minor record that stops abruptly at the time of her alleged death. I verified that there is a Lawrence Henderson with a record for pimping and domestic violence... and then I went to his house and arrested him for parole violations yesterday."

"Okayyyyy... so he's in the county jail right now?"

"Yep."

"You aren't out playing knight in shining armor for the late Ms. Wright's sister, mom, friend, whatever, are you? Wait- don't answer that, you've been in enough trouble just lately. Just let me suggest that would be a bad idea, okay?" I nodded. "I mean, hey, we'll certainly go over and talk to him, see what we can find out, okay? But I gotta tell you, just looking through the computer, this isn't even a cold case to us. This is a never-heard-of-it case. Nobody ever reported Tasha Wright missing."

"She may have been among the Jane Does at the morgue."

"Yeah, almost three years ago." Frasier sighed. "Our backlog… look, never mind, we'll go see what we can find out. Is there anything else you can tell us?"

"That she was beaten to death in the back room of some dump nightclub on the north side called the Golden Lounge. The bartender is an old-timer named Virgil, possible witness."

Castanello nodded. "That would certainly not be the first very bad thing to happen at the Golden Lounge. We've visited that shithole a few times."

"What's your cell number?" asked Frasier, "I'll get back to you when I've got something."

Before Detective Frasier could get back to me, Lieutenant Myles certainly did, cornering me after night shift roll. "What is this bullshit, Witkowski? I specifically told you the perimeter of where you go when you're assigned here- County Cemetery- period! What part of that sounded like 'go do some off-the-books, vigilante parole check-up, unauthorized by the agent I might add, in the ghetto, by yourself, with saying shit to anybody'? You're really lucky things didn't get violent with this Henderson, okay? The guy has a record a mile long."

"Lieutenant, I received an anonymous report that Lawrence Henderson had committed a murder. I did report it to Detectives Frasier and Castanello."

"Well, you should have left it to them. Don't let this happen again, I don't care what you've got, understand me? You don't leave that damn graveyard."

"Yes, sir."

That night I drove a short distance into the cemetery and parked. I killed the lights and nursed a cup of coffee while I thought things over. It wasn't long and there was a sharp rap against my window. Tasha stood there. I rolled it down.

"So, how's it going, Handsome? Can I get in?"

"I guess."

She went around to the passenger side and climbed inside, then slid close to me. She looked exquisite. Even her scent, a perfume I could not identify, was intoxicating. "Everything okay?" she whispered in my ear.

"I reported everything to a pair of veteran detectives. If anybody can solve your case, they can. Then I got chewed out for leaving the grounds to arrest Henderson. I gotta be honest, Tasha, I kinda feel like you're using me."

Her eyes locked with mine. It felt hypnotic. "Of course I'm using you. I'm using you to get justice. You've known what I was from the first moments we spoke. You can only see me in a graveyard in the middle of the night, what does that tell you? I can't rest until the one who murdered me pays for it. So, yeah, I'm seducing you into helping me. Feel free to leave any time it's not worth it. But I need justice, and I'll do anything to get it." I had no quick answer. Tasha put her finger to my lips. Her other hand took mine and placed it on her crotch. "Don't say anything except this- just tell me this isn't the best you've ever had." I could not.

The next morning, Detective Frasier called me. He did not have good news. "Me and Castanello interviewed Henderson down at the jail. Or, more exactly, we read him his rights and got told to 'fuck off'. I think you're info is probably right on, but it's going to be hell to prove especially with no body or cooperating witnesses. We went to the Golden Lounge and got told to 'fuck off' there too, so it's kind of a dead end at this point. Anyway, we were lucky to even get an interview with Henderson. His parole officer already signed the paperwork for his release, which, I don't have to tell you, is fast."

"He's paying him, the P.O. is taking bribes from Lawrence Henderson. The fucker offered me a bribe on the ride to the jail."

"I kind of surmised that. But, again, very difficult to prove."

"So there's nothing that can be done? This guy can just kill with impunity, do whatever he wants, violate his parole right in front of the police, and walk?"

"Hey, hey, you know how these things work. You did a good thing. He's on our radar screen now. Guys like him fuck up. And when he does, we'll put him away. But, seriously, Witkowski? Listen to me. You've done enough now. Let this whole Tasha Wright thing rest, for your own sake."

Detective Frasier was giving me good advice. But it was too late. Because she couldn't rest. And neither could I.

The next night, I asked Lieutenant Myles if I could use my accrued vacation time early and not come in for the next two weeks. "Witkowski, as long as I don't have to explain you to the front office, I don't give a ripe shit." Much as I had suspected, cemetery patrol was a unique purgatory designed just to keep me out of the brass's hair. I would not need a replacement because no one cared if I showed up or not.

Ironically, I spent more time in the county cemetery over the next few weeks than when I was assigned there. Every evening, I would load up my car with food, booze, blankets, wood for making a little campfire, and go spend the night with Tasha. The place was a wasteland. Nobody cared. Besides, who was going to bust me?

It was a sweet time. We partied, she fucked my brains out, we talked. I mean really talked, about our lives and how they had ended up the way they did. I hadn't talked with someone like that in years- okay, ever.

One day, Tasha sent me to the house where her mother lived. I was in regular clothes and had my own car. Awkward as hell, I knocked on the door. A haggard-looking older woman opened it, a cigarette dangling from her lips, the smell of liquor strong on her at ten AM. "Yeah?"

"Ma'am, I am, I mean, I was, I mean, I'm a f-friend of Tasha. I was wondering if you had any of her stuff, like yearbooks or something, that I could see."

"You one of her tricks from the strip club? You some sick fucker looking for a thrill?"

"No ma'am, I never saw her dance."

"Uh huh. You one of those half-assed cops who haven't lifted a finger to find her?"

"No ma'am, just a friend."

"Really? And how did you meet my daughter?"

"We met at the public library."

She chuckled grimly. "Yeah, okay, whatever. Look, you sit on the couch." A few minutes later, she came out with a pile of papers. I could see there were yearbooks from eighth grade to junior year of high school, notebooks covered in doodles, job applications, and just a pile of miscellaneous ephemera. "Take it. Shit, maybe you'll get something out of them. I'm done. She's been out of my life for years."

"T-thank you, ma'am. Thank you very much."

She stood silent for a moment. One tear slid out of her left eye. "She was a really good girl. I mean way back, when she was little. She had, y'know, a pure heart. But the world takes everything and twists around and makes it all wrong. I don't know what happened to her. I don't want to know. But she was good once." I just nodded. She took a deep drag on her cigarette. "Aren't we all, y'know?"

That night, and every night that week, Tasha went through her old things. She told me a hundred stories and I told her a hundred back. It was sweet, but even more so, bittersweet. Because nobody ends up where they start out dreaming of. Everybody becomes something very different than they ever thought they would.

I extended the time I had off by calling in sick and using accrued holiday time. I didn't go back to work for about a month. But finally, I knew things would have to come to an end. Tasha made her request. The one I couldn't say 'no' to. It started with buying a shovel, heavy duty gloves, and garbage bags.

My first night back to work, I came in clean shaven, uniform pressed, boots shined. I checked out a squad car and headed to the county cemetery. About one AM, I drove to the Golden Lounge.

It was a week night and not a large crowd. I parked the car right in front of the entrance and turned on the red and blue lights. Someone shouted , "5-0!" and several people ran off. I walked in. There at the bar was Lawrence Henderson. I walked to about ten feet away.

"Hey look, pig, you are making a big mistake coming in here, in my fucking place! I don't know what bullshit you're on-"

"I'm here about the murder of Tasha Wright."

"Fuck you and that bitch! You can't prove anything! You can't put a case on me! You can't charge me! You can't even arrest me!"

I sighed. "I guess you're right." I drew my gun and shot him five times in the chest. When he fell to the floor I walked over and fired one more bullet through the top of his skull. Then I aimed in on the bar tender. He threw his hands up. I spun around, looking to see if anyone was drawing on me from behind. The few people who hadn't fled were either crouched on the floor or frozen against the walls. I turned on my heel, walked back to the car, and drove away, headed back toward the cemetery.

I had no illusion that I would get there. The radio was going crazy with calls from dispatch and patrol officers talking over each other. Within minutes, the communications traffic went from "shots fired" to "officer involved" to the shift commander ordering radio silence and calling me for my present location. I didn't answer. Then my cell phone went off. "Hello?"

"Yeah, Witkowski? This is Jimmy Bender."

Bender, Sgt. James Bender, was a hostage negotiator for the department. We had worked together as regular deputies. He was a good person. He had gone places. I had just shot a guy to death in front of a room full of witnesses. "Hi Jimmy."

"Hey, yo, Witkowski, man, I don't have to tell you there's a lot going on right now. Where are you, exactly?"

"Look, Jimmy, I'm not going to hurt anyone else. I want to surrender peacefully."

"Great, that's what I want, too. So what's your location, so we can end this the right way?"

"I just have one condition, Jimmy, before I turn myself in."

Ominous silence for a moment. "Uhm, okay, Witkowski, what's your condition?"

"I want a proper burial for Tasha Wright."

"You want what for who, now?"

"Talk to Detectives Frasier or Castanello, they'll tell you about her case. She was dumped in a mass grave as a Jane Doe. Now, you got a chaplain working tonight?"

"Yeah. Reverend Gomez is the duty chaplain."

"Have him call me ASAP." I hung up. Then I pulled into an alley and killed the lights. I could still hear sirens howling, seemingly everywhere.

A few minutes later, my phone rang. "This is Minister Jose Gomez, Sheriffs' Department chaplain."

"Hi, Chaplain, this is Deputy Witkowski, currently wanted fugitive and murderer. I need to talk to you about something important."

"Please, tell me what's on your mind."

"I want to surrender peacefully, to end this, but I need one thing from you."

"What's that, son?"

"I need your word, as a man of God, that you'll do a proper funeral and burial ceremony for a murder victim."

"Of course."

"No, Rev, no departmental BS, no excuses. I need your word, as a servant of God, that you will do a Christian funeral and burial service for Tasha Wright."

"I give you my word, in the name of Christ, that I will do a funeral for her, and that if her body can be found, I will do a burial ceremony."

"Don't worry about that, Rev, I've got it right here. Have Jimmy call me and I'll come in."

The surrender was almost an afterthought. Once I told Jimmy I was driving up Center Street, he directed everybody to block it off about a mile ahead of me.

There was a lot of firepower present- the department's armored entry vehicle, the mobile command post, a county bus parked sideways blocking the street, with four squad cars side-by-side in front of it, lights flashing and spotlights on (but empty, I'm sure).

"Driver halt!" boomed a loudspeaker. I stopped, put the car in park, and killed the engine. "Turn off the vehicle and throw the keys out of the window." I knew the drill. I complied. My dashboard was lit up by spotlights from the rear as the SWAT team moved in. "Driver- exit the vehicle and get down on your knees." I did so, leaving my gun belt on the seat. Next to Tasha.

So now I'm here, the seventh floor of the County Mental Hospital. I was ruled incompetent to stand trial for the murder of Lawrence "Big Money" Henderson. I probably never will be found competent, and I'll probably never leave here. It's taken a year and a half to get them to trust me with loose leaf paper and a small, dull pencil. But when I get to go to the dayroom and look out the heavy-duty reinforced window, I have a great view of the County Cemetery. I can look right down on Tasha's grave, the marker is large and easy to spot. Donations paid for it after the story hit the papers.

She visited me one last time. I was here. It was the day Reverend Gomez officiated her funeral and burial. She hugged me and it felt so real. "You released me. I can move on now."

"Where you going, Tasha, heaven?"

Her face was so beautiful. Her eyes locked with mine. She winked. "I don't know, but I know when you get there, I'll be waiting. See you in your dreams…"

And she does. Oh yes, she does.

Techno Tendencies

David Owain Hughes

Paraphilia.

That's the word Izzy had read online concerning her… needs.

It was the closest of the 'philia' words used to specify her kind of attraction –sexual need or affinity to something in particular – the love or obsession with something.

Her magnetism? Electrical equipment or 'buzz goods' as Izzy liked to refer to them.

Paraphilia: a term that describes sexual arousal in response to objects or situations that are considered abnormal or odd in some societies. Such as paedophilia or necrophilia.

Of course, there are other words similar to paraphilia to describe my unusual sexual behaviour, such as objectophilia and mechanophilia, she thought, pressing her mobile phone tight against her shaven, naked pussy in readiness and anticipation of the incoming phone call.

Mechanophilia and objectophilia however, were not fitting words in her eyes. These words best described a person who had a sexual attraction to machines such as bicycles, motor vehicles, helicopters, ships, aeroplanes, robots, androids, computers, tablets, buildings, bridges, etcetera…

Izzy did not have a mere attraction to electrical goods. No. She had a sexual one.

She liked to fuck them.

Gyrate her hips and pussy against them.

Grind on them.

Push the smaller ones inside her.

Tease her G-spot with them.

To have their powerful buzz take her; to make her scream and beg for more. And if they didn't, couldn't, please her, or weren't up to the job she would threaten to take their batteries away or cut their plugs off. It was as simple as that.

You either do as I say or you're history. Fit for the scrapheap!

Izzy continued to press her mobile against her. Her pubic bone was starting to ache, but she didn't care. She was longing for a techno release. She bit her bottom lip and turned her head to look at the small clock on her bedside table. It was a few minutes-to six o'clock. On the hour, she expected an early morning wakeup call from the app on her phone.

But of course, her electrical goods were inanimate objects, and couldn't listen to her commands and demands. Izzy knew that. She wasn't totally crazy. Still, she liked to bully and pressure them. To hold power over them. It made her sexual experience with a new device even more pleasurable.

Whenever a new machine she was capable of playing with entered her home, she would always give it a harsh, mistress-like dressing down before permitting it to please her. Allowing it enter her and to make her G-spot swell.

"Listen up, maggot!" she would say, circling the tool like a vulture whilst delivering her well-worn speech. "The washing machine and shower head are the number one and two around here! Don't ever think you can muscle them out of their positions. Got it? The best you can hope for is nestling yourself in between my favourites. The most yearned for spot around these parts is to become one of my 'go-to' items. You got that, pal? Am I making myself clear? Do I need to speak up, or do you need to clean 'em spuds out of your ears, darling?!"

The machine would never talk back.

Never.

But sometimes, just for shit'n'giggles, Izzy would put batteries into the item or plug it in, and when she spoke, she would operate that particular device under her spotlight as though it was answering.

It's like the Spanish Inquisition, she thought. Only here, my captives get to fuck me and make their tyrant come!

And come…

…and come…

…and come again!

"You'll get one chance and one chance alone, sailor!" she'd continue. "Now, I'm not asking for Niagara Falls on your first attempt, but I do expect a good session. A session that will allow you a second go at my pussy, maggot, and if the second effort is improved, then it will guarantee you a spot within my kingdom until you are spent. Until your components can give no more. And if you can't please, then you will be cast aside. I'll either rip your guts out or cut your plug off. Or I'll cast you down lower than the non-fucking dildos! Are we understood?!" This last bit was usual yelled into the 'face' of the appliance.

When her phone started to vibrate, thanks to the prearranged phone call, she was momentarily startled, but that soon turned to one of joy. Her cunt became juicy, a tingle jolted through her pleasure nub as the mobile continued to ring. Thanks to the app she had chosen, the call wouldn't stop until she answered or her voice mail kicked in.

Izzy had disconnected her voice mail months ago, so there would be no disturbance, unless Opie, her two-year-old son, was to walk in and catch her lying there naked and gasping. If he should, he wouldn't know what was going on. Not only that, he normally sleeps until seven or eight. *That is why I get up and play early…* she thought, trying to keep herself from reaching an early orgasm. Izzy loved delaying her first one, which came stronger if successfully postponed.

She clenched her jaw and ground her teeth – her tongue pushed at them. Izzy buried the back of her head into her pillow, her tits pointed skyward. Her nipples were erect and looking like eraser heads on pencils.

"Oh-ugh!" she gasped, desperately trying to hold her orgasm off. She clamped her free hand to her tit and teased the nipple, not that it did much for her. It was all about the pussy and her G-spot.

"Oh, fuck!" she whispered. Her thighs started to shake. Izzy pressed her knees together but didn't ease the pressure on her mobile, which was becoming slippery. Her fingers were saturated. She bit down on her lip so hard, she could taste blood – a small trickle of liquid drizzled down her chin and pattered against her chest.

She arched her back and pushed herself up off the mattress with her feet. When Izzy reached her bowed zenith, she looked like a humpbacked bridge, with her soles and the top of her head as her only support.

Her hands remained busy.

"Fuck! I'm…I'm…C-c-c-coming!" she gasped, snatching at breaths.

Her Richter scale was pushing an eight-point-five

She licked her dry lips. When the first orgasm ripped through her body like a bolt of energy, she felt herself turn to jelly – her legs, which were concrete-like pillars mere moments ago, turned to yielding masses of flesh, blood and bone.

"Ugh!" she quivered, her hand that had been grabbing, moulding and teasing her tit, shot to her side and clutched the duvet. Izzy's grip on the bedding was so intense she thought she was going to rip through it. Tears pearled at the corners of her eyes.

As the orgasm burned out, she collapsed onto the bed like in the scene from The Exorcist when the hoofed fella leaves Regan's spent, drained body.

But she didn't allow the ecstasy to stop.

A second, almost as powerful orgasm rushed through her, followed by a timed third and a fading fourth. Six was her record with her mobile. Apart from the washing machine and shower head, Izzy's phone was the next best thing. It was also the device she had kept the longest. It had outlived a washing machine and two shower heads. It was also the gadget she kept on her at all times.

Izzy removed the phone from her snatch and looked at the juice-covered screen. She then put her thumb to the little green phone and answered the call. She didn't bother putting the speaker to her ear, but she heard the voice talking, which sounded tinny.

"This is your automated wakeup call. The time is now 06:18. Good morning…"

Izzy disconnected the call and pulled the covers over her. She had another couple of hours before she had to get up and sort Opie out with his breakfast and get him ready for playgroup.

She wiped the screen clean on her bedding, knowing she had to change it today anyway.

An extra few juices ain't going to harm it!

When she was satisfied the phone was clean, back and front, she popped it on her bedside table and closed her eyes. She allowed her mind to wander; to try and take her excitement off the arrival of the new household product, which should be with her later this afternoon.

Got the wine chilling in readiness, which will go well with the Indian takeaway I think I'll order, she thought. Yep, it's just going to be me and my new man! She smiled. Of course, I'll have to wait until Opie has gone to bed before the pleasuring can begin…'Man'. That's a laugh!

It had been three years since Izzy had been with a bloke. Since she'd had penetrative sex with a human, which had been with Opie's dad, Felix. He'd been a one-night stand. A drunken fumble. Izzy did not regret this. It had produced her beautiful son. She'd always wanted to be a mum but had never thought it would happen.

Felix, who she had thought would flip-the-fuck out and distance himself like a weak-kneed ass, had been, and remained, a magnificent dad. He pulled his weight, provided money, care and a home for their son on weekends. Regularly, he would turn up and take Opie out for her to have some alone time or to attend her part-time job as a barmaid.

Being a single, twenty-something mum was hard, but Izzy was determined to make something of herself. Twice a week, she went to night school to train to become a hair and beauty artist. She didn't want to remain on government benefits.

As much as Izzy tried to focus on life, her job, her studies and her son, her bizarre sexual need did tend to distract her. It didn't completely rule her world, as she had a strong hand over it, but still… it occupied a lot of her thinking, and did, at times, push all other responsibilities to one side.

When did it start? She wondered, feeling restless and turning over in bed. A long time ago… longer than I care to remember!

Izzy had tried to cure herself through meditation and medication. There was nothing the doctors could suggest. She'd tried classes, but nothing seemed to work. She needed the electrical buzz.

Sex toys did little. Just like men, they were a cheap imitation.

University, of course! There had been much experimenting.

From before her higher education had started, Izzy had a string of boyfriends and casual fucks, but none of them could blow her mind. At first, she'd thought she may have been gay, but that turned out to be a negative.

A human tongue did nothing. Man or woman.

Once, while at University and staying at a friend's house, Izzy had allowed her friend's bulldog to lick her pussy clean after discovering bestiality online. The unusual porn had stirred something within her, and she'd been game to try it. To see if she could finally find something that would get her off.

The act had occurred after stumbling home half-cut, to find the pooch lying on her bed. Izzy had coaxed the dog into tongue-fucking her by smearing chocolate all over her twat. Even though the experience had slightly thrilled her and made her come just the once, it didn't quite do it for her.

And then, just like that, Izzy found her thing.

After University broke for the summer, she invested in a phone so she could stay in touch with friends. When the thing had started vibrating in her pocket, sending shocks of pleasure through her pussy and triggering multiple orgasms, Izzy had been keen to test a new avenue.

Whenever she had a spare few minutes and wanted to get herself off, Izzy would use her phone. As soon as she realised that she was falling for what her mobile could do for her, she tried other objects, with equally stimulating results.

However, that summer her mother fell ill, her life as well as her plans to continue exploring her sexual awakening were put on hold.

Once her mother had finally succumbed to the cancer eating her from her inside out, and after Izzy had finished grieving, she got her life and sexual desires back on track. She didn't allow her pregnancy to stop her, either. With a new house came plenty of electrical goods to play with. She was finally happy as she explored her techno tendencies, and moved through life as a single mum. There would be no more men. Ever.

Every new electrical gadget that came through the door, she tested with her fanny before putting it to work: toothbrush, razor (firstly, remove the blade), exfoliating machine, back massager, blender, hand mixer, oscillating fan, food mixer, handheld vacuum cleaner, screwdriver, whisk, tumble dryer, dishwasher, shower head; all can be laid against one's nether regions when in the "on" position. She'd pretty much tried everything there was to test.

Well, I can't just lay here all morning thinking about my pussy! Izzy rolled over and threw the covers off her body. Once Opie's fed, ready for playgroup, and is sitting watching his cartoons whilst I get ready, maybe I can have a little play in the shower!

Happy with that idea, she got up and crossed the landing to her son's bedroom door, which had bright coloured tiles on it spelling out his name.

"Opie, baby, it's time to get up!" she tapped on his door lightly and walked in to find her boy sleeping. She couldn't help but smile.

With Opie fed, dressed, and playing in his chair in front of cartoons, Izzy had taken to the bathroom for her customary morning shower.

A girl can't have too many orgasms in a morning! She wiped the mist from the bathroom mirror and looked at herself. At her body. She didn't think much of herself, but plenty of men had lusted after her. Told her how gorgeous she was. One fella, with whom she had been friendly, had told her that she had a "stripper's arse," that she "belonged on a pole".

The memory brought a smile to her face and she turned to show her bare backside in the mirror. It was ample: 'booty,' some would call it.

"Nothing wrong with a little junk-in-the-trunk, I suppose," she uttered, turning front and centre in the glass once more. "It offers a bit of cushion-for-the-pushin'! If only someone would come along and put some of that arse fat in my tits, then we'd be talking."

Not that her small-ish breasts or size sixteen figure bothered her. Truth be told, she was happy within her skin. However, Izzy found her face and long red hair to be her best features.

She cast all thoughts from her mind and stepped into the shower. Hard, hot rays of water assaulted her body, making her groan. Her nipples instantly turned hard. She imagined the shower's water as a tongue: licking, lapping and caressing her body. It poked its watery organ into her bellybutton, flicked her nips and invaded her anus. The thought alone was enough to take her to the brink of climax, but she managed to hold back.

Izzy squirted shower gel into her hands and slowly massaged and stroked it onto her skin, causing a divine amount of lather. She gently glided her hand over her twat, not wanting to take the matter out of the shower head's hands, so to speak, as she cleaned herself.

That's your area… she thought, biting her lip. It's all for you! For you to take care of.

A shaky breath escaped her.

"Oh, God! I don't think I can hold off…"

Her skin prickled with gooseflesh.

"So, there's a new bit of electrical muscle coming home to play later today?" Izzy opened her eyes and noticed the shower box affixed to the wall had formed a mouth. It was talking to her. It sounded jealous. "Surely it won't replace me, your trusted shower head?!"

At that moment, the water seemed to hit her harder as it worked its way into all the desirable cracks.

"N-n-n-no!" she managed. A shriek escaped her. "You're my number two. Always will be. But you know you could never match the supreme power of the washing machine! He-h-h-he'll always be my number one." Izzy continued to soap her body slowly.

"Oh, I know that. I'm more than happy to be your number two, my beautiful Izzy. But I don't want to be overthrown by a new device!"

The water infiltrated the hood of her pussy and swirled around her G-spot.

"Ugh!" she gasped at the unexpectedness. "You are a rude boy!"

"Take me off my hook and press me against your cunt, Izzy. Please."

In her mind, the showerhead had a smooth voice, soft like blended chocolate. "And if I m-m-make you wait?!" her lip was starting to hurt from where she had it clamped between her teeth. She loved it when her electrical friends got jealous of each other.

"Then I will keep teasing you."

"Oh, you bad, bad boy!" Another yelp escaped her. Izzy put a hand to the shower wall to steady herself. Her legs felt weak, her thighs started to tremble.

"What is the new device?!" he asked.

"That's for you to find out! Now, satisfy your madam!" Izzy said, slowly removing the showerhead and pressing it against her pussy. Instantly, an orgasm pulsed through her, and she juggled the showerhead, almost dropping her man and collapsing to the floor.

As she lowered herself to the shower floor she huddled into a ball with her legs jammed together, crushing the showerhead against her privates.

"Oh!" She screamed and panted, hoping Opie wouldn't hear her over the gush of water. She writhed and thrashed her legs – her right knee struck the wall but she didn't notice in her moment of euphoria.

Her mind swayed and bobbed like a ship lost in a storm. Whilst the showerhead did its thing, buried in her twat, she thought about the new machine she was expecting. It was like cheating in her mind: as she was being fucked by one gadget, Izzy had another on her mind.

It was delicious.

A second and third orgasm tore through her body, followed by a powerful fourth – it was like being struck by lightning.

Yeah, ride the thunderstorm! she screamed inside her head.

After a fifth climax racked her body, the showerhead slipped from her relaxed hand. Her body spasmed as she lay there catching her breath and trying to recover. She felt on fire. Her cheeks were flushed and burning. Her forehead, too. Sweat poured from her.

"You're so good to me!" she wheezed.

The shower didn't respond.

"Maybe I'll come back later today before I try out the new electrical device. Maybe I'll allow you to warm me up ahead of my romantic evening. You'd like that, wouldn't you? It would make you feel some form of manliness, wouldn't it? You dirty bastard!"

"Yes!" it said.

"Oh!" she exclaimed. "You're such a dirty motherfucker!" Izzy smacked her fist against the wall in pure joy, before getting to her unsteady legs and turning the shower off. She got out, wrapped a towel around her body and stepped out of the misty room.

Before crossing the landing to her room, she popped her head around the banister. Izzy could hear her son laughing and playing.

Thank God! Izzy felt guilty when she left Opie on his own so she could pleasure herself, but she didn't dwell on it. I'm a good mum. He wants for nothing and is loved.

That evening, after a long, tiring day of looking after and playing with Opie, cleaning the flat, making them food and running errands, Izzy was finally able to relax. She lay on the sofa in her pyjamas feeling spent and limp-like. And then her eyes fell on the large box that had been delivered earlier in the day. They lit up – a surge of fresh energy engulfed her. A tingle of pleasure shot through her.

Izzy felt instantly rejuvenated.

She sat bolt-up right. "I'd forgotten about you!" she purred, slipping off the sofa and onto all fours. Slowly, Izzy slinked over to the huge box, sashaying her arse as she went. "I'm sure I can make my rudeness up to you…"

When she got within touching distance, she seductively ran her index finger down the mass of cardboard. It reminded her of a fortress, with its sharp edges and reinforced industrial tape.

"Impenetrable!" she mouthed, taking her finger back and then running her tongue up the box. "Your size is impressive." To Izzy, her drawl sounded sexy. "Would you like me to dress up for you? Shave my legs and make them soft? I bet you'd like that!"

She pressed her tits against the box and threw her arms around it. Izzy gave it a bear hug. "You smell so nice. Fresh. Factory fresh. Maybe I should rip you open and roll around in your padding first? Would you like that? Your bubble wrap will go pop, pop, pop, pop," she teased, "like staggered machine-gun fire! I won't need to give you my speech. I already know you're going to be impressive. I was going to let the shower head warm me up first, but I don't think I'll waste my time. You have my attention."

Izzy then pressed her mouth close to the box, as though whispering in its ear, "My knickers are wet."

She then tittered, and continued, "Before I get ready, I'm going to take you out of the box."

After spending the next fifteen minutes unpacking the new electrical item and disposing of its wrapping, she'd slipped into a pair of sexy black stockings, complete with suspenders and garter.

She didn't bother wearing knickers or a bra.

To conceal her nakedness for the time being, Izzy had slipped into a thin robe.

"I'll reveal myself once I'm good and ready!" she'd said to herself.

The plan had been to eat and relax with a few glasses of wine before jumping straight into the sex games with her new fella. But she couldn't wait.

Her pussy was snapping and foaming at its entry for the electro buzz that it knew was coming. Not even a lion tamer could keep my girl in place at this point! She'd thought, patting her privates.

When she got back to the living room, she stood before the new gadget with her legs apart. "So, you think you're man enough?! I've got a lot of faith in you."

The machine didn't answer.

"Going to do your talking with your mouth, hey?! I like the strong, silent type," she teased, letting her robe hit the floor. Izzy then hurriedly plugged the machine in and brought it close to her. Before lying down, she grabbed all its impressive extensions. "My, what a lot of toys you come with!" she exclaimed excitedly.

All around her, she felt the other various appliances had their jealous eyes on them, giving her that added thrill. "I hope you boys enjoy the show!"

Before Izzy started her new wet-and-dry vacuum cleaner, she removed the nozzle that could have an assortment of different heads attached to it and placed it against her G-spot. She then hit the on button. The robust machine snatched at her, teasing her into an immediate, powerful orgasm. Her eyes rolled. She didn't think she would be able to withstand another, and so switched the machine off.

"Jesus Christ!" she huffed. "You're incredible!"

Izzy heard a few unimpressed groans from around the room – even her mobile phone sounded inferior. "Now, now, boys – there's no need to pout. You'll still get your chances!"

She giggled, whilst she sorted through the numerous heads: brushes, scrubbers, extensions… The list went on.

Before the night is out, I plan to go through them all!

As time ticked by, Izzy tried and tested the variety of heads and made a mental list of the ones she liked and didn't.

When she came to the last attachment, she felt a slight sadness. Her heart sank.

Our time has almost come to an end. Probably a good thing, because I don't think my mini can take much more!

The final interchangeable head was long and slender, reminding her of a bamboo shoot. When she clicked it into place, it added a good foot to the nozzle.

It must be used for reaching all those awkward, hard to get to places. Plus, with it being slender, it could be slipped into tight gaps. Or…up tight gaps!

A smile spread across her face as she lowered the pipe and put it to her pussy. In her eagerness to feel pleasure, Izzy failed to notice the sharp, jagged edge at the top of the pipe where a piece of its plastic had snapped off.

It looked like a spearhead.

"Ooh! A turbo button!" she squealed at seeing the function on the vacuum. When she hit the button, the pipe was viciously sucked up inside her cunt. Izzy felt it rip into her walls and tear through the flesh as it snaked its way inside her.

"Ugh…No!" she screamed, collapsing onto her back. She tried to rip the pipe out of her, but it had gone too deep and was attached to her insides. "The off button…"

She tried to get up, but the agonising pain in her stomach pinned her to the floor. She felt a wetness puddle out from between her legs. She guessed it was blood. Izzy became faint. The room started to spin. "Get out!" she screamed and kicked at the machine.

Her outburst did nothing but help the attachment slip further up inside. An excruciating pain ripped through her, and she felt something in her rip open. Her stomach rippled. Blood trickled from her mouth and nose.

Izzy's uterus prolapsed and the pipe gobbled it up, wheezing and choking with the effort as it tried to swallow it down to its bag.

"Help!" Tears flooded out of her. She screamed and screamed.

Finally, Izzy managed to sit up slightly. Her hands fell off the attachment and found a pool of blood between her legs. With nothing holding the pipe back, it pushed further up inside, impaling her. She felt like one of Vlad's victim's.

Her abdomen split open, the structures ripped. Soon her bowels and everything else inside her would be sucked up, hollowing her out like a Halloween pumpkin.

She tried to hit the off button, but the vacuum slipped away from her reach as Izzy laid her slippery fingers on it.

"Opie!" she screamed. "Opie!" A faint hope arose in her when she heard her son's feet come rushing down the stairs. "Help m-m-m-mummy...!" She was starting to faint. Something was being forced free in her. The vacuum was beginning to make a choked, blocked sound. Smoke funneled out of it.

Before she fell onto her back again, she watched as her son rushed to the pipe and pulled on it.

"Aaargh!" she screamed, witnessing Opie's face being splashed by her blood. She started to spasm.

Her son yelled as yanked on the vacuum's extension.

Then, the pipe came free.

"Look mum! There were sausages inside you!" Opie said in amazement.

Izzy felt a moment of supreme disgust and embarrassment as she watched the powerful machine claim her intestines and other parts of her guts. She felt everything split away from inside – her blood was pumping out from between her legs.

"Ugh…uch" she gurgled, her head hitting the floor as her life was sucked out of her.

Mistress Perdition

J.J. Smith

Through years of living the vampire lifestyle that Perdita had loved since she was a teen, she estimated that she had downed about a pint of human blood a teaspoon at a time. While many people would find that repugnant, Perdita didn't believe it was. Rather, she believed it was an alternative lifestyle that was no one's else's business. But drinking all that blood didn't prepare her for the repugnant taste that now filled her mouth; a taste that reinforced her belief that she now knew what excrement tasted like. However, even though what she was eating truly tasted like shit, she couldn't stop herself from peeling one off; popping it into her mouth; chewing (not gagging); swallowing; and then moving onto the next crusty treat. As she did so, Perdita tried to cover up the taste by imagining she was consuming thick, coppery blood because that was fun compared to this. She so much wanted to return to that innocent era in her life when drinking blood was kids' stuff; to that time before the Boogie Lady entered her life and life suddenly became all too real. So, to get her mind off what she was doing, Perdita's thoughts turned to that last vampire ball.

***

The teaspoon of fresh blood looked like children's cough syrup, but this isn't kids' stuff, thought Perdita who anticipated the rush she would get whenever she downed the liquid. While the blood may have been drawn from her own arm using an insulin needle she stole from her father, she believed drinking it elevated her into the vampire convention's hip elite. Nothing else in Perdita's world made her feel as special as the kinship that developed around drinking small amounts of the liquid life. Vampirism was a lifestyle Perdita had loved since joining a role-playing group in high school. The feel of the dark velvet clothes; the sense of going on an adventure every week; the comradeship when around like-minded people, it all excited Perdita, who swallowed the blood with a dedication that reinforced her commitment to never relinquish the standing she had achieved among the roughly 1,000 Vamps Convention attendees. She then washed the blood down with some red wine, and departed her hotel room for what she considered the event's highlight, the convention ball

Nothing excited her more than the ball, for that was where all the magic occurred. Perdita did not attend her own high-school prom, not because she wasn't asked, but because she refused to go and force a smile and pretend she was having a good time with people who hated her, and whom she hated back. But as a regular at several vampire and horror conventions she was a social butterfly. Perdita especially enjoyed those conventions that had a dance, or a ball as part of the program. She loved them so much that she would prepare for the ball weeks in advance, and she obsessed over every detail of her appearance. The reason being that it wasn't Perdita who entered the ballroom on those occasions, but rather it was her alter ego, "Mistress Perdition," a persona she assumed for the duration of a convention. Therefore, it was important to make Mistress Perdition as mysterious and glamorous as the characters in the vampire novels Perdita loved. While she was a plain looking girl, she knew how to apply makeup and pick the right Goth clothes so she stood out in a crowd. Makeup and the right clothes, combined with attitude—and her willingness to drink blood—drew the attention of the convention's experienced vampires, and they eventually opened their ranks to her.

Because she wanted to keep her standing in the upper tiers of vampire convention society, it was essential for Mistress Perdition to make a grand entrance into the ball, and Perdita had it down. She posed in the doorway long enough so that others sitting at tables could view her and be filled with envy. As part of her routine, Mistress Perdition would work the room, moving from table to table like a genuine socialite.

Following that strategy, she greeted each table's seated occupants, and as she was doing that at the Vamps Ball, a somewhat sexily dressed woman caught Perdita's eye, mostly because the woman looked so out of place. She was wearing a kimono that wasn't wrapped very tightly and therefore sporadically opened from the waist down offering glimpses of the woman's bare thighs and panties, which were black. She was a blonde, and her hair fell to her shoulders in such a way as to suggest she had been lying down just prior to attending the ball. Perdita wondered if the woman's character was a street-walker vampire. If so, it was exactly the type of dangerous friendship Mistress Perdition would seek out. So Perdita quickly approached the newcomer hoping to recruit her into Mistress Perdition's clique before anyone else bagged her. She introduced herself and asked the woman's name followed by an invitation for a drink.

"I'm Princess, and yeah I'll take a drink."

"Wonderful, I'll get us champagne," Perdita said drawing out her words to sound sophisticated.

"Is there anything stronger than that?"

"I'm sure there is."

"How 'bout whiskey?"

"Sure," Perdita said, feeling a little dumbfounded. That must be her character, she reasoned as she led Princess to a table. Once she retrieved the drinks, Perdita sat and daintily sipped her champagne while Princess downed the glass of bourbon as if it were a glass of ice tea on a hot summer day. They sat quietly for a few awkward moments—the music making normal conservation difficult—but Perdita was determined to move the evening in the proper direction, so she asked the newcomer if she'd like to dance.

The newcomer took a few long seconds before saying "yes" and once out on the dance floor it became obvious that Princess' had some questionable dance skills for she moved like a stripper, flashing parts of her body, especially to some of the male vampires. While Perdita attributed the behavior as being Princess' character, she was suddenly self-conscious about dancing with the woman and was anxious for the song to end. When it was over, she turned to the table, but Princess pulled her close, her eyes growing large, and saying, "That was great, do you want to get high?"

Surprised, but not lacking in experience, Perdita said, "You've got smoke?"

"Do I," Princess replied grinning.

This woman made Perdita nervous, so a joint sounded like a good way to calm herself, so after a few second, she said, "Sure, why not."

In a move, Perdita wasn't prepared for, Princess grabbed Perdita by the back of her head and pulled her forward, covering the shocked vampire gamer's lips in a kiss. However, it wasn't a normal smooch, for smoke, lots of smoke, shot out of Princess' mouth and down Perdita's throat in what marijuana users called a shotgun. The smoke hit Perdita's lungs, and its effects hit her head like a sledge hammer. For Perdita, the rest of the night was a blur, and the next thing she knew was waking up in her hotel room. It took her a few minutes, but she eventually recalled that she was still at the Vamps Convention, and that she badly needed a shower and breakfast.

***

During that day's convention activities, a woozy Perdita heard several times about the spectacle she had made of herself the previous night with the newcomer. She heard how she and the woman—no one seemed to know her name or if she was even a convention attendee—was quite an item, and that the pair couldn't seem to get enough of each other. When Perdita asked what each person who said that meant, they all replied with the same answer, "kissing." Constant kissing. Slightly embarrassed at such an open display of affection—lust really—Perdita nonetheless continued with the rest of the convention, the activities of which occurred rather routinely, leaving her both relived and disappointed that Princess never appeared again.

***

Nearly a fortnight had passed since the convention, and Perdita was leaving the coffee shop where she worked as a barista. It was Friday evening, and she was full of energy for she planned to spend her weekend gaming. As Perdita neared the bus stop, which was her main mode of transportation, she was surprised to hear someone call her using her character's name.

"Hey Mistress! Mistress!"

Perdita turned and saw it was Princess, who was approaching her from behind. This time Princess didn't look as ragged as when they first met. She looked sexy in black spandex pants, and a leather jacket. Once Princess had reached her, Perdita said, "Um…hi…where did you come from?"

"I've been around."

"How'd you find me?"

"Don't you remember, you told me where you work? I'm not surprised you don't remember, you were pretty wasted that night."

"I looked for you at the con, and couldn't find you. No one there knew who you were."

"You mean the hotel? Hell, I saw a party and went for it."

"You crashed the Ball?"

"If that's what it was, yeah. But 'crashed,' I just flirted with the guy at the door, showed him my tits, and he let me in."

Perdita was both shocked and impressed. "Well what's up?"

"I was about a block from the coffee place when I saw you leaving. Want to go to a party?"

"A party, really?"

"Yeah, really."

"When?"

"Now. It's already started, but we can show up anytime we want."

"I'm not dressed for a party."

"You look fine. Don't worry about how you're dressed, this crowd is casual. I told them about you, and they said bring her."

"Where is it?"

"Across town. We can take a cab, I'll pay."

Perdita considered that the gaming wasn't until Saturday afternoon, and that she didn't have anything specifically planned for that night. So why not, she thought, and said, "OK, I'm game."

Princess then hailed a taxi.

****

The ride was long, nearly 45 minutes, and it ended in a rundown neighborhood that had empty lots peppered in between dilapidated houses with boarded up windows and front yards full of weeds, dirt piles and garbage.

"Where are we?" Perdita said as she exited the cab, repeating a question she had asked when the cab left the business district, and entered an area of the city famous for shootings, prostitution and drugs. The first-time Perdita asked their location, Princess responded with an icy glare, but now—in an excited state—she said, "We're home. I'm going to take you to the Boogie Lady." She again took Perdita by the arm, but now she led her to the back of a gloomy looking dwelling. Once there, Princess knocked three times on a windowless door.

"Who is it?" said a menacing sounding voice from the other side.

"Princess," she replied and that set-in motion the sound of something large and heavy being moved behind the door. The entrance was then creaked open just enough to let the two into the hall, which was pitch black and smelled of body odor. The dark made Perdita nervous, but light from around the frame of a door at the top of a flight of stairs eased her anxiety. Which was good because the entrance was slammed shut behind them. "Watch your step," Princess said ascending the stairs, and she hadn't taken more than two steps when the door at the top opened, flooding the hall with much needed light. Perdita could now see the large man who'd let them in as he wedged a thick steel pipe between the door and stairs. It must be a barricade, but why? She thought. She then looked at the man, and believed he was as thick and tough looking as the pipe.

Perdita was filled with apprehension upon entering the room at the top of the stairs. She wasn't sure what to expect, but it turned out to be nothing more than an ordinary living room filled with very worn sofas positioned into a square around a center table that was just a large wire spool painted black. The spool/table was filthy with cigarette ash, empty beer bottles, crumpled up cigarette packs, bits of foil and paper and several lighters placed next to several glass and metal tubes, the ends of which were burned black. There were also four plates in various spots, and on each plate, were various amounts of small plastic bags with white chunks of what looked like chalk and powder. The nervousness she felt walking up the stairs quickly turned to outright fear causing Perdita to want to turn and run, but the door leading back to the stairs was shut and secured with a thick lock. In addition, bolts were jammed at the top and bottom of the door.

"Princess, who's your friend," said a large woman who reclined on one of the sofas.

"This is Per…Mistress Perdition."

"Hey new girl, you want to do a hit," said a strange man who was sitting on a two-seater sofa with another woman very close to his side.

The invitation caused the woman next to the man to sharply bark at Princess, "You'd better keep that whore away from my ticket!"

The anger and menace in the woman's voice seemed real, and if Perdita had been filled with fear, she was now terrified. "I should just go," she said, the fear in her voice unmistakable.

"No!" Princess said just as sharply as the woman who'd called Perdita a whore. She then turned to the woman and said, "Rock Jaw, you shut the fuck up. We're going to see the Boogie Lady."

"Then do it," Rock Jaw replied with a sneer. She then turned to the man—who had taken a long drag from one of the glass pipes—and she moved so her face was directly in front of his and waited. The man held the smoke as long as he could, and just as he exhaled, she placed her lips over his and sucked up the stream of smoke that shot out of his mouth. Perdita noticed that Rock Jaw seemed to instinctively know when the man was ready to exhale because she pounced on smoke like a vampire attacking prey.

A part of Perdita told her to turn her head and not watch, but there was another part of her that was fascinated by the whole exchange, so she kept her eyes glued to the scenario.

"I can hit you with a shotgun like that, just like I did at the hotel," Princess said. "But later, I need you to wait in there," she said pointing to a curtain which hung across a doorway to a room off the room.

Would anyone call that room a parlor? Perdita thought. Just as quickly her mind replied, No one would even call this a home, it's drug house. "I think I should go now," Perdita then said much firmer.

"No! It'll be all right as long as you're with me," Princess said sharply.

Perdita knew a veiled threat when she heard one, so she did as told and moved past the curtain into the small room, which was a bedroom of sorts. It was just as dirty as the outer room—but with a strong stench of urine—however, unlike the outer room, the only furniture was a mattress tossed on the floor that had a couple of filthy blankets on it. Surrounding the mattress were piles of very dirty clothes, and littering the floor were pornographic magazines with titles like "Cumbuckets" and "Young, Dumb, and Full of Cum." Perdita was familiar with the mainstream men's magazines, but she knew nothing about such hardcore filth. The titles alone appalled her.

Next to the mattress was a cardboard box that was being used as a table. On it were a lamp and a plate, and on the plate was a cigarette lighter and glass pipe. Perdita looked back at Princess, who said, "Go on…sit. Look at a magazine. I'm in some of them."

"Getting pissed on!" yelled someone from the other room. That was followed by uproarious laughter.

"Fuck you cunts!" Princess replied.

"Okay, but new girl, I wouldn't eat the Piss-cess' pussy," the voice said evoking more laughter.

Perdita was suddenly more afraid to be in the other room, so she spread a blanket on the mattress and sat. Princess hadn't pulled the curtain all the way back and Perdita could watch as Princess approached a second door—obviously leading deeper into the drug house—and knock. The new door was different, it was a Dutch door, but when the top half opened, it revealed that someone had cut a regular door in two and haphazardly attached the upper half to the doorframe. Peering out of the homemade Dutch door was a crazy-looking, dirty man.

Princess said to him, "Here's the money. I need to see her because more people want time with me."

The man nodded and opened the bottom half of the door, but before passing through, Princess turned and looked at Perdita and said, "Just sit for a few. I'll be right back, and then we'll party." She then disappeared into the next room and both halves of the door were solidly shut.

Perdita sat down on the mattress in such a way that she could see through the open folds of the curtains and around the breaks created by the positioning of the sofas. She watched, almost hypnotized, as the addicts picked up pieces of the white substances, packed them into an end of glass tubes and used the lighters to heat them up and smoke the contents. All the drug users held the smoke as long as possible, and when some of the women were ready to exhale, they blew the smoke into condoms as if they were blowing up a balloon. After a moment to catch their breath, they would suck the smoke back into their lungs and hold it again. As she watched, Perdita saw the woman named Rock Jaw looking back at her through the curtain opening. After a few uncomfortable seconds, Perdita dropped her head, but kept Rock Jaw in view from the top of her eyes. She saw Rock Jaw whisper something to the dingy looking man who'd asked Perdita if she wanted a hit. He listened intently, and nodding in agreement, he placed some of the substance in the glass pipe and handed it to Rock Jaw. She quickly smoked it, and when she finished, he repeated the process, but this time for himself. What was different this time was the man stood as he smoked the drugs, and as he placed the pipe to his lips, Rock Jaw opened his zipper, pulled out his penis, removed her dentures and immediately began fellatio. At the same time she was giving him head, the man held up the lighter and ignited the drug. Perdita's curiosity was immediately replaced by shame and fear and she feverishly started thinking up excuses to get out of the house. However, at that instant one of the women approached her.

"Hi sweetie, I'm Shelly, want to get high?"

Perdita looked at her feet and squeaked out a pathetic sounding, "No."

"No! Then what the hell you doing here?" said Shelly, the menace in her voice unmistakable.

"Princess brought me."

"Oh, Princess brought you, so you think because you're with Princess your shit don't stink?"

"No, I don't think that."

"Think what?" Shelly asked.

"That my shit doesn't stink."

Shelly started laughing and said, "You damn right, but soon enough you're going to find out that shit stink isn't so bad." After a few seconds she said, "You're going to see the Boogie Lady so you might as well get started now," and she produced a glass pipe. When Perdita didn't lift a hand to accept it, Shelly's offer became a command. "Take it!"

Perdita took the glass pipe and said, "Are you all some kind of drug addicts?"

"Nah, we smoke Boogie socially," Shelly said laughing.

"I have to go," Perdita said starting to stand.

"Sit down!" said Princess, who was now standing in the doorway. The command made Perdita move back so she was again sitting on the mattress. Princess then moved to a spot between Perdita and the exit. "Shelly offered you a hit, you're going to take it, aren't you?"

Perdita knew she didn't have a choice, so she said, "I don't know what to do." She was then provided with quick instructions on how to manipulate the pipe and lighter so the maximum amount of "Boogie" smoke would be inhaled.

Eventually, Perdita could not stall any further. Shaking, she placed the pipe between her lips and brought the lighter to the end. Drawing on the flame the smoke traveled up the glass stem and quickly hit her lungs. The air in the room became thicker and had an unreal quality about it, like they were underwater. While Perdita might have thought the room's air changed, she couldn't express it because her ability to speak was gone. She also couldn't get her legs to stand; but why would I want to stand, when I can just sit here and float? she thought. Followed by, Only sex was this good. No! Make that only great sex is this good, and she was suddenly filled with the need to fuck someone. As desire grabbed hold of her emotions, Perdita was only vaguely aware there was such a thing as time and that the night had turned into the next day. Because the hits of Boogie kept coming and Perdita found them more and more enjoyable, it could have been mid-morning or early evening, Perdita couldn't tell because the party never stopped as Princess, or Shelly, or Rock Jaw, or any and all of them kept the Boogie coming, which kept her from sleeping, but she didn't care because all she wanted to do was to keep smoking that wonderful pipe.

At some point—Perdita had no idea when—the room either changed or she was moved somewhere else, because as she reclined she realized she was no longer on a mattress on the floor, but she was lying on a bed. The sheets were filthy, and there was a woman whom the addicts called Boogie Lady. Even in her drugged state, Perdita understood the woman to be the addicts' dealer, their pimp and—in some crazy way—their leader. But for someone who must have been making a lot of money off her customers, the Boogie lady was grimier than any of the other women—all of whom never seemed to bathe—and the woman's uncleanness was unmistakable by the way she was dressed, or rather not dressed. She wore a silk kimono that was old and covered in stains, and not tied in the front. It stayed on her by sitting on her shoulders and, because it hung open, her dirty and scarred body was easily visible. The strange thing was, the woman—she was no "lady" no matter what they called her—held herself in such a way that it indicted she didn't care that everyone could see the scores of scary black scabs and needle marks covering her lower arms, neck, legs, pelvis and belly.

While the Boogie Lady appeared to be in a sad, pathetic state, there was no mistaking the control she had over the addicts who hovered around and moved in and out of the area like worker drones as the queen filled narcotics orders. While doing so the woman would issue commands as if she were a prison-gang boss, but dealing with the addicts never stopped her from keeping an eye on Perdita, or from providing Perdita with shotgun after shotgun. The woman had an uncanny ability to sense when Perdita was coming down, and would act to keep her nice and high. But just as quickly as when brainlessness took over Perdita, her consciousness reemerged.

***

The sound of a door lock clicking snapped Perdita out of the drug induced, trance-like state she was in. She awoke to find herself lying on a bed wearing a kimono, and she hadn't touched the door, yet the lock clicked. She moved to the door, pulled, and found it opened. Recognizing an opportunity to escape she ventured out of the room into a corridor, where she heard distant voices. She really did not want to go in the direction of the voices, but she had no choice, so she moved down the hall to the foyer area and the source of the sounds. In the foyer stood about a score of people who weren't anything like the house full of crazy addicts Perdita had partied with. To begin with, these people were clean and dressed in the latest designer clothes. Their wealth was unmistakable. With the beautiful people was the Boogie Lady, and in front of the Lady was a single person cot, on which someone laid who was covered by a sheet.

The Boogie Lady was apparently acting as ring master of this circus, for once Perdita entered the room—is if on cue—the Lady then addressed the crowd. "Ladies and gentlemen, the subject of tonight's demonstration has arrived." There was some clapping, but the Boogie Lady held up a hand and said, "There's no need for applause, but I do want you to examine her beautiful, pure body." Turning to Perdita, she said, "Remove your robe."

Shocked by that command, Perdita's hands tightly grasped the front of the kimono holding it shut, to which the Boogie lady said, "Now Perdita, you weren't so modest when full of Boogie." Suddenly, as if she were in a trance, Perdita couldn't stop herself from opening the robe and letting it fall to the floor. There she stood revealing her naked body to the roomful of strangers, but it wouldn't have mattered if the world had been watching for she would have done as commanded. "Beautiful isn't she, the pureness of her young milky white skin, unblemished and unburdened by past sins," the Boogie Lady said. She then turned her attention to the cot and who it held saying, "Now look at this species of drug whore." She then pulled back the sheet to reveal Princess, who was also naked Princess. The Boogie

Lady continued with the presentation, "As you've likely ascertained, both of these women are my slaves. On the bed is Princess, she's been a follower of mine her entire life, and she's been going on specific assignments the last two years the results of which you'll soon see."

The Boogie Lady then pointed at Perdita and said, "Standing there is Mistress Perdition. She's very new, and, as you can see, she's not undertaken any assignments, which makes her perfect for this demonstration." The Boogie Lady then gestured at Princess and said, "Now I'm going to properly prepare her for this demonstration." She then closed her eyes, took a deep breath and blew onto Princess as if she were blowing out the candles on a birthday cake, except the Boogie Lady exhaled more than air. From her mouth shot a column of smoke that smelled just like Boogie. If her mouth had been a chimney it couldn't have expelled more smoke, for the bed—and more importantly Princess—was totally enveloped. After a few seconds, the Boogie Lady stopped blowing, and the blanket of smoke quickly dissipated. What it revealed caused a collective gasp to pass through the crowd. For along with the smoke, went the mask that had concealed the scores of thick, crusty, black scabs that each had a tinge of red that pockmarked Princess' body. Princess raised her head and looked at the ugly scabs, she seemed confused, and weakly said, "Mother…mama…"

The Boogie Lady bent slightly and said, "Hush dear, you'll be fine soon." She then again spoke to the crowd. "Each blemish was acquired within the last two years, but not through disease or injury, but by the process you are here to witness. As long as she's the carrier, the scabs will never heal, but I can disguise them so she can move among normal society unnoticed, or I can remove that covering as I did for this demonstration. But while the scabs won't heal, they can be removed through the process you came to see." She then turned to Perdita and said, "Come here." Despite her fear, Perdita obeyed and approached the Boogie Lady. Once in close proximity, the Lady pointed to a stool placed next to the bed and said, "Sit." Perdita complied and the Lady then said, "You may begin."

As if she were a robot that had been pre-programmed, Perdita reached for a scab located in Princess' cleavage and peeled it off. She then placed the hardened blood into her mouth, and everyone in the room heard the crunch as she bit down on the crusty, hardened blood. Like everyone else in the room, Perdita had in her life smelled excrement, either her own, or the stink left in a public toilet, and when she took that first bite that smell exploded onto her taste buds. As a blood drinker, Perdita believed she had tasted the extremes, but she'd never tasted anything as repulsive as the scab. She literally tasted what shit smelled like. She wanted to spit it out, and wash her mouth out with rubbing alcohol, but she couldn't, she so wanted to retch, but was unable to do that. Despite her desire to stop, she was compelled to swallow the scab, filling her with nausea. For good or ill, mostly ill, the scab was staying down. Perdita then moved onto the next scab, peeling it off of Princess' left breast and eating it just as she had the first. She then moved onto the next scab, and the next and the next after that. Princess' entire body was covered with the scabs, including her face and pubis. As if the scabs themselves weren't enough to make her nauseas, Perdita found that several had hairs on them. In her mind she gagged at the thought of those pieces of crusty shit-tasting blood, given extra zest by strands of hair follicles, some curly, but she was still unable to stop. And the scabs with hair from parts of Princess' body that were relatively hairless weren't the only hairy scabs that she consumed. Perdita peeled several from Princess' scalp and from her unshaved armpits. As disgusting as the hairy scabs were, they were rivaled in their ability to turn one's stomach by the scabs on the soles of the woman's feet. Princess was not a stickler for cleanliness as evidenced by the filthy, greasy nature of the drug house she called home, and that was reflected on the underside of her feet which were black with dirt, and some of the scabs had small pieces of garbage attached to them. But that didn't stop Perdita from eating the filthy things.

In a surprise to Perdita, and the attendees, when removed, the scabs revealed no lacerations underneath, just bare skin. Apparently, the scabs didn't actually cover wounds, but rather, they were the wounds. In addition, and likely because of her trance-like state, Perdita didn't notice that for every scab she consumed, one appeared on her body in approximately the same spot that it had been on Princess. However, even if she had noticed, Perdita would not have been able to stop herself from eating more.

As Perdita downed scab after scab, the Boogie Lady continued with her presentation. "As you can see, the sins Princess' has eaten within the past two years are now manifesting on Mistress Perdition. The same will happen when one of my followers eats your sins, no matter how mortal in nature. Like Princess, you can be awake and watch it happen, but you'll need to be under the influence of my special Boogie to get your sins to appear. Again, these services aren't cheap, but rest assured that a member of my group will carry your sins away. What I can't guarantee is that you will not have to answer to civil authorities for any laws you may have broken—that's what lawyers are for—but those who engage these services will be viewed in a new way. You will be seen as pure and innocent, and that will change people's opinions of you, including judges and juries."

The demonstration continued until the last scab, located right next to Princess' anus and smeared with feces, was consumed by Perdita. Princess then stood, donned her robe, and took her place next to her mother, who ordered Perdita to stand and said, "Ladies and gentlemen, I give you Mistress Perdition." There was applause. When it was over, the Boogie Lady said, "You may examine her, but do not touch the scabs, they are now her sins to carry."

Perdita then went on display, and the beautiful people formed a line and filed past her taking time to closely examine her scabbed body. A very stylishly dressed man then asked, "Why do they do it?"

"The people you see here, I've ensured their obedience. They will follow my commands to the letter."

Another man asked, "What happens to her?" The Boogie Lady looked at the questioner as if it were the stupidest thing she had ever heard, so the questioner meekly followed up with, "I mean now that she's carrying all those sins…"

"None of your concern," she said as if talking to a five-year old.

When Perdita heard that, she remained still as a mannequin, but alarms went off in her mind that screamed, Yes! What's going to happen to me?

The Boogie Lady looked directly at Perdita as if to suggest she knew what the duped sin eater was thinking and said, "I'll tell you once they've gone."

After all the guests had an opportunity to examine Perdita, she was released from the "hold"—for lack of a better term—that kept her on display. She then donned the kimono and held the front tightly closed. The Boogie Lady approached her and said, "Go back to your room and sleep."

"But what about…?" Perdita said pointing to a scab on her arm as a tear formed in her eye. Considering how scared she was, Perdita was surprised how calm she sounded.

"In the morning," was the reply. "It will all be taken care of in the morning." Perdita then did as she was told.

***

The police raid on the house occurred at dawn. Dressed in black jump suits and helmets, automatic rifles aimed in every direction, they conducted a blitzkrieg like assault on the dwelling and found it contained only one occupant, who was found lying on a bed in one of the bedrooms, her entire body covered in scabs, including her face.

She was transported to a hospital, at which she awoke and started screaming "I didn't commit them! I didn't commit these sins I'm carrying, I'm being punished for sins I didn't commit!" She also screamed for the Boogie Lady, pleading for her help, and had to be sedated before being transported to a mental hospital.

No drugs were found in the house, but to keep from being sued, the police charged Perdita with trespassing. She was processed, including having her fingerprints and mug shot taken, and her photo was then posted on a police website designed to discourage drug use. Anyone who saw the mug shot found it difficult to believe it was Perdita because she not only didn't look the same, she didn't look human.

The hospital tried to have Perdita committed, but eventually released her to the custody of her parents, both of whom cried every time they looked at her. At her parent's home she hid in her old room, only emerging from seclusion to eat. Alone, she tried removing the scabs herself, and at first she was elated when they came off. However, in a cruel joke, almost immediately after she peeled one off an identical scab appeared at the exact spot, and the scab that was removed would disintegrate into crumbs. That reinforced her conclusion that a sin would only stay off if someone else carried it. So she waited until the next time a vampire gaming was scheduled when she slipped out of her parent's house to attend the session.

She had been careful to cover herself with a hoodie sweatshirt, and large sunglasses that concealed her cheeks. Despite the disguise, once she entered the gaming room, which was in a fantasy game store, the gamers stopped play and focused their attention on Perdita. There was a long few seconds of awkward silence that Perdita broke. "It's me...Mistress Perdition," she said.

The man who owned the store and who was also a vampire gamer, said. "We haven't seen you since the con, what happened? There were things said..."

With tears streaming down her face, she said, "I'll tell you if you want, but first I need to ask for help, help from the drinkers here. I don't know who else to ask."

"What do you want?"

She then removed her sunglasses, pulled back the hood, and rolled up the sweatshirt's sleeves. The gamers winced, but couldn't look away. Some wondered if she was a leper, other's if she'd contracted AIDS, but the real shock came when she pointed to the scabs on her face, and then to her forearm, and said, "I need help removing these."

The store's owner said, "I don't know what we can do? Shouldn't you go to the doctor for that?"

"I need the gamers who are drinkers, to each...eat some...just a few mind you...of the scabs."

"What! What the fuck are you talking about?"

"I know it's asking a lot, but they're not really scabs...they are...they look like scabs, but they're really sins. Not my sins, but the sins of other people. I can't get rid of them unless someone eats them. If it's spread out over a lot of people no one will have to carry all the sins."

"Lady, I don't know what's wrong with you, but get out!"

"Please help me. I don't know where else to turn."

"I said get out, and don't come back here or I'll call the police."

Perdita then dropped to her knees, and with tears bursting forth, said, "Please help me...we, the community...the vampire community, we're a family. If you don't help me I'll stay like this for the rest of my life, and then when I die I'll have to answer for someone else's sins."

Picking up the phone, the owner said, "I'm calling the police."

Perdita then fell onto her side and rolled into a fetal position and cried. She stayed that way for about 20 minutes, when her mother arrived and said, "Please honey, come home with me." Perdita was confused, she had been expecting the police and the look on her daughter's face prompted the mother to add, "They called me to come and get you. They know you're sick and they really don't want to call the police, but we have to go."

Realizing that they would never help her, Perdita stood, rolled down her sleeves and pulled the hood over her head. Her mother held her arm as they left, and once outside the store, Perdita saw her reflection in the window. Looking back at her wasn't the fantasy life of Mistress Perdition, but the real living hell that was Perdita's existence. Desperately seeking an escape, Perdita saw a bus approaching, and she bolted. Running into the street, she was able to get ahead of the bus, but she had to stay ahead of it in order to beat it to the bus stop, and board the vehicle before her mother realized what she was doing. Nearly out of breath, she made it to the stop, and was quickly on the bus as her mother, still across the street, was just reaching the opposite corner. Perdita had no idea where the bus was headed, but she didn't need to know, she only needed it to get away from her old life. Looking out the window, Perdita couldn't keep tears from flowing as she saw her mother still chasing the bus for it was likely the last time she would ever see the woman who gave birth to her, who raised her, and who now was screaming her name pleading for her to come back.

***

A small story about the police raid had been published in the newspaper, and it included the address. Using that information Perdita eventually found the house. There were huge locks on the doors with signs warning all not to enter. She walked to the back of the house and found a basement window that wasn't locked, and she used that as her way in. The basement was dark, but enough natural light streamed in so she found her way upstairs, and to the room where she became a sin eater. The room didn't have any furniture, just garbage thrown everywhere. Perdita slowly picked a corner, sat and waited.

Several hours passed so that it was late into the night before her presence was acknowledged. The door to the Boogie Lady's private room opened and a light illuminated a large cloud of smoke that emerged from the room. Along with the smoke appeared Princess. Perdita stood as Princess approached the sin eater so they were less than a foot apart. The two stood silent for about a minute until Perdita said, "Take me back."

After a few seconds Princess removed her shirt to reveal about a score of scabs peppering her torso. "Because of all the new customers mama has me busy, but I don't like working that hard. So show me how much you want to be with me."

Perdita understood, and she reached out and peeled a scab off of Princess' chest and chewed it up and swallowed it down. Looking down, she saw the sin appear on her chest on top of scabs that already occupied that space.

Princess then smiled and produced a glass pipe full of boogie. As she went to light it, Perdita raised her hand and said, "Can you make the high like the one at the ball?" Still smiling, Princess nodded and brought a flame to the pipe. Drawing up some smoke, she leaned toward Perdita—who had closed her eyes—and covered the sin eater's lips, the sweet smoke filled Perdita. When Princess finished giving the shotgun, she turned back to the room from which she came.

Perdita held the smoke in her lungs as long as possible, as she held the smoke, she heard Princess say, "You'll have to perform. As long as you do, mama will keep you supplied with smoke. You'll eat, have a place to sleep, stay high, and look hot. You'll have to do a few cops—I hope you like anal—but we mostly do the other thing now. When you do that, the scabs will appear, but once you turn over the client's money, she'll hide them so you look hot again." As she spoke, Princess stepped into the room from which she'd emerged. Perdita listened, but the smoke made it all seem so unreal. The boogie gave her a rush that filled her with ecstasy, and that feeling was further enhanced when she heard Princess say, "Hey, you boogie hoes, Mistress Perdition is back in the house." But the only response was mocking laughter.

Zombie Hooker: a Love Story

James H Longmore

ONE:

The fat, dead guy ambled along the sidewalk, his uneven gait rolling his ample body from side to side like a badly laden truck. His face bore the unmistakable gray pallor of death, his skin mottled and peeling. The man's feet - one bare, one sporting a black patent slip-on - shuffled and scraped the ground as he made his way along the familiar route to the office where he'd once worked.

He swung a battered tan, leather briefcase in his right hand; it had fallen open months ago and spilled its cargo of paperwork out along the street and now it flapped empty. In the guy's left hand was a TV remote, which he held to his ear as if in the midst of an important telephone conversation. His cell phone, one could presume, was back at home lying atop a TV set that had not received a transmission since the emergency broadcasts had ceased. Of course, the man was dead and incapable of making a call, even if the cell towers had not stopped working when the whole world went to hell and back.

The corpse shuffled onwards, driven by an inane instinct that condemned him to repeat his old routine *ad infinitum*. His eyes stared straight ahead, blinking occasionally, with only his peripheral vision to prevent him from stumbling into his surroundings.

He didn't acknowledge the girl who stood on the street corner, he never had. Her skin was the same hue as his, her eyes almost as dead. She wore a tiny skirt that had ridden up to exhibit her soft, sensual folds where thigh met buttock, and a skimpy halter-top that exposed her decaying, pallid flesh.

The girl watched the dead businessman in his derelict thousand-dollar suit as he staggered by. She recognized that he walked this way every day at this same time, on his way to an extinct job in a ruined downtown office block. In the deepest recesses of her decaying brain she remembered him; this was the guy who had walked by her every day when his suit had looked like a thousand dollars and his briefcase had been firmly shut.

The girl waited on the street corner that she'd called her own for almost two years. She had staked her claim to the prime piece of hooker real estate after its previous incumbent had vanished. She'd turned up eventually, in a services area on Interstate Ten, wearing a garish off-cut of rolled-up carpet. They'd never found the woman's head - or uterus, liver and heart for that matter.

Prior to her death during the outbreak six months ago, the hooker on the corner had been a real, natural beauty. But now, her copper-red hair lay plastered to her head, her pretty face was swollen, drab and lifeless save for fading blue eyes that somehow still managed to sparkle.

She dressed as she always did, her curvaceous figure squeezed into a stretch mini-skirt that showed off slender legs adorned with spiked heels, and metallic top that displayed her ample breasts and a firm belly from which dangled a long diamante belly ring, now hanging precariously from a sliver of rotten skin.

In the Before Time, out on *her* corner for the twelve 'till three lunchtime shift, it had never ceased to amaze just how many office workers needed to fuck in the middle of their working day. Still, it was all good business, especially on alternate Fridays.

When three o'clock came around, the hooker's ingrained routine would drive her back home to her less than salubrious apartment above the Smoke Shop to prepare for regular clients and in-calls.

Even though the Johns didn't seem to come by anymore.

Sure, cars still drove by, but nowhere near the number that used to crawl past in the old days. Back then, there'd been the regulars, the new and the voyeuristic out to catch a glimpse of forbidden flesh with all of the frisson of Victorians espying a well-turned ankle. Cars that did happen by now all maintained a steady speed and had their windows firmly closed; their occupants peering out at the hooker with frightened eyes. And she would faithfully wait out her three-hour shift, no longer caring if anyone was going to stop and ask if she was *doing business*. Things were different now.

One car - silver, German – still happened by every now and then. It would slow down, and she would dip her knees the best she could to catch the driver's gaze. All to no avail as the car would simply race away like a timid animal. Somewhere in the back of the hooker's mind, she *knew* this particular vehicle. It was from the Before Time, but her decaying mind couldn't quite place it.

The reverberating crack of a gun shot barely registered a reaction with the hooker and as she watched with her blank expression, the suited man slumped without ceremony to the sidewalk. Half of his head was gone and the gray-green muck of putrescent brain matter dribbled out of the yawning hole in his skull. He lay there oozing and twitching in a spreading pool of his own slop.

The hooker slunk around the corner and pushed herself hard against the cold, gray brick of the building that had once been a popular nightclub. Experience had taught her that where there were gunshots, there were cops.

And those, she hid from because some things never changed.

A garish red Challenger crawled by. There was a buzz-cut redneck type hanging out of the window with a rifle clutched in his scrawny hands.

"I got him, Olden!" He shouted at his driver. "Blew his fuckin' brains out first shot! Yeee-ha!" He hollered his war cry as he pumped another couple of bullets into the fat guy's corpse by means of celebration. "One less of them dead fucks to worry about - they should give me a fuckin' medal or sumpthin'!" He flipped off his victim, pulled his denim-clad torso back into the car and his partner floored the gas.

The Challenger was barely a small red spot on the horizon when a blue-and-white cruised by. The uniforms within peered out through the safety of wire-clad windows like curious carrion birds at a kill. Satisfied that the fat guy was well and truly deceased, they sped away. Soon, a black mortuary van would swing by and pick up the businessman's corpse for incineration.

The hooker skulked in the shadows until the cop car was gone. She knew that she couldn't afford to be seen by the Exterminators or the cops otherwise she, too, would end her days oozing gunk onto the sidewalk.

Being a prostitute *and* being one of the undead were not a good combination in these troubled times.

With the suit guy already forgotten, the girl crept out from the shadows and began walking.

It was three PM - time to go home.

TWO:

August S Phillips adjusted his silver-plate cufflinks a third time, twisted the crisp, white shirt sleeve around his thick wrist. He paced back and forth in his cramped living room and studied his reflection in the faux-Viennese mirror that hung above the mantel. He'd been presented with the cuff-links two years ago in recognition of twenty years' loyal service to the United States Postal Service; they'd even put on a champagne reception with an array of nibbles, some of which he'd never even heard of.

That had been a proud day.

A mailman's life suited August. He was a man who enjoyed his own company and he got to work pretty much alone. He had the chance to play the extrovert on his route with a nod and a smile and the occasional light banter to those he had gotten to know over the years. Then he could retreat back to the sanctuary of his tiny home and go back to avoiding the social contact that had always made him feel awkward.

It wasn't that he didn't like his colleagues at the USPS. They were a friendly bunch and some of them had even called around to the house, back in the Before Times. Mom had still been alive then, and she did fuss so when they called him *Augie*. She hated that nickname, said it made him sound like a fucking retard.

And she'd pronounce it *reeeeeetard* in her inimitable Southern drawl.

Always a quick one with the expletives was Mother. A pure heart and a foul mouth, the Reverend had described her when they'd laid her to rest; her final words on God's Green Earth as a coronary destroyed her heart had been '*motherfucking cocksucker*'.

The mail service was only just starting to get back on track after the terrifying events of six months ago. The USPS had paid August for all the time he'd been hunkered down at home with only a shotgun and an emergency radio service for company. August figured that people still needed to get their mail, even through a zombie apocalypse.

That's what they were - *zombies* - and that's what they called them. Call a spade a spade, Mom had always said, and she was never shy when it came to spade-calling. August had always been amused at the folk in those old zombie films who referred to the shuffling antagonists as *those things*, like they didn't know what the dead people who were trying to eat them actually were. Had none of them ever *seen* a zombie film before?

From Day One, they had referred to the reanimated dead as *zombies*, no point beating about the bush in a global crisis, August reckoned. Call them what you will - Walking Dead, Living Dead, the fucking Dead Dead if you prefer - they were just regular people who wouldn't - or couldn't - lie down and stay dead. Something kept them going, driving their putrefying bodies with an irrepressible urge to feed on the living. So far, no explanation had been offered as to what had caused the unholy plague, although the supermarket tabloids that and conspiracy theorists had had plenty to say.

From what August had gleaned, it had all been pretty much Obama's fault.

The whole thing had been a surreal nightmare filled with groaning, decaying people that stank to high heaven and would sink their teeth into your flesh as soon as look at you. No amount of horror movies could have prepared the population for the disgusting reality of the dead preying on the living, it was all too much like some nasty dream.

But it *had* actually happened and August - along with a significant number of others - had gotten through it. And, as they say, life goes on.

What a terribly appropriate phrase that had turned out to be.

August fussed at himself once again. Was the tie right for this shirt? Was this the right shirt for this tie? Did the pants make his look fat? Was his hair too shaggy? He stared at himself in the mirror and studied the middle-aged man who stared back at him. It had seemed a mere blink of an eye since he straightened the black bow-tie that he'd proudly tied himself as the finishing flourish to the hired prom suit as he waited for his Limo ride to Haley Johnstone's house to show.

Those had been years brimming with hope, with endless possibilities of the vast world beyond the suburbs of the spreading city. August and his recently graduated classmates had stood with their toes on the threshold of the fantastic adventure that was *LIFE*, poised to embrace and devour everything that it had to offer.

And then college had happened. For everyone except August. Dad was long-gone and Mom was working herself in to an early grave with two jobs just to make the mortgage payments and put food on the table.

And somebody had to take care of Davey.

August glanced at the faux-oak framed photograph of Mom that sat on the mantel below the mirror. Her prematurely aged face smiled out from behind the UV-proofed glass, her brown, twinkling eyes surrounded by heavily lined skin. Her frail, liver-spotted scalp was clearly visible through the fine wisps of frost-white hair that looked windswept no matter how much she brushed it.

Next to the photograph was Mom's matt black, ceramic urn. It was decorated with gold-leaf angels and on its lid perched the engagement ring Dad had brought back from a business trip to Amsterdam. Dad had not been able to afford a proper ring when he proposed, so he'd surprised her many years later with a belated white gold and diamond ring along with a particularly virulent strain of *Chlamydia* that had almost put paid to her fertility and which she claimed to her dying day was responsible for Davey's *condition*.

Davey was what Mom had called *special*.

Davey was the eldest of the two boys, by three years and change and was so *special* that he'd eat his own shit and scream blue murder all night long like the Devil himself was sticking it up his ass. He'd tear off his clothes and run off down the street and the police would bring him back with sympathetic smiles and platitudes and then Davey would smash up the house and try eating the silverware.

There'd been the days when Davey was catatonic, it brought some welcome peace to the house even though and August and his mother had to take turns to wipe the kid's ass when his bowels let go. August struggled to see how not being able to wipe your own goddamned ass was deemed *special*, but there you had it.

August had been nominated Carer-in-Chief the minute he'd graduated high-school. Mom couldn't afford home care for Davey and she would be damned – *God-*

fucking-damned - if she was going to stick her eldest son in a state facility.

Haley Johnstone had gone to MIT to do something *sciency*, and all her promises of keeping in touch and coming home for *every* vacation went quickly by the wayside once she tasted freedom. The handful of friends August had managed to make in school also spread their wings and left the city as quickly as they could - and Ronnie Labouchardiere had travelled to England to major in something scientific under Professor Stephen Hawking.

And there's another special person who can't wipe his own ass.

Naturally, August had never married, never allowed himself close enough to anyone again after Haley's correspondences had dried up. He'd tell everyone – including himself - that he was waiting for the right girl to come along. In reality he knew in his heart that the right girl had already been and gone.

August had put Davey in a private nursing home the day after their mother had passed.

He'd also ignored the old girl's wishes to be buried and gone ahead and had her body cremated; in August's opinion, there was far too much inner city land taken up to accommodate dead folk. And what a marvel that hindsight had been; he would have hated the thought of Mom up and walking around like the rest of the corpses.

He'd paid for Davey's sanatorium out of his own wages, and visited his brother once a month to assuage his guilt at palming off his own flesh and blood to complete strangers.

Davey wasn't a problem anymore. August reminded himself on occasion that he really ought to feel guilty about what had become of his brother, but the harsh truth was that what he did feel was relief. When the dead had resurrected and the fragile fabric that held society together began to shred, Davey along with life's other unfortunates were rounded up and disposed of in hastily-built incineration units around the city. For many of them, it had been a mercy.

Paying for the Davey's care had put a large hole in August's finances, effectively tying him to the small house in which he had grown up and inherited. It also meant that he had to watch every penny and save wisely to pay for the companionship that he craved.

Again, with little guilt, August had built himself a cosy routine of saving for his once a month treat - twice when he got his bonus - of female company.

He'd met Danielle, *his* Danielle only a few months before the world as he - as *everyone* - knew it had changed for ever.

August took out his wallet, fished out the picture he had of the two of them together. They'd had it taken in the photo booth next to their favorite coffee shop. They'd fallen into it giggling like a pair of love-struck teenagers and Danielle had sat on his knee. Danielle's happy smile shone out from the small photograph and they looked for all the world like lovers.

August had been feeling extra lonely recently, ever since they had taken Martha-May away. That flea-bitten tortoiseshell cat with the torn ears and one eye had been older than dirt and had been the final legacy from his mother. The cat had had smelled bad, was cantankerous and a little too quick with her razor claws for his liking, but he missed her. There was always comfort in having another living thing to come home to.

Hot on the heels of the dead folk climbing out of their coffins, all mammalian pets were rounded up and destroyed; cats, dogs, mice, hamsters, rats – even though there had been not a single instance of anything other than humans *turning* and no evidence from what was left of the scientific community that they could, or ever would.

August had considered arguing that point with the people who came to take Martha-May to the incinerators, right up until the soldiers in biohazard suits had pointed ludicrously big, black semi-automatics at his face.

He *had* made a cursory protest, but the soldiers had advised him in calm, gas-mask muffled voices that they really didn't have the time for his bullshit and that they would be more than happy to shoot him should the need arise. There'd been no alternative but to take them at their word on that one, considering the circumstances.

Gazing at the photograph of his happier self, August realized that never in his life had he felt so desperately, utterly alone.

There had been occasions in the recent weeks on which he'd found himself making an excuse to drive by the street corner where he had first met her, although he told himself that it was only to check that she was alright. He'd drive slowly by, heart racing, hoping against hope that she had survived the madness and would still be there. He'd circle the block as slowly as he dare, his old route by the abandoned office buildings, the litter-strewn streets and *their* coffee shop.

The coffee shop was a wreck now; windows smashed, chairs and tables spilled out onto the sidewalk like innards from a gutted carcass. Next to it, the photo booth was just a burned out shell. It saddened August to see it like that; it had been their special place, where pretence became real - if only by the hour. There had been days he'd paid Danielle just to sit, drink the over priced coffee and talk like he imagined a real girlfriend would. There'd be no sex on those occasions, just companionship and at least the façade of affection.

As he spent more time with Danielle, August had become convinced that he saw something in those liquid blue eyes that hinted at something more than just a business transaction. And that had made him incredibly happy.

In his heart, Danielle had been his constant companion throughout the mayhem and chaos and inescapable presence of death. His memories of her had buoyed up his spirits in even the darkest of hours and given him the motivation he needed to stay alive through the hellish carnage. And he missed her so much that it physically hurt.

August had been rewarded with a glimpse or two of Danielle on his latest sorties. She'd been in her usual place on the corner of the street and he'd slowed his car down to a crawl, still too afraid to roll down the dark-tinted windows on his Mercedes, let alone stop. His heart had skipped a beat or two as she bent her knees to peep into his car, and he imagined that their eyes had met for the briefest of moments.

He'd seen enough of her sickly countenance to know the condition she was in, but her eyes were still alive and they sparkled for him.

And then he'd driven on.

August fiddled absently with his car keys and ruminated on the decision he'd finally made; today would be the day.

The City streets were pretty much cleared of zombies now. The cops and licensed exterminator gangs were still out and about shooting the few remaining dead folk on sight but it had been a couple of months since the city had seen a zombie-related death. August thought it would be fun if they put one of those *'xx days with no*

Zombie killings' boards up - one with interchangeable numbers.

He'd heard that the dead were becoming less aggressive and that the Government were planning to use the lesser decayed ones to replace the tradesmen who were gone now. That was good news for sure; you just couldn't get a plumber for love nor money these days and August's garbage disposal had been all screwed up since the electricity came back on and now it barfed chewed crud back up into the sink whenever the dishwasher drained.

Snorting down his nose at the thought of calling in a zombie plumber, August plucked the ring from his mother's urn and headed out.

THREE:
The hooker pushed her apartment door. It swung open. No need for locks these days; very little to steal, no one to steal it.

Out of habit, she closed it firmly behind her.

The three flights of concrete stairs that made her apartment block look and echo like some crumbling mental institution had taken their toll on her atrophied legs and she was exhausted; it had taken a full hour and a half to climb them today. And that was a half hour longer than it had taken her yesterday.

The hooker shuffled across the tiny room, her head lolling slightly to the left and arms swinging loosely by her sides. She aimed for the bathroom, missed and stumbled into the nursery in which stood a cheap pinewood crib. The room was no bigger than a walk-in closet, but before she'd died, the hooker had made it nice by painting it eggshell-blue and adhering Disney character stickers to the walls.

Inside the crib, nestled amongst the glassy eyed, stuffed animals lay the remains of her child, its head crushed by the silver stiletto shoe that was embedded in its soft skull.

Her baby boy – Jethro - had been eleven months old when he'd taken ill. He'd been bitten by one of his playmates at the day care center and the incident had been dismissed as nothing more serious than *it's what babies do* and a write-up in the Boo-Boo Book. But that was in the time before things really turned to shit.

She'd instinctively known that there was something seriously wrong with her baby, but by then the hospitals had been stretched beyond capacity, the streets too dangerous for her to venture out. She'd watched helplessly on her TV the events unfolding in the City, and then mirrored all over the country as the dead took to walking around and biting chunks out of people.

When, finally the TV played only static as the networks closed down, the hooker had known that her baby was going to die. And even worse than that, she had known that dying wasn't the worse thing that was about to happen to her offspring.

So she'd taken off her shoe and put the mite out of his misery.

The tiny corpse had finished rotting. The last of its fluids had drained out, congealed and dried on the hardwood floor beneath the crib. All that was left now were dried up, mummified remains that looked nothing like the pink, squealing bundle of life that she'd nurtured at her breast.

Before he'd died, little Jethro had bitten a lump out of his mother's cheek.

The hooker's stiff fingers crept up to touch the suppurating hole in her cheek as a vestige of memory maintained the connection between the wound and the tiny corpse in the crib. She made her way out of the grim nursery by homing in on the harsh sunlight that bullied its way through the narrow, filthy window next to her bed.

Instinct buried in the deepest recesses of the hooker's subconscious informed her that now was the time to prepare for the afternoon clientele, although she wasn't quite cognitive enough to register that said clients never came actually calling any more.

She wriggled out of her mini skirt and peeled the halter off over her head. As she did so, she pulled her right nipple away from its sagging mound and it plopped to the floor. She stood in front of her mirror in black panties and heels and contemplated.

Her body was still firm, her breasts remained full if somewhat downward facing, and the left one was still adorned with a large, dark pink nipple. Her stomach was flat and the outline of toned abs descended towards her pussy, interrupted by the thin, white smile of her caesarean scar. She had a few stretch marks here and there from her pregnancy but those were largely masked by the grey pallor of the decaying muscle beneath her skin.

The hooker peered hard at her own face as if trying to recognise it. Her clumsy hands reached for the cluttered array of make-up scattered over the dresser and she padded a soft foundation brush over her face. She grimaced as the bristles sank through the wound on her cheek and tickled her tongue. She pulled the brush out and it made a faint sucking sound as it squelched from face, the bristles glistening wet and clumped together with rot.

Eye shadow next, daubed on in haphazard fashion with poorly coordinated movements and, as hard as she tried, more went onto her forehead than her eyelids.

Finally, the lipstick. She picked out a bright red, glossy color that accentuated the scabbed remains of her lips and spread it around her mouth the best she could, and over onto her shallow cheeks.

Satisfied with her makeup, the hooker stepped away from the mirror. She dropped to her knees and they let out a sharp report as tendons snapped. She scrabbled around under the metal-framed bed and her thin, brittle fingers pulled out a half dozen shoe boxes, each one labelled in teen-girlish red sharpie. She picked up the box that read *'A..S.P'* and placed it on the bed.

She'd used the boxes to store the gifts that her regular Johns bought for her, kept deliberately separate so she'd know which one was from which guy. In reality, the gifts tended to be more for the client's benefit than for hers, typically outfits that they paid her to wear. There was fetish stuff - leather, latex, cheap PVC mostly, clichéd, role-play outfits (French maid, Catwoman, schoolgirl - a Princess Leia gold bikini), and sex toys of all shapes and sizes.

Some of her more thoughtful clients bought her dresses and outfits that were not fetish although they did tend towards the shorter, revealing styles; as expensive as modest wages would allow, clothes they couldn't get their wives to wear.

The box that she tugged open had a rough-edged heart drawn onto the lid in baby pink lipstick, an echo of happier times. She pulled out a small, black dress, struggled to her feet and pulled it on. The soft fabric of the dress scuffed away small clumps of her scalp which then clung to the shimmering fabric.

The dress clung to the hooker's every curve and accentuated her body with sensual lines. It came to an abrupt end at the curve of her pert bottom, tucking into that sexy crease between thigh and ass. The collar was high and fastened by a small zip at the nape of her neck and the back was simply non-existent; the flimsy material scooped low to expose her entire back and just the slightest hint of buttock cleft.

She had dim, distant memories associated with the dress. Memories that hung around the less decomposed parts of her brain; of smiles and kindness, caring and compassion.

Coffee.

Although the hooker couldn't remember the *why*, she put on this dress at the same time every Wednesday.

The hooker smoothed the dress over her slim frame and her remaining nipple stiffened at the touch of her wasted hands. She sat down on the edge of her bed with her legs outstretched and stared blankly at the disintegrating toes that peeped out from the ends of her shoes.

And she waited.

FOUR:

August's palms were moist and he felt the sweat trickling down his back. He genuinely couldn't think of a time when he'd felt more ill at ease. August gulped down deep breaths and told himself that it had been walk through the apartment block and up three flights of litter-strewn stairs that had made him overheat, and not that he was as nervous as hell.

He'd parked his car a couple of blocks away - old habits die hard, he supposed. Danielle's neighborhood had never been the most pleasant to walk through in the Before Time, and when zombies had become a *real* problem, slums and drug-infested tenements such as this had been the first to be cleaned out by the Army. They'd systematically swept through and shot indiscriminately at anything that moved, living *or* undead. Then, they had rounded up whoever was left, and shot them as well. The resulting corpses were thrown into the back of garbage trucks and carted away to the incinerators and neighborhoods like this had become some of the safest places to be.

August's footsteps echoed in hollow rhythm on the concrete walkways as he walked. Like most places nowadays, the apartment building had succumbed to the smothering, empty silence.

He fiddled absently with the ring in his pocket and felt like a teenager on a first date. After six months of his whole world - *the* whole world - being turned inside out and upside down, August would have thought that any lingering anxiety he may have had of hearing the word '*no*' from a girl would have been diminished. But sadly no, the fear of rejection was as deeply ingrained in him as with any man and although things were different now , there were some things that *never* changed.

One more deep breath and August knocked on the door.

FIVE:
Stirred by the timid knock on her door, the hooker struggled from the edge of her bed. She stood up, wobbled as her ankles threatened to give way in her precipitous shoes and steadied herself against the dresser. A cascade of make-up paraphernalia fell to the floor with a plastic clatter. She shuffled towards the door and grasped the handle on her third attempt.

Opened it.

"Hi." August said, feeling awkward, very much like Hugh Grant on Andi McDowell's doorstep. "It's wonderful to see you again." As polite as his mother had taught him. "You look beautiful."

The hooker stepped aside to allow August in, holding onto the doorframe as she stumbled slightly. August thought that she looked pleased to see him, fancied he saw a smile on her rotting lips. He looked into her eyes, searching for that remnant of the Danielle she had been before. To his absolute delight, August saw that her eyes were still the same iridescent blue that he had fallen in love with, albeit sunken into her skull some and marred by cloudy cataracts.

The rest of her, however, didn't look so good.

Her skin had the sickly bluish-gray pallor that was common amongst the dead, it was cracked, split and oozed a foul green/brown slime. In places, eruptions of liquid putrescence pushed to the surface and threatened to burst through like miniature, pustulant volcanoes.

Danielle's body seemed far thinner, more angular than when August had last been this close to her and the soft flesh of her prominent cheeks was now peeling away to reveal the yellowing bone beneath. Clumps of his love's red hair were sloughing from her wasted scalp, and stuck in the viscid ooze of her face like ancient creatures in a tar pit.

A stink of rot and decay wafted from the hooker like some gruesome perfume but like all survivors, August had grown used to the pervading stench of death and it barely bothered him.

August noticed that Danielle had on the dress that he'd bought for her to wear during their liaisons - *their* dress – and it gladdened his aching heart. She had been waiting for him. Did he dare hope that this was a sign that she felt the same way as him?

"How have you been?" His wilted attempt to make small talk was met with a guttural grunt. "I'm sorry I haven't been around for a while. But, you know how crazy things have been." He stopped himself short and felt embarrassed at his *faux-pas*. He was babbling again, always did with Danielle, damned nerves.

August clamped his tongue firmly between his front teeth to force himself to stay silent. The last thing he wanted to do right now was to put the gal off with his incessant, jibber-jabber. He followed Danielle towards the bed that had been the scene of many trysts. Unfortunately, it looked a little less inviting than he remembered it, the covers were crumpled in an unruly heap at the foot of the bed to leave the bare mattress exposed and there were ominous-looking stains splashed across the mattress in dried patches that spanned the spectrum between dried blood red and the greenish-black of putrefaction.

Despite the sickening lurch in his gut at, August smiled at Danielle and fiddled with the ring in his pocket. The gold felt warm and smooth and the huge diamond dug into his fingertips.

The hooker turned to face her client and something that could easily have been a smile forced itself across her face. She reached both hands behind her neck and plucked at the zipper with uncooperative fingers.

"No." August pulled her arms away. "Leave it on."

SIX:
The hooker's lips split open and wept a rust-red fluid beneath the tawdry lip gloss as her face contorted into a seductive smile. Her eyes burned into August's with animal lust and something intangible that he just couldn't quite put a handle on.

She bent forwards to reach beneath the hem of her dress, hooked her bony thumbs through the waistband of her panties and slid them down. As she did so, viscous globs of snot-green slime snaked downwards along her legs and pooled between her feet. Delicate tendrils of the putrescent gloop made translucent strings between her thighs as they slopped noisily to the floor.

It made August think of melted cheese on fresh from the oven pizza.

August undressed; taking care to slip the ring onto his left pinkie finger, diamond facing inwards. Didn't want to ruin any surprises now, did he?

Danielle climbed onto the bed and reclined with her arms above her head to create an illusion of sexy.

August's eyes wandered up along Danielle's legs and peeked beneath her dress. There he saw her ruined vulva; once deliciously pink and slick and inviting, now it glistened with the silvery green of suppurating flesh. Base instinct overrode disgust and August's penis twitched to life.

August climbed onto the reeking bed and lay beside his love. He stroked her body and reacquainted with every line and curve. His hand rose with the twin mounds of her breasts and dipped with the hollow of her flat belly. And then August ventured down towards that special place where he found a slick, inviting wetness into which his fingers sank. And when he pulled his sticky fingers out of her, Danielle delighted him by licking the discolored rot from them.

Danielle rolled August over on to his back and heaved her decaying body on top of him. She straddled him as one would a steer and her stiletto heels dug into the soft meat of his thighs, just how she remembered he liked it. The hooker positioned her dripping sex just so and lowered herself down on to August's penis.

August gasped as he slipped with ease between Danielle's labia and slid deep into her vagina. She was pleasingly wet for him, so much so that her juices drenched his groin and soaked into the mattress under his plump ass. August groaned at the delightful moisture that made their bodies slick, although he understood that it was more the by-product of her putrefaction than of arousal.

But he was happy to pretend for the sake of love.

The hooker ground herself hard against August, using her hands to support herself against the wall above his head. As she made love to him, a cacophony of grunts escaped from her throat and gave the impression that she was truly enjoying their copulation.

August squirmed and bucked his hips as the pressure in his dick built towards an unbearable, almost painful crescendo. It had been an age since he'd done this, and there had been only so much frustration that onanism could alleviate.

August thrust his fingers into Danielle's hair as he came and dislodged her left ear. It slid down her neck and hit his chest with a *splat*. The hooker clamped his hips tightly with her thighs and grunted with her own orgasm.

SEVEN:
It was done.

The hooker looked down at August, his face and torso flushed red in the afterglow, his eyes half closed.

August looked up at his Danielle and for the first time in six months felt entirely at peace. She had always accepted him for who he was; there had never been the need for pretence. In that respect, she was the one who had found his awkwardness *cute*.

"Thank you." He said, forever the consummate gentleman. "You are exquisite."

Taking her hands from the wall, Danielle placed one on either side of his chest and lowered her face towards his. She smiled again and her peeling lips parted to display discolored teeth.

"I love you, Danielle." August blurted out. He liberated the diamond ring from his sweating finger. "And I was going to ask you if you would -"

A rasping snarl spewed from the hooker and she lunged at August's exposed throat, her teeth bared in an obscene grin, mouth dripping its fetid juice, August struggled as his lover's teeth sank deep into his neck and he felt some snap off in his flesh. He opened his mouth wide to cry out, but no sound came save a strangled mewling noise as the air whistled through the rip in his windpipe. He tried to push her away but she was too strong and he could feel his life drain away along with the blood that Danielle slurped from his lacerated throat.

August tunnelled his fingers into Danielle's hair and in a macabre emulation of their recent passion; he drew her closer to him.

EIGHT:

August S Phillips and the hooker walked along the street hand-in-hand. They had the slow, unsteady gait of the living dead and they looked for all the world like besotted lovers.

He was naked with a scarlet bib of blood covering his chest, she wore spiked heels and the tiny black dress that showed off her shapely legs, clung to her rounded buttocks and exposed the sensuous curve of her spine. The engagement ring hung loosely from the remnants of the fourth finger of her left hand, the diamond glinting in what light remained from the bloated, setting sun.

They shuffled their way towards their coffee shop.

There they would sit amongst the debris and ruins of a world that once was, and wait patiently for someone who would never come to serve them. And neither of them would care, because they were together and in love and because things were very much different now.

THE END

Other HellBound Books
For You To Enjoy

**All available now in paperback and eBook
from Amazon, iBooks, Barnes & Noble, Kobo etc.
For full details, visit our official website
www.hellboundbookspublishing.com**

**Or
Download our App from iTunes / Google Play
– or simply scan the QR Code below**

Depraved Desires

A mind-blowing collection of the very darkest erotica from the very best minds in the business!

Desires - we all have them, even if we won't admit it. Some are considered normal, and probably healthy. But what about the others?

Those haunting stirrings within that rail against societal norms and the bounds of decency?

Depraved Desires delves into the writhing depths of carnal appetites and sin, peeling back the veneer to reveal tales of wanton lust and supernatural depravity...

The terrifying prospect of knife play; a cosmic liaison; a

classy party that turned out to be more than a hired call girl ever expected; or when a sinister fantasy becomes reality - all will shock you.

Whether your desires drive you mad or your madness drives your desires, delving within these pages will take you to places where those itches live, the ones that demand to be scratched.

Shopping List

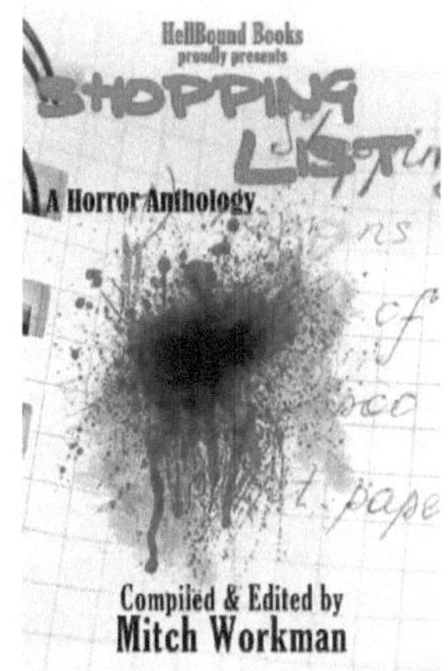

A simply superlative collection of spine-tingling horror from the very best minds in the business!

We decided upon the shopping list theme for this particular volume as an antithesis to those wildly successful writers (they know who they are) of whom it is often said *'we would read their damned shopping list if they published it!'*.

Well, we have given twenty-one of the hottest authors in the independent horror scene the unique opportunity to have their own shopping lists read by you - along with their most terrifying tales of course!

Stories of gut-wrenching terror from:
Kathy Dinisi, Robert Over, Christopher O'Halloran, Eric W. Burgin, Russ Gartz, Mark Slada, Jeff Baker, Tim Miller, Nick Swain,JC Raye, Jovan Jones, Ben Stevens, David F. Gray, Brandon Cracraft, M.S. Swift, Kevin Holton, David Owain Hughes, Bertram Allan Mullin, Jeff C. Stevenson, Sebastian Crow and S.E. Rise

Sángre: The Color of Dying
By
Carlos Colón

Carlos Colón's first published novel is the story of Nicky Negrón, a Puerto Rican salesman in New York City who is turned into foul-mouthed, urban vampire with a taste for the undesirables of society such as sexual predators, domestic abusers and drug dealers.

A tragic anti-hero, Nicky is haunted by profound loss. When his life is cut short due to an unforeseen event at the Ritz-Carlton, it results in a public sex scandal for his surviving family. He then rises from the dead to become a night stalker with a genetic resistance that enables him to retain his humanity, still valuing his family whilst also struggling to somehow maintain a sense of normalcy.

Simultaneously described as haunting, hilarious, horrifying and heartbreaking, Sángre: The Color of Dying is a breathtakingly fun read.

Nightly Visits
By
Stephen Helmes

When you close your eyes, where do you go? What do you see? The moment you drift off into that world of the unknown, you are on a rollercoaster ride, speeding down a track that takes you anywhere it wants to take you.

Often it takes us to places that we would never voluntarily go when we're awake, into a world of darkness, tragedy, and fear. In this virtual reality world, you do things that you would never do when you're awake, such as jumping from a plane without a chute, or opening the door to a room when you know there is something behind it waiting for you to enter.

But dreams can also tell you stories of love, wit, and treasures. You may wake laughing, crying, or screaming, because your dreams know your weaknesses. They know your every thought, and they know how to attack.

That's not what Nightly Visits is *about*. THAT'S WHAT *NIGHTLY VISITS* IS!

**A HellBound Books LLC
Publication**

www.hellboundbookspublishing.com

Printed in the United States of America

www.ingramcontent.com/pod-product-compliance
Lightning Source LLC
Chambersburg PA
CBHW030648120726
47905CB00001B/109